THE Sight

SPIRIT WALKER SERIES
BOOK ONE

EBook ISBN: 978-1-7364582-8-0

Trade Paperback ISBN: 978-1-7364582-9-7

Cover design by Fiona Jayde Media

Edited by Kelly Colby

Published by WIP Publications

WIP Publications EBook Edition 2022

WIP Publications Trade Paperback Edition 2022

Printed in the USA

Get your writing in progress www.wippublications.com

For younger me.

1

The wind outside seemed to whistle, as if demanding to be acknowledged. Yet no one challenged it, no one said anything at all.

Marceline glanced around the treehouse she had shared with her best friend Katy since they were kids. It was their own secret hideaway they'd stumbled upon on an abandoned property that they had been returning to for nearly a decade. As Marceline leaned back against the wood wall and tried to straighten her legs as much as she could in the narrow room, the entire structure wobbled, sending the lantern hanging in the middle of the tight space swaying.

The orange hue of the lantern bounced across Tag's face. It again struck Marceline how handsome he was and also how out of place he was in the tiny box only Katy and Marceline had occupied until now. Even so, it felt nice to be shoved into a snug space with him.

"Easy there," Tag said, breaking the uneasy silence. "You'll send the whole tree crashing down."

Katy snorted. Marceline could tell she was relieved she

didn't have to be the one to speak first. "Trust me, if this tree hasn't fallen down after a Marci and Katy cover concert, this thing isn't going anywhere."

Marceline shot Katy a look that said, *Why would you say that right in front of him?* But Tag just chuckled. "I'd love to get a front-seat ticket to that show."

He smiled at Marceline, and she held his gaze for a long moment, only remembering they weren't alone when Katy cleared her throat loudly, preparing her vocals.

Marceline wanted to throw a hand over her friend's mouth to protect poor Tag's ears, but she settled for laying a hand on Katy's shoulder. "As much as I would love to relive that for Tag, has anyone heard from Nate? He should be here by now."

"Good question," Tag said, shuffling his long body like a giant in a dollhouse to grab his phone from his pocket. "He hasn't texted or anything."

Marceline frowned. "That's weird." As silence settled again, the wind picked up. Marceline's head started to ache suddenly, which she couldn't help but notice had been happening more frequently over the past few weeks. She mentally shrugged it off, blaming it on the stress of a new school year.

The gusts outside almost began to sound like whispers. It almost sounded like the word "Help" over and over again. She nearly asked if anyone else heard it when the hatch entrance to the treehouse was abruptly thrown open.

Katy let out a high-pitched squeal, throwing her hand dramatically across her heart.

Marceline had to admit she wasn't pleased at the sight of Nate, Tag's best friend, sticking his head through the door in the floor.

"Nice of you to show up," Tag said.

Nate didn't respond in his usual snarky manner. His eyes were strangely wide and unblinking, and he was breathing heavy. Nate glanced around the treehouse. "What do you think of ghosts? Real or fake?" he gasped.

Marceline rolled her eyes. Nate was probably trying to pull some prank, coming in here pretending to be afraid. "Fake, obviously."

Tag shrugged before he answered his friend thoughtfully. "I don't know. I think they're real. Not in the spooky, haunting way, just in the nice, watching-over-us way."

Marceline smiled at this. She hadn't pegged Tag as the superstitious type.

"I hope they're not real," Katy said, shivering.

Nate's face was still pale and drawn, and he was nearly shaking.

Marceline frowned at him. "Nate, are you okay?"

After a shaky exhale, Nate said, "What if I told you all I just saw the real Anna?"

"Anna? The one people dress up as every year?" Tag asked. He was the only one of the group who hadn't grown up in Catori Springs, who didn't know all the quirks of the strange mountain town.

Katy nodded with an eye roll. "Yep. They dress up like post-life Anna for the Coffin Races every October. Whoever makes the best dead person wins. It's kind of disgusting if you think about it."

Marceline shrugged. "It's tradition. Anyway, Nate, you're probably just drunk and seeing things."

"I saw her, the real Anna," Nate insisted.

"You saw someone *dressed* like Anna," Marceline corrected.

"No," Nate said forcefully, "she was *see-through*. Come see! She was on the bench across from the Grocery Elf."

Katy groaned. As much as Marceline wanted to brush this off, Nate was acting very spooked and abnormal, and he did have a gleam of sweat across his brow even on the chilly night, so he probably had run all the way here. Didn't mean he was telling the truth, but the interruption was welcomed. Anything to break the awkward silence between her best friend and the guy she had a crush on, both of whom had nothing in common.

Katy leaned closer to Marceline, gripping her arm as if to brace for impact. Katy had always hated scary stories ever since they were little. Marceline put a steady hand on Katy's and squeezed.

"Okay, lead the way then," Marceline told Nate.

Tag rose to his feet, promptly banging his head on the short treehouse ceiling. He rubbed his head sheepishly.

Marceline pretended not to have seen and made her way toward the exit.

"Why would we go toward the ghost?" Katy cried.

"We're not going toward any ghost," Marceline assured her under her breath.

One by one, each of them crawled down the ladder behind Nate, into the high weeds that surrounded the abandoned McCormick Estate. Barely visible through the trees, there was a large, once-beautiful manor that was now a vine-covered, dark and dingy structure to the right of the treehouse. To Marceline's knowledge, it hadn't been lived in for decades.

Marceline gripped her arms in the wind and nearly jogged to keep up with Nate, who held a bottle of clear liquor. That certainly didn't help Marceline believe his story.

Tag turned to her. "What is it you Catori people do at this Coffin Race again?"

"The activity is in the name, Tag. Come on," Marceline teased.

Katy, who had reluctantly jogged to catch up with them, explained, "The participants create a coffin on wheels and then race it up and down a hill. Each coffin has to contain an 'Anna,' who, in case anyone didn't know, is based upon a real person."

"What's the story there?" Tag asked.

Katy raised her hand excitedly, as if she were in a classroom. "I wrote a paper on this for history last year. I got this." She paused to clear her throat. "The real Anna Thompson and her husband, James, came to Catori Springs in the late nineteenth century to receive treatment for Anna's tuberculosis. When she sadly died only a few months later, James and a few other men from town carried her coffin up thousands of feet to bury her at her desired location in the mountains. About twenty years later, as the weather eroded the area where she was buried, the coffin washed back down the mountain. To honor the real Anna's slide down the hill in a coffin, the Catori townspeople recreate it every year."

Marceline nodded at the familiar story. She'd never missed a Coffin Race. There was even a baby picture of her dressed in the white gown with a red velvet jacket that was customary of an Anna costume.

Tag's nose crinkled. "Isn't that kind of disrespectful to the dead to be dressing up as this lady and recreating the fall of her corpse down a mountain?"

"It's tradition," Marceline said again, as if that could explain an entire town's actions.

They were nearing the Grocery Elf when Nate stopped in his tracks. "She's gone."

"Who, Anna?" Marceline asked, resisting another eye roll. This paranormal crap never fazed her. Katy, on the other hand, was nearly cowering behind her.

"I swear, just a few minutes ago, a woman in old Victorian clothing was sitting on that bench under that streetlamp," Nate said, dramatically pointing as he spoke. "I thought it was strange she was dressed like Anna when it's not even around Halloween, but hey, it's Catori Springs. This town is full of freaks, so I didn't think much of it. Then the lamp started flickering, so I turned to the Anna woman again, and she looked right back at me, smiling."

"So, was this Anna a friendly ghost?" Tag asked, a smile threatening at the corners of his mouth.

"I'm not finished yet," Nate snapped. "This lady in the Victorian gown smiles, and at this point I didn't even realize that I could see the back of the bench she was sitting on right through her. I looked away, but I could feel her staring at me so intensely."

Tag snorted. "Dude, you were scared of a lady on a bench watching you?"

"A see-through lady, yeah, man, I was, and you would've been too. It was like I couldn't move. I turned back around. Then, the woman's eyes glowed red. She got up, screamed bloody murder, and sprinted at me full-speed, still screaming her head off."

Katy let out a frightened squeal and gripped Marceline's arm tighter, burying her head into Marceline's shoulder.

Marceline tried to keep a straight face. "What'd you do?"

"I started hauling ass to the treehouse. When I turned back a second later, Anna wasn't there. Like she disappeared into thin air."

Tag made a *poof* noise and gesture.

"Like I said, you're probably just drunk," Marceline said, unfazed by the story. She turned to lead the group back to the treehouse.

"I'm not drunk this time," Nate protested. "Really, I swear. This bottle's not even open."

Marceline shook her head. As they neared the edge of the property where the treehouse was, she checked her phone and groaned. "Crap. I've got to hurry back. It's already past my curfew again."

"You need a ride?" Tag asked.

"No, thanks, though. It's a short ride, and you know my dad wouldn't be happy to see your truck dropping me off after curfew again, especially on a school night."

"Fair enough. Nate, let's get going too."

Katy hugged Marceline. "I'll let the boys drop me home since it's on the way. See you tomorrow, Marci."

Tag lingered by her on the sidewalk. "Sure I can't drive you?"

Marceline smiled. "I'm sure. Barb will get me there in no time."

"Barb?"

Marceline's cheeks colored as she patted the handlebars of her red cruiser bike. "Barb is the name I gave my bike."

Tag laughed. "See you tomorrow, Marceline . . . and Barb."

Marceline immediately felt butterflies before hopping on Barb and turning the opposite direction from the rest of the group toward her house.

They had only recently started hanging out with these boys over the summer. Before, it had always been just her and Katy hanging in this treehouse with a bag of chips, jamming out to music, talking about crushes.

Marceline rubbed her bare arms, shivering. She was in denial of summer's end, still wearing shorts and a T-shirt even as the early-September temperatures had started to drop into the coolness of fall. Normally, she'd love this weather, but right now she just wished she had a jacket.

The wind made the trees that lined the streets wave at her menacingly. Their branches clacked against each other loudly. As much as she would hate to admit it, the strange sound gave her goosebumps.

Passing the bench and streetlamp where Nate had claimed his story happened, she couldn't help but envision the Anna-looking woman dressed in Victorian clothing, screaming and chasing Nate. Not that she believed his story, but if the ghost of Anna was haunting Catori, Marceline wouldn't blame her, considering they celebrated the desecration of her grave once a year. She picked up the pace, when she felt a sudden breeze gust past her as if someone had just run by with enough speed to blow her hair back. It was probably just the wind, even so, Marceline turned back over her shoulder, squinting as she thought she saw the silhouette of a woman in a long gown and a hat with her back to her. This woman's hair and dress weren't billowing in the wind as they should have been. Everything about this woman was eerily still.

Marceline nearly jumped off her bike as she rode over a fallen tree branch. When she turned back around, the figure was gone. Marceline laughed at herself. Normally, she was never fazed by ghost stories. Maybe it was the combination of the story with the windy, unusually chilly night that made her feel slightly creeped out.

Shifting her gaze straight ahead, her mind trailed to other things. The way Tag had held her gaze, the way his voice had sounded when he called her by her full name. *Marceline.* Everyone called her Marci. Everyone but Tag.

For the past few years, until she heard him call her by her full name, she hadn't really liked the sound of it. *Marceline* had always been what her mother called her, and it had always sounded beautiful coming from her mom's lips, decorated by her mom's lovely French accent. Ever since the day her mom had left, the sound of her full name, *Marceline,* was nothing more than a painful reminder of what was missing. But now, hearing it in Tag's deep voice, she had a new appreciation for the longer version. Maybe she could be a Marceline instead of a Marci after all.

Marceline and Tag had met last semester in Calc II. He was the new guy, a cute new guy at that, and everyone wanted to get to know him. So naturally, Marceline, who avoided any sort of conflict at all costs, stayed away. She was more the type to envision an encounter in her head, where in such scenarios Marceline would always have the best comebacks and witty one-liners, when in reality, Marceline was the mumbling, "I'm sorry" girl when conflict struck, even when she wasn't really sorry.

When Tag and Marceline got paired up to work on an assignment together, Marceline was weary. She thought she'd have to do all the work and that Tag was just a stupid jock, held to a lower standard because of his good looks.

But he'd surprised her, completing his equal share of the work. They paired up for every project after that, and over the year, Tag invited her to a few parties that were filled with the jocks and the cheerleaders, not nobody's like Marceline, but she went anyway, bringing Katy as her social sidekick. She and Tag were friends and nothing more.

Still, tonight, the sound of Tag's lips delicately forming the word *Marceline* rang in her ears, carrying her all the way home.

Quietly, she unlocked the front door of her home and removed her shoes. It was dark, and she crossed her fingers, praying that meant her dad and stepmom had gone to bed early. She took one tiptoe, and the entire floorboard creaked. *Perks of an old home,* she thought sarcastically. The lamp flicked on in the living room.

"I told you ten sharp, Marci," came Dad's voice from the recliner near the window.

She held up her phone. "I'm, like, ten minutes past, cut me some slack."

Dad sighed. "The curfew isn't 10:10; it's 10 p.m. sharp."

"It's 10:09 to be fair," Marceline couldn't help but mutter. She looked around the empty living room, glad to see her stepmom hadn't joined this reprimanding.

"Late is late. And ten is a very generous curfew, considering your behavior this summer and the fact that it's a school night."

Marceline resisted the urge to roll her eyes, as she knew it wouldn't help the situation. Her dad had found a six-pack of beer under her bed this summer, then she'd box-dyed a few strands of her hair purple the night before school picture day without asking. He'd ending up allowing her to keep the purple, but she'd only just gotten un-grounded and knew she was walking on thin ice. "You're right, I'll be back on time next time. I'm sorry."

Dad's face softened as he rose from the recliner, his knees cracking in protest. "You know I don't like you biking home alone at night either."

"It's Catori. Nothing bad ever happens here," she replied.

Dad huffed.

"Well, maybe if you actually let me get my driver's license, I wouldn't have to walk."

Dad shrugged. "You know my rules. Once you can follow them consistently, then we can discuss you getting your license. But coming home late definitely doesn't help."

Marceline turned to walk upstairs so Dad wouldn't see her eye roll. She was about to turn seventeen, but her dad wouldn't so much as allow her to get her learner's permit. Nearly everyone else in her grade could drive already. It was almost getting embarrassing.

"Marci?"

She looked back.

"I love you, bean."

Despite herself, Marceline couldn't help but crack a half-smile. "Love you too, Dad. Night."

2

Marceline groaned when her alarm went off in the morning. No matter what sound she set to wake up to, it was always an unpleasant shock to the system. Her brain felt as though she'd been kicked repeatedly. She rolled back over, eyelids falling back down, but was quickly woken again by the weight of two bodies crashing on top of her.

"Wake up, Marci!" Theo, her nine-year-old brother, giggled.

"Marci!" Peter shouted, cupping his hands around his mouth.

"I can hear you. I'm up, you little punks," Marceline grunted, tossing a pillow at the boys. They laughed and jumped on her bed until she sat up.

"You're going to want to do something about that," Peter said, gesturing to her hair.

"Yeah, yeah, you'd better go do something about that stinky breath. Get out, let me get dressed."

Marceline heard her stepmom congratulating the boys on a job well done behind the closed door. Marceline rolled her eyes. The boys would do anything Delilah said. She was the cool mom to them, not as strict as their dad and more present than their real mom.

In her closet, Marceline pulled on a baggy T-shirt and jeans and laced up her Converse. She glanced at corner of the mirror where the last picture she'd taken with her mother was pinned up. It was from right before she'd left. Marceline had just turned ten. Peter had only been six, and Theo only three. Though part of her always had the thought of taking it down, she remembered her mom placing it there for her, and she felt compelled to leave it.

Their mother, Apolline, only ever called infrequently. Maybe a few times a year. Apolline travelled the world and didn't have a cellphone, so they could never call her; it was always them waiting for Mom to call. The last few times she'd called, Marceline hadn't even been home, not that she really wanted to be. Talking to her mom always felt like an unpleasant chore. Why bother talking on the phone when they hadn't seen each other in person in nearly seven years?

Marceline carefully straightened her hair, trying to get it to lay flat. Since she'd added purple streaks, she'd noticed her hair was drier in those areas, but she didn't care. She liked the color. Once her frizzy, wavy hair was somewhat tamed, she applied her makeup, trying to emphasize her plain features. She tried to chisel her non-existent cheek bones to look sharper, contour her nose to not be so flat, add black eyeliner to make her wide, dark brown eyes pop. Ironically, the one feature she had in common with her mother, her eyes, was one of the few features she really liked about her face.

As she came downstairs to the boys already at the table eating oatmeal, Delilah looked up from the morning paper and smiled. "You look nice, Marci."

"Thanks," Marceline replied shortly, not making eye contact. She rubbed her temple to soothe her headache.

Something about Delilah's constant bright smile was too much for a half-asleep Marceline to handle. It made her want to shake her stepmom and ask, "How can you be so happy all the time?" Marceline had in fact never seen Delilah in a bad mood since she and her dad had started dating. She'd figured once Delilah moved in after the wedding, she'd have to let the cracks show, eventually. She couldn't be perfect all the time. Yet, after over a year of living together, Marceline had still only ever encountered Delilah with that wide smile. Was she a robot stuck on the happy setting, or was she just good at hiding her other emotions?

"You look like a racoon with that black stuff on your eyes," Peter laughed through a mouthful of his breakfast.

"Well, at least I don't smell like a racoon like you do," Marceline chimed back.

Dad joined them in the kitchen, pausing to kiss Delilah on the top of her head. "A little heavy on the eye makeup, Marci. Is goth still a thing these days?"

"It's not goth, Dad," Marceline said, sighing as she popped a piece of bread in the toaster.

"You need a ride to school, bean? I can drop you off before the boys."

"I'd rather take my bike," she replied.

"Suit yourself," Dad said.

Marceline grabbed her toast and backpack and slipped out the back door to avoid more morning conversation before she was fully woken up. She stopped to grab Barb the bike from the garage before making her way to school.

As she rode up, she saw Katy getting out of her old Subaru. Marceline quietly rolled up right behind her and rang the bell, making Katy just about jump out of her shoes.

"You're in a good mood," Katy laughed.

"Maybe Delilah's illness is rubbing off on me," Marceline

said, pausing to lock up Barb. Katy looped her arm around Marceline as they began walking toward the front doors of the school.

"Happiness is not an illness, Marci. And you shouldn't hate someone for being too happy."

"Yeah, yeah," Marceline said. She looked up as she heard the familiar roar of Tag's truck turn into the parking lot.

Katy rolled her eyes. "You two are so ridiculous."

"What two?"

"You and Tag. Obviously, you like each other. What's holding you back?"

"Tag doesn't like me," Marceline said quickly.

"Please," Katy scoffed. "You see the way he looks at you and is always offering you rides home? The guy's crazy about you."

Marceline shook her head. "We're just friends."

Then again, Marceline couldn't help but remember one night at the beginning of the summer at a party at Nate's house. They'd been sitting out by the fire as the others had gone inside when he pointed out a shooting star. "Look," he'd said, grabbing her shoulders to point her to the sky. Sure enough, a bright light shot across.

"Whoa," she'd breathed. She'd felt Tag's big hands on her shoulders, and she'd leaned back into him. His arms had tightened into an embrace, and he had gently spun her around and slowly moved toward her face. Her brain had been screaming at her, *He's going to kiss you, you fool! Lean in!* But before anything happened, Tag's attention had been pulled away by Nate, and that was the end of any romantic moment.

For her, the shooting star they'd seen that night had continued right through her heart, but she guessed it must not have felt the same for Tag. After that night, he'd never brought it up again. It was as if it had all been a dream.

"I think he's going to ask you to Homecoming," Katy said in a sing-song tone.

Marceline countered, "He'll probably go with little-miss-perfect Lacey again."

As they turned the corner toward their lockers, the girls were stopped in their tracks.

"Marci, Katy!" came a squeaky voice.

Marceline found herself being hugged tightly by a small, pink-cheeked girl. Pulling away, she saw Bijou Eyota staring up at her. Marceline and Katy had taken swim lessons with Bijou when they were younger, but over the years they'd grown apart. Bijou still spoke the same, her voice light and flowy like a cloud. She also still had her trademark long dark hair in two braids and shiny brown eyes, looking like a doll. This was the first year her parents had cracked and allowed her to come to public school after homeschooling her. Bijou was a year younger than them, but somehow seemed simultaneously much wiser and much less grown up.

"It was the first quarter moon last night. Did you both set your intentions?" Bijou asked.

"Uh, no," Marceline started.

"I did," Katy said brightly.

All their heads turned as a loud whistle echoed through the hallway. Nate passed by, shooting a wink and blowing a kiss in Katy's direction.

Katy feigned gagging and turned her back to Nate.

Bijou giggled. "When will he take the hint you're not interested?"

Katy rolled her eyes. "Trust me, I've given him more than a hint. I've expressly told him there's no way in hell. Maybe he thinks he's so irresistible even someone who doesn't like boys will just be so turned on by his masculine charm."

"And what charm is that exactly?" Marceline asked.

As Katy and Bijou kept talking, Marceline's head pulsed with a searing headache. She zoned out, her vision going blurry. She pinched the bridge of her nose. "Marci?" Katy said, squeezing her shoulder. "You alright?"

Marceline sighed and clenched her teeth. "Just another migraine."

Katy frowned. "You've been getting an awful lot of those lately. Maybe you should get it checked out."

"I'm fine." She looked up to see Bijou eyeing her, looking concerned. Marceline cleared her throat and repeated, "I'm fine. It's probably just because my period's starting soon. I'll see you both at lunch."

Marceline started toward her first class of the day, Spanish. Though the high school had only a few hundred students, the old building had been built nearly as tall as it was wide, meaning the students walked up and down flights of stairs constantly. Walking the steps to the third floor for class was a battle as her headache worsened with each step, but she gritted her teeth and made it.

3

W hen the final bell rang, Marceline made her way back to her bike.

As she was zipping her lock in her backpack, a shadow appeared behind her. "You didn't tell me your birthday was next week," came Tag's voice.

Marceline's heart caught in her throat as she turned around. Birthdays had never been big in Marceline's family. Her dad would get her a strawberry cake from B's Sweet Treats, her favorite, and she'd eat dinner with the family. Katy was always there on her birthday, but other than that, it was nothing special. She swallowed. "Let me guess. Katy told you?"

"I have my sources, but it doesn't matter. So, what are you doing for your big day? Turning the big one-seven, right?"

Marceline smiled. Suddenly her headache had all but disappeared. "Seventeen, yeah, crazy to think I'm that old. I'm not doing much. My dad said I could have off work next weekend for that and for, uh . . . ," she trailed off, not wanting to use the word "Homecoming" in case Tag felt she was pressuring him to ask. He was probably going with his on-again, off-again fling, Lacey, anyway.

"So what you're telling me is that you need some epic birthday plans. I can probably help with that," Tag said, flashing her a smile that Marceline thought should put him on the front cover of magazines. His hazel, nearly golden eyes glinted against the sun, and the freckles around his nose and across his strong cheekbones seemed to bounce as he spoke.

Marceline had to remind herself to blink, then responded, "Oh, no, my birthday isn't something epic to be celebrated."

"You should be celebrated every day, Marceline, but especially on your birthday."

For some reason, the notion of her being celebrated nearly brought tears to her eyes, which she quickly blinked away. "The sun is so bright," she muttered lamely to disguise her sudden show of emotion. She smiled shyly at Tag. "Okay," she said, letting her hands fall from her backpack straps. "Let's celebrate my seventeenth. What awesome things are you thinking of?"

Tag smiled widely. He put his hands in his pockets. "We need to start celebrating right away. A birthday should be celebrated an entire week, and since yours is next week, lunch on me tomorrow. We could go off campus to Luigi's?"

"Oh, yeah, that'd be groovy," Marceline said. *That'd be groovy? Really, Marceline? What year are we in?* Her cheeks colored brightly as she tried not to cringe at herself. But who cared, if Tag wanted to use Marceline's birthday—which was a whole nine days away—as an excuse to take her to lunch, so be it.

"It's a date," he said.

Marceline's eyes bulged, and she bit her lip as she tried to not let her internal freak-out show on her face.

He checked his phone. "I've got to head to football practice, and don't you have to go to work, anyway?"

She nodded. "Supposed to be there in five minutes."

"Yikes, don't let me hold you up."

"I don't mind, really. The mid shift can wait a few minutes, and my stepmom isn't as crazy about punctuality as my dad."

Tag laughed. "You've got to learn a thing or two about getting places on time. First, you missed your curfew last night, now you're going to be late to work. I'm starting to think I'll be waiting around at Luigi's with my food getting cold," he said with a wry smile.

"I'll never be late if food is involved. And you're right, I've got to go. Have a good practice," she said, patting his arm awkwardly. She instantly started to remove her hand, but Tag caught it and held it for a moment. Marceline looked down at his hand, then down at her shoes, not sure how to respond. She couldn't dare a look at his face.

"I'll see you for lunch tomorrow. Get her to work safely, Barb," he said, releasing her hand and patting the back tire of her bike.

Marceline blushed that he'd remembered her silly name for the bike. She waved before riding through the parking lot and onto the main road, resisting the urge to look back. Had Taggart Holiday really just asked her on a lunch date for tomorrow?

———

As she pulled up to the Grocery Elf, the awful but classic sign depicting a creepy elf with wide eyes that were nearly crossed visually confronted Marceline, as it always did. She could see Delilah through the front windows.

"How was school?" Delilah greeted her as she came through the chiming door. Delilah didn't say anything about Marceline being late, and Marceline knew she wouldn't tell her dad either. Sometimes Marceline wished Delilah would show some sign of human emotion instead of being so nice all the time.

"It was fine, boring."

"I hope your classes get more interesting for you," Delilah said sympathetically. "So, we got a shipment in today. If you have time tonight, there's some new product in the back that needs tags and to be put away."

Marceline nodded as she tied on her apron. "Will do."

Delilah had started as a regular employee back when she was a mountain-bike-riding-tourist who'd stumbled upon Catori Springs. She'd fallen in love with the small mountain town and gotten a job at the Grocery Elf, where she met Josh, Marceline's dad and the owner of said grocery store, married the guy, and became a stepmom to three kids. Best of all, her marriage also came with the exciting new title of manager of Grocery Elf, a title Marceline had vowed she herself would never have.

Delilah left for the night not long after the afternoon rush, leaving Marceline to work the rest of her shift with Sheldon, a nice, quiet, older guy who had worked there forever.

The store closed at eight on the dot every night, and Marceline and Sheldon had their routine down pat. She restocked while Sheldon wiped down the windows and counters, then after closing, Sheldon counted out the drawer while Marceline mopped.

Right before closing, as Marceline was stocking the cereal aisle, the chime above the door sounded. Marceline cursed under her breath. A strange woman with dried blood below her nose walked in. She looked to be mid-thirties, Japanese, and she had short, greasy black hair to her chin with some dyed streaks of gray throughout. Sheldon looked up from the back window, but Marceline nodded to indicate she'd help the customer.

Damn tourists. It was always tourists stopping in town on

the way to the mountains who came in right before close, never the locals who respected the closing time.

Fortunately, the woman was quick. She picked out a loaf of bread and a jar of peanut butter and brought them to the counter. She pointed to the two-gallon water jugs. "Two of those," the woman said in a raspy voice.

Up close, the youth Marceline had thought she'd seen from a distance showed cracks, literally. There were deep lines ingrained in the woman's skin. The woman's almond-shaped eyes were such a dark brown they were nearly black, and they seemed to sink right into her, making Marceline feel the woman's tiredness herself. Marceline caught a brief whiff of sweat as the woman turned her head, which was strong enough to overpower the smell of the floor cleaner in the mop bucket behind the counter.

Marceline tried not to stare at the dried blood under the woman's nose. As she scanned the woman's items, she couldn't help herself. "You've got a little . . . ," Marceline trailed off, gesturing under her nose.

The woman just stared at her, not reaching self-consciously toward her nose or seeming surprised at all. The silence, combined with the *stop talking* look in the woman's eyes, made Marceline shiver.

Marceline cleared her throat. "That'll be $15.74."

The woman pulled a small pouch from her jacket pocket, counting out the exact change.

Without a word, the woman grabbed her bag and left through the chiming door.

4

The next morning, Marceline woke up with a headache worse than the day before. The kind of headache that made her nauseous, and every step rocked her brain. But she was meeting Tag for lunch, and that was all the motivation she needed to go to school.

Bijou approached her as she was walking into school. "How are you doing, Marci?"

"Good, good," Marceline replied, distracted by her throbbing head.

"Have you ever noticed how overwhelming public school is?" Bijou burst as she dodged a group stopped in the hallway. "I've never spent the whole day, every day, every week with this many other people my age."

"I'm sure it's a shock to your system," Marceline said. She nearly winced as they entered the building.

Bijou's brow crinkled, and she began rummaging through her backpack. "I almost forgot. I brought you this to help with your migraines." She handed Marceline a small tincture.

It surprised Marceline that Bijou had remembered. "What? For me? What is it?"

Bijou instructed her to take the cap off the tincture, which released the aromatic scent of peppermint. "Peppermint essential oil can help relieve headaches," Bijou explained. "Just apply it to your temples as needed."

Marceline remembered that Bijou's parents were the owners of a metaphysical healing store in town and figured this was some sort of natural healing method. "Wow, thanks so much, B. I really appreciate this."

Bijou gave her hand a gentle squeeze before heading toward her locker. Marceline couldn't contain a smile lifting the corners of her mouth as she looked down at the small vial in her hands. Marceline wasn't used to having friends like this outside of Katy, who noticed her and wanted to help and support her, who gave her little gifts. Katy was her best friend, always had been and always would be, and for a while, Marceline had convinced herself Katy was all she needed. It was nice to open herself up to other people like Bijou and Tag.

The peppermint surprisingly worked like a charm at relieving Marceline's headache. She applied it once every class.

In fourth period English, the teacher allotted quiet time for them to begin reading the newly assigned book, *Frankenstein.*

Marceline pulled out the tincture and used the roller to apply it to her temple.

"What's with the peppermint?" Katy whispered.

"Got it from Bijou. It's been helping my migraine."

"That's great. Bijou is so sweet. I'm glad she's here this semester."

"Me too." Marceline paused then, trying to sound nonchalant, said, "Oh, I almost forgot to tell you, I can't go to lunch today."

Katy frowned. "You've got some other plans?" Marceline

didn't exactly have a wide group of friends. Occasionally, Marceline would join Katy's choir group or her student council friends for lunch, but it was always at least the two of them.

Katy was the social butterfly. She had friends in student council, in choir, in yearbook club, but she had always made Marceline her number one, and for that, Marceline was so grateful. But it could be lonely seeing how easily her best friend connected with others, while she was only ever invited out because she was Katy's friend. She'd sit in the corner, not speaking unless Katy pulled her in to a conversation. It was very unlike Marceline to be the one who had plans.

"Actually, yes. Tag asked me to go on a lunch date yesterday." She stared down at her book, avoiding Katy's reaction.

"What?" Katy squealed. She lowered her voice back to a whisper when the teacher shushed her. "I told you he liked you. Did he call it a date?"

Marceline glared at her. "Don't look so smug. Yes, he called it a date, but I feel like that's a normal thing. He probably wants to talk about school or football or something."

"Or Homecoming," Katy said with a wink.

When the bell rang, Marceline got a text from Tag. *Meet at my locker?*

"I've got to go. Talk after lunch?"

"Someone's getting a Homecoming date," Katy chimed.

Marceline ignored her and headed toward Tag's locker. He was talking to Lacey, his ex. He glanced up when he saw Marceline coming. "Marceline, hey!" he called. Marceline approached and smiled at Lacey, who kept a straight face. "You know Marceline, right Lace?"

Lacey nodded. "I'd recognize that bad, box-dyed purple hair anywhere." Marceline's smile faltered at the insult. Turning to Tag, Lacey continued, "So, did you want to go to lunch today?"

"Marceline and I already have plans," Tag said.

Lacey raised her eyebrows and flipped her hair, wafting them with an overly flowery scent of perfume. Marceline crinkled her nose. "Ah, well, have an excellent lunch with *Marceline*."

Marceline didn't know her name could sound like a contagious virus, but somehow Lacey had said it with enough disgust to warrant one needing to douse oneself with hand sanitizer afterward. Marceline couldn't help but laugh as Lacey walked away. Tag looked at her questioningly.

"That girl does not like me," Marceline explained.

"What makes you say that?" Tag asked, shutting his locker.

Marceline could've kept laughing at Tag's obliviousness. She wanted to say, *Didn't that whole conversation hint at that?* Instead, she shrugged. "She just seemed a bit cold toward me."

"She's not always like that. I think you two would actually get along really well. She's smart like you are."

Marceline felt eyes following them as they walked out the front doors together. The bright light of the sun made her head pulse with pain, but she wasn't about to pull out her peppermint tincture and rub it on her face in front of Tag. The ease of the conversation was doing some to relieve the headache. They walked across the street to Luigi's and ordered a pizza. As they had an open campus lunch, the place was already filled with many students.

Sitting across from one another in a booth, Tag sniffed the air dramatically. "Is that peppermint?"

Marceline's cheeks colored. "Oh, yeah. Bijou gave me some peppermint essential oil."

Tag smiled. "I like it."

Marceline smiled back. "So, how's football going?"

"It's been great. We might even have a chance of making it to State this year."

Marceline raised her eyebrows. Their school had been

notoriously bad at all sports for as long as she could remember. Most kids, if they were serious about sports, would transfer to the high schools in the bigger towns surrounding them. This was the first time in a long time a Catori Springs High sports team was actually good.

"I know that sounds crazy," Tag continued, "but we've been dominating. We're playing Pine Crest next, so that will really tell how good we are. You coming to the game on Friday?"

Although never one to attend football games of her own volition, when a cute boy asks you to attend a football game, you attend a football game. Tag had asked her to come to all the home games so far that season. "Wouldn't miss it," Marceline said.

Tag smiled. Their server brought them their pepperoni pizza and took their number.

"Are you sure you don't want to split the bill with me?" Marceline asked.

Tag shook his head. "Nah, it's your pre-birthday birthday lunch. You can get the next one."

Marceline hesitated. "So, there will be a next one?" She couldn't force herself to make eye contact with Tag, so instead, she glanced out the front window of the restaurant, watching the stream of passersby.

As the sidewalk cleared, Marceline nearly gasped. It was as if her senses were simultaneously heightened and turned off. Her ears stopped picking up specific sounds; everything was muffled, but her breath was loud. She could feel her heartbeat in her throat. Outside was the faintest vision of a woman dressed in a long, flowing white gown. Anna. Only she wasn't walking. Her feet hardly moved at all, dangling as her body was propelled forward, hovering an inch above the ground.

Anna turned toward her, making brief eye contact. Nate had told the truth, after all.

"Marceline?" Tag asked.

She broke her gaze from the woman outside and shook her head. "Sorry, I was just looking at—" Marceline blinked; the woman was gone, nowhere to be seen on the street. "Um, never mind."

She must have just imagined it after hearing Nate's story the other night. But still, how could her eyes have deceived her so badly in broad daylight? Her brain slowly unscrambled as she recalled what Tag had said earlier. "Sorry I got distracted. About what you said, I'm having a good time too. I'd like to do this again."

Tag cleared his throat and looked down at his hands. He looked nervous, which Marceline had never seen before. "I like you, Marceline. I'm sorry it's taken me so long to say or do anything about it. This summer I tried to push the feelings away. It scared me to want to be with someone like you."

Marceline's heart hammered. "Someone like me?"

"Someone who doesn't care about all this high school stuff. You're so smart and kind. You always make whoever you talk to feel so important. People come to you like magnets, and yet, it doesn't go to your head."

Was he talking about her? Marceline didn't think people noticed her at all, especially not coming to her like magnets.

Tag continued, "I just . . . I guess what I'm trying to say is I wish I could go back and redo this summer. All those times I dropped you back home, I always wanted . . ." He shook his head. "I can't go back now, but I want to make up for lost time and just tell you how I've been feeling. I've made up my mind, and I don't want to pretend like the feelings aren't there because it's scary. I like you. A lot."

Marceline didn't know what to say. Her heart was pounding so hard she could feel it against the table. All this time she'd thought it was all in her head. That a guy like Tag wouldn't like a girl like her. Her mouth was suddenly so dry. Even if her brain could have formed words, her mouth couldn't.

Tag was looking at her expectantly. *Say something!* her brain screamed.

"Thanks for telling me," Marceline finally said slowly, collecting her thoughts. It took everything in her to try to appear calm. She wasn't sure she was totally ready to let her guard down yet and show him her true feelings, but she reached across the table and squeezed Tag's hand. "Next lunch is on me."

5

Katy did an entire little dance number when Marceline told her what Tag had said at lunch. "Can I just hear you say that I was right? He's liked you this whole time."

"I guess you were right," Marceline admitted.

"So, what'd you say after he told you he liked you?"

"I told him, 'Thanks for telling me.'"

Katy stopped in her tracks and laughed.

"What? What's so funny about that?" Marceline snapped.

"You are absolutely savage. I love that about you," Katy said in between laughs. "You don't just tell people what they want to hear. You say what you're really feeling in that moment."

"Was that the wrong thing to say?"

"No, I think that was fair. You've been waiting months for the guy to finally say how he feels. At the same time, if you would've just told him how you were feeling earlier, maybe this process could've moved along faster."

Marceline sighed. "I know. I was just scared to say anything."

"He was too, apparently. So why don't you seem excited

right now? Do you not like him like that anymore?"

Marceline thought for a moment. "No, I definitely like him. It's just overwhelming, and I—"

Katy put her finger to Marceline's lips. "Nope, no, no. You've got to go tell him you like him. Don't leave anything up in the air anymore, just put it all out on the table. Why not?" Katy put her arm around Marceline's back and steered her toward Tag's locker.

"I guess you're right," Marceline relented.

Katy let out a wistful breath. "If you know of girls in this school who have a secret, romantic crush on me, tell them now is the time to confess to me."

"Sorry, Kat. I only know of some boys who have crushes on you."

Katy crinkled her nose. "No thanks."

They turned the corner to Tag's hallway. He was still by his locker. Marceline tried to turn around, but Katy held her firm. "Go," Katy commanded, giving Marceline a little push.

Marceline walked as slowly as she could toward Tag's locker. He looked up to see her approaching and smiled. She didn't return the smile.

"What's up?" he asked.

Marceline took a deep, settling breath. "I should've told you this earlier, but I've been scared to tell you too. I like you, Tag."

Tag's smile widened, and he reached for Marceline's arms. The bell rang, but neither moved for a second.

"Thanks for telling me," he said.

Marceline smiled, looking up into his golden eyes. She started to feel the same way she had last summer when they'd nearly kissed. Was he slightly leaning toward her, or was that in her head? Marceline felt her hands sweating. Were his eyes closing?

"You two, get to class!" a voice scolded, causing them to

jump apart. Marceline glared at the person who'd shouted; Nate, and he was laughing. Tag smiled back weakly. Why did Nate always seem to get in the way?

———

Thursday, Marceline was feeling the best she had felt in days. The peppermint Bijou had given her had really helped her headache.

Before she worked the close that evening, Katy and Bijou offered to ride their bikes with her.

Katy wasted no time grilling her. "When is Tag going to ask you out?" she said in an impatient whine.

"Why are you more excited about this than me?" Marceline asked.

"Well, you should be more excited than me about this! It will be perfect; Homecoming is the day after your birthday. You can go with your hunky boyfriend—"

"Not my boyfriend."

Bijou giggled. "You two would make a beautiful couple."

Switching the focus, Marceline asked, "What about you, B, anyone catch your eye?"

Bijou turned a light shade of pink. "Oh, me? No, no boys for me right now. My parents want me to focus on school."

Marceline smiled at the prospect of tiny Bijou, with her pigtail braids and her baggy overalls, flirting with a boy.

After their bike ride, Marceline went to work her usual three-thirty-to-eight shift with Sheldon.

Marceline noticed early into her shift that her peppermint tincture was empty. She reminded herself to stop by Bijou's parents' store to get more soon. The shift felt extra long, her head pounding with each movement. It got so bad at points she had to stop and hold on to a shelf to keep herself from doubling over. Marceline hadn't wanted to admit to herself how much of a problem these headaches were becoming, but they were almost unbearable. Maybe she'd tell her dad that night.

At quarter to eight, without speaking, Marceline and Sheldon began their closing routine. Sheldon was in the back counting out the drawer, and she was restocking soup cans when she heard the door chime. Another migraine was sneaking back up on her, making her eyes sting. Her vision got slightly blurry, so she closed her eyes and stood up. Knees quivering, she leaned into the shelf she'd just stocked, knocking some cans to the ground. She opened her eyes and found the lights flickering. The pain in her temples was electrifying.

Suddenly, a voice spoke to her. It was only a whisper, but it was as if she had her earbuds set to the highest volume setting. "Beware the Homecoming dance. Don't let history repeat itself."

Her knees completely gave out, and she found herself crashing to the floor. Her vision went black, and she lost all sensation.

When she came to, the woman from earlier in the week with short, black and gray-streaked hair was kneeling beside her. The woman's nose was bleeding again, only this time it was fresh, dripping blood.

Marceline tried to sit up, her head still spinning. She felt nauseous as the metallic smell of blood assaulted her nose. "What happened?" she asked her.

The woman didn't answer. She just got to her feet and left the store, the bell on the door ringing behind her.

Marceline quickly got to her feet and continued stocking the soup cans. When Sheldon came up from the back, Marceline greeted him like normal.

"Marci, you've got a nosebleed, doll," Sheldon said, pulling a tissue from the counter and bringing it to her.

6

After work, Marceline rode her bike around the neighborhood, trying to clear her mind. It was long past dark, nearly nine. She kept riding her bike past her house and circling back. Her mind was racing. Who had spoken to her? It couldn't have been the black-haired, nose-bleed woman. The voice had been too masculine sounding. But what was that woman doing in the store at that moment? Why didn't she say anything? Why had Marceline's nose also started bleeding? What did it mean, *Beware the Homecoming dance?* What history was she to not allow to repeat?

Once she felt ready to head inside, she laid her bike in the garage and opened the door to the kitchen. The sound she heard stopped her in her tracks.

"Are you coming to visit, Mommy?" Theo asked.

Their mom's sigh shot static through the speaker. "Oh, my loves, I want to see you all so badly. I will try to make a trip to the U.S. soon." Marceline's heart tightened at the sound of her mom's voice, velvety and drawn out with her French accent.

She knew her mom wouldn't come visit. She hadn't ever been back, and Marceline doubted she ever would.

"Can we come to you?" Peter asked.

Marceline felt her heart break. It hurt her the most to see how her brothers still clung to their mom's irregular phone calls.

"I would love nothing more, but I'm not staying in kid-friendly places, darling."

Marceline rolled her eyes. She was still standing in the garage, not ready to turn the corner to join the call. She didn't want to be there at all. Just as she was about to turn back out the way she came, her mom said, "Will your sister be home soon?"

"I think I heard the garage. She might be home now," Peter said.

"Oh, that is good news. I need to speak with her."

Marceline felt her entire body shake. There was such an overwhelming dread to speak to her mom. Her mom had made her choice, and it wasn't to be with her husband, with her kids, where she belonged. Every time she and her mom spoke, Marceline felt like she reverted to her child self, back to when she was ten and the world seemed so small.

She turned before she could hear another accented word, wiping a tear from her eye. She couldn't even find comfort at home. But she didn't want to be alone to think about what had just happened at the store.

She felt tears roll down her cheek. With shaky hands, she reached for her phone. She thought about calling Katy, but she didn't want her to worry. She needed comfort. Her fingers were dialing before she'd even thought it through.

Tag picked up on the second ring. "Hey, Marceline."

"Hi," she responded through a shaky breath. Just hearing

his voice took her mind off the emotions of the night so far. "What are you up to?"

"I'm just working on homework. Actually, have you done your stats assignment yet?"

"No, I haven't," she said, feeling her heart release at the normalcy of the conversation. She sniffled.

"Are you okay?" Tag asked.

Another tear rolled down her cheek. "Can I see you?" she asked in a choked, quiet voice.

She immediately regretted saying it, but before she could say anything else, Tag responded, "Want me to pick you up?"

"No," she blurted. Having Tag's loud truck come roaring up to her house at night would set her dad off on an over-protective rampage. She thought about taking her bike to Tag's house, but he lived pretty far toward the highway. There were always strange people under the bridge to the highway. As she considered, she finally told him, "Meet me at the treehouse in ten."

"I'll be there."

With a deep breath, she wheeled Barb back out and set off down the street. She'd be back before anyone noticed. It was a quick ride to the abandoned McCormick Estate. The estate was on a big plot of land. It backed into the pine trees which sprouted all along the edge of the mountain range that surrounded the entire town of Catori Springs. Marceline had heard many ghost stories over the years from the townspeople that had taken place at the abandoned estate. What had once been an elegant, well-kept mansion built by the town's founders had long since fallen into disrepair.

The treehouse on the property had always been a safe space. Since they were little kids, Marceline would tell her dad she was going to Katy's, and Katy would tell her parents she was going to Marceline's, and they'd secretly meet at the tree-house. It was disguised by so many trees surrounding the estate that no one could see it from the street. It was secluded, and for some, that may be scary, but it had never bothered Marceline and Katy, as they always had one another.

Walking her bike toward the low iron fence surrounding the estate, she noticed a light was on in the main house. That was unusual. Just as quickly as she'd seen it, the light went off. Maybe a headlight from the street had reflected off the glass, but she hadn't noticed any cars. She shook it off as a trick of her eyes.

As she waited for Tag, Marceline started to worry she'd overstepped her relationship with him. They weren't dating, after all. What was she thinking inviting him in the middle of the night to the treehouse? She hadn't spent much time alone with Tag, let alone with any boy she wasn't related to, ever. She hesitated, holding Barb's handlebars uncertainly. Maybe she could text him never mind. She jumped as she heard the familiar roar of Tag's truck. Well, too late now. His truck door slammed closed, and she turned as he made his way toward her.

"Hey," she greeted him shyly.

He opened his mouth to speak, but she quickly turned her back, busying herself by leaning Barb against the iron fence. She stepped her long legs over the fence, and Tag followed suit. He wordlessly walked behind her into the trees until they came across the bottom of the treehouse's ladder.

She climbed up first, with Tag coming behind her. She pushed the latch door up and heaved herself in.

Tag pulled himself up and carefully shut the door. He reached for the lantern hanging above them, and with a click, they could suddenly see one another with a vaguely orange hue. Both of them were awkwardly standing on their knees until Marceline leaned against one of the walls. Tag sat next to her.

He turned to face her and grabbed her hands. "Are you okay?"

Marceline nodded, swallowing a lump in her throat.

"No, really, you can tell me if something's wrong," he said. "You sounded upset on the phone earlier."

"I just didn't want to be alone," she confessed. She wanted to pull her hands away to move her hair from her face, some way to fidget, but he held firm. If she looked into his eyes, she was sure she would tear up again.

"Do you believe in the supernatural?" she blurted.

Tag laughed, but quickly sucked it back in. "Sorry, I didn't mean to laugh. That was just unexpected." He pulled his hands away and scratched his head as he leaned back, sending the treehouse swaying. "To be honest, if you would've asked me that before I moved to this town, I would've said hell no. But you heard that story from Nate with the Victorian woman chasing him, plus there's been countless other stories just like that. I'm not sure I believe in everything supernatural, but there is at least something weird in this town."

Marceline nodded again.

"Why? Did something happen to you?" he pressed.

Marceline thought about telling him about what happened at the store or about seeing Anna while they'd been on their date the other day, but she knew it would sound crazy. She shook her head and smiled. "No, nothing happened. I was just trying to take my mind off . . . my mom."

"Your mom?"

"She—" Marceline paused to swallow. "She left us almost seven years ago. A few weeks after my birthday."

"I'm so sorry, Marci—"

"She's in France, or somewhere in Europe, I don't even know," Marceline burst out, the sound coming out like a sob. She laughed dully as another tear rolled down her cheek. "And she calls and acts like everything is perfect, like she isn't thousands of miles away. She hasn't been to visit. She doesn't even have a phone for us to call. It's different every time."

Tag clasped her hands but didn't say anything.

"I don't like to talk to her. And I don't like that I don't like to talk to her. She's my mom, I shouldn't be this angry at her. But I'm so mad at her it hurts. I'm the oldest, I knew what it was like when she left. How hurt my dad was, how confused my little brothers were. Hell, how confused we all were. I still don't know why she left us. I feel guilty, like if I had only—"

"Don't," Tag said. "Don't blame yourself for any choices your mom made. You were just a kid."

Marceline heaved as another sob came through her chest. She released Tag's hands to wipe her eyes.

"I'm so sorry, this is all out of nowhere," she said.

"It's okay, I can only imagine how hard that is for you."

Marceline took some inhales through her nose, releasing them through her mouth. "I'm okay," she muttered, more to herself than to Tag.

He didn't say anything as she calmed down, then she turned back to him. "So, you know any other ghost stories?"

Tag smiled gently. "Lots. And I'm a very good storyteller."

7

arceline and Tag had somehow moved even closer together in the tight space while he told her ghost stories. Some of the ones he told were so ridiculous, she was wiping tears from laughing. She leaned her head on his shoulder. "Thanks for cheering me up," she said quietly.

"Anytime," he said. Their faces were so close together that when he spoke, his breath tickled her cheek, wafting the scent of spearmint gum.

As Marceline turned to look up at him, his eyes were already shining down on her. In the back of her mind, she heard Katy encouraging her, telling her not to leave anything up in the air anymore. Without a second thought, she laid her hand on Tag's cheek, pulled his chin down to her level, and pressed her lips against his. He pulled away after only a moment. She could tell he was surprised, and so was she that she'd done something so unlike herself. Her cheeks instantly burned. "I'm sorry, I—"

He interrupted her with another kiss, pulling her in deeper. She'd been kissed before, sure, but never like *this*. Before, she'd always been hyper aware of the feeling of two pairs of lips touching, but now it was as if these lips were only extensions of the entire body. She felt this kiss everywhere.

She felt his hands reach for her waist, and she put her legs on either side of his lap. He pulled her up, and she faced him, knees locked around him. Her jeans had pulled away slightly from her lower back, and she felt his hand run softly across her bare skin, sending tingles up her spine. Her hands acted of their own accord, wrapping up in his short, soft hair.

He pulled away and took a deep breath, looking like he didn't want to stop. Marceline was out of breath, feeling light-headed.

"I don't want to rush anything between us. I meant what I said. I really like you." His tone was serious. He took another deep breath. "Will you be my girlfriend? I don't know if that's rushing into it, and you don't have to say yes, I just—"

She interrupted him with another peck. "I'd love to be your girlfriend."

He smiled and kissed her again, long and tender, hands cupping her face.

———

On the way back home, Marceline felt light as a feather, like she could be blown away into the sky, and she'd still be lost in her own world. A world in which she was Taggart Holiday's girlfriend. She laughed to herself as she thought of Katy's reaction. She thought about calling her before she got home.

She pulled off to the side of the road and pulled out her phone. It was almost 1 a.m. She'd definitely wait until school tomorrow.

She turned right to head home, past the Grocery Elf, when her vision blurred as her head instantly felt like it was going to explode. She screamed in pain as the same voice yelled in her ears, "Beware the Homecoming dance. Don't let history repeat itself."

With her eyes closed, she raised her hands to grip her head and felt herself hop the curb. Regaining her senses, she pressed the brakes, but it was too late. She smashed into the stop sign, the force of her body uprooting the pole from the ground as they both hit the ground. Whole body shaking, she quickly pulled herself up. Her arm was bleeding, and she'd ripped the side of her jeans, but she was okay. She looked down, gasping as she saw Barb, her frame bent at a bad angle. Beside Barb was the stop sign, which had dislodged from its pole. She cursed under her breath and grabbed the dented bike with one hand and the stop sign with the other. As she moved through the crisp air, wheeling Barb beside her, the hairs on her arms were standing straight up. Her teeth chattered. She couldn't be out here another moment, so she took off in a run down the road, away from the Grocery Elf, away from the voice.

8

Marceline stowed Barb in the garage, scared of the damage she'd caused, both to Barb and with her furious father. She shone the light from her phone on the poor battered bike and was confused why she'd taken the stop sign with her. Part of her shaken brain was thinking maybe people would think some kids in town had stolen the sign, not that someone had crashed into it.

Now, of course, she had the stop sign, and the damaged bike, to lead her directly to the accident.

As she nervously opened the door to the house, she flinched, as if waiting for her dad to come barging downstairs at any moment, but all was quiet in the Lees household. Every step she took seemed to creak louder than the last, echoing in the sleeping house.

She was careful not to hit the stop sign on anything as she slowly made her way up the stairs and into her bedroom. She closed the door behind her and stowed the stop sign under her bed.

She didn't know how she'd explain where she'd been all

night and what had happened to Barb, but that was a problem for the morning. Then she collapsed onto her pillow, eyes closing immediately.

———

Marceline woke up to her alarm, never having gotten under the covers. She was still wearing yesterday's clothes. Her hands were covered in dirt from the ordeal last night. There was dried blood under her nose and on her arm from where she fell, and smudged makeup under her eyes. She needed a shower, bad.

She slowly opened her bedroom door, peeking both ways before crossing the hallway to the bathroom. Fortunately, it was open, and she darted in. She locked the door behind her and only seconds later, a hand was pounding on the door. "I have to pee!" Theo yelled.

"Go downstairs!" Marceline shouted back.

"Marci, can I just go real quick?" Theo whined.

Marceline responded by turning the water to the shower on. Theo gave one final defeated kick to the door, then she was in the clear.

Dressed and ready for school, Marceline came downstairs, fearing the worst. She gulped to find her dad sitting at the kitchen table alone, drinking coffee.

"Where is everyone?" she asked.

"I had Delilah take the boys to school," he said. He offered her a mug.

"Thanks," Marceline said gratefully, reaching out to pour herself some coffee. "I'm going to need the caffeine today."

"I'll bet you are after the night you had," Dad said.

Marceline felt the blood drain from her face. "I can explain—"

"Please do, Marci. Please explain to me why you didn't come home until nearly 1 a.m."

Marceline swallowed and closed her eyes, holding back tears. "I'm so sorry."

"You're sorry? Marci, what has gotten into you these last few months? Ever since you've been hanging out with that Tate guy—"

"His name is Tag, Dad."

"Tag, whatever. Ever since you've been seeing him, you've made really poor choices. Coming in at one in the morning. On a school night, nonetheless. You have a curfew for a reason, Marci. You must respect my rules if you're going to live under my roof." Marceline couldn't think of what to say. "Were you with him last night?"

She groaned. "Dad, it's not Tag's fault. These have all been my bad choices."

Dad's stare was unrelenting. "What do you have to say for yourself?"

Marceline grasped for words, coming up empty-handed. Her breath caught in her throat as tears pooled in her eyes. "I promise I'll pay for the damages—"

"What damages?" Dad's eyes bulged with anger, unblinking.

"Barb. I sort of crashed her."

"Crashed? Marci, do you know how much that bike costs? How could you crash a damn bike? You've been riding since you were five years old."

Marceline's breath was so quick, but each time she sucked in air, it felt like none was getting to her lungs or brain.

Dad sighed and put a hand on Marceline's back. "Breathe, Marci." He sat her down in a chair.

"I'm so sorry," she gasped.

Dad sat in the chair next to her and put a hand on her back

while her breathing slowed down. Deep inhale through the nose, exhale out the mouth.

"Are you okay?" he asked after she'd caught her breath.

Finally, she looked up at him. "I'm fine. When I came home and heard mom on the phone with the boys, it freaked me out. I just needed to ride my bike to clear my head."

Dad nodded. "What did you hit?"

Marceline hesitated, then answered, "The stop sign outside the Grocery Elf."

"Did you at least come to a complete stop?"

Marceline cracked a small smile. "After I hit the sign, yes."

"Were you hurt?"

Marceline shook her head. "I feel fine. It was stupid, really. I just wasn't paying attention and lost control." She hesitated. "I've also been having some pretty intense migraines lately. That may have had something to do with it." That was an understatement, and she'd left out the part about the voices and the nosebleeds, but at least she'd finally told him.

Dad sighed, and his face softened slightly. "Your mom used to get those a lot. They could take her out for a few days. I'll bring you home some migraine medicine she used to take." He sighed again. "Marci, I want you to know you can always talk to me about anything, about your headaches, your mom, school, boys—whatever."

Marceline nodded.

"But," Dad continued, "you did break my rules. I'm going to have to ground you again. No more ten o'clock curfew. You come straight home after work or school, you understand?"

Marceline nodded again.

"I'll pay to fix your bike for now, but you're going to pay me back with your paychecks every month."

Marceline raised her head. "How am I going to get to school and work and back until Barb's fixed?"

Dad smiled. "I guess you'll have to take Peter's old bike."

"No, come on. He hasn't even fit on that thing in a year. How am I going to ride it?"

He shrugged. "Your problem to figure out. Or you can walk, up to you." He stood, zipping his jacket. "And promise me you won't spend any more time with that Tom kid."

"Tag, Dad. And I can't promise that. I have class with him, and he's my . . ." She paused. "Tag's my friend. He's a really good guy. I think you'd like him if you gave him a chance."

Dad's frown only deepened. "Just be careful. Only see him at school, okay?"

Marceline looked down at her coffee. Her phone buzzed with a text from Tag. *Birthday week lunch today?* Of course Tag remembered her birthday was exactly a week away. She smiled as she texted her response.

9

She desperately missed Barb on her walk to school, which seemed so much further than usual. At the same time, Marceline wasn't exactly excited to walk closer to the scene of the accident, fearing she'd experience the same pain she'd felt the night before.

Fortunately, as she passed the Grocery Elf, it was nothing more than the now-usual headache.

She greeted Katy at their lockers. "You won't believe it," Katy said before Marceline could get a word out.

"Believe what?"

Katy rolled her eyes. "You know how excited we've been to have the Homecoming dance at the Richmond Manor?"

Marceline nodded.

"Well, now the school is saying it's out of the budget. After we already paid the deposit!" Katy looked at Marceline for her reaction.

Marceline feigned disgust. "No!"

"Yes! And so now we have to have the dance in the boring old gym."

"Ah, I'm sorry, Kat. I'm sure it will still look amazing."

"It will," Katy said brightly. "Why do you look so tired?"

She knew her eyes were likely puffy, but she'd done her best to mask it with makeup. "It's a long story," Marceline began. She trailed off as she saw Tag walking toward them. She smiled, and he leaned over and kissed her. It gave her butterflies deep in her stomach, reminding her of the night before.

"Hey, Katy," he greeted.

Katy did nothing to hide the shock on her face. "Hi, Tag. Where's my kiss, since you're kissing all your *friends* these days?"

Tag looked down at Marceline and raised his eyebrows. "You didn't tell her yet?"

"I was about to."

"Tell me what?" Katy demanded.

"I asked Marceline to be my girlfriend last night."

Katy turned to Marceline, eyes about to pop out of her sockets.

"I said yes," Marceline confirmed.

Katy enveloped Marceline and Tag in a hug. "I knew you two would make the best couple," her muffled voice said from mid-hug.

Tag kept his arm around her shoulders. "So, are you going with Marceline to the game tonight?" he asked.

Marceline's face fell. Before Katy could respond, Marceline said, "Actually, I'm not sure I can go anymore. I'm sort of grounded again."

"From breaking your curfew last night?" Tag asked. Katy raised her eyebrows at this, and Marceline promptly avoided eye contact.

"That, and I got into a bit of an accident on the way home."

"Are you okay?" Tag and Katy asked nearly simultaneously.

Marceline held a hand up. "I'm fine. Barb, on the other

hand, is not. Oh, and the stop sign across the street from the Grocery Elf was an unfortunate casualty."

"That was you? Everyone's been talking about the missing sign."

Marceline nodded. "So, I've got to work extra shifts to pay for fixing Barb, and I'm also not supposed to be going anywhere but school and work."

"What about Homecoming?" Katy asked.

Tag looked expectantly at Marceline.

Marceline looked down at her feet to avoid both their stares. "I'm not sure. We haven't talked about that."

"But it's only a week away," Katy said, her pitch rising in panic. "Let me talk to your dad. I'm sure I can convince him to let you go to the dance."

Marceline smiled. "You are persuasive."

The first bell rang, signaling them to make their way to first period. "Talk to you both later," Marceline called on her way to the dreaded staircase up to the third floor.

———

Bijou intercepted Marceline on her way to meet Tag for lunch.

"Katy told me what happened. I'm sorry to hear about your bike. I hope you're feeling okay."

Marceline nodded. "Thanks, B. I'm feeling fine." After a silence, Marceline said, "Hey, what's the name of your parent's store again? I want to buy more of that peppermint oil you gave me."

Bijou smiled. "It's called Moon Opal. It's just two blocks down from the Grocery Elf."

"Thanks again for bringing me that. It did wonders for my headaches."

"I thought it might." Bijou leaned closer. "I get headaches like that sometimes, especially here at the school."

"Must be the stress," Marceline said.

Bijou narrowed her eyes slightly. "Yes, must be the stress. Anyway, have a good lunch. Looks like your boyfriend is waiting for you."

Marceline turned around. Sure enough, Tag was waiting patiently by her locker. "Talk to you later, B." She met Tag by her locker and smiled at him. "Is it my turn to buy you a pizza from Luigi's?"

"I actually had something different planned," Tag said, taking her hand as they started toward the front door.

Instead of crossing the street to the restaurants and park where most of the students ate, Tag led her down the left side of the street.

"Where are we going?" she asked.

"Patience," Tag said.

Marceline was silent for a moment as she allowed Tag to pull her along. "About your game tonight. I'm going to try to come after work."

"I don't want you to get into any more trouble with your dad. If you can't come, it's okay, really. Besides, it's kind of my fault you were grounded in the first place."

Marceline again felt tingles run up her back as the memories struck, but she shook her head. "It's no one's fault but mine. I knew better than to miss my curfew."

"So, what happened? How did you crash?"

Marceline bit her lip. As much as she wanted to share the truth with him, it felt like too much too soon to tell him about her intense migraines, especially after she'd already had an emotional breakdown right in front of him the night before. Telling him about hearing disembodied voices warning her about the Homecoming dance? Well, that just wasn't going to happen. "I, well, I saw a rabbit crossing the road," she lied. "And I lost control trying to avoid it."

"That's one lucky rabbit," Tag said. "I'm just glad you weren't hurt."

They walked until they reached the edge of the Aspen Leaf Cemetery.

"The graveyard?" Marceline asked. The pain started to itch its way back into her head, burning from the temples.

"We just have to cross it to get to where we're going," he promised. "You're not scared of cemeteries, are you?"

"No, I actually find them peaceful for the most part," Marceline said. The Aspen Leaf Cemetery, in particular, was peaceful. It was situated on a hill, but each row of graves was on its own ledge, appearing like a pyramid. The scenery from the graveyard was beautiful, backing up to the mountain range and overlooking the town and river below. They walked up the middle path of the cemetery until they reached the top, then took a right. Her head was aching with every step, but she tried to stay present. She wanted to apply more peppermint oil, but she hadn't brought any with her.

They were high enough to overlook the entire city, past the boundaries of Catori Springs.

"Wow," Marceline breathed.

"Beautiful, huh?" Tag said. He took her hand again and squeezed. "I like coming here to think sometimes." He led her to a gravestone. It was engraved, *Freya Holiday*. "My mom died not long after we moved here freshman year," Tag said quietly. "Lung cancer. We moved here because she thought the mountain air might help. It didn't cure her or anything, but at least she was at peace. She loved this little town."

Marceline squeezed his hand. "Oh, Tag. I had no idea. I'm so sorry for your loss."

"I know what it's like to miss your mom," Tag said under his breath.

Marceline swallowed. "I'm sorry I was complaining last night. Our situations are not the same at all. At least my mom is still here, even if she's not . . . here. I can't imagine how hard that must have been to lose her."

"Don't apologize. Both are hard," Tag conceded.

Marceline nodded, sensing he didn't want to elaborate. She rubbed a hand on his back for a silent moment, honored he had shared such a vulnerable side of himself with her.

He led her to a shaded area not far from the gravestones. There was a blanket set out and a picnic basket. "How did you—"

"I have fourth period free, so I came up here to set up."

"It's beautiful. I can't believe you did this," Marceline said incredulously.

They sat, and Tag opened the basket to pull out sandwiches, cookies, and sparkling water. "My sister helped me pack this," Tag admitted.

"You both did a great job," Marceline said, happily taking a bite of a turkey sandwich.

"There's one more surprise. Can you grab it?"

Marceline reached to the bottom of the basket and held up a small piece of paper that said, *Marceline, will you go to Homecoming with me?*

In the back of her mind, Marceline could hear the voice telling her to beware the Homecoming dance, to not let history repeat itself. Inside, she felt nerves tightening around her chest. Outside, Marceline smiled.

Tag said, "I know you're grounded and all, but if you're able to, will you go with me?"

Marceline leaned over and threw her arms around his neck,

laughing as he fell onto his back, and she landed on his chest. "Of course I'll go with you, Tag."

Tag smiled and leaned up to give her a kiss. Then he frowned. "Your nose is starting to bleed."

Marceline self-consciously rolled off of Tag and covered her nose with her hands. He handed her a napkin. She closed her eyes. What was going on with her?

10

Since they had a game that night, Tag didn't have practice right after school. He offered to drive Marceline to work before he had to get ready for the game. Marceline happily agreed.

Outside the store in Tag's truck, he offered to come inside and meet her stepmom.

"That's probably not a good idea," Marceline said. "My dad doesn't want me hanging out with anyone while I'm grounded, especially not you."

"Why especially not me?"

"Well, he sort of thinks you've been a bad influence on me this summer."

"What? Why would he think that?"

Marceline bit her lip. "Katy's mom told him we were hanging out with you a lot, and I got in trouble this summer. I guess he just connected the two in his mind. Don't worry, he'll change his mind. I've been telling him what a good guy you are."

Tag sighed. "Great. How am I going to get him to let you come to the dance with me next weekend?"

Marceline saw the clock and realized it was time to go. She felt nerves return as she recalled what had happened the night before. She figured it had been stress-related, but part of her wondered if something was seriously wrong with her, if she had hallucinated the entire thing.

She lightly laid a hand on Tag's face and turned his head toward hers. "It'll happen, alright?" She leaned forward and gave him a kiss. The heat from the kiss made her cheeks hot. She wasn't sure she'd ever get used to being able to kiss Tag. "Kick ass at your game tonight. I'll try to be there."

She walked into the front door of the store and was confronted by Delilah's watchful eyes.

"Hey, Delilah," Marceline muttered.

Delilah took a deep breath and smiled. "Was that your boyfriend out there?"

Marceline hesitated, then nodded.

"He's awful cute," she pressed.

Marceline felt her cheeks start to burn. "He is."

"How long have you two been together?"

"Not long. He only asked me out a few days ago." Marceline paused. She had an idea. If she could convince Delilah to like Tag, maybe she could convince her dad. "His name is Tag. I really like him."

Delilah bit her lip as recognition flowed through her features. "I think your dad wanted you to keep your distance from that boy."

"Dad's wrong about him. Tag is generous, hardworking, and funny. I would love for you and Dad to meet him."

Delilah's face softened. "I'd like to meet him too."

Forming a plan, Marceline added, "He's playing one of the important games of the season tonight against Pine Crest. The

Catori team is supposed to be really good this year, and Tag is the quarterback. I know I'm grounded, but maybe you, Dad, and the boys could go since Dad's been trying to get them into football? You could see Tag out there." If Marceline knew anything about her dad, football could be the hidden key to his heart, a way to change his perspective of Tag.

Delilah nodded and smiled. "I'll ask your dad when I get home. I'll see if I can also get him to make an exception on your grounding."

Marceline smiled back. "I appreciate it, Delilah."

———

The night passed slowly and, thankfully, without any migraine or loss of consciousness activity. Other than a headache, which was an unfortunate constant these days, Marceline felt fine. Delilah let her know before she left that Marceline was still instructed to go straight home after work, but the rest of the family was still going to go to Tag's game. Dad made it clear he'd been thinking of taking her brothers anyway, and this just happened to be a good night for them.

She felt guilty for not being at Tag's game, but she couldn't have ridden her bike to it even if she wanted to. Plus, she'd learned her lesson from breaking the terms of her grounding.

At home, it was quiet, as the family hadn't yet returned from the game. She decided to pull out her laptop and research her symptoms. Hallucinations, headaches, nose-bleeds. Most pages pointed to severe migraines or anxiety, but some of the scarier depths of the web pointed toward serious medical conditions like tumors, nerve issues, and aneurisms.

More than her health concerns, she was also worried about what was meant by history repeating itself at the Homecoming dance. She'd been putting off researching this as much as she had avoided researching her health concerns.

Marceline had a thought. Katy knew so much of Catori Springs's history. Maybe she'd know something about what had happened at the Homecoming dance in the past.

Knowing Katy was at home tonight and not at the football game, Marceline dialed. Katy answered the phone on the second ring.

Marceline didn't wait for pleasantries. "Do you know of anything bad or tragic happening at a past Catori Springs High Homecoming?"

"Nothing more tragic than Freshman year's under water theme," Katy scoffed. "Why?"

"Oh, it was just something I heard in passing at work. Someone mentioned something about history hopefully not repeating itself at Homecoming this year."

Katy hummed. "Interesting. I'll see what I can find out for you." Marceline could hear her typing in the background. "Honestly, Marci, I don't know why you can't google this yourself," she chuckled.

Marceline shrugged even though Katy couldn't see. "You're better at it than me."

"Ah, here we go. Whoa!"

"What?" Marceline asked impatiently.

"I found an article. Let me send it to you." Marceline's laptop dinged with a text containing a link. Marceline clicked at the same time Katy said, "I had no idea there were deaths inside the school. All on the same day, too, years apart. How strange."

Marceline scrolled through the article, skimming its contents. There'd actually been a number of deaths at the school. They were known as the September Five, because all had occurred in September, but two specifically had happened during the Homecoming dance. There was no foul play marked in any of these deaths, and all were ruled either suicide, freak accident, or medical issue, but it was mysterious why they had all occurred in the month of September. This year's Homecoming dance was on September 18th. Marceline shuddered. Was that what she was supposed to prevent? Another Homecoming death?

"Poor kids," Katy murmured.

Marceline thanked Katy for her help and shut her laptop. She couldn't think about it too much or she'd make herself sick, maybe sicker than she already was. She crawled into bed. She couldn't remember the last time she'd been in bed before 10 p.m., especially on a Friday night. But she was exhausted, and it was exactly what she needed.

———

It surprised Marceline to wake up with the sun shining on her face. She was amazed she had actually slept through the night, considering she'd gone to bed so early. She rolled over to check her phone and saw a text from Tag.

Can I call? he'd texted at 10:34 p.m. Marceline smiled that he'd wanted to talk to her. He'd sent another text an hour later, letting her know they'd won the game and that he'd met her dad. Marceline sat up in bed, panic washing over her.

She couldn't imagine under what circumstance her family would have spoken to Tag. Had her dad angrily approached him after hearing he was her boyfriend from Delilah? Marceline was nervous to find out, but eager.

She pulled the blankets off and padded down the stairs, smelling pancakes and coffee.

"Hey, hon," Delilah called, flipping a pancake. "Want some breakfast?"

"Sure, thanks," Marceline replied coolly, undecided if Delilah was the culprit. Marceline busied herself pouring a cup of coffee.

"Oh, and could you work a mid instead of a close at the store today? Tiffany needs to switch."

"Yeah, no problem," Marceline said. She lingered by the counter, about to ask her how the game had gone last night, when she heard footsteps coming down the stairs.

"How about them Catori Cougars!" Dad cheered.

Marceline smiled. "I heard they won last night."

"They didn't just win, they killed them! That boyfriend of yours sure is talented." Marceline froze. She slowly looked up to explain, but Dad continued, "He has such an arm. And a clear head! Never rushing into the pass, making smart decisions. He's the best this town has seen in some time. I'll bet he's going to get plenty of D-1 offers."

Marceline looked accusingly to Delilah. They made brief eye contact, then Delilah looked back down to the pan. "I'm sure he will," Marceline said, taking a sip of her coffee.

Dad leaned against the counter, looking more serious. "After speaking with the young man last night, I'm afraid I was wrong about him. He seems to have a good head on his shoulders."

"He does," Marceline agreed. "So, in what circumstance did you talk to him?"

"I found him after the game. I knew you'd been hanging out with the guy recently, and Delilah had mentioned you wanted to go to the game to watch your *good friend* play, plus he played a heck of a game, so I wanted to meet him."

Marceline's mind was racing, trying to picture it. At least Delilah hadn't ratted her out. "And?"

"And I knew what a *good friend* was code for. The kid was polite, respectful. He also asked if he might be able to take a certain someone as his Homecoming date next weekend."

Marceline raised her eyebrows.

"I told him if he performed as well as he did last night at the home game next Friday, he could take you."

"Dad!" Marceline laughed, hitting Dad's shoulder.

"I have to say, you must really like this guy. The fact that you're willing to spend your birthday at a football game says a lot."

Marceline blushed.

Just then, the doorbell rang. "Who's here at eight thirty in the morning?" Delilah asked.

Dad shrugged and walked to answer it while Marceline stayed in the kitchen.

"Good morning, Mr. Lees. Sorry to bother you so early, but this is important." Marceline recognized Katy's voice.

Marceline rushed to the door. "Katy?"

Dad stepped aside, allowing Katy to step inside. "Don't worry, Marci, I've got this," Katy whispered.

"Katy, wait—"

"Mr. Lees, I'm here to present to you the argument why you should allow your daughter to attend this year's Homecoming dance, even though she's grounded."

"Please, go ahead," Dad replied, amused. He sat down at the kitchen table.

Well, this was happening. Marceline didn't bother stopping Katy's rampage. "You want some pancakes, Kat?" Marceline asked.

"Later," Katy said in a serious tone. "For starters, it's Marci's birthday. She deserves some slack. Second, Marci needs to come to Homecoming to support me, her best friend since the first grade. You see, I was in charge of planning this year's dance, which is *Alice in Wonderland* themed, and I worked really hard to make this day special for everyone. Plus, Homecoming is a rite of passage for all high schoolers, and it is an imperative event all high school students attend to have a well-rounded experience. There will be plenty of chaperones, so no funny business will be happening. I'll make sure of it myself. Now—"

"Katy, enough," Marceline laughed. "He already said I could go."

"Really?" Katy squealed, tossing her notecards on the table.

"I said you could go on the condition your quarterback does well at his game."

Marceline rolled her eyes.

"Well good thing Tag is a great quarterback. Now I can actually enjoy these pancakes." Katy sighed.

"You would've enjoyed them anyway," Marceline said.

11

Marceline took advantage of her family's usual Saturday hustle and bustle to leave for work earlier than she needed, claiming she had a long walk.

Really, what she needed was a few extra minutes to stop into Moon Opal for more of Bijou's magical peppermint oil.

Marceline walked quickly to make up the added distance past the Grocery Elf to Moon Opal and back. As sweat beaded on her forehead, she found herself dreadfully missing Barb and cursing herself for damaging the mode of transport she'd taken for granted.

From outside, the sign with purple lettering and a crystal ball reading "Moon Opal Metaphysical Store" stood out against the red brick building. The witch store, as tourists liked to call it. To be fair, Marceline was pretty sure they sold wands. That was about as witchy as it got. In the store window, Marceline saw lines of impressive crystals and geodes. Taking a deep breath, Marceline pushed the door open, resulting in the same *ding* the door to the Grocery Elf made.

There was low, wordless music playing that Marceline

would expect to hear in a yoga class or mid-massage, and her nose was quickly filled with the overpowering scent of what could only be described as *earthiness*. There was a diffuser in the corner misting the smell throughout the space. No one greeted her as she entered, and there seemed to be no one behind the front desk. If she wasn't on a time crunch, Marceline would've considered taking a longer look around at the assortment of candles, incense, herbs, oils, books, and jewelry that were displayed on every available surface, but instead she made her way to the back shelf where she saw oils stacked. As she got closer to the back, nearer to the beaded curtain leading to the back of the building, her ears started to buzz.

Marceline paused, reaching a finger in her ear as if she had water lodged it in. She could make out muffled voices, but they were indistinct, with no comprehendible words. Tempted to peek her head into the back curtain, Marceline felt the buzzing from her ears shift down the rest of her body, as if she wasn't supposed to go back there. Curiosity kept her frozen in place rather than running away.

The beads were thrown open as, suddenly, Marceline regained her hearing.

"Forget it!" shouted a short, dark-haired woman. The woman spared a last glance over her shoulder, making brief eye contact with Marceline. It was the same woman who Marceline had seen at the grocery store with the bloody nose, who had found Marceline passed out and left without saying a word. The woman's nose wasn't bleeding this time. She narrowed her eyes at Marceline but didn't say anything before storming out of the store. What was that woman doing here?

The beads pushed open once more. "Don't come back here," another woman, who looked nearly identical to Bijou, seethed. Mrs. Eyota. "Dark witch," she muttered under her breath.

Marceline raised her eyebrows. That was a strange

comment. What had this mysterious woman done to the Eyotas?

Mrs. Eyota turned her gaze to Marceline, her face shifting from one of rage to a more friendly smile. "How can I help you, dear?"

Marceline couldn't find her words for a moment. "I—I'm Bijou's friend. I was looking for more peppermint oil. She let me try some before."

"Ah, yes," Mrs. Eyota said, her eyes darkening again. "You're the Lees girl. I'm afraid we don't carry the oil you're looking for."

"Oh," Marceline said, surprised. "Okay, is it not in stock at the moment or . . .?"

Mrs. Eyota cocked her head as she stared at her for another moment until the swishing of the beaded curtain broke their gaze.

"I've got some more here, Mama," came Bijou. She smiled at Marceline, handing over two identical tinctures.

Marceline picked up on a shared glare between Bijou and her mom. "Thanks, Bijou. You're a lifesaver. How much do I owe you?"

"11.99," Mrs. Eyota said, eyes never wavering from Bijou.

Marceline paid quickly, thanking the Eyota ladies before booking it to work. Whatever had just happened inside of Moon Opal, none of it sat right with her. Something was off, and she didn't know what. She'd have to ask Bijou later.

Even though she felt uneasy, at least she had her peppermint oil again to relieve her migraine.

———

As the rest of the weekend passed sans weird shit happening, Marceline was more convinced she'd hallucinated the whole thing. She still shuddered as she recalled the voice saying, *Beware the Homecoming dance.* What did that mean, anyway?

Monday, Marceline had plans to go to lunch with Katy and Bijou. As she waited near her and Katy's lockers, she heard Nate's obnoxious laughter down the hallway. She bit her lip as he fist-bumped the guy he'd been walking with and turned toward her. As much as she didn't want to admit that maybe Nate had told the truth about seeing Anna, she'd also seen her after all, and now that she'd heard this voice warning her about the Homecoming dance, she had to know she wasn't crazy.

Building her courage, Marceline approached Nate. He looked surprised to see her, but he managed to smirk all the same.

"Hey there, Marceline," he said. Marceline hated the way he said her full name. Mockingly, the syllables drawn out like the word was exhausting to spit out.

She resisted an eye roll. "Hey. I wanted to ask, have you had any more paranormal sightings?"

Nate's smirk widened into a grin. "Seeing ghosts now, are we? Welcome to the club."

Marceline couldn't help an eye roll this time. "I didn't say I'd seen any. Just thought I'd ask."

"Sweet of you to care, Marci, really, but no, I haven't seen dear old Anna since that night." His eyes narrowed accusingly. "But you have, haven't you?"

"Of course I haven't," Marceline said quickly. "And you didn't either. You just saw someone in costume." She wasn't so sure that was true anymore, but she couldn't give him the satisfaction of validating his ghost story. That would also validate her own, which she wasn't ready to do.

"If you say so," Nate replied. His eyes looked past her. Spinning around, she saw Katy and Bijou walking toward them.

"She's never going to be interested, you know," Marceline snapped.

Nate sighed longingly. "A man can dream. Anyway, see you and your fine friend later."

Katy's nose was wrinkled when she approached. "What'd Nate want?"

"To tell me how fine you are."

Bijou giggled, and Katy shrugged. "I guess he's not wrong about that. You ready for lunch?"

"Starving."

They walked to the park across the street from the school, sitting on the grass with their packed lunches.

"How was your grounded weekend?" Katy asked.

"Not so bad, actually. I didn't feel grounded. I think it's because my dad has been so excited about the football team actually being good this year. He's, like, proud of me for dating the quarterback of the 'best team this town has seen in years.'" Marceline couldn't help an eye roll as she held up air quotes.

Katy laughed. "How was your weekend, B?"

Bijou shrugged. "I just worked at my parents' store this weekend."

Marceline tried to make eye contact, but Bijou wouldn't look up from her sandwich. She needed to ask Bijou about the encounter she'd witnessed that weekend inside Moon Opal.

Katy cleared her throat loudly. "Well, since neither of you bothered to ask me, I had an eventful weekend."

"Did you?" Marceline asked, eyebrows raised. "What happened?"

"Well," Katy began, unable to hide a wide smile. "Ever since Marci had her romantic rendezvous in the treehouse with Tag, I thought maybe I'd invite someone there myself."

Marceline blushed profusely at the mention of her and Tag in the treehouse, but she cocked her head with curiosity. Katy was the type of girl who would see a pretty girl for two seconds across a crowded restaurant and plan their entire love story in her head before her meal arrived. She fell fast but had not had a girlfriend of her own yet. "Was this someone a girl?"

"It was a girl . . ." Katy grinned as she trailed off, then she briskly leaned into Bijou's shoulder. "It was Bijou! You know, we hadn't ever invited her up there? How rude of us!"

Marceline smiled at Bijou. "What'd you think of our little hideout?"

"Well, emphasis on little," Bijou joked. "But it was cute! I loved all the trinkets you had in there."

"Speaking of trinkets, I need to stow the stop sign I ran over in there."

"You kept that? That will be an awesome addition!" Katy squealed. "But we didn't even get to the crazy part yet. Go on, B."

"Well," Bijou started, "we saw a light on in the McCormick Estate."

Marceline raised her eyebrows, remembering how she'd thought she'd seen one that night with Tag, but thought she must've imagined it. "Someone was in there?"

"That woman you saw at Moon Opal, her name is Amina. My mom wouldn't let her read tarot cards at the store. That's why she was so upset the other day. There's been rumors Amina has been hiding out in the old McCormick Estate, offering her tarot readings from there."

"Tarot card readings?" Marceline asked skeptically. She'd heard of those before, with so-called psychics pulling random cards from a deck and claiming they could tell your future.

"I want to do that. I want to have my fortune told," Katy said eagerly.

Marceline frowned at her. Coming from the girl who was scared of ghosts and butterflies, why would she want to go have her future told in a creepy abandoned mansion? "You believe in all that?" she asked Katy.

Katy shot her a look as if to say, *Don't be rude*, but Bijou just smiled.

"I'll try anything once. Plus, they actually can tell the future, right Bijou?"

Bijou nodded. "Of course there are frauds, but the ones who are actually devoted to the craft, who are in tune with the world, can pick up on bits and pieces of your life; past, present, and sometimes future. I've heard Amina's readings have been very accurate. Maybe she could convince you it's not all nonsense," Bijou said, looking at Marceline.

"Oh, we have to go!" Katy chimed, then her face fell. "Do we have to meet the reader at the McCormick Estate? Isn't that place, like, haunted?"

"I've heard that," Bijou said. "But I don't think we'll be seeing any spirits." She flashed a look toward Marceline, then quickly darted her eyes away. Marceline found it odd Bijou had been avoiding her gaze all morning. What had changed in their relationship in a single weekend?

Katy smiled. "I'll trust your word, B. What do you say, Marci, want to come?"

Marceline shrugged. "I mean, I'd be open to going, but I'm still grounded. I can't go anywhere but to school and work."

"Well, aren't you allowed to go to the football game on Friday night?" Katy asked.

Marceline nodded. "Yeah, but that's only because Tag is playing and it's my birthday."

"Maybe we can go after the game?"

"I don't think my dad would make any exceptions for me to go to some woo-woo tarot card reader. No offense, B," Marceline protested, glancing to Bijou, who shrugged.

"We can tell your dad we're going to the Homecoming bonfire after the game," Katy insisted.

"I really think you need to go," Bijou spoke up in a quiet voice. "I think there's something you need to find out there."

Bijou finally looked into Marceline's eyes, only this time Marceline looked away. Her brain flashed to that voice, so loud in her head, warning her about the Homecoming dance.

Katy held her hands up triumphantly. "See, you need to go get the tarot reading. Besides, I'm sure Tag will do great, we'll win the game, and your dad will be in a great mood. We can convince him. Plus, Nate's been nagging me all week to go to his party Friday night. Now I at least have a real excuse not to."

Marceline sighed and found herself agreeing to go. As Katy started showing Bijou pictures of the Homecoming dresses Marceline and Katy had picked out a few weeks ago, back when Marceline thought she'd just go as Katy's date, Marceline tuned out.

For some strange reason, she knew Bijou was right. She also had the nagging feeling there was something she needed to find out at this tarot reading.

12

At the dinner table the night before Marceline's birthday, the house phone rang. The clinking of forks seemed to stop instantaneously. Everyone knew what that meant. The only one who called that number, and the only reason they even had a landline, was their mother.

"I'll get it," Dad said after a few seconds. He scooted back his chair and rose.

"Can you believe Mom is calling twice in one month?" Theo said excitedly.

Peter shot Marceline a look. "I think she's probably calling for Marci's birthday."

"Oh," Theo said, face falling slightly.

"You can still talk to her," Marceline said, pushing back her chair. "I don't need to talk to her." She was about to escape up the stairs when her dad's voice stopped her.

"Marci? It's for you. It's your mom."

Marceline almost continued up the stairs, but between Peter's and Theo's stares, Marceline relented. She couldn't remember the last time she'd talked to her mom. It was probably time to rip the Band-Aid off. She took slow steps toward the phone, dread bubbling up in her stomach. Tonight's dinner of spaghetti and meatballs suddenly wasn't sitting so well. When she reached her dad's outstretched hand and took the phone, she took a deep, steadying breath.

"Hello?"

"Marceline?" her mom's voice called.

She couldn't breathe; couldn't speak.

"Marceline, are you there?"

Marceline swallowed an unexpected lump in her throat. "Hi, Mom." The word felt strange to say out loud to her own mother.

"Darling, how have you been? I've missed your voice." Despite everything, her mom's accent still flowed over Marceline like warm honey. Marceline hadn't realized how much she'd missed hearing it.

"I'm good. Just busy working at the store."

Her mom laughed lightly. "Ah yes, the Grocery Elf. Does it still have that awful front sign I painted?"

Marceline walked toward the living room to separate herself from the watchful faces at the dinner table. "Dad will never take it down," she said, taking a seat in her dad's recliner.

There was a beat of silence. "I wanted to wish you a happy birthday, darling. Seventeen is a big landmark in our family."

"Thanks," Marceline replied hollowly.

"You know, Marceline, turning seventeen comes with a lot of changes and . . . responsibilities. You must be careful."

Was her mom really about to lecture her about responsibilities? Her mother, the woman who had betrayed her ultimate responsibility to be a present mother, was the last person on earth Marceline would listen to about responsibilities.

"I've got to go do some homework, actually," Marceline said quickly.

"Wait," her mom said, her voice almost desperate. "Before you go, Marceline, remember what I always told you about envisioning light when you were scared as a little girl? A mental force field of light will always protect you in the darkest of moments."

Marceline wondered why her mom had offered that random, cryptic pocket of advice. "Okay . . . thanks," she replied awkwardly.

"Whatever happens, you are braver than you know. Your life changes once you turn seventeen, but I know you will get the guidance you need. Happy birthday, darling."

Marceline ended the call before she allowed her mom to spew anymore encouraging words. If guidance was what she thought Marceline needed, why wasn't she there to offer it herself?

When Marceline woke up, she didn't immediately remember that she was now seventeen. As she looked in the mirror, applying eyeliner around her tired brown eyes, it hit her: these were the first hours of the seventeenth year of her life. She set down her makeup and stared. She didn't look any different, didn't feel any different. What was so special about birthdays, anyway? Why was a number part of a teenager's defining traits? *I'm Marceline Lees, I'm seventeen, I have purple hair . . .* that really needed some touching up, she realized, running her fingers through the faded purple strands, once a dark plum color, now a light lilac shade that almost faded into the rest of her brown hair.

Suddenly, she gasped. In the mirror, she saw her wrist was shining with what looked like a shiny silver bracelet. She rubbed her wrist, but the bracelet wasn't protruding; it was as if it was implanted in her skin like a tattoo. She crossed the hall to the bathroom. Once there, she noticed her other wrist had the same white marking that shone silver when light hit it. In the sink, she started scrubbing. Maybe her brothers had put some kind of a fake tattoo on while she was sleeping. It wasn't coming off.

She held her wrists up, inspecting the curious, single, thin circles. The white almost blended in with her pale skin, but when she held them up to the light, they shone a blinding silver. What were these markings, and where did they come from?

No one in her family seemed to notice the bands on her arms either. Marceline wouldn't put it past her family to plan some elaborate practical joke for her birthday, in which they pretended not to see these bands on her arm.

The more she looked at them, letting the sun shine almost silver against the crisp white band, the more unnatural they looked. More than the fact that they weren't washing off, they blended seamlessly with her skin. She could hardly eat the cake Dad had gotten her for breakfast.

As Marceline got up at her usual time to walk to school, Dad said, "You probably don't have to leave quite as early today, birthday girl. Your mode of transportation has been restored."

Marceline's eyes widened as she checked out the front window. Lo-and-behold, Barb was sitting propped on her kickstand. Only, it wasn't Barb. Marceline opened the door and went to her.

"Old Barb was too far gone to be repaired. I upgraded you to the new version," Dad confirmed.

Marceline rubbed her hands over the unfamiliar handlebars, feeling a strange mourning for her fallen first bike. She couldn't be ungrateful, though. Looking at Dad, she smiled. "It's Barb2.0. Thank you."

"Happy birthday, Bean," he said, hugging her.

Marceline had gotten so used to walking, her legs felt wobbly on Barb2.0, but she quickly found her rhythm. She was so lost in thought, she walked right past her friends without meaning to, straight through the front door of Catori Springs High. Her ears didn't recognize the fact that they were singing happy birthday to her until she was halfway to her locker. Then she turned around, finally smiling.

Katy, Tag, and Bijou concluded their song and smiled at her.

"For a second, I wasn't sure you were going to turn around," Katy scolded, reaching for her and pulling her into a tight hug. "I know you don't like your birthday much, but come on, that was a great performance!"

Marceline laughed. "I was completely zoned out, but your singing voices really brought me back. Thank you," she said, reaching to hug Bijou next. Tag leaned down last, offering her a kiss and a long hug.

Pulling away, her friends filled her arms with flowers, cupcakes, and cards. "What is all this?" Marceline asked, amazed.

"First, eat a cupcake," Katy demanded.

"I already had cake with my family this morning," Marceline protested.

"Eat!"

Marceline took a cupcake to oblige. Katy tried to force a "Birthday Girl" sash around her, but Marceline held her off.

After the crowd had cleared and the first class bell had rung, Marceline grabbed Katy before she left for class.

"Something super strange happened this morning," she whispered.

"What?" Katy said back loudly, then reading Marceline's tone, she said more quietly, "What happened?"

"I woke up with these," Marceline said, pushing up her sleeves to reveal the white bands on each of her wrists.

Katy squinted. "No, you've always had that mole on your wrist."

"Not that," Marceline snapped. "The white bands."

"What white bands?"

Marceline thought maybe she couldn't see without direct light shining on them. She pulled her toward the stairwell, where the light streamed in through the large windows. "See?"

Katy shook her head and shrugged.

"Stop messing with me. You can't see these?" Marceline asked, running her finger along the white bands, which were now shining bright silver.

Katy frowned, looking confused. "I don't know what I'm supposed to be seeing. Is this some kind of trick?" The second class bell rang. Katy swore. "You always make me late," she complained, racing away and leaving Marceline alone in the stairwell, eyeing her newfound silver tattoos.

Why couldn't Katy see them?

Without wanting to sound even more strange, but needing answers, Marceline showed her wrists to Tag at lunch and told him she'd had to scrub all morning to wash off the fake tattoos her brothers had put on her while she slept. She asked if he could see any parts of the tattoos remaining, but he shook his head no, even as they shone so bright in Marceline's eyes that she had to look away.

After school, she stopped by Tag's locker. Nate was there already, and he called out when he saw her approaching. "QB's girlfriend is coming. Think fast!"

He tossed a football. It was coming right toward Marceline's face. She held her hands up, not catching the ball, but successfully protecting her face. It bounced against her arms and shot back to the ground.

"Hey man, not cool!" Tag protested.

Nate bent down to pick up the football that had rolled back to his feet. "No one got hurt, just having fun, right, Marci?"

Marceline swallowed and nodded.

"So, Marci," Nate continued, "you coming to the party at my house after the game tonight? I've heard we have a special birthday to celebrate!"

"I already told you she's grounded," Tag said.

Nate scoffed, "Grounded? Well, whatever, you're already grounded. How hard is it to sneak out again? What's the worst that could happen, you get double grounded?"

"I'll try to be there, Nate."

"Good, because I don't want my boy here missing out on anything his senior year."

"I'm not missing out on anything, man," Tag protested.

Nate held up his hands and shrugged. "See you tonight, bro. Bye, Marci. Happy birthday, by the way."

Marceline waved. Nate had always been a bit of an asshole, but his attitude toward her had worsened since she and Tag had started dating. She tried to mentally shrug it off and smiled at Tag. "I came to wish you luck before the game tonight."

Tag returned her smile and kissed her lightly. Marceline felt herself blush again. That sensation never got old.

"I'm just happy you're going to be there tonight."

"Me too. You're going to do great."

Tag wrapped his long arms around her. Marceline was quite tall herself, towering over her petite friends, but it felt nice to be significantly shorter than Tag. She leaned into him for a moment before pulling away.

"See you tonight," he called to her.

13

The excitement in the crowd was contagious. The Homecoming game usually brought with it the largest crowd of rowdy students. Many in the student section had their faces painted, which Marceline and her friends had all passed on to not make fools of themselves later at the McCormick Estate.

The first quarter was not good for Tag. He threw two interceptions and was unable to complete many passes. Marceline was chewing her lip so hard she was sure it would bleed. She could see Tag standing on the sideline while the defensive team was out, holding his helmet, taking a sip of water. The stress was apparent on his face. She thought how much pressure he must be feeling, all eyes on him. Her heart ached for him. She wanted to tell him none of this mattered, to hug him and bring him peace, but of course, this game did matter for him and for the people in the stands. Marceline hardly noticed when the buzzer signaling the end of the first quarter sounded.

Nearly halfway through the fourth quarter, it was 28-21, with the Catori Cougars down.

Tag threw a pass to a receiver who was on the five-yard line. The receiver caught it but was quickly tackled, and the ball slipped out of his hands. Players from each team jumped onto the ball, the referees blowing whistles.

"What's going on?" Katy asked.

"I think they just fumbled the ball," Marceline explained.

Katy rolled her eyes. "Like I know what that means."

Marceline sighed as the referee signaled that the ball went to the other team. "Our team lost possession."

The Cougar's defense held the other team. Marceline found herself as enthused as the face-painted superfans in the student section, cheering at tackles, joining in the chants.

The clock was winding down. The Cougars had possession again, and they were slowly but surely moving back up the field. With a minute left, Tag threw another pass toward the end zone. This time, the receiver jumped and caught it, running the final two steps to the touchdown.

"What happened?" Katy asked again, trying to see around the group of jumping, screaming students in front of them.

"Just cheer," Bijou said wisely.

As most of the crowd dispersed, Marceline stood alone, waiting for her family. Katy and Bijou waited for her near the stadium exit to get permission from her dad to go with them.

"Can you believe that, Marci?" Marceline heard her dad say from behind her. His hands clapped onto her shoulders.

She smiled. "I can't believe they went for two."

"They wouldn't have done that if they didn't have a quarterback they could trust to win the game for them! Can we head down to the field? I'm sure you want to see your quarterback."

"I'm sure *you* want to see your quarterback," Marceline shot back.

Dad put his arm around her shoulders as they descended the bleachers.

As the team released from their huddle, the players jogged their way over to the bleachers. Tag came straight for them.

"Great game, son!" Dad called out.

"Thanks, Mr. Lees. Started out a bit rough, but we pushed through. I'm glad you could make it," Tag replied, looking at Marceline.

Her dad cleared his throat. "Well, with that second point at the end, I think you earned taking my daughter to the dance. What do you say?"

Tag's face brightened. "I'm looking forward to it."

"You still have to adhere to my curfew," Dad said sternly. "Back by eleven, and absolutely no funny business."

Marceline smiled at Tag. This was the best present her dad could have given her. Well, that, and there was one more thing.

As Tag jogged back to the locker rooms, Marceline turned to her dad.

"So, Dad."

"So, Marci," Dad said in a mocking tone. He nodded toward Katy and Bijou at the top of the bleachers. "Let me guess, you want to do something with your friends tonight. You know you're still grounded, even if it is your birthday."

"I know. It's just this silly school tradition. They wanted me to come with them to the Homecoming bonfire. But I understand. I'll just tell them I can't . . ." She lingered at the bottom of the bleachers, shooting an overly dramatic look of disappointment toward her dad.

"Alright," he sighed. "You can go to the bonfire. But I want you back before eleven, understood? Every minute you're late tonight will be docked from your Homecoming curfew tomorrow."

"You're the best," she said, giving him a hug.

Next on her birthday to-do list, confront this mysterious tourist-turned-tarot-card-reader about leaving her on the floor of the Grocery Elf without making sure she was alright, why this woman had constant nose bleeds like Marceline did, and why she was so hated by Mrs. Eyota. Though she wasn't particularly excited about the tarot reading itself, Marceline was ready for some sort of explanation at last.

———

When they reached Katy's car, Marceline got in the passenger seat while Bijou climbed into the back seat. "We shouldn't be gone too long," Bijou assured Marceline, almost reading her mind. "We'll definitely be back before your curfew. The readings are only fifteen minutes each, and I'm just tagging along."

Katy turned out of the parking lot. "Oh really? Why won't you get a reading, B?"

Bijou shrugged. "We're kind of on a time crunch. Plus, I've had many readings before in my life. You two haven't."

"I know you're the birthday girl, and I shouldn't be greedy, but I'm so excited to get my first tarot card reading! Can I go first?" Katy squealed, looking briefly at Marceline.

"Sure, I don't care about the order," Marceline said, laughing lightly. She started to feel ill with nerves as they drove the short distance to the McCormick Estate. "How do we even know this woman is still at this house reading tarot cards tonight? Surely she's got better things to do on a Friday night."

"I booked us an appointment," Bijou explained.

"Are you telling me this woman has a business website or something?" Marceline asked with raised eyebrows.

"No, but maybe she should. She wasn't exactly the easiest person to track down, but I saw her on the way to school yesterday morning. She knows we're coming tonight."

Katy parked across the street from the estate.

Marceline and Katy leaped over the short iron fence as they

had hundreds of times. Bijou followed suit, more clumsily, and the three of them made their way toward the dark house. The house was made of stone, with intricate detailing along the top peaks of the roof. There were several chimneys on the roof. One, Marceline noticed, had smoke coming from it. All the many windows had curtains drawn shut.

"It's so spooky," Katy muttered.

Marceline didn't want to say it out loud, but she also felt creeped out, like there were invisible hands reaching out and lightly running along her skin, causing goosebumps to appear up her arms and down her neck. Marceline's head had also started to pulse angrily, like the blood was starting to freeze in her temples again.

14

arceline paused uncertainly. "Do we just walk up to the front door?"

"I think we go around the side," Bijou called, having left the two to wander toward the right side of the mansion. "Yes, there's light coming from over here."

Katy gripped Marceline's hand. "Why did I agree to this? I hate being scared."

"You'll be fine," Marceline assured her. "There's nothing scary here. It's all in your head." Marceline hoped Katy believed her words more than she did.

They met up with Bijou on the right side of the house. Marceline took a deep breath. Bijou knocked on the side door. It was silent for a moment, then the doorhandle turned. Answering the door was the Japanese woman with spiky black hair and gray streaks. The woman pursed her lips at the three of them.

Bijou took a step forward. "Amina, right? We spoke the other day. These are the friends I was telling you wanted readings."

Amina nodded once, then opened the door wider to allow the girls to step in. The floors creaked as they entered the candle-filled space. There was a sheet on the floor with four pillows in each corner and two in the middle on either side of a small table. The candles on the floor and on the short table in the middle of the room were flickering, as if there was a draft in the room. The walls had peeling, floral wallpaper and a long, dusty bookshelf on the right wall. There was a couch that was pushed against the wall that also had an off-white sheet on it.

As Amina walked around to sit on the pillow on the other side of the table, her silhouette cast by the candles mirrored her movements on the walls. She sat and made eye contact with Bijou. "Have a seat. Whoever is first, sit with me in the center."

Marceline released Katy's hand to encourage her. Katy walked bravely to the pillow across from Amina and sat cross-legged.

"I've never had one of these before," Katy admitted.

Bijou nudged Marceline, and they both sat on the pillows at the corners of the sheet on the floor.

"It's quite simple," Amina said. "Spirit speaks through me and uses these tarot cards as expressions to communicate what we need to hear about the past, present, and future. Is there anything specific you'd like to know, or do you want a general reading?"

"Oh, general, I guess," Katy said.

Amina flipped a sand timer over and began shuffling her deck of cards, eyes closed. The cards had drawings on them, some had numbers, and they had words Marceline couldn't make out. Amina laid the cards face down on the table and fanned them out in a circle.

"Pick a card while focusing on your past. Don't look at it," she instructed Katy.

Katy's hand moved over the circle, then she reached for one and handed it to Amina.

"Now, pick one for your present." Katy was quicker this time, reaching for one directly in front of her.

"Now your future."

After Katy handed over the third card, Amina flipped the first card over. "Two of swords," Amina said quietly. "You had to make a difficult choice recently. It's in your nature to avoid confrontation with authority figures, but you were at a crossroads, and you had to face your reality."

Katy nodded slowly. "Yes, I guess I did."

Amina nodded. "You see her chains," she said, pointing to the card. "You see her swords held up? Her blindfold? You were on guard always, but you were blind at the same time. Blinded by fear, by feeling the need to hold yourself back." Then her voice softened. "It's good that you told your parents. I know that couldn't have been easy for you."

Marceline wasn't sure what Amina was talking about, but she saw Katy's surprised eyes fill with tears.

Amina continued, "Telling your parents about your sexuality was necessary for you in your process of accepting who you are yourself. It was hard, I'm sure, but you're moving on the right path to fully embracing and loving yourself."

Marceline frowned as she looked at Katy, but her eyes were locked on Amina's. Marceline wondered why Katy hadn't told her she'd come out to her parents.

Amina flipped the next card. "Page of pentacles," she announced softly. As the light from the candles bounced against her face, Marceline noticed Amina looked very tired, in a way that required more than sleep to resolve. "You're a smart, rational person. Now that you've released your secret, you've moved forward with full steam ahead. Right now, you are in a great place, acting on your dreams and goals, your educational achievements."

Katy nodded and smiled. "I feel more like myself. I love being busy with school and activities. When I hadn't told my parents I was gay, I was too exhausted all the time to enjoy what I love the most."

Amina flipped the final card and frowned. "Your future shows unpredictability. Ten of pentacles, reversed, signifies loss. Let me see." Amina closed her eyes again and laid her hand on the card. It was silent as the candles flickered. When Amina's eyes opened, she looked directly at Marceline. "Be careful who you trust."

Katy followed Amina's gaze to Marceline. "What do you mean?"

Amina pressed her lips together firmly. Marceline was starting to feel lightheaded. "Let me see your palms," Amina said.

Katy held out her hands, and Amina took hold of her right hand, thumb tracing her palm. "Your head and heart line are separated, showing your rational side. You're a planner, I can see that."

Katy's eyes lit up. "What else can you see from my palm?"

Amina turned Katy's palm to look at the pinky-side edge. "You will have three significant relationships in your life, one marriage, if I'm not mistaken."

"Any kids?" Katy asked.

Amina stared at Katy's pinky, bending it back slightly. "I see two kids. A boy and a girl."

Marceline rolled her eyes. Like a palm could tell someone all that. Amina continued to tell Katy about her future, where she'd meet her wife, what state she'd go to college in, her career. This woman was just blowing smoke up Katy's ass, and Katy, eyes gleaming excitedly, was eating it all up.

"Time is up," Amina said. "That will be twenty dollars."

Katy reached into her purse and pulled out the cash. "That was amazing, thank you."

Amina pocketed the money, and as she did, her sleeve rolled up slightly, revealing a tattoo just like Marceline's. Only hers was darker, more gray than white. Amina noticed her looking at the marks and narrowed her eyes.

Marceline could hardly believe what she'd seen. It was unmistakably the same marking, just a different color.

Amina asked the room, "Who's next?"

Katy volunteered her. "She is."

Marceline rolled up her own jacket sleeve, revealing her white band. Stepping forward, Marceline said, "Before we begin, I've got some questions you need to answer."

The smile fell from Katy's face, replaced with a look of confusion, but Bijou nodded, understanding somehow. Amina glanced down at Marceline's wrist, then made eye contact with her again. This time, Marceline's head pounded. She vaguely noticed in her periphery, the candles became dimmer.

"This one's different," whispered a man's voice.

Marceline felt shivers run up her spine, and her eyes darted around the room. "Who said that?"

"Said what?" Katy asked, looking around.

"Out," Amina commanded, looking to Bijou and Katy. "I need to speak with this one alone."

"We're not going to leave," Katy protested, looking at Marceline.

"Out," Amina repeated more sternly, gazing at Marceline.

Bijou walked to take Katy's hand, but she shook her off. "Marci?" Katy asked.

Amina locked eyes with her. "I can help," she said.

If this was the only way to get answers, Marceline was willing to be alone with this woman and the unexplained voice only she could hear. Petrified, but curious, Marceline found herself nodding. "It's okay, Kat, you can go. I'll meet you outside."

As soon as Bijou and Katy left the room, the flames from the candles that were nearly burnt out shot high with seemingly new flames. Marceline sat on the pillow across from Amina. Up close, Marceline could see deep wrinkles in Amina's skin. She was older than she looked. She planned to ask her about the bands, what had happened at the grocery store, why her nose was always bleeding, just like hers. Before she could say a word, Amina gripped her hands; they were as cold as ice.

"Now," the man's voice whispered again.

The candles' flames shot higher still as Amina whispered strange words under her breath. Marceline began to feel hot, like her blood was boiling. Unable to move or speak, a man's strong, invisible arms kept her seated.

Marceline tried to scream, to run away, but all she could do was look at Amina's concentrated face, her brow furrowed as she furiously whispered words, quicker now, louder. Desperately, she remembered what her mom had told her to do when she felt scared as a little girl. "Envision light surrounding you, protecting you from any darkness out there. A force field of light."

Marceline focused on a bright light shielding her, the light moving from her core to her feet, to the top of her head. Amina opened her eyes, surprised. Marceline felt the hold on her release.

Standing up, Marceline yelled, "What were you doing to me?"

Amina's eyes narrowed as a drop of blood started a slow trickle from her nose. "You've got a lot to learn."

Marceline didn't want to be in that room another second.

She burst out of the house, gasping as she felt the fresh air on her face. Katy and Bijou, who were sitting on the steps, looked up, alarmed.

"What happened? You were in there forever," Katy said.

"How long?" Marceline demanded.

Katy shrugged and looked at Bijou. "I don't know, thirty minutes?"

Bijou nodded.

Thirty minutes? It had felt like five. Marceline didn't answer as she walked past them down the steps, trudging through the long weeds. "I need to get back home before I'm late again," Marceline said.

Katy jogged to catch up to her, grabbing her shoulder. "Marci, stop. What the hell happened in there?"

Marceline shook her head. "That woman is a scam artist, that's all."

Katy frowned. "Your nose is bleeding."

Bijou met them in the middle of the lawn. "Are you alright?"

Marceline felt drained of energy, like she hadn't eaten or drank in days, like she was alive on fumes. "I'm okay," she mumbled. "Can we just please get back before my curfew?"

Katy nodded, and they continued to the car silently.

Inside, Marceline had another question. "Why didn't you tell me you came out to your parents?"

Katy sighed. "I didn't mean to purposely not tell you. It just wasn't as big of a deal as I thought it was going to be. It was almost like they already knew."

"I'm happy for you," Bijou said gently.

"And proud of you," Marceline added.

15

Marceline worked her morning shift at the store on Saturday, still feeling the weight of the night before. She was exhausted, moving like a zombie all morning, and she was distracted, thinking about what she had heard, felt, and seen. The tarot reading had provided the opposite of what she'd came for. She needed answers, and yet all she got were more questions. With the Homecoming dance that night, and Marceline no closer to understanding what she was supposed to do to prevent history from repeating itself, Marceline felt a growing pit in her stomach, which she could hardly focus on over the pain of her pulsing skull.

Her dad even asked if she was okay as she kept forgetting which buttons to press on the point-of-sale system.

"I'm fine, Dad. Just have a headache," she responded as she scanned items for a customer and bagged them in brown paper bags.

Her dad nodded sympathetically. "You are your mother's daughter with those headaches. Caffeine might help. Take what you need. Just make a note."

Marceline nodded. "Thanks."

She must have applied an entire tincture of Bijou's peppermint oil during that shift. In the back of her head, she kept hearing that voice echoing, "Beware the Homecoming dance. Don't let history repeat itself."

Around noon, Marceline's shift was over, and she made her way to the back office to grab her belongings. She checked her phone. She had a text from Tag, a text from Bijou, and twelve texts from Katy. Marceline had never been so popular in her life. Tag's message was sweet, telling her he couldn't wait to see her tonight, letting her know he'd be by to pick her up around five so they could go to dinner. Bijou asked how she was feeling and wanted to know what time she was getting to the dance. Katy, who was busy setting up the dance for the night, had still managed to send her messages wondering what the hell had happened to Marceline at the psychic the night before.

Her last message read, *I'm just worried about you, Marci. I've never seen you like that before. Like you'd seen a ghost.* As Marceline read Katy's last text, a new one arrived. *Kill me, this setup is taking forever. You're going to look hot at the dance tonight, and I'm going to barely have any time to shower beforehand.*

Marceline smiled and texted back, *I promise I'm good. Tell you more tonight. And you've never looked like a hot mess in your life.*

Katy responded seconds later with an eye roll emoji. *At least I know I won't have to impress any future girlfriends at this dance.*

Marceline was still standing in the back office of the store, holding her phone, when her vision blurred like the color was being sucked out of her eyes. The temperature dropped as drastically as if she'd entered the walk-in freezer, and her hearing went deaf apart from a single voice, whispering into her ear.

"The anniversary of death is coming. Protect your school, Marceline, and no lives need be taken."

Marceline winced at the pain in her skull, trying to cover her hands over her ears, but the whispering wouldn't stop. She felt blood dripping from her nose, but she willed herself to stay conscious.

"How do I stop someone from dying if there's no foul play?" she gasped to the empty room.

"The previous deaths were not accidents or self-inflicted," the voice answered her. "They were murders. She seeks another sacrifice to take her place. You must stop her."

At once, the atmosphere in the back office returned to its normal color and temperature. Marceline dropped to her knees, panting. She wiped her hand against her bloody nose. "Who? Who seeks another sacrifice?" she asked the empty space with as much force as she could muster. The desperation made her voice crack. "And how do I stop her?"

This time, no voice responded.

16

With a gasp, Marceline woke up in a cold sweat. She had been having some sort of nightmare, running from something she couldn't see. She sat up and looked at her phone. "Oh crap," she muttered, throwing the blanket off. It was already 4:15. Tag would be there in forty-five minutes.

After work, she'd been so drained from yet another strange encounter with a disembodied voice that she'd fallen asleep on her bed.

First order of business, she had to shower off the sweat. Even though she had to worry about a potential murder at this dance, she still wanted to look good while she fought this supposed killer off. In her closet, she located the dress she'd picked with Katy weeks ago, a simple black dress, short, with spaghetti straps. She quickly put it on and plugged in her curling iron.

"You're cutting it kind of close, aren't you?" Delilah said, peeking her head through the bathroom door.

"I overslept," Marceline explained, with a hair clip between her teeth.

Delilah hesitated, clearing her throat. "Can I help you at all?"

Marceline sighed, looking at the time again. 4:30. She had planned on curling her hair, but now she only had time to straighten it. She considered asking Delilah to curl it, but seeing Delilah's smiling face, Marceline couldn't give her the pleasure. "No, I'm good."

Delilah nodded. She turned to leave, but hesitated. "So, are you excited to go to the dance with Tag?"

Despite her worries, Marceline couldn't hide a brief smile from her lips. "Yes, but kind of nervous. I've never gone to a dance with a date before." She'd only ever gone to dances in the past to show Katy support, but they weren't exactly her scene.

"I know it might seem like a big deal to take a date, but if it's with the right person, it should feel as fun and easy as going with friends."

Marceline nodded. Hanging out with Tag had always been low pressure. She supposed going to a dance wouldn't change how they interacted with one another. No need to be nervous. She was, however, nervous about the whole "murder" thing. Part of Marceline hoped it was all in her head, which would mean there was something seriously wrong with her, just because her brain couldn't fathom the latter. What if history did repeat itself tonight?

As much as she wanted to just enjoy her first dance with her boyfriend, she knew she'd have to be on the look-out. The only problem was, how was she supposed to know what to do or who to look for?

Though Marceline was too lost in thought to even attempt small talk, Delilah seemed determined not to leave the bathroom, watching her get ready, hands twitching like they wished they were busy doing something.

"Stunning," Delilah said, smiling at Marceline in the mirror.

Marceline smiled back weakly. "Wait, I have the perfect earrings." Delilah rushed down the hall and came back a moment later holding dangly gold earrings. Marceline had to give it to her. They were the perfect earrings.

"Thanks, Delilah." Marceline returned to her room to put on her shoes when she heard the front door open. The familiar, clunky steps of her brothers running to the door sounded, then she heard another voice. *Tag.*

Marceline's stomach flipped, and she took a deep breath. She quickly applied some of Bijou's oil behind her ears and on her wrist and added the vial to her wristlet. "Marci!" Dad called. Marceline took a deep breath as she smoothed out her dress. She took a last look in the mirror, tucking a strand of purple hair behind her ear, then started down the hallway. As she came down the stairs, she locked eyes with Tag, who immediately burst into a wide grin. He was wearing a crisp white button down with a black tie to match her dress. Marceline smiled back.

"You look beautiful, bean," Dad called, Delilah standing at his side.

"Thanks, Dad."

Her dad posed her and Tag in the usual spot by the stairs for a round of pictures. Tag's hand found its way firmly around her waist. "Bean?" Tag whispered between clenched teeth.

"That's a story I'll never tell," Marceline whispered back.

"Now I have to know."

"Well, hopefully, some of the fifty pictures aren't blurry," Dad said. "Could I get one with my girl?"

Tag offered to take the picture, and Marceline hugged her dad, who looked a bit teary-eyed. He quickly sniffed and cleared his throat.

"Have fun at the dance, kids. Back by eleven, okay?"

"Back by eleven, and no funny business," Tag confirmed on the way out.

He held the door to his truck open, offering her a hand up. After he buckled himself into the driver's seat, he turned to her. "Can I just say how amazing you look?"

Marceline laughed, but she felt like she was going to puke. "You do too."

Tag pulled out of the driveway, and at the stop sign at the end of the street, he turned to her again and gently pulled her face toward his for a long kiss. "I've been wanting to do that," he said, returning his hands to the wheel and putting his turn signal on.

Marceline's face felt hot, and she reached over to hold Tag's hand while he drove. "Where are we going for dinner?"

"We're actually just headed to Nate's house, if that's okay. His parents are gone, but they got dinner catered to the house."

"Oh, that's fine," Marceline said, looking out the window. She'd hung out with Nate a lot with Katy and Tag that summer. He was alright in small groups, but in larger groups, he became a whole other person; loud, obnoxious, and sometimes rude. At parties, he was the guy who broke things for fun and challenged others to drinking contests. She hoped this dinner wouldn't be as rowdy as his other parties had been.

At Nate's house, there were already several cars parked in the driveway. "Who's all here?" Marceline asked.

"Oh, I think just Nate, Marco, Luis, Brady, Sabrina, Molly, and Lacey."

Marceline bit her lip. Just seven people who she wasn't exactly friendly with. Of course Tag's ex would be there. She wished Katy could join her, but she'd be too busy setting up the dance. She'd invite Bijou, but Bijou wasn't the social sidekick Katy was; she'd probably feel more uncomfortable than Marceline with this group.

Seeing the pained expression Marceline failed to hide, Tag said, "It'll be fun. They're all just here to have a good time. We don't have to stay long."

Marceline forced a smile. "It'll be fun," she agreed, trying to convince herself the same.

Nate's house was enormous. The modern exterior backed against the mountains and was on a very sloped driveway. Marceline's heels felt like they might snap at the vertical angle. Tag opened the door without knocking, holding it open for Marceline. There was music playing and laughter, but when Marceline entered, it was as if the music was muted, and all conversation stopped. Marceline smiled and offered a wave.

Nate was the first to return her smile, and he walked over, throwing an arm around Marceline and offering a hand to Tag. "It's the birthday girl!" he shouted. His breath already smelled like booze. "There's food on the counter. Help yourself. In the meantime, what can I get you to drink?"

"I'm driving," Tag said.

Nate scoffed. "Did I forget to tell you we got a limo? Come on, man, it's your last Homecoming! You've got to make it memorable, or unmemorable, you know, depending on how the night goes."

Tag laughed. "Okay, one drink. I'll have a whiskey Coke."

Marceline was hardly paying attention to the boys' conversation, having noticed in the background the girls were whispering to one another, shooting daggers in her direction. Then Marceline did a double take. To her horror, she realized Lacey was wearing the exact same dress as her.

"What about you, Marci?"

Marceline swallowed. "I'll do the same, I guess."

"On it!" Nate made his way to the table that held an assortment of alcohols and mixers.

Marceline grabbed Tag's arm, about to tell him her situation, when she heard Lacey's voice. "Tag, don't you look hand-some!" Lacey's arm snaked around Tag. Again, Lacey's flowery perfume assaulted Marceline's nose. "Marci, I see you have good taste."

Tag looked both girls over and laughed. "Holy crap, what are the chances you would both have the same dress?"

"What are the chances?" Marceline replied meekly.

She and Tag went to grab plates to fill with the array of pastas and salad. Before she'd finished filling her plate, Nate barged between them, sloshing some drink on the floor.

"Before you eat, we all have to take a shot," Nate declared. Every person circled around with their own mini, red Solo shot cup. Lacey shot Marceline a challenging look, and she grabbed the shot. "Cheers to the memories," Nate chanted, then added, "and to Marci's birthday."

Everyone reached their cup in to tap one another's, then Marceline threw the shot back, her whole body shivering as the whiskey burned its way down her throat.

Tag's arm wrapped around her waist. He whispered in her ear, "Want to drink more before since we can't go out after? We're taking a limo there."

Marceline thought she'd need something take the edge off this night and the enormous pressure she felt to prevent the repeating of tragic history, so she nodded.

17

Marceline's head was fuzzy, and she felt off balance. More than the drinks, her enormous responsibility of keeping someone safe from dying at the dance made her sick with worry. Stepping out of the limo at the school, she grasped Tag's arm for support.

"Looks like someone can't walk in heels," Lacey laughed. "Tag, you'd better be a gentleman and hold her hand on the way in."

Marceline's cheeks colored, but Tag offered his arm, which Marceline took.

The hallway leading into the gym was filled with prints on the walls of rabbits, cards, books, clocks, as if they were falling down the rabbit hole into Wonderland. There was an impressive balloon arch outside the door to the gym with a cardboard cutout of the Cheshire cat.

Inside, the lighting was purple hued, and there were streamers all along the rafters of the gym. Marceline saw Katy and Bijou standing at the edge of the dance floor. She took

Tag's hand and led him over to her friends, grateful to see the friendly faces.

Katy's mouth formed an 'O.' "You two are the hottest couple I've ever seen!" she exclaimed. Katy wore a dress that hugged tight around her chest and flared out at the thigh in a red color that stood out against her pale skin and sandy blonde hair. Bijou wore a silver, silky dress that came to her mid-calf. It looked too big on her tiny form.

"You both look beautiful," Marceline said to her and Bijou. "Kat, you've outdone yourself. This place looks amazing."

Katy smiled and bowed. "Thank you, thank you. *Alice in Wonderland* theme was my idea after all, so I had to deliver. Only took the entire student council and me about twelve hours to do all this." Katy's eyes traveled around, then they widened. "Don't look now, but Lacey is wearing the same dress—"

Marceline held up a hand. "I know. We had dinner with her and a few others at Nate's house."

"Ah," Katy said, shooting Marceline a look that said, *We will talk about this later.* "So, guess what? A girl in my tech class told me she was excited to see me at the dance. That's got to mean she's into me, right?"

"Well, there's a chance," Tag acknowledged.

"I'm going to go find her. Bijou, want to come?"

Bijou shrugged and hooked arms with Katy, waving to Marceline and Tag.

"I'll catch up with you later," Marceline promised. She turned to Tag, who put his arms around her waist, turning her toward him.

"Want to dance?"

Marceline hesitated, knowing she needed to at least try to stop this potential murder, even if she had no clue if she was crazy or if this whole thing was real. The words of warning crept into her mind again. She couldn't live with herself if history repeated when she could have prevented it.

Even so, she still didn't know where to look for this killer or if there was even a murderer to look for. One dance couldn't hurt. "I'd love to," she replied. Tag kissed her, and she melted into it, pressing her body close to his.

He pulled away and offered her his hand to pull her toward the groups of dancing kids.

———

Marceline and Tag danced to only a few songs over by his friends, but Marceline was distracted. She thought of everything she knew about the past murders-ruled-accidents at the school, specifically about the ones that had occurred at the Homecoming dance. Strangely, the cause of death for the ones at past Homecoming dances had been broken necks. Her mind was racing with all the ways a person could die via a broken neck, and she very quickly was no longer in the mood to dance. She whispered in Tag's ear that she was going to the restroom.

"Want me to walk you there?" he asked, arms wrapped tighter around her. She leaned in closer for a moment, swaying, then she pulled back.

"No, you stay and keep dancing. I'll be right back."

He leaned into her ear again, breath hot against her neck. "I'll be waiting." She was too stressed out to even react, and she slowly released his hand, pushing her way through the crowd to find her friends.

She found Bijou standing alone by the same table they'd seen her at earlier. Bijou smiled when she approached.

"B, what are you doing here all alone? Where's Katy?"

Bijou nodded to their left. Marceline turned to see Katy giggling with a girl, holding hands as they danced. "I didn't want to third wheel. Plus, I'm having fun just people-watching. This is my first school dance. I still feel like I'm getting used to all this."

Marceline nodded, glancing around the dance floor. "Okay, strange question. If you had to choose someone at this dance who could potentially be a murderer, who would you pick?"

Bijou's brow furrowed. "I would hope no one at our high school was a murderer."

"But if you had to pick?"

Bijou made eye contact with her, frowning, like she realized Marceline was being serious. "Well, I'd imagine it'd be difficult to get away with that in broad view of the entire school. A murderer would probably be lurking in an unlit hallway or something."

Marceline thought about where someone may be able to not be caught, where someone may be able to get away with murder. Somewhere with no cameras. "Do you want to come with me to the bathroom really quick?"

"Sure."

They exited the gym, but there was a line to get into the women's bathroom. "Let's go to the second floor," Marceline suggested. On the staircase, Marceline felt a sinking sensation in her stomach, like maybe she was too late.

Bijou took her hand and gave it a squeeze. "We will find who you're meant to find."

Marceline wondered how Bijou knew to take her seriously, but she didn't question it. There were a handful of girls in the second-floor bathroom, but none who seemed out of the ordinary.

Each of the school's bathrooms were right on top of one another, and all were right beside the staircase. Without speaking, they made their way back to the staircase to head to the third-floor bathroom.

As soon as they reached the top stair, Marceline's head began to throb. Nausea filled her as a migraine gripped her skull like a giant hand, squeezing, intensifying in pressure. The hallway was dark on the third floor, with only some dim light coming from the staircase leading to the floor below. The only other light streamed in from the moon outside the window in the staircase. Marceline hesitated outside, suddenly scared of what she'd find.

Luckily, the lights switched on automatically when Marceline pushed open the bathroom door.

"Hello?" Marceline called nervously. She and Bijou were quiet for a moment, and no other sounds were made. "I think we're alone in here." Though half of Marceline was relieved, half of her was terrified. Where else would someone go to murder someone in the school?

"I'm going to use the bathroom," Bijou said gently. "Then we can keep looking, okay?"

Marceline nodded, unable to find words. She leaned onto the pedestal sink, closed her eyes, and then opened them to find her gaze in the mirror. Her eyes moved down to observe the white bands on her wrists.

"Marci?" Bijou called, her voice even higher than normal.

"Mhm?" Marceline grunted, starting to grow light-headed. Her vision was growing colorless and blurry again, but she couldn't tell if it was all in her head.

Bijou let out a nervous sigh. "I know some strange things have been happening to you lately."

Marceline wondered how Bijou knew, or rather, how much she knew at all, but before she could respond, she noticed goosebumps forming all up her arms. She shivered.

Bijou continued, "I just wanted you to know that I'm here to listen and, you know, my family is . . . like yours, and I can help you through this."

Marceline could barely hear Bijou's words. It was getting very cold, and her ears started to feel like she had cotton balls stuffed in them. As she glanced up, she saw a silhouette behind her in the mirror.

She turned around quickly but saw nothing in front of her. She shook her head; she really was losing it.

Turning back to the mirror, she heard a whisper in her ear. "Marci." This wasn't Bijou's voice. This voice didn't sound within the bathroom at all; it was as if it came directly into her ears.

Marceline's eyes widened as she saw the silhouette appear in the mirror again. Marceline slowly turned around. The bathroom lights flickered. Behind her, she could see a girl with long blonde hair and bangs, wearing a short, sequined, light blue dress.

It didn't hit Marceline until she realized she could see the tiled wall on the other side of the girl, that the girl was transparent. The girl started flickering in tune with the lights.

"Help me," the girl breathed. The sound, though only a whisper, echoed like it was full volume in her ears. Marceline swallowed back a scream. She didn't want to alarm Bijou if this was just another mind trick. The see-through girl moved through the door, out to the hallway. Marceline followed her.

When the door swung closed behind Marceline, the silhouette became clearer, but she was still flashing in and out of visibility. The colors were faded, though tinted an ominous shade of blue. "You're the first who's been able to see me, Marci," the girl said. Her voice sounded so sad.

Marceline didn't know how to reply.

"You've got to get me out of here."

Marceline struggled to find words. "What can I do?" she asked.

The girl made her way toward the stairs. Marceline noticed

the girl's feet didn't touch the ground, just dangled beneath her as she drifted, just like Anna's had. Marceline felt adrenaline running through her. She didn't know if she should run, scream, or try to wake herself up from this nightmare.

"I need to be free," the girl whispered. "I need . . . a sacrifice." Her last words sounded hard, more intimidating.

Marceline shuddered. *Sacrifice* was the same word the voice had used when warning her about the murder at the school. She didn't think that was a coincidence. "What do you mean, a sacrifice?"

The girl started crying, her sobs echoing in Marceline's ears. "Someone has got to take my place in this hell of a school. I can't do this anymore." The ghost's shoulders heaved as she buried her face in her hands. "If you were in my position, you would do the same."

Marceline took a small step forward. "I'm not sure I understand how I can help you."

The girl lifted her head from her hands. This time, fury replaced the despair on her face. Her transparent figure flickered red. "I need a sacrifice."

With that, the transparent girl came rushing toward her at full speed, her mouth opened in a silent, desperate scream. Marceline instinctively held her arms over her face to brace for impact, but the only thing she felt was an extremely cold gust of wind. As fear gripped her, the only thing Marceline could think to do was to try to envision the light shield her mother had reminded her of, but she became lightheaded. She felt blood gushing from her nose as she stumbled backward, falling back against the lockers.

Marceline opened her eyes as the door to the bathroom swung shut again. Bijou was walking toward the staircase, eyes unblinking and looking straight ahead.

"Bijou," Marceline called. Bijou didn't turn her head, just kept walking. "Bijou, what are you doing?" she cried.

Marceline rose to her feet as Bijou got to the edge of the staircase. Slowly, Bijou threw a leg over the railing, about to drop off. If she succeeded, Bijou would make the long fall all the way down to the first floor. Another Homecoming death.

Marceline rushed to her and grabbed ahold of Bijou's arm.

"Help!" she screamed as she struggled to pull Bijou's stiff body back from the railing.

With all her strength, Marceline flung Bijou over the railing, but the force of Bijou's body crashing against her made her lose her grip. Bijou's limp body went tumbling down the stairs.

Marceline tried to scream again for help, but the flickering figure of the ghost appeared before her, glowing red as she reached for Marceline. The blood rushed to Marceline's head as she desperately envisioned light surrounding her. Marceline felt herself falling, losing consciousness. She mumbled, "Bijou," before collapsing.

18

She was floating. No sound reached her ears. Her vision was black, all her senses were off. She was rocking like she was floating on a wave. Floating . . . like the figure of the girl she'd seen in the hallway. In the hallway where Bijou fell. *Bijou.*

Her eyes fluttered open, and all her senses regained at once. The light hit her eyes, and she immediately closed them again as pain shot through her skull. "Patient is awake," she heard an unfamiliar woman's voice say. "Marci, can you hear me?"

Marceline's eyes opened again as she felt a gust of wind; they had exited out the front doors of the school. She was being pushed on a stretcher. "Where's Bijou?" Marceline muttered.

"They have already loaded her into an ambulance," the woman said.

Two men lifted the stretcher Marceline was on down the stairs. The lights of the ambulance and police cars flashing made her struggle to keep her eyes open. She could hear the roar of conversations behind her.

"What's happening?" Marceline asked no one in particular.

The woman rejoined Marceline's side. "We're going to take you to the hospital. You hit your head on the edge of the staircase. You likely have a concussion, and we need to check its severity."

They wheeled her to an ambulance that was at the curb closest to the school. They raised her stretcher up to lift her into the ambulance.

"Wait, no," Marceline tried to yell. She was hoarse. "I don't want an ambulance. Just call my dad." She tried to sit up, but a strap over her chest held her in place.

"Your father has already been called. He's on his way. We can wait for him," the woman said calmly. "In the meantime, we're going to check you out."

Marceline nodded, and they unstrapped her to allow her to sit up. The blood rushed to her head, and she gritted her teeth to stay upright. The woman shone a flashlight into each eye. "Do you know where you are?" the woman asked.

"At the school," she answered softly.

"What are you here for?"

Marceline tried to swallow and found herself struggling to form words. "The dance."

"What's the name of your school?"

"Catori Springs High School." Out of the corner of her eye, Marceline saw a white shirt push through the growing crowd of students standing outside the school.

"Tag!" Marceline called.

He pushed past the school security guard trying to hold him back and ran to her. The woman checking Marceline out stopped her tests for a moment as Marceline reached up to wrap her arms around Tag.

"Are you okay?" Tag asked, releasing the embrace and holding her hands.

"I'm okay," Marceline replied meekly.

"What happened? People are saying you pushed someone down the stairs. I know that's not true, but what happened?"

Marceline cringed as she recalled the events. "Well, I guess I kind of did. But I was trying to stop Bijou from jumping over the rails."

"Off the third floor? That would've—"

"It wasn't her . . . I mean, she wasn't herself. There was someone else forcing her to." A ghost was the murderer the voice had been warning her about. How could she have known?

"Who?"

Both Tag and the medical technician stared at her.

Marceline didn't answer as she suddenly felt chills again running up her arms. Looking back at the front doors of the school, she saw Katy running toward her. To Marceline's horror, Katy was being trailed by the same ghost girl from before. Katy rushed down the stairs, and, as if there was an invisible force field, the ghost following her slammed to a halt at the end of the stairs in front of the building. The ghost's eyes followed Katy menacingly. In a whispered voice that was only heard in Marceline's head, the ghost girl said, "She's next."

Marceline started crying as she looked from the ghost to Katy, her best friend. "Leave her alone!"

A searing pain entered her skull again, and distantly she heard Tag asking the EMTs for help. "What's wrong with her?"

"She has a severe concussion; she might be reacting to all the noise. We need to get her loaded in immediately."

Marceline lost bodily control. She started shaking and her eyes rolled back. Her ears were filled with screams.

19

Marceline woke up and tried to roll over in her bed, but she felt a tug from her arm. She groaned as she opened her eyes and the light hit. Looking around, she realized she was in a hospital bed hooked up to an IV.

Her dad was there. He took her hand as she began to stir. "Hey, hey. You're safe. I'm here. We're at the hospital."

The lights were dim in the room, and the blinds were pulled. Marceline wondered what time it was. She tried to talk, but she was extremely parched. Dad handed her a glass of water with a straw.

"You really scared me, bean," Dad said as she drank.

She stopped sipping and cleared her throat. "I'm sorry, Dad."

Marceline tried to sit up, but Dad gently laid her back down. "The doctor said you need to rest for a few days. No school or work."

Marceline felt her mind trudge through the night's muddied events. She rubbed her forehead. "I don't know what happened. I passed out, and I don't remember much."

"You did more than pass out, sweetie. You hit your head so hard you had a seizure. Luckily, you were already in the ambulance, so they could take care of you."

"A seizure?" Marceline shuddered. She felt goosebumps again when she thought about the vision of that ghost appearing, red hued, screaming in a creepy, muted whisper. Marceline didn't think she could face that building again. How hard was it to get a GED? Of course, if she didn't go back, then Katy was in danger and didn't know it.

"They did some scans of your brain. Everything has come back normal. They just wanted to keep an eye on you overnight."

Normal? There was obviously something very not normal about Marceline's brain. Her eyes filled with tears. She wanted to tell him about everything, but the words wouldn't come. What would she say? Sometimes she heard voices that caused her brain to feel like it would explode, made her nose bleed, and had at times caused her to pass out? What would she say about the ghost she'd seen at the school?

"It's okay, you're okay," he soothed, rubbing her hand. Dad let out a deep breath. "Honey, what happened? What made you and your friend fall?"

Marceline closed her eyes as she pictured Bijou's slack body toppling down the stairs. Her heart filled with guilt. "Can I see her, please? Can I see Bijou? Is she alright?"

"She's in surgery now, or just about out now, I'd imagine."

Marceline's eyes widened as her heart started thumping with panic.

"Bijou is fine," Dad assured her, taking her hand. "Don't worry, she just needed some pins in her arm. It broke in the fall."

Marceline groaned. Bijou was in surgery getting pins in her

arm, and it was all Marceline's fault. She'd somehow made this ghost appear, who proceeded to possess her friend, trying to get her to fall to her death. Plus, the ghost had done something to Marceline, something that make her brain feel like it had caught fire and had resulted in a seizure. Marceline knew she couldn't ignore this problem anymore. It clearly wasn't all in her head. She had to get answers. Instantly, the short black-haired girl, Amina the tarot reader, popped into her head.

"Do you remember what happened?" Dad asked gently.

She sighed. "I can't remember anything." She wasn't ready to disclose everything just yet. She took another gulp of water. "My head hurts."

Dad let out a small chuckle. "Well, stop hitting your head, bean." Dad's face grew more serious. "Marci, your blood alcohol levels were one of the tests the doctors did. You were drinking tonight. Did that have anything to do with you and Bijou falling?"

Marceline closed her eyes, feeling her intense guilt grow. Her guard had been down since she'd been tipsy. Maybe none of this would have happened if she had been in more control. She sighed. "Bijou didn't drink anything. I remember that much."

He leaned forward and kissed her hand that he still held. "Get some rest. I'll be here when you wake up again."

———

They released Marceline from the hospital in the morning after all her tests came back clear. She had a severe concussion and had to stay away from bright lights and screens for a week, but she could rest at home now.

That morning, the police had questioned her to give a statement about what had happened. Mainly, they wanted to know if Bijou had been trying to harm herself and if a seventy-two-hour hold in the hospital was needed to protect Bijou from herself since Marceline had told Tag and the EMT that Bijou had tried to jump. Marceline had to backtrack, saying "jump" was the wrong choice of words. She told them they'd been sitting on the third-floor railing when Bijou slipped. Marceline tried to catch her but had accidentally dropped her once she'd pulled her over the railing. She said maybe it was the adrenaline that then made Marceline herself lose consciousness.

Mysteriously, the school's cameras on the third floor had all stopped working after the clips of Marceline and Bijou walking into the bathroom. The only other witnesses, a couple of girls who had been on the second floor at the time, had heard Marceline screaming Bijou's name and shouting for help, so there was no reason to suspect foul play. It was determined to have been a strange and unfortunate accident.

Before they went home, Dad allowed her to go visit Bijou, who was resting after her surgery the night before. Marceline hesitated outside the door, nervous about what Bijou might remember. What if she only knew Marceline had pushed her down the stairs?

Footsteps approached behind her. "After you," the nurse said, offering a smile. Marceline nodded and walked inside.

Small Bijou was laying in her bed watching TV. She looked up when Marceline approached and smiled. "Marci," she said. "How are you feeling?"

The nurse entered the room behind her and wheeled in a small cart.

Marceline took a few steps and sat at the chair beside Bijou's bed, taking her outstretched hand. "Me? I'm fine. How are you? I'm so sorry about . . . everything."

"Why are you sorry? It's not your fault," Bijou said gently. Marceline wanted to tell her it was her fault, but she wasn't sure what was going on yet. The nurse sanitized her hands and started to remove the IV from Bijou's arm.

"Are you getting released too?" Marceline asked.

"Later today," the nurse confirmed. "Where are your parents?"

"Mom's at home getting me some new clothes, so I don't have to wear my dress home. Dad's getting some food," Bijou explained to the nurse, then looked to Marceline. "Where's your dad?"

"He's just waiting downstairs to take me home." Marceline paused as she eyed Bijou's cast on her right arm. It stretched from her shoulder all the way to her elbow.

"Shoulder fracture," Bijou explained. "I'm just glad I'm left-handed, so I can still do things. You have to sign my cast."

Marceline felt sick with guilt. She shook her head. "I'm so sorry this happened."

"Hey, stop, I know it's not your fault. I'm sure my clumsy self just slipped, and you tried to save me."

"You don't remember?"

"I remember going to the bathroom with you, that's about it."

"Oh," Marceline said slowly.

"Should I remember something else?" Bijou asked.

The nurse, who had finished removing the IV from Bijou's arm, also looked up at her.

"No, that's pretty much what happened," Marceline said quickly.

Footsteps sounded as another person entered the room. "Mama, you remember my friend, Marci," Bijou called.

Marceline distantly remembered in the bathroom before

the accident, Bijou told her that their families were the same . . .
Did that mean Mrs. Eyota could see ghosts too?

Mrs. Eyota's closet must be filled with only long black
dresses and skirts, and today was no exception. She scanned
Marceline over with a guarded but fierce expression. "The Lees
girl," she said flatly.

"That's right," Marceline confirmed. The intensity of Mrs.
Eyota's gaze didn't waiver. Marceline could tell she wasn't
welcome.

"I hope you feel better soon, B," Marceline said, standing
up.

"You too. Thanks for coming by."

Marceline didn't look back as she nearly ran from the room,
ready to leave this hospital.

———

At home, Marceline immediately crawled into bed. Dad had
brought her phone into her room and left it charging on her
nightstand. She saw she had missed calls from Katy and Tag.
Marceline knew she wasn't supposed to be on her phone, but
she needed to make a quick call.

Katy picked up on the first ring. "Marci, oh my God, are
you okay?"

"I'm fine, just have a concussion. I won't be in school next
week."

"I was so worried about you. Seeing you scream and then
start seizing . . ." Marceline could hear the tears welling through
the phone.

"I'm fine," Marceline said again. "I don't have much time.
I'm not supposed to be on my phone. I called to ask if you could
do me a favor."

"Of course, anything."

Marceline took a deep breath. "Could you look more into those deaths that happened at the Homecoming dance?"

She heard Katy's sharp intake of breath. "Sure, I can do that. Can I ask why?"

Marceline heard footsteps coming up the stairs. "I've got to go. Bye, Kat. Love you."

20

After a week, Marceline was cleared to return to school. It had been a week with a lot of rest, more than she thought her body was capable of. She'd thought with minimal human contact and no electronics or reading allowed, she'd have been bored, but she had hardly kept her eyes open the entire week.

Her mom had tried reaching her, but thankfully Marceline had the excuse of the concussion to avoid speaking with her.

Marceline didn't know what was happening to her, why after she'd turned seventeen, she'd suddenly sprouted these strange markings on her arms and started to hear voices and see ghosts. She needed answers.

Marceline had a sneaking suspicion her mother knew what was happening to her, and yet, she had never even tried to warn her. Why hadn't she been here to help Marceline through whatever it was that was happening to her since she'd turned seventeen? She wasn't ready yet to have this conversation, but at the same time, if she couldn't figure out what was happening herself, she'd have to lose her pride and ask her mom for help. The only other person she could think to ask would be Amina, the tarot reader, but both sounded like equally terrible options.

The Sunday night before her return, Marceline was in bed when her phone vibrated. Marceline read a text from Katy. *I'm outside. Let me in, or I'm breaking in.*

Marceline laughed and shook her head. She peeked her head around her curtains, and sure enough, she saw Katy parked out front. It was 10 p.m., so the rest of the house was in bed. Marceline tip-toed downstairs, unlocking the front door as quietly as she could. Katy was standing there, rubbing her arms and bouncing from foot to foot. "It's getting cold out," she complained. Marceline shushed her, and they tip-toed to her room.

Katy plopped onto Marceline's bed as she had thousands of times before, removing her backpack.

Marceline held a warning finger to her lips. She wasn't sure if she was still grounded, but either way, Marceline wasn't allowed to have people over after 10 p.m. on a school night.

"So," Katy said in a low voice, leaning back onto Marceline's pillows. "I did the research you asked me to do." Marceline swallowed nervously and joined her on the bed. Katy shuffled through her backpack, pulling out a manilla folder. "How are you feeling, by the way?"

"Better," she replied. Marceline held her tongue. While she was feeling more rested, above all, she was nervous to go back to school, to face the ghost.

Katy narrowed her eyes but didn't say anything. She knew Marceline well enough to know she wasn't saying the whole truth, but Marceline was grateful she didn't press, at least not yet. Katy started pulling freshly-printed pages of old news-paper stories from the folder, laying them on Marceline's bed.

"The first death at the school happened the year the current building was built, in 1954. A fourteen-year-old girl, Tabitha Lamare, died 'under suspicious circumstances.' I couldn't find much other information about this one."

Marceline could barely swallow as Katy flipped through the files, explaining each of the other September Five's deaths. In 1968, Dale Brown had passed away suddenly from an aneurism. In 1984, Todd Washington had slipped and cracked his head open. And in 1999, Suzy Somers died from hanging, this one at the Homecoming dance. Marceline gulped at that. One of two broken necks at the dance.

Katy continued, "The most recent death at the school happened in 2004. Her name was Kendra Macintosh."

Marceline's heartbeat quickened.

Katy bore into Marceline's eyes. "It was ruled a suicide. On September 18th, which was the night of the Homecoming dance that year. Weird, the same exact date as ours this year. Anyway, at the dance, Kendra jumped from the third floor to her death and broke her neck."

Marceline felt tears in her eyes. She thought about Bijou, how close she'd been. She closed her eyes and swallowed. "That's awful."

"It is," Katy agreed. "But what's worse is that some speculate it wasn't really a suicide, that she'd been pushed or . . . forced. But you seem to strangely already know that bit."

Marceline ignored the last sentence. "Forced?"

"There were no witnesses, but Kendra's friends and family all said she was always a happy girl. No one had suspected she'd been sad at all, let alone suicidal. She was a senior in high school, the student body president, captain of the basketball team. She was popular, she had a boyfriend . . . Doesn't mean someone with a seemingly perfect life can't also be secretly depressed, but it's strange there were no signs."

"Wow," Marceline said. She stared down at her hands. She didn't know what to think. Was the flickering girl she'd seen at the Homecoming dance who tried to force Bijou off the ledge the ghost of Kendra, Tabitha, or Suzy? Or was she someone else entirely?

"Earth to Marci," Katy called, waving a hand in front of her face. "I can see you're lost in thought, but I'd like to be let in. Why did you have me do this research? Something bad happened at the dance, I know. I've never seen you so terrified."

Marceline struggled with how much she should say. Would Katy think she was crazy? At this point, Marceline was so desperate to tell someone about what was going on, she didn't care. "I saw something, or I guess I should say *someone*, in the third-floor bathroom when I went with Bijou at the dance."

"What do you mean, saw someone?"

"I don't know who it was. It was a transparent girl, flickering in and out—"

"Marci, stop. Are you telling me you saw a ghost?"

Marceline sighed. "I don't know what I saw."

Katy cursed under her breath. She already looked scared.

"The girl said she needed help," Marceline continued. "And I know this sounds insane, but I think she took over Bijou's body. She was trying to sacrifice her."

"Whoa, whoa, whoa, 'took over' as in possessed her? And what do you mean sacrifice her? Was she trying to kill Bijou?" Katy looked equal parts terrified and concerned.

"All I know is the girl kept saying she needed a sacrifice, then I felt this colossal force throw me backwards, and next thing I know, I see Bijou, looking straight ahead, walking toward the railing. I tried to call her name, and she didn't respond at all. I pulled her back over the railing, but I dropped her, and she fell. I tried to save her, and I hurt her," Marceline said, tears falling down her cheeks.

Katy leaned across the bed and wrapped her arms around Marceline, rocking side to side. "It's not your fault, Marci. From the sound of it, you saved Bijou's life."

Marceline sniffled. "So, you don't think I'm crazy?"

"If the most skeptical girl I know is saying she saw a ghost, it has to be real."

Marceline let out a shaky breath. "Thanks, Kat."

"Is this what you were so freaked out about after the psychic? Did she say something?"

Marceline sighed. "I don't know what happened with the psychic. But I'd been hearing a voice lately at work, telling me to beware of the Homecoming dance."

"Stop it! I have chills," Katy squealed, running her hands over her arms. "I'm kidding, don't stop telling me. How long has this been going on?"

"A few weeks," Marceline admitted.

Katy smacked Marceline's arm. "What is the point of having a best friend if you don't even tell me shit like this? I'm here for you, Marci, always. I'm mad at you for dealing with all this supernatural stuff alone."

Marceline let out a sigh of relief. She threw her arms around Katy. "I love you, you know?"

Katy buried her head in Marceline's hair. Her voice was muffled. "You better. Who else would believe their best friend when they tell them they're hearing voices and seeing people who aren't there?"

Marceline released her and shrugged, smiling. She looked down at the bed, where Katy had laid out the old newspapers. "Wait a second. This is her."

"Who?"

Marceline pointed to the newspaper displaying Kendra Macintosh's photo. "This was the ghost I saw."

It was the same girl with blonde bangs, only her face was softer, kinder, alive. Though the ghost she'd seen looked exactly the same age, the ghost version seemed much older than this photo. Hardened by time and by death.

21

Marceline slowly rode Barb2.0 to school, savoring her time alone and collecting her thoughts. She knew she'd have to confront Kendra. She needed to figure out how to send her away for good and how to protect her friends.

Tag met her at the doors to the school, giving her a gentle hug. She had to assure him five times she felt alright for him to allow her to walk into the school, but he eventually let her pass, promising to take her to lunch.

Marceline continued to her locker, where she met Katy. "I'm coming with you," Katy said.

Marceline didn't even ask how Katy knew her plan, but she tried to act unassuming. "To Spanish with me? You might be a little lost. The conjugations we're working on are tough."

Katy rolled her eyes. "I'm not talking about first period." She lowered her voice and whispered, "I'm talking about you going to see that ghost."

"Even if I was planning on talking to the ghost this morning, which I'm not, you're not coming with me," Marceline said forcefully. Marceline couldn't have another Bijou moment.

Plus, she hadn't told Katy how she'd seen the ghost point at her and say, *She's next*, and she didn't plan on telling her. "Where's Bijou, anyway? Is she back at school yet?"

Katy's eyes shot down. "About that, Bijou's parents pulled her out. They're going back to homeschooling her."

Marceline sighed, the guilt twisting her stomach.

Reading her mind, Katy said, "It's not your fault."

Marceline tried not to roll her eyes. Of course it was her fault. It certainly wasn't Bijou's fault. The first bell rang. "I'm going to class."

"You sure you're not going to a certain third-floor bathroom to try to summon a certain ghost?"

"I'm not in the mood for that. I'll try later."

Katy nodded, looking unconvinced. "Right, well, let me know when you do go."

Marceline headed up to the third floor, only she wasn't headed to Spanish.

The only way Marceline could think to find out what was happening to her that didn't involve asking the two people she didn't want to talk to most was to go straight to the source.

She went to the other side of the floor, above the gym. She couldn't look at the staircase. The final bell rang as she stood outside the bathroom door, summoning the courage to push it open. Part of her wondered if the ghost was still there or if she only appeared during the Homecoming dance.

She took a deep breath, envisioned light, then entered the bathroom. It looked significantly less scary with the lights on. She walked to the mirror she had first seen the ghost in. This time, there was no figure looming behind her reflection. Working up her nerve, she clamped her shaking hands into fists.

"Kendra?" she called. She waited a moment. There was no response. "Kendra? That's your name, isn't it?" Marceline walked around the small bathroom, seeing and hearing nothing. "I'm sorry you died. I'm sorry you're stuck here. I'm just trying to help you." Marceline waited a few more minutes, then, deciding Kendra either wasn't there or didn't want to talk, Marceline took a few steps back toward the door.

As Marceline put her hands on the door, the energy in the room shifted. She pushed, but the door wouldn't budge. Marceline started to feel chills again, then her vision dulled until every object lost its color, even her own reflection in the mirror. She blinked, then, behind her in the mirror, she saw her. This time, Kendra wasn't flickering. She was solid, appearing more present, even though she was still transparent.

"Kendra?" Marceline addressed her uncertainly.

"You know who I am?" Kendra's voice was small, like a little girl's.

Marceline nodded. "You died here."

Kendra's lip quivered, but she held her face flat.

"Why did you try to hurt my friend?" Marceline asked.

Kendra's face abruptly changed in emotion from sad to enraged. "I just want out of this place," she cried. "Please, you see how cold it is here all the time? No color. No warmth. No joy. You're the first person who has seen me, who has talked to me, in years. I'm alone all the time, watching teens deal with stupid problems and go through puberty over and over. That was bad enough experiencing it for myself. Now I'm forced to watch others do it? It's awful being stuck here. I can't take it anymore."

Marceline couldn't help but feel a bit of sympathy for the poor, trapped girl. "Why do you think a sacrifice would get you unstuck?"

"Because that's how it works. That's how I got here. I was at the Homecoming dance just like you were when I was possessed by the ghost before me, and the next thing I knew, I woke up dead. She did to me exactly what I tried to do to your friend, and she made me jump from the third floor to my death. You don't see her still here, do you? She got out when I got in. The only way for me to get out of here is to have someone else die here."

Marceline shook her head. "I'm sorry that happened to you, but why would you want to take someone else's life? To give them the same fate you've had?"

"Better anyone else than me," Kendra replied darkly.

Marceline switched her tactic. She needed all the information she could get. "Why are you trapped here? Why didn't you move on or whatever normally happens when someone dies?"

Kendra floated back and forth across the bathroom. "It doesn't matter. You don't really want to help me, not after what I did to your friend. What I tried to do to you."

"What you tried to do to me?"

Kendra sighed impatiently. "For some reason, I couldn't get inside your head. With your friend, it was much easier to take over."

Marceline shuddered but tried to keep her voice level. "I really do want to help." She took a step closer. "Why are you trapped here?" she repeated.

Kendra huffed and crossed her arms. "My soul is stuck. This place is holding on so tight. There was someone stuck here before me, but they got out when I got here."

"Suzy?" Marceline guessed. The girl who'd died before Kendra.

Kendra's eyes darkened. "Yes, but don't ever say her name."

"Why now? Why did you wait until now to start trying to sacrifice people?" Marceline asked.

Kendra laughed darkly. "Trust me, it's not like I haven't been trying to possess people. All these girls who come in here, wasting their lives talking about boys and parties and how their hair looks. They deserve to die."

Marceline tried to contain her panic at Kendra's disregard for human life. She wanted to keep Kendra calm, to reason with her. "How were you able to possess my friend?"

Kendra's face brightened, and she put on a smug smile. "I'm quite proud of that, actually. I've never had the strength to fully possess someone before. I get stronger around my death-iver-sary, so it just worked out. Except, I suppose it didn't work since I'm still stuck."

"I'm sorry you're stuck, but how can I help? I don't want you to kill anyone. Do you know of any other way?"

Kendra's face fell back into a bitter scowl. "There's no other way. Replacing the soul here is the only way to get me out."

Marceline shuddered at the thought. A life for a life. But why was anyone stuck here in the first place? "There's got to be another way," Marceline pleaded. "Wouldn't you have wanted that chance? Rather than Suzy killing you to take her place, wouldn't you have rather she'd found peace another way?"

"There's no such thing as finding peace, not in Catori. I've been searching for years." Kendra's entire body was shaking. She was slowly fogging over with a blue hue.

"There has to be peace. Maybe I can—"

Kendra's entire demeanor changed; her coloring turned a red hue as she rushed into Marceline's face. "Take my place, or someone else will. The next full moon is coming, and someone will die."

Fire shot through Marceline's skull, and she gritted her teeth. "I'm not scared of you," Marceline said through the pain. Kendra's face pulled back in rage as she circled around her. The pain intensified, but Marceline managed to force out, "Leave me and my friends alone!"

Marceline broke through Kendra's force and pushed the

door open, nearly falling into the hallway. As she stumbled, her vision still blurry, she was surprised as arms caught her.

"Are you alright?" Katy asked.

"What are you doing here?"

Katy helped pull Marceline upright. "I came here right away. I knew you weren't going to Spanish." She reached into the front pocket of her bag and pulled out a packet of tissues, handing one to Marceline.

Marceline held it to her nose, pulling away a freshly bloodied tissue.

"What happened in there? I tried to come in, but the door was locked."

Marceline shook her head. "I tried to sympathize with her, to figure out how I could help her be free, but she didn't want my help. She just wants to cause destruction."

Katy's eyes widened in fear. "Great, an angry, forever-teenage, bratty ghost girl is on the loose in our school."

"I'm going to stop her," Marceline promised, taking Katy's hand.

Katy released her hand to rifle through her backpack again. This time, she pulled out a fresh sheet of paper on which she wrote, *Out of Order*. "For now, let's try to keep people out of there."

Despite the overwhelming dread, Marceline couldn't help but frown. "You just have tape in your bag?"

"You never know when you'll need tape, Marci, case in point, and you know I'm always prepared for anything."

22

S he couldn't shake the way Kendra had looked at her with
so much burning hatred. It distracted her through all of
her classes. Kendra had told her she would try again on the
anniversary of her death, which, Marceline remembered from
Bijou's constant updates about the lunar cycles, was October
1st, this coming Friday.

Her head ached, but this time she wasn't sure if it was due
to her concussion or from her encounter with Kendra. Even the
peppermint oil from Bijou didn't seem to help, which was also
running low. What would she do for more peppermint oil now
that Bijou wasn't at school anymore and Marceline clearly
wasn't welcomed at the Eyotas' store?

For lunch, Tag met her by the front doors. "Ready for some
pizza?" Tag wrapped his arm around her as they walked.

"Always. And I'm buying this time," Marceline replied.

"How are you feeling?" Tag asked in a more serious tone.

"Tag, I'm fine. You don't have to ask me every five seconds,"
Marceline said. Her tone was unexpectedly more snappy than
she'd meant it to be. Tag quickly removed his arm from her

shoulders, and Marceline sighed. "I'm sorry. My head is still hurting. I'm a little on edge."

"I understand. I'm just worried about you. Sorry I'm annoying you." There was an edge to his tone, a hint of irritation.

"It's okay, don't apologize," Marceline mumbled. They were silent the rest of the walk to Luigi's. Part of her felt bad for showing this side of herself to Tag, for getting annoyed with him for the first time, but she figured it had to come out sometime. Couples got annoyed with one another. It wasn't the end of the world.

As they entered the restaurant, the door nearly hit the person at the end of the line, who happened to be Nate, standing beside Marco and Brady. "Well, well, well, if it isn't the cutest couple in school."

"What's up guys?" Tag said, greeting his friends.

Marceline was not in the mood, but she forced a smile.

"Why don't we all sit together?" Nate suggested.

Marceline instantly wanted to burst out, *NO*, but she turned to Tag, hoping he could read the desperation in her eyes. "Sure, why not? We're all here," Tag said.

Marceline suppressed her groan.

"I'll just buy. Marci, want to grab us all a table?"

Marci? He never called her that. "Sure," Marceline replied through tight lips. She walked around to sit at an open booth.

As she sat, Marceline's head pounded, and she felt shivers crawling up her arms. The volume of voices in the restaurant was hammering her ears. There seemed to be more voices than there were people. She tried to cover her ears, but she noticed the sound was like when Kendra spoke to her, like amplified whispers directly to her skull.

Looking up, it slightly horrified Marceline to see more transparent bodies floating around, as if they, too, were there for lunch. There was a group of men floating near the counter. One of them floated straight through the counter and along the wall to the kitchen. He wore an apron, like he was still working, even in the afterlife. Each of the other three men turned to look at her, making eye contact. None of them moved, seemingly just as curious about her as she was about them. Marceline closed her eyes, focusing on her light like her mom had advised, sending away her fear.

Marceline jumped as two hands landed loudly on the table. "Hey, Nate," Marceline said with strained politeness as he scooted into the bench opposite her. Looking around him, she noticed the other ghostly men were gone.

"You coming with Tag to my party on Friday, Marci?"

Marceline wanted to roll her eyes but resisted. "I can't."

"Why not? Because of your little stunt at the Homecoming dance?" Nate's tone was full of over-done concern, and Marceline glared at him.

"I just don't want to," Marceline replied coolly. They stared one another down until the others joined them, Tag sliding in next to her.

"What were you two talking about?" Tag asked.

Nate crossed his arms across his chest. "Marci doesn't want to come to my party on Friday."

"Well, she has a concussion. She can't even drink. Plus, are you still grounded, Marci?"

"I don't know," Marceline snapped. She closed her eyes and ran her fingers over her eyelids.

The boys all grabbed slices of pizza, but Marceline stayed leaning back against the booth.

Nate took a large bite and, in between chews, said, "So, Marci, I also heard you got possessed by a ghost and threw your friend down the stairs. That true?"

Marco, who was taking a sip of soda, spit it back into his

cup as he tried to cover a laugh. Brady stared straight down at the table. Marceline's eyes narrowed, clenching her jaw as she stared at Nate.

"Of course not, dude. Why the hell would you ask that?" Tag said.

"I didn't ask you, Tag. What really happened, Marci?"

Marceline's eyes turned toward the door to the kitchen, where one of the ghost men with sad eyes watched. Marceline tried to swallow, but it got stuck in her throat. Her vision started blurring.

"Let me out, Tag," Marceline muttered.

Tag refused to budge. "Marci, come on—"

"Let me out," Marceline repeated, more aggressively. He obeyed this time and slid out, and Marceline ran out the front door. She felt bile rising in her throat. Once outside, she dropped to her knees, retching into the bushes. She coughed, her whole body shaking. She felt a hand on her back, making her jump.

"Are you okay?" Tag asked. "I'm sorry. Nate was being an asshole. That's just how he is."

Marceline furiously wiped her mouth. "Some friend you have."

Tag took a step toward her, brow furrowed. "You don't look well. Can I drive you home?"

"I'm fine, Tag," Marceline insisted angrily. "You just . . . enjoy your lunch with your friends. I'm going to find Katy."

"Wait," Tag called. He grabbed her hand and forced her to face him. "Want me to come with you?"

Marceline's head was on fire again. She held a hand to her temple. "No, I just need some time alone."

"Are we . . . okay?" Tag's eyes were full of concern.

She sighed. "We're fine," she assured him. She squeezed his hand before turning to walk back toward the school.

23

By the end of the day, Marceline was feeling exhausted. Though Dad had told her she didn't have to work for another week, Marceline had insisted. It was Monday, the day the mysterious tarot card reader, Amina, always came by to grab her usual peanut butter and loaf of bread.

At the Grocery Elf, Marceline was grateful it was slower than normal. They had tasked her with the simple jobs like taping this year's Coffin Race announcement poster on the front door of the store. Marceline took her time on that.

Delilah stayed later to help her put away stock, as she was moving slowly. Delilah kept asking if Marceline needed to go home early, but Marceline insisted she was fine.

Delilah finally left her alone with Sheldon. Marceline made her way to the back area to grab another load of stock to put away. As soon as the door closed behind her, she felt an instant chill, a feeling that was becoming familiar. She sighed. Was this her life now? Being haunted everywhere she went?

"Who's here?" she called impatiently into the empty room, wanting to get this over with. "Come on, show yourself."

The lights in the stock room dimmed. Marceline sighed again, rolling her eyes. She was no longer fazed by this whole routine. She turned and saw a transparent hand pass through one of the shelves, which quickly retracted back behind. Marceline walked over, peeking around. "Hello," she said to the short transparent man who was hiding behind the shelf.

The man, who'd been cowering, finally looked up at her. He was an older man, maybe around seventy. He still wore a name tag which read, 'Joe.' "Ah, you've found me. Yes, you can finally hear me now. Well, happy belated birthday, dear," the man said in a shaky tone Marceline instantly recognized.

"You're the one who was warning me about the Home-coming dance," she said. "Who are you?"

The man still trembled. He opened his mouth to speak several times before words finally came out. "Can I just say, Marceline, what a privilege it's been to watch you grow up?"

Marceline cocked her head, confused.

Joe continued, "Your mother and father bought this place when you were still inside of your dear mother. You see, I was the owner of what was Joe's Convenience Store before my wife sold this place to your parents. I've seen you almost every day for the past seventeen years. It's surreal to finally speak with you. You've been like a daughter, or rather, grand-daughter to me, I suppose, as your mother was like a daughter to me."

"You knew my mom?"

"Ah, yes. She had a gift such as yours. The two of us were friends. She's the only one I've been able to really speak with all these years. It was a sad day when she left Catori."

"My mom could see ghosts too?" Marceline felt like a balloon that'd been pricked with a needle. She'd suspected this, but this confirmed that it was true. Whatever she was dealing with, her mother had dealt with it too. It made it even worse in her mind that her mother had left, knowing at some point Marceline would have to deal with all this on her own.

"Why yes, she never told you? Oh dear, I really did not mean to spill any secrets . . . Anyhow, Marceline, my name is Joseph Price. You may call me Joe."

"Hi, Joe," Marceline said slowly. "Why were you hiding from me?"

"I know that it costs you needless energy when you speak with ghosts. And I suppose I was nervous about speaking to another human again. I've become a bit of a recluse all these years alone."

Marceline hadn't thought about that. Maybe that was why her nose bled and her head hurt. Maybe every time she was close to a ghost, those were physical indicators her energy was being expended. "So, about the Homecoming dance—"

"Sorry if I spooked you, I wanted to really sink the message in to be careful. I was trying to warn you."

"You definitely warned me, though it was cryptic. I didn't know who or what I was looking for, but it certainly wasn't Kendra—"

"Ugh!" Joe shouted, raising a fist in the air. "Kendra did something terrible, didn't she? I knew she would. Is she still there, or did she, well, get a replacement?"

"You know about Kendra?"

Joe rolled his eyes. "Don't even get me started about that brat. She's big in the Catori ghost community. Every Halloween she goes on and on about how much she hates these innocent teenagers—"

Marceline had to interrupt Joe to get a word in. "You've talked to her? I thought Kendra said she was stuck in the school and couldn't leave?"

"Yes, we all are stuck in the locations where we've died," Joe said impatiently. "But on Halloween, we are all released for the day and can go anywhere. Anyway, Kendra has been waiting, growing in power until she could strike. Did she succeed in taking another's life?"

Her head was spinning from talking with someone who knew more about all this than she did. Marceline shook her head. "Almost. She tried to get my friend to throw herself off the third-floor staircase." Marceline launched into the tale, Joe clutching his heart and grunting in disgust at the mention of Kendra's actions.

"A disgrace of a ghost, that Kendra," Joe spat. "I'm glad she's still stuck there. But bitterness is a potent source of power for a miserable soul such as her. Please be careful around her. I knew that, since you were seventeen now, she would try to use your power to find peace. There's some rotten rumor that killing a Spirit Walker would give them the ability to find peace."

"Spirit Walker . . . What is that?"

Before Joe could answer, the door to the stockroom burst open and Sheldon hustled inside, letting out a deep sigh of relief when he saw Marceline. "Gosh, girl, if you need a break, just tell me. I was worried you'd fallen and hit your head. Josh and Delilah would kill me if I didn't keep an eye on you."

Marceline let out a small smile. "I'm fine, Sheldon. No need to worry."

Sheldon frowned back. "You've got another nosebleed, doll." He pulled a package of tissue from his pocket and handed it to her before closing the door behind him.

Sure enough, when she swiped under her nose, there was fresh blood. Marceline called out to Joe again.

"Back to work, Marceline. I don't want to distract you," Joe chided. "Plus, I'm not the best person to be answering these questions. Since your mom isn't here, you may want to ask that other Spirit Walker who comes through here sometimes."

"What's a Spirit Walker?" Marceline asked again. "And who else is one?"

Joe grunted impatiently, twitching nervously. "You are a Spirit Walker, Marceline. You can see and communicate with the dead. And don't ask me who the other Spirit Walker is like you don't already know."

Marceline was almost positive Amina was the other Spirit Walker he was talking about, but she didn't get the chance to confirm it, because Joe vanished into the back shelves.

Joe stayed away from Marceline the rest of her shift, even though she was desperate to talk with him more.

It felt good to know there was a term for what was happening to her and that she wasn't the only one out there. Now it was just a matter of either asking her mom, which Marceline wasn't prepared to do, or getting Amina, who didn't seem like the friendliest person, to listen to her.

Finally, five minutes to eight, the door chimed. Marceline turned around quickly. She spotted the back of Amina's short black-and-gray bob making her way toward the front shelves. Marceline set down the cereal boxes she was holding and walked toward the bread aisle.

As she turned the corner, Amina innocently held her hands up. "I'm just here to buy some food," she said defensively.

"Well, good thing you're in a grocery store that sells food," Marceline replied, but quickly regretted her sassy remark.

Amina glared as she quickly grabbed a jar of peanut butter and turned her back.

"Wait," Marceline called in a loud whisper. Amina continued moving down the aisle until Marceline pleaded, "Please. I need your help."

Amina stopped in her tracks and slowly turned back around.

Marceline's eyes filled with tears. "I don't know what's

happening to me. My friend almost died last week because a ghost possessed her, and now something bad is about to happen again at the school, and I don't know how to stop it. I've been feeling things, seeing things for weeks, but it's gotten worse since I turned seventeen. Please, I don't know who else to ask for help."

Amina's eyes looked past her. Marceline turned quickly and saw Joe dart behind a shelf. Amina nodded. "Come back to the McCormick Estate tonight." She spun on her heel and continued back toward the front counter. Sheldon nonchalantly checked her out, and Amina left without so much as another look in Marceline's direction.

But Marceline felt hopeful. She would get some answers tonight.

24

After work, Marceline hopped on Barb2.0, but this time she went the opposite way from her house, toward the McCormick Estate. Pulling up, she leaned her bike against the wrought-iron gates.

The weeds that had been green, tall, and wildly overgrown last time she was here were still just as tall, but they were now brown, as if the life had been sucked out of them. It was likely the result of the colder weather, but Marceline couldn't help but feel unsettled by the lifelessness. The weeds scratched at her skin as she walked. She still felt the same sensation of hands lightly rubbing her arms. Though it hadn't crossed her mind last time, now, knowing what she did, she wondered if actual ghost hands, invisible, made contact with her. She calmed herself, thinking if there were hands, she'd be able to see them now. Still, she shivered at the thought as a breeze rustled through the weeds.

Before Marceline had reached the steps leading to the side door, it opened, seemingly on its own. Amina was sitting in her same spot on the pillow across from the small table. The candles were ablaze. Marceline took a deep breath of the fresh night air before entering, fearing it might be her last.

"Marci," Amina greeted in a dull tone. She gestured to the pillow across from her.

"Amina," Marceline said as she slowly lowered herself onto the pillow.

Amina reached for Marceline's hands, examining the markings on her wrist. "You've got your fledgling bands. You're officially a Spirit Walker," Amina said, cocking her head to the side. Her eyes seemed to invade every crevice of Marceline's face. "I could sense you had the Sight when we first met."

Marceline stared blankly. It was that same word Joe had said. "Spirit Walker? Sight?"

Amina raised her eyebrows. "You mentioned at the store you had started to see things, see ghosts, no?"

Marceline nodded slowly.

"It's called the Sight. When you can see the lower dimension. Those who have the Sight are called Spirit Walkers."

"The lower dimension?" Marceline asked in a small voice. She didn't like not knowing things. She didn't like asking questions, but now she didn't have a choice. In this moment, she was completely clueless. Everything about this was uncomfortable for her. Plus, she wasn't sure if she could even trust this woman.

"Where the lost souls go?" Amina said it as a question, but her tone made it clear what she was saying should be common knowledge. When Marceline showed no sign of understanding, Amina sighed. "You really know nothing, huh?" She sighed again. "Well, if you're here for more protection, let's get this over with." Amina busied herself rolling up her sleeves, revealing her darker bands.

"What do you mean, more protection?"

"I thought you'd figured it out by now. Why do you think you couldn't see any spirits the past few days? That night you were here before, I tried to give you some of my energy to keep you safe."

"Is that what you did that night? Transferred your energy to protect me?"

Amina nodded. "I knew you were freshly Realized, and without anyone around you to protect you, you'd be quickly overwhelmed by the spirits in this town. I gave you enough protection to block spirits from you for the past few days."

"Well, it hasn't worked," Marceline said. "The day after my birthday, I was at the school for a dance. A ghost named Kendra came to me."

Amina sat forward, intrigued. "This must be a powerful spirit to break through my protection."

"It was her death-iversary, so she was powerful. At least, that's what she said. But she was flickering, not how the ghosts normally look. She must have had to use a lot of energy to appear in front of me. And then she tried to possess me and my friend."

"Did this spirit succeed in possession?"

"She couldn't take control of me, but she did take control of my friend. She almost killed her."

Amina nodded thoughtfully. "This spirit has taken a turn down a nearly irreversible path toward darkness. Once a spirit possesses a human, it makes finding peace that much more difficult for them. You kept her out of your head, that's good. At least you know how to protect your energy from the spirits who are trying to feed on you."

Marceline shook her head no.

"On some level, you must already know how to protect yourself, whether you know you know or not. You did it to me when I was trying to attach my energy to you. You got me out. How did you do that?"

Marceline thought of her mom's advice. "I just envisioned a bright light protecting me," she said, feeling lame.

Amina's face lightened. "You were taught a little something, after all. That's exactly what you need to do to protect your energy. It's called an energy shield. Golden light is the highest vibrational color. Only good spirits can get through golden shields. But if you ever need to be completely shielded, nothing can permeate a lead shield. Remember that."

Marceline could hardly believe it was that simple, that her mom's method was actually protecting her. This whole time she'd thought it was a placebo, only making her feel more protected. She didn't know it actually helped, even slightly. She bit her lip as she considered the second half of what Amina said. "Like, an actual lead shield?"

Amina's neutral, hard expression softened slightly as she pursed her lips. "Trying to distance myself from you clearly did more harm than good. I didn't realize I'd have to teach you *everything*." She sighed. "You can envision a lead shield just as you envision your golden shield. It all starts in your head."

"Can you teach me how to do a shield like that?"

"You can already do it; it just takes practice and concentration. It gets easier over time. Right now, as a new Spirit Walker, you actually hold more power than me. It's just that your power is not under control yet. Once you learn how to direct it, you'll be able to cast all the shields you want."

"But how do I direct it?" Marceline struggled to keep her voice level, to not allow her frustration to show. Amina acted like everything was so easy. How was she supposed to know how to do these things?

"I didn't sign up to be a teacher," Amina said with narrowed eyes. "I thought you would've been told at least the basics, then I could just give you protection until you were strong enough to protect yourself."

"Why did you bother to help me at all, then?" Marceline pressed.

"As much as it may seem that way, I'm not completely heartless. Passing through town, I noticed a young Spirit Walker on the verge of Realization who was clearly clueless, and in our world, clueless means vulnerable."

"Why?"

Amina continued, "You and I, we attract spirits. We sense them, we see them, and these spirits like to be acknowledged by Spirit Walkers. It strengthens their pull to our dimension. But it's almost a literal pull. They can invade your spirit, attaching to your energy for nourishment, feeding on and draining you. That's why I felt the need to protect you in your first days of Realization. Otherwise, the spirits would have fed on you too much."

Marceline thought of being in the hospital. She hadn't seen any spirits while she'd been there, which now, looking back, was strange since she'd seen them about everywhere else. Amina's protection must have kept all the many spirits at the hospital at bay. She was thankful for that.

She looked back up at Amina. "You mentioned earlier a place where lost souls go. Does everyone go there when they die?"

"Not everyone, fortunately. When people die, ideally their soul crosses over and finds peace immediately. But it's not always that easy; some souls get stuck in the lower dimension."

"The lower dimension. Is that, like, Hell?" Marceline asked.

Amina smirked and shook her head at the question. "Not at all. The stuck souls in the lower dimension don't live in Hell as you might imagine it, with a fiery, evil devil wreaking havoc. They live here, more or less, watching the world change around them, with no one, apart from other spirits and those with Sight, able to see them. Another important difference between

Hell and the lower dimension is that not all souls who get stuck in the lower dimension are bad. Some just are lost."

"So why do only some get stuck?"

"There's no certain answer as to why it happens, but many believe it's because that soul has unfinished business here on Earth, or they want to watch over their loved ones. Some unconsciously trap themselves as a form of self-punishment for actions in their life. Some just aren't ready to leave quite yet."

"Can't they just decide to cross over when they're ready to move on?"

Amina smiled sadly. "No, sometimes it can take a long time for a soul to find peace. There aren't directions for that either, how to find peace. It just happens eventually, or we, as Spirit Walkers, can sometimes help them along."

Marceline first thought of Joe, trapped in the Grocery Elf all these years. He wasn't a bad person. She felt sad thinking of him watching her family all these years, with no one to talk to. Even Kendra, an angry ghost, had an obvious sadness that permeated around her. Kendra appeared lonely more than anything. Then Marceline shivered as she thought of Kendra's fury making the insides of her head light on fire.

Marceline sighed, looking down at the table lined with crystals and candles. "I feel ashamed to say this, but ghosts scare me. I don't want to see them at all, to sense them. They make me sad, uneasy, and some even cause me . . . physical pain. I feel like this is a curse."

Amina nodded. "I know how you feel. Having the Sight can be a curse, but it is a gift too. We have a unique ability to help those who otherwise couldn't be helped. Some can be scary, but like I said, not all trapped souls are bad. A lot of them are just looking for help. That's what I do. I try to help souls crossover."

"That's your job? People hire you to do that?"

Amina smiled grimly. "The work is mostly unpaid. Wherever I go, I look for souls to release. But I do have a website that sometimes gets bites. My technical title is 'Ghost Hunter,' but I don't like to think about it that way. Plus, I don't have to hunt too hard. I just try to bring souls to peace. The work can be inconsistent, so I read tarot cards on the side."

"So, you pretty much get stuck souls . . . unstuck? Where do they go?" Marceline was starting to get annoyed with herself with all the questions she was asking, but Amina, as much as she claimed she didn't want to be a teacher, didn't seem to mind. In fact, her voice grew more animated the longer she talked.

"Pretty much," Amina agreed. "To be honest, I don't know exactly where they go, but it's peaceful most of the time. Every soul's version of peace is different. Like I said, it is up to the spirit to find their peace, but there are some things Spirit Walkers like us can do to help speed up the process."

"Just so I make sure I fully understand, Spirit Walkers are people who have the Sight, like you and me," Marceline said slowly.

"Correct."

"You said we can help spirits find peace. What does that entail exactly, sucking them into special vacuums like in *Ghost Busters*?"

Amina's eyes widened in horrified surprise, but she blinked, her eyes turning intense and slightly angry again. "Our job isn't to punish these poor souls further, it's to help them find peace. Some need a simple cleanse to be freed from the place they died, some require rituals or prayers. Once they are free and a hundred percent willing to leave this Earth, we can open the portal that sends them on their way. The solutions are entirely dependent on the circumstances."

Marceline still sat with her arms clasped around herself, still uncomfortable. "We can open portals? How?"

"Short answer, yes. But we aren't going to go into all that right now. Your little newbie head will explode with too much information."

Though curiosity felt like it was literally burning her insides, Marceline nodded. Everything she'd learned so far today was enough to make her head explode. She did still have one burning question she couldn't help but blurt. "Are you on a job right now?"

Amina hesitated, then said, "I'm just here for a little while until I get another job somewhere else. But this town is overrun with spirits, I'll say that. Even stranger, my usual methods of peacefully dispelling spirits don't work here."

"You can't dispel spirits in Catori?" Marceline asked.

Amina looked down, appearing almost ashamed. "Not yet, at least." Her tone had a hint of determination. Amina absent-mindedly stroked the lines on her wrists.

"These markings . . . they mean we're Spirit Walkers, right?"

Amina shrugged. "They mean we're magical, yes."

"Why are ours different colors?"

"Yours are white, the purest color. Every fledgling starts out white and pure. It's your choices that determine the color. The darker the magic you use over time, the darker the color of your stripe."

Marceline wondered what Amina had done to darken her stripe. Almost reading her mind, Amina snapped, "My past is my past. Once your stripe turns a shade, it stays that way. One dark spell marks you forever."

"Got it," Marceline said, eyebrows raised as she turned away from the intensity of Amina. "Only those of us with the Sight can see the bands, I've noticed."

Amina shook her head. "Every magical person can see them, including all spirits, which is why they always know when you're a Spirit Walker."

"Are there a lot of spirits in here?" Marceline asked, gesturing around the room.

"There are. I've been blocking their presence with my own protection shield while you've been here."

"Your shield is big enough to cover this entire property? Mine doesn't seem to work like that."

"It will. It just takes time and practice. You're still new; your powers are untapped and undirected. One day, you will be able to cast protection over larger spaces and even cast protection on individual people. I didn't want to overwhelm you by walking onto this property with all the ghosts here, because, believe me, they are all very excited about two Spirit Walkers being here, but there's one I want you to meet. He's a friend of mine. Maybe he'll help change your opinion of spirits. Do you want to meet him?"

Marceline started to feel lightheaded, but she found herself nodding.

Amina closed her eyes, grimacing slightly. "Sometimes, it's hard to let just one in. They are all waiting at the door, so to speak."

Marceline watched in awe as the candles flickered angrily. A few of the candles went out completely as a cold gust of wind swirled through the room.

"Marci, meet Rush. Rush, this is Marci, as I'm sure you remember."

To her left, a half-transparent young man materialized, seemingly out of thin air. Marceline shivered, though she didn't know if that was because of the chill ghosts brought with them or the idea that this whole time, she'd been sitting next to a ghost she couldn't see.

"It's a pleasure to formally meet," he said. He looked to be maybe around twenty. He was wearing a suit. If he weren't slightly see-through, Marceline imagined he'd be quite attractive. His face was chiseled; he had prominent cheekbones, a protruding but straight nose, and full lips. He had kind eyes. He smiled shyly.

"Was it you that night I heard when Amina was trying to transfer her energy to me?"

"It was," Rush replied, looking at Amina. "We wanted to protect you."

Marceline swallowed, feeling more relaxed by Rush's kind demeanor. "Well, thanks. Nice to meet you, Rush."

"That's just what Amina calls me. You can call me Russel if you'd like," he said.

"Russel," Marceline said weakly. It still wasn't lost on her that she could talk to ghosts. It was sort of overwhelming. "So, how long have you . . . been here?" Marceline didn't know if it was rude to ask a person how long ago they'd died.

Russel looked amused. "I died in 1955 when I was nineteen. I was working as a waiter here at the McCormick Estate when it used to be used for events. It was a wedding. I was at the top of the stairs when I lost control of my body. A force, coming from inside me, pushed me down the stairs."

Marceline gaped. There seemed to be an ongoing theme of ghosts pushing people down stairs.

"Don't worry, I'm not a vengeful ghost who will take another's life to 'take my place.' Some think they have to kill someone else to escape the lower dimension," Russel said bitterly.

"What happens when ghosts, um, murder people?"

"Well, they certainly don't find peace," Amina said. "Their spirit vanishes, though I don't know where they go. Anytime I've seen a spirit leave this dimension not toward peace, it certainly doesn't look like a pleasant place to go."

"Why would they kill if they don't even find peace when they leave here?"

"Some are so desperate, they do it," Russel explained. "You

see, being a ghost wouldn't be so bad if you could travel anywhere in the world. But we can't stray far from where we died."

Marceline shifted uncomfortably in her seat. "That kind of brings up why I needed to talk to you, Amina. The ghost at my school, Kendra, keeps telling me she needs someone to take her place."

Amina and Russel exchanged a glance. "You've been communicating with her?" Amina asked.

Marceline nodded. "I just want to help her, to get her out of the school, but without harming anyone. How do I do that?"

"I don't think you can help her," Russel said quietly.

"Why not? You said you send spirits to peace all the time. It's your job." Marceline looked to Amina accusingly.

Amina sighed. "I told you, this town is different. It's tricky sending spirits away here. There's a strong spiritual hold in Catori Springs. I haven't figured out how to send spirits away here yet."

"What do you mean? How can it be any different from anywhere else? Just tell me what you do. I can at least try it with Kendra," Marceline argued.

Amina's face grew hard and cold again, back to the way Marceline was used to seeing her. "No," she said, crossing her arms.

Marceline stood up in anger. "So you won't help me get rid of her? I'm just supposed to let another innocent person die and get trapped in the school?"

Amina glared at Marceline. "I didn't say I wouldn't help you. I'm just saying I don't know how to do it yet. Give me a few days, I'll figure it out."

"We don't have long!" Marceline yelled. "She's going to try again on Friday, the anniversary of her death."

"I won't let anything happen," Amina said with a firmness

that put Marceline more at ease. "In the meantime, keep your distance from Kendra. If she's willing to stoop to possession, she's too far gone to try to bring peace to, but don't tell her that. Not until we know how to get rid of her. Protect yourself." As Marceline rose to leave, Amina called to her again. "Oh, and Marci? Don't tell anyone you were here."

25

This was the first secret Marceline had ever kept from Katy, but she didn't want to worry her, or worse, put her best friend in any danger. Marceline told Katy at school she was "figuring it out," leaving out the part about returning to the McCormick Estate and talking to Amina. Katy hadn't seemed convinced, but Marceline didn't want to give her any more information than that. She hadn't even told Katy about being a Spirit Walker or having the Sight.

All day, Marceline distracted herself during school by practicing her light shield. Though she'd desperately wanted to return to the third-floor bathroom, she'd heeded Amina and Russel's advice and stayed away from Kendra.

Marceline was eager to know more about herself, what she was, and how she could stop Kendra, but her searches for anything about Spirit Walkers had proved to be entirely fruitless. Tonight, after work, Marceline would get the reassurance from Amina herself that she'd be able to send Kendra away for good.

At work, Joe had praised her for learning from a mentor. He muttered something about wishing she could learn from her mother, the best of the best, but when Marceline shot him a glare, he vanished into the back room.

Now, as Marceline waded through the weeds at the McCormick Estate, she noticed there wasn't the usual light coming through the windows on the right side of the house. It was so dark she couldn't see a step in front of her. She made it to the side door, half-expecting it to fly open and to see Amina sitting there cross-legged. The door didn't open for her as it had before, but it was unlocked. Marceline took a deep breath before pulling it open.

A gust of cold air blew at her through the open door. She closed her eyes at the force. Instantly, she felt the same feeling of hands reaching out to her. This time, they felt more real. She opened her eyes again, and there was an entire horde of ghosts closing in, hands clawing toward her. Each touch stung like icicle stabbing into her skin. Their whispers were deafening in her ears.

A scream escaped her throat as she tried to back up. Her foot slipped on the first step, and she fell down the other two, landing on her back. Tears came to her eyes as the over-whelming feeling of exhaustion and pain hit her. She couldn't breathe; she could literally feel her life force being stolen.

"Marceline," came Russel's voice above the other increasingly loud whispers. "Remember what Amina taught you."

She closed her eyes, envisioning the lead shield Amina had told her about. The other times she'd thought about light as a means of protection, it felt like something so simple couldn't possibly *do* anything. This time, though, knowing it wasn't just some weird tip from her mother, that it was actually a viable method of protection, something clicked. This time, she felt the light begin at her forehead. It stretched down to her heart, through the soles of her feet. She could feel it pulsing at the same rate as her heart.

The whispering and the feeling of hands grabbing her started to die down. She felt herself take a deep breath, then she forced the shield out of her body, clearing the area in front of her. When she opened her eyes, all the ghosts were gone apart from the one she'd kept the door open for.

"Good job, Marceline," Russel praised.

Marceline picked herself off the ground, plucking a clump of weeds from her hair. "Thanks," she said between deep inhales, trying to catch her breath. "I didn't realize how many of you were here."

"Nearly two dozen of us, I reckon." Though he was floating a couple of inches above the ground, Russel was taller than Marceline had imagined. Over a full head taller.

Marceline took another deep breath. She couldn't believe she'd actually done it on her own. She'd protected herself without anyone's help. "Where's Amina?"

Russel sighed, looking down at her. "She's not here."

"Where'd she go?"

"She had to go on another job, but she said she'd be back before Friday."

Marceline blinked like she had misheard. "But it's Tuesday, and she hasn't even figured out how to send away spirits here yet." Marceline heard her voice rising with panic.

"She'll be back," Russel assured. "She'll know what to do."

Marceline's hands shook with frustration. She couldn't just wait around for some flakey ghost hunter to come back and tell her what to do. She'd have to take matters into her own hands.

"Marceline, wait," Russel called. Marceline turned. "There's a spell book inside that may be of some use to you. Amina left it behind."

"A spell book? You're joking, right?" She would've laughed, but she didn't have the energy.

Russel just raised his eyebrows. Marceline's frown deepened as Russel's face remained unchanged.

"I'm not a witch," she scoffed, crossing her arms over her chest.

Russel frowned back, following her lead and also crossing his arms. "What do you mean you're not a witch? You can talk to the dead, and you can produce an invisible shield with your mind. That sounds like magic to me."

"Yeah, but that's all I can do," Marceline protested. She knew she was arguing for the sake of arguing, but she couldn't stop herself.

"Is it?" Russel pressed.

As Marceline considered this, she realized there might be even more to this Spirit Walker lifestyle that she was still unaware of. "Since you seem to know so much, tell me, what all can I do?"

"I'm afraid you'll have to figure that out for yourself."

Despite her frustration, Marceline was curious. She stomped back up the stairs, picking up the book laying in the middle of the emptied altar. It was leather-bound and heavy, but there was no writing on the outside to indicate its contents. "Thanks for nothing," Marceline mumbled under her breath.

"You have a lot to learn, Marceline, be excited," Russel called to her. She could hear the amusement in his voice. She rolled her eyes.

26

"A spell book?" Katy asked skeptically. She turned the book around in her hands, examining it at arm's length.

"That was exactly my tone," Marceline said, joining Katy on the floor of the treehouse. Marceline had texted Katy to meet her there since she was already at the McCormick Estate. Plus, it gave her a chance to continue practicing her energy shield, which she now had surrounding the entire wooden box.

Despite wanting to protect Katy from this new, apparently magical, world, Marceline couldn't help but want to share this with her. Anytime she learned something new all her life, the first person she'd wanted to tell had always been Katy.

"Where'd you get this creepy thing?" Katy asked, letting it drop with a resounding thud to the floor. Dust flew up around the book, but Marceline wasn't sure if it was from the treehouse floor or from the spell book itself.

Marceline hesitated. She hadn't wanted to tell Katy about her returning to the McCormick Estate, about Amina, or especially about Russel. Marceline bit her lip, trying to decide how much to say. Katy raised her eyebrows and held her hand up as if to say, *So?*

"I ordered it online," Marceline said sheepishly.

"Really?" Katy picked up the book again and inspected it. "There's no barcode or anything."

"It was from some weird website," Marceline quickly explained.

Katy stared accusingly, using her finger to wipe a line of dust off the front cover. "But what were you even doing looking for a spell book?"

Marceline sighed. "Well, I figured I might be able to get some use out of it. Clearly there's something supernatural going on with me, and all the things I looked up online said to perform rituals to get rid of evil spirits. I didn't think a spell book was that out there, considering the circumstance."

Katy seemed satisfied with the response. "I guess you're right." She paused, letting out a dejected breath. "I wish Bijou was here. She'd know all about this witchy shit."

Marceline agreed. Bijou was the one who'd introduced them to Amina in the first place. She'd also told Marceline her family was "like hers" at the Homecoming dance. Bijou would know more about this. "I'll try to call," Marceline said. The phone went to voicemail after a few rings. She dialed again, also to voicemail.

On the third attempt, a woman answered. "Don't call again, Lees," the woman hissed. It sounded like Mrs. Eyota. The line went dead.

"What the hell was that?" Katy asked.

"I think her mom blames me for what happened with Bijou," Marceline said, face falling. She secretly agreed with Mrs. Eyota.

"It wasn't your fault; it's this bitch Kendra's," Katy said

firmly. She grabbed the spell book again and laid it in front of Marceline. "Go ahead, Ms. Witch. Find your magic spell."

Marceline braced herself before flipping it open. To her surprise, as she continued flipping, all the pages were blank.

"I can see why it didn't have a barcode on it. It's a journal. 'Dear Diary . . .'" Katy laughed.

Marceline frowned. For some reason, she heard Russel's voice in her head telling her to remember what Amina had taught her. Marceline placed her hand on one of the blank pages and closed her eyes. She envisioned light spreading through the book, words sprouting on the pages. When she opened her eyes, her white arm bands were shining silver, and Katy was gaping at her.

"How'd you do that?" Katy asked.

Marceline shrugged, looking down at the pages that were suddenly filled with cursive, hand-written words.

"Seriously, Marci, how did you do that?" Katy repeated, eyes wide.

"I really don't know," Marceline mumbled, looking at her hands as if they didn't belong to her body. The bands on her wrists had returned to their normal white color. "I've got to go. Can't be home too late. See you at school."

She climbed as quickly as she could down the ladder, suddenly sick from seeing the horror on her stunned best friend's face. Marceline was starting to think it had been a mistake to tell Katy anything at all.

———

As Marceline was grabbing some books out of her locker in the morning, her locker door suddenly swung shut.

"Hey," Marceline complained as Katy came into view. Part

of her was relieved it wasn't another ghostly entity slamming her locker door.

"You could try a serenity prayer. Or a positive mantra," Katy said.

"What are you talking about?"

"To get rid of Kendra," Katy explained impatiently. "I did some research last night. Look in that spell book of yours for something about a serenity prayer or positive mantra you could try reciting. Oh, and I got you some sage to burn." She reached in her bag, pulling out a bundle of wrapped sage. "Just, please, whatever you do, don't burn down the women's restroom, or if you do, tell them I had no part."

Katy wasn't looking at Marceline like she was crazy or like she was some cursed monster. She was looking at her like she'd always looked at her, as a friend who was always going to support her.

"Thanks, Kat," Marceline said, grateful in more ways than one. She took the sage from her.

Marceline saw Tag walking toward them out of the corner of her eye. She spun the opposite direction. She knew she was avoiding Tag for no real reason, but the thought of having to lie to him about all these new discoveries in her life made the pit in her stomach expand. "I'm headed to class. See you at lunch."

27

Marceline practically ran out of the building after class to avoid running into Tag.

Even though she'd been seeing him in third period statistics every day, talking about probability and distributions was the extent of their conversations. She sent a quick text: "Have a good practice, sorry we keep missing each other."

She didn't have to work that day, so she went straight to the McCormick Estate. It looked significantly less terrifying in the daylight. She paused at the edge of the property, preparing herself for the onslaught of spirits that would attach themselves to her the moment she crossed the iron gate. As she crossed the barrier, her protection up, she encountered no one.

She opened the side door. "Amina?" she called. It was silent. Marceline sighed. "Russel?" It was silent still. In her mind, she tried to conjure him, trying to just release Russel's spirit from the crowd of spirits on the property.

When she opened her eyes, Russel was sitting on the couch with the off-white cloth draped over it.

He smiled. "You're really getting the hang of this."

Though Marceline felt the same pride in herself, she ignored the compliment. "She's still not back?"

Russel shook his head.

Marceline sighed, trying not to panic. There were only two days until Kendra's death-iversary. She plopped the spell book onto the empty altar. "Can you help me, then?"

"I can try to be of some assistance," Russel said. "But I'm no witch."

Neither am I, Marceline wanted to yell. Instead, she asked, "Have you heard of a serenity prayer? Or a positive mantra?"

Russel nodded, floating closer to Marceline and joining her on the opposite side, where Amina normally sat. "Both are commonly used to open communication with spirits. They're a polite way of announcing yourself as a Spirit Walker to a spirit."

Marceline's face fell. "So, they don't work to dispel spirits?" Dispel was a word she'd learned from the spell book. It meant to send a spirit to peace. There were mentions of dispelling spirits all over the book, but no explicit instructions on how to do it.

"Not in my experience. But from my understanding, everyone requires different methods to find peace. Some may need some feeling of serenity, some positivity spoken over them, for them to find peace."

Marceline sighed. "I've been looking through this book all day, trying to find some way to help spirits find peace. Most of this is just going over my head. I thought this one serenity spell might work."

"Well, you can try," Russel said, offering Marceline a gentle smile.

"On you?" Marceline asked, suddenly nervous.

Russel shrugged. "Sure, there's no harm in you speaking serenity over me. But I don't want to get your hopes up. Amina has tried nearly everything in that book; burning sage, smudging, crystals, prayers, even a few banishing spells, not the aggressive kind, though."

Marceline tried not to let it deter her that nothing in the book had worked for Amina. She decided to light the sage Katy had given her anyway, allowing it to create gentle smoke swirls in the air as she rested it on the altar beside her crystal. "I hope this works," Marceline whispered, flipping through the pages until she got to the correct one. She sincerely wanted Russel to find peace, to be free, but selfishly, she also wanted to try this out on a spirit who wasn't hostile like Kendra.

On the page before the spell, the writer had recommended lighting at least six candles. Fortunately, Amina had left behind candles and a pack of matches. Marceline spaced them around the room and lit a match. Her heart was pumping fast.

She cleared her throat. "By the power of all my good karma, direct connection to Source, agape love, and selfless acts, I ask the universe to please direct all good entities in this house to peace. To please send them on a path to feel no pain, to feel only warmth and joy. I pray to you, universe, may their souls find rest at last."

Marceline felt moisture from her eyes and realized she was crying. A drop of blood spattered onto the altar, and she realized her nose was at it again. She was definitely going to have to up her iron intake. She looked up, disappointed to still see Russel sitting across from her. He, too, had a look of intense emotion on his face. She thought it was disappointment.

"Thank you for trying, Marceline. That was beautiful," he said softly.

Marceline bowed her head. "I'm sorry it didn't work."

If this wasn't going to work, she was going to have to figure out another way to get rid of Kendra. Marceline had a feeling she wasn't going to have more than one chance with her.

"No, no, don't be sorry. I don't expect to find peace for many more years to come," Russel said sadly. His hand reached out as if to grab hers, but he pulled back. Marceline sensed there was more to Russel's story, but for another time. She had to get back.

She rose to her feet, swiping the blood under her nose with the back of her hand. "I'll see you, Rush," she said.

"Goodbye, Marceline. Be well."

———

Marceline had barely walked through the garage door when Peter called to her. "Marci, Mom is on the phone!"

Marceline sighed, dragging her feet on her way across the kitchen. She didn't have the excuse of her concussion to avoid this any longer. It was time to confront her mother.

Theo smiled. "She's here, Mommy. I love you too, Peter says bye." He handed her the phone. Marceline made sure to grab it with the hand that was not smeared in dried blood. Theo darted from the room, and Peter started to follow.

"You're not staying?" Marceline asked her brothers, holding the phone away from her.

Peter shrugged. "Mom said she needed to talk to you alone."

Marceline hadn't talked to her mom by herself in many years, but she was eager to know her mom's excuse for abandoning her now, knowing full well what Marceline would have to go through when she became fully Realized. An anger replaced her dread. Anger she hadn't allowed herself to feel to its fullest extent, ever. She took a deep breath before holding the phone to her ear. "Mom."

"Marceline," her mom's voice breathed. She sounded sick, like she had a cold. Her voice was unusually raspy. "How are you doing, my darling?"

"You knew," Marceline seethed into the phone. "This whole time, you knew what was happening to me. This whole time I thought I was going crazy, I thought something was seriously wrong with me. This curse is all your fault."

Her mom was silent on the line. Then Marceline heard what sounded like a shaky, wet inhale. "I'm so sorry, Marceline, I should have realized earlier, but I guess I foolishly hoped you hadn't inherited the gene. Your father told me about your headaches, your bloody noses, then the whole situation at the school got me thinking . . . I'm so sorry I haven't been there since you've gotten *la Vue*."

Marceline's stomach dropped. *La Vue* was French for "the Sight."

Her mom continued, "I meant to be back by now, by the time you were seventeen. To guide you through this time, to help you—"

"Why aren't you here, Mom?" Marceline asked. Tears burned in her eyes.

"One day you will understand. But for now, please, practice your light shield. It will save your life. And don't interact with the spirits, avoid it at all costs."

Marceline shook her head, sighing. "It's too late. I have to fix things."

"Marceline," her mom thundered, voice suddenly intense. "Listen to me, you will never be able to fix things, to help the spirits, at least, not in Catori Springs. All you can do is survive by avoiding all spirits until you go away to college. You have to leave that town as soon as you can. You're not cursed, my darling, the town is."

28

Marceline's hands shook as she grabbed books from her locker. What had her mom meant, the town was cursed? Did she mean an actual curse? The call had cut off abruptly, and the pile of seemingly unanswerable questions continued to grow.

All night she'd been scavenging through the spell book, looking for any way to peacefully dispel spirits, but in truth, she wasn't even sure what she was looking for, and she wasn't sure it would work on Kendra, anyway, since she had possessed someone. Marceline didn't want to have to try anything risky when she was actually in front of Kendra. It was scary to think about attempting to banish her, failing, and facing Kendra's wrath, especially when she was at full strength. So instead, Marceline had hatched another plan.

"You look tired," came Tag's voice.

Marceline's whole body lurched at the unexpected sound. She had been exceptionally jumpy lately. She offered a smile to Tag. "Haven't been sleeping well," she replied, leaning forward to kiss Tag on the cheek. It felt forced. She didn't know why she was acting so weird around him, why everything had been going so well only to feel so off now.

Tag awkwardly shoved his hands in his pockets rather than put an arm around her like he normally would. "Have I . . . Have I done anything to make you upset?"

"No, of course not. Everything is fine with us," Marceline said quickly, reaching to grab Tag's hand. She squeezed, but he didn't squeeze back.

"I don't know. You've seemed really distant the past week. Plus, you and Katy have been sneaking around corners every time I try to approach you."

Marceline sighed, and a guilty sensation sprouted in her stomach. She knew it was selfish to be avoiding him. It was hard not being able to let Tag in, but she knew it would only complicate things more if she told him. What if he thought she was crazy? What if him knowing this secret put him in some kind of danger? Until she knew more, she knew she couldn't risk it. "I'm sorry," she said earnestly. She struggled to choose words to hopefully set him at ease. "I guess I've been stressed lately and not feeling well, but I know I've been a crap girlfriend. Can we go to lunch today?"

Tag's face brightened slightly, and he nodded, offering a small smile. "I'd love to have lunch with you." The first bell rang, and Tag ducked his head toward her face, hesitating. Marceline met him at the other end and gave him a quick peck. She knew if she'd observed that kiss as a passerby, she would've cringed at the awkwardness.

"See you at lunch," Marceline called, making her way toward the staircase. Once out of view, she jogged up the stairs, skipping every other step. She knew she was likely still going to be late to first period again, but she was at least going to make

an effort to keep this conversation with Kendra short and hopefully sweet.

Marceline walked quickly to the third-floor bathroom
before she lost her nerve. The last bell rang; she was officially
late to class. She pushed open the door to the bathroom.

"Kendra," she said calmly. She couldn't allow the anxiety to
appear in her voice. "Kendra, I'm here to talk, please."

Marceline mentally dimmed her shield and felt a shiver, almost
like a finger tracing along her shoulders. She spun around in an
entire circle until she settled on Kendra, looking completely unin-
terested, pretending to lean against a wall. It was an act; Marceline
knew she'd float right through if she actually leaned back.

"What are you here to talk about, Marceline?" Kendra said
drearily, as though her words were one long sigh. "You've had
your shield up all week. I've just been *dying* to talk to you."

Marceline felt some confidence regain at Kendra's acknowl-
edgment of her shield. "Like I said before, I'm here to help you.
You can't kill someone to take your place. It doesn't work like
that."

Kendra rolled her eyes. "You're just saying that. That's how
it worked for me, that's how it's always worked as far as I'm
concerned."

Marceline shook her head. "No, it's not. At the McCormick
Estate, there are around thirty spirits. Some of them were killed
by other spirits in the first place, but you know what happens to
spirits who kill people? They might go away, but they don't find
peace. Don't you want to find peace, Kendra?"

Kendra's eyes flickered. "I don't know if I believe in peace."

"It's real," Marceline said. "It's warm, it's full of joy. Don't
you have family, friends you'd like to see one day? You won't see
them here, and you certainly won't see them where you'd go if
you killed someone here to take your place."

Kendra's face grew sad, and she looked down as if to hide the show of emotion. "I wasn't always this way, you know. I had hope I would find peace." Marceline opened her mouth to spout more optimism, but Kendra shut her down with a single hard look. "You can call me a bad person all you want, Marci, but I can't be stuck here anymore. I've been trapped here as many years as I was alive. This is torture. Of course I want to see my family, but I can't even leave this damn school."

Marceline nodded. "You must miss them."

"I miss everything. Sitting in a car. Playing a CD. Dribbling a basketball. Holding someone's hand. I hate it here." Kendra sunk to floating above the floor, pulling her knees to her chest.

Marceline crouched down beside Kendra, wishing she could put a hand on her shoulder. Though Amina had said Kendra, by possessing someone, had made it that much harder for her to find peace, Marceline couldn't help but feel sympathy for Kendra. Being trapped with no one to talk to would be maddening for anyone. If there was a way to find peace for Kendra, Marceline wanted that for her, as long as she didn't try to harm anyone again. "I'm working on a way to get you out of here, peacefully. I know you're planning on possessing someone on Saturday, but I don't think that will fix your problems. Give me until the next full moon to find a way to help you find peace, to get your soul unstuck, okay?"

"But I'm going to be at my strongest tomorrow," Kendra argued. "I can't waste my chance. How can I trust you?"

"If I can't find a way to free you in a month, then you can use me as your sacrifice."

"You?" Kendra scoffed. "I tried to get you last time, and it didn't work, remember?"

Marceline nodded. "That's because I had an energy shield up to protect me. If it comes to it, I'll let it down. I'll let you do what you need to do."

"I still don't know if I can trust you," Kendra said, eyes narrowed. "I need more than empty promises."

Marceline hesitated. She wanted to earn Kendra's trust, but she also didn't want to make it harder to dispel Kendra later. "I'll let my guard down for just a moment now. But you can't do anything, okay? Just to show you that you can get into my head."

Kendra rose to floating, and Marceline closed her eyes as she let her shield dim all the way out. "Now," she whispered.

Instantly, Marceline felt her vision grow blurry, almost completely black. Her whole body ached like she was in an ice bath as she watched with horror her hand lift to her face without controlling it. It felt like the motor side of her brain was completely switched off. Her body walked around the bathroom without her control. She felt her train of thought switching off, but she couldn't allow Kendra to take complete control. She tried with everything in her to envision a light breaking through her blurry vision, then she felt her body, her controlled body, fall to the floor, shaking.

Kendra glared at her accusingly. "You still had some control."

"That's because I didn't know if I could trust you," Marceline said, rubbing her arms to try to erase the chill that had overtaken her body. "But I give you my word, I'll allow you to have complete control next time."

Kendra cocked her head to the side. "You'd really sacrifice yourself? Knowing what your life would be like stuck here as a ghost?"

Marceline thought of Kendra standing behind Katy menacingly. "To save someone's life, I'd gamble my own."

Kendra nodded thoughtfully. "I'll wait until the next full moon. If you don't deliver, you're taking my place."

Marceline shuddered, thinking of Bijou nearly jumping. "You can trust me. No one else's life has to be at stake."

Kendra smiled darkly before becoming completely transparent. "Thirty days until the next full moon," her voice whispered in Marceline's ears. Thirty days from tomorrow's full moon fell on Halloween. *How fitting*, thought Marceline grimly.

<h1 style="text-align:center">29</h1>

Near the end of fourth period, Marceline got called to the front of the classroom. Katy shot her a reproachful look, but Marceline shrugged. Marceline grabbed the pink slip; it was a note from Ms. Steel, the guidance counselor, to head to her office immediately.

Marceline wanted to crumple up the paper on the way back to her seat, but she resisted. She let Katy read the note, and she shot her the same accusatory look, but Marceline still shrugged. Katy wished her luck.

She dragged herself toward the front office, thinking it might be the dreaded conversation about what had happened at the Homecoming dance. She'd been trying to prepare herself for what to say, but every time it didn't make sense. How could you explain that a ghost possessed your friend and tried to make them jump off the staircase without sounding like a crazy person?

Ms. Steel greeted her with her pursed lips as she came into her room. "Marci," she said flatly, "I'll be quick."

Marceline took a nervous breath as Ms. Steel shuffled through some papers.

"Sorry I had to pull you out of class. I didn't want you missing more, but I had to talk to you sometime. You've had an awful lot of tardies lately. I know you were recovering from a concussion, so there's some slack, but you've got to start getting to class on time."

Marceline could have danced with joy at this scolding. "I won't be late again," she replied quickly.

"Good," Ms. Steel said, setting down her papers. "How have you been since the accident?"

"Fine, I'm recovering well."

"It must have been traumatic to see your friend fall."

Marceline hesitated before nodding. The image of Bijou's limp body tumbling down the stairs was still burned in her memory.

"Your teachers all say you've been distracted this entire year, even before the accident," Ms. Steel said.

Marceline resisted an eye roll. "My grades are fine."

"Have you given any thought to college?"

Marceline saw a pamphlet on the shelf behind Ms. Steel's desk. She thought of her mom's words, *You have to leave that town as soon as you can.* "I've been thinking of Western State University."

Ms. Steel's eyes brightened. "That's fantastic! I think I have a pamphlet. Ah yes, here we go." As the final bell rang, signaling the beginning of lunch period, Ms. Steel dove into the details about how Marceline's ACT scores were definitely high enough, how she could apply, how scholarships and financial aid worked. Marceline tried to look interested, but she tapped her foot impatiently, thinking of Tag waiting for her. She sighed as a weight rested on her stomach.

Ms. Steel finally let her go fifteen minutes into lunchtime.

She checked her phone, seeing the text from Tag she hadn't been able to read during Ms. Steel's spiel. *Bailing on me again?*

She didn't take the time to respond. She just ran across the street to Luigi's but paused outside the door. From the front window, she could see Tag sitting at a booth next to Lacey, across from Nate, Marco, and Brady. Lacey was laughing at something Nate said, like Marceline hadn't been able to. Why couldn't Marceline be normal and get along with her boyfriend's friends? But worse, why was her boyfriend sitting with his ex at lunch, looking very much couple-like?

Lacey, mid-laugh, glanced out the window, making cold eye contact with Marceline. Though her first instinct was to look away, Marceline forced herself to hold Lacey's gaze. It was Lacey who broke first, looking down to take a bite of pizza. Marceline stared until Tag turned, seeing her. His face seemed to lose color when he saw her. He offered a small wave.

She could have gone in. Sat at that table and forced herself to laugh at the boys' jokes. But Marceline felt like there wasn't a spot for her at that table. She nodded once to Tag before turning to walk back to the school. Part of her half-expected Tag to follow her, but he didn't.

———

Tag hadn't texted her back the rest of the day. After the way she'd treated him, maybe he didn't want anything to do with her anymore. Maybe he just needed some space. Marceline tried not to think about it. Joe had picked up on her gloominess at work and kept his distance.

How was she supposed to keep anyone safe when she hardly knew herself what she was capable of? She wished she could learn something, anything, to help protect her friends. She was desperate to the point she wished her mom would call.

If Marceline had her number to dial, she would have. After work, she returned to the McCormick Estate. If Amina couldn't help Marceline figure out how to dispel spirits in Catori, Marceline knew she was going to have to try something else to stop Kendra. Marceline wanted to practice on Rush first.

Walking into the dark estate, Marceline called out, "Rush?"

Russel was waiting for her on the couch. He offered her a smile. "Amina's not here."

"Good, because I'm here for you," Marceline said.

Rush raised his eyebrows. "To what do I owe the pleasure?"

"I have a spell I want to try." Marceline set the heavy spell book on the altar. Rush opened his mouth, but Marceline held a hand up to silence him. "Just one little spell. I want to make sure it works in case I need to try it on Kendra."

"Amina wouldn't want you practicing and wasting your magic. She's going to figure out how to dispel in Catori. Just be patient," Russel said.

Marceline sighed as she busied her hands, lighting the candles around the room. "It's not that I don't trust Amina will figure it out eventually, but I don't have time to wait, and I can't take any chances. The full moon is tomorrow. I have to have a backup."

Rush floated close to her. "I will help in any way I can."

Marceline gave him a small smile. "Thank you." She crouched down and flipped open the spell book, returning to the page she had bookmarked with an old photo booth strip of her and Tag she'd had on her bedside table.

"Who's that?" Rush asked. "If you don't mind me asking."

"That's Tag, my . . . ," Marceline trailed off, lightly running her fingers over the image. They'd taken it the summer before they started dating. She could still remember the feeling of Tag's arm hooking her around the waist and pulling her closer as she'd nervously sat next to him on the bench as far away as she could so as not to touch him. It had pleasantly surprised her in the first of the four pictures, her mouth in an opened 'O' while he smiled and stared right into her eyes. "He's my boyfriend."

"You look happy," Russel said.

Marceline looked down at the smiling, naïve girl in the photos. It was hard to believe that was only a few months ago. That girl with the big crush finally got the guy of her dreams, and here she was, throwing it all away. Tag deserved better than to be ignored because she couldn't deal with her problems. "I was. I mean, I am," she corrected herself.

She took another settling breath, then under her breath she whispered the phrase from the spell book. She wasn't certain of the language or if she was saying the strange words correctly, but she didn't falter. She tried to sound as sure of herself as she could.

When she opened her eyes, Rush was gazing at her intently. "Did it work?"

"Let's see." Marceline reached out and for Rush's hand.

Russel flinched instinctively. "What are you—"

"I cast a spell to allow me to make physical contact with spirits. I'm temporarily in the lower dimension with you," Marceline explained. "Do you mind if I hold your hand?"

Russel shook his head and slowly reached out. Marceline intertwined her fingers with his cold hand. Russel let out a breathless laugh. "You feel so warm. I haven't touched another since . . ."

Marceline allowed the silence following Russel's words to fill the space. She just nodded and smiled. She was growing light-headed and knew she couldn't keep herself in this dimension for much longer.

She held his hand for another moment until she felt blood

run from her nose and, without warning, her hands came crashing around air rather than Rush.

"I'm sorry I couldn't hold it longer," she said, wiping her nose.

Russel shook his head. "Thank you, Marci," he whispered. "I didn't know how much I'd missed feeling warm, feeling physical contact."

Marceline wished she could take his hand again. "Thank you for letting me test that on you." More than the fact she was able to touch Russel, it confirmed she would be able to drop herself to the lower dimension even temporarily. If she could physically stop Kendra, even for a moment, maybe that could save a life if Kendra tried something tomorrow.

30

Pulling up to her house, Marceline was surprised the lights were still on in the kitchen. She smelled the sweet scent of cookies baking in the oven as soon as she opened the door from the garage.

"She's home!" Theo called excitedly.

The scene in the kitchen made Marceline smile. Delilah and the boys were wearing flour-coated aprons, and Dad was sitting at the counter with half a cookie in his mouth. It reminded her of a memory of her own mom. When Theo was still tiny enough to be wrapped to her mom's chest, Peter still toddled around the tile floor, her dad's forehead had fewer wrinkles, and Marceline was . . . happy.

"Your favorite," Theo said, bringing her a chocolate chip cookie. He was still the size that made Marceline want to grab him and squeeze his little round cheeks, but she resisted.

"Wow, these smell amazing. What's with the late-night baking on a Thursday?"

"It's to convince you to do something for us," Peter said, crossing his arms.

"These are bribe-cookies?" Marceline asked through a full mouth, feigning horror.

"What the boys are trying to say, Marci, is that they want you to be 'Anna' this year."

Ah, the boys wanted to participate in this year's Coffin Races. Four pairs of eyes peered up at Marceline, begging like starving puppies.

"Come on," Peter burst. "Delilah already agreed, we can compete like we always wanted to!"

Marceline thought back to this time last year. Delilah and her dad hadn't even been married six months yet, and the boys hadn't felt comfortable with her enough to ask her to participate. They'd been wanting to compete since they were little and could barely run, but their family had never had the right number since their mom left, as you needed four coffin pushers plus one "Anna" inside the coffin.

"Please, Marci?" Theo pleaded.

Marceline finally broke her stoic face with a wide smile. "Of course, I'll be Anna."

There was an eruption of cheers in the kitchen. They had three weeks to prepare, about the same timeline Marceline had to solve the entire mystery of the trapped ghosts in Catori and dispel Kendra.

"I'll work on your costume," Delilah said excitedly.

———

Marceline couldn't sleep, worrying about Kendra keeping her promise. Tomorrow she'd be her strongest self. She could easily take someone over, make them do . . . anything.

Plus, there was Tag on her mind. He hadn't responded to her texts, not that she could blame him. What was she thinking, shutting him out like that? He was so kind and understanding to her, always. She could trust him. Even if she couldn't share all the specifics of what was happening with her, she didn't have to completely ignore him for a week. Thinking of him sitting there with Lacey at lunch made her stomach hurt. She couldn't let him go, not without trying to fix what damage she had caused.

She eagerly checked her phone as soon as she woke, feeling deflated at her lack of notifications.

Before first period, Marceline marched straight to Tag's locker. She almost turned back around when she spotted Lacey was already there, standing in between Tag and Nate. Marceline greeted them all, forcing herself in between Lacey and Tag. She was not going to let this girl swoop in.

"You having a party this weekend, Nate?" Marceline asked.

Nate smiled. "Saturday night. Are you going to be there?"

Though Lacey tried her hardest to ignore Marceline's presence completely, her eyes flicked toward Marceline at the mention of the party.

"Sure, I'll be there," Marceline said.

Nate's smile widened while she felt Tag's eyes burn into the side of her face.

"Excellent," Nate said. "Bring Katy. You know I always welcome her presence."

"I will." Turning to Tag, Marceline asked, "Can we talk for a second?"

Tag nodded and gently put a hand on her back to lead her down the hall, away from the crowds. Both took a deep breath, then said simultaneously, "I'm sorry."

Marceline held her hands up to speak first. "I'm so sorry I was late for lunch yesterday. I got called to the guidance counselor's for lunch."

Tag frowned. "Marci, if you don't want to hang out with me, you can just say that."

"I really did get called in about all my tardies," Marceline said.

Tag cracked a smile. "That I believe. Punctuality has never been your strong suit."

"And I'm sorry I've been blowing you off lately. I've been going through kind of a rough time. It's hard for me to open up about it, but I was wrong for shutting you out."

Tag nodded. "Apology accepted. I'm sorry I reacted the way I did to you distancing yourself. I should have just respected your space instead of trying to get you to talk before you were ready."

Marceline stepped forward, and Tag extended his arms to pull her into his chest. She sighed. She had missed him.

She pulled away, biting her lip. She wanted to hold her tongue, but the jealously of seeing Tag with Lacey, again, was still burning in her. "I don't like feeling like I'm competing for your attention."

Tag scoffed. "Are you kidding? I've been competing for your attention for the past week."

"I already apologized for not giving you attention, but at least I wasn't spending that time cuddled up with my ex."

"Cuddled up? Marci, I haven't done anything wrong. Lacey is still my friend," Tag said firmly.

Tag's use of the name Marci instead of Marceline hurt her more than it should have. She reacted as though he'd struck her in the face. She sighed. "I don't want to fight anymore. I'm sorry."

Tag tucked a piece of Marceline's hair behind her ear. "I don't want to fight either. I really think you should give Lacey a chance. You two could be friends."

Marceline forced her tone to sound even. "I'll give her a chance."

Tag offered her a smile. "See you tomorrow at Nate's? Want me to give you a ride?"

Marceline smiled back. She knew she had somewhere to be after work that night, but she couldn't tell him that. "I might ride with Katy since she doesn't have anyone to go with."

"As long as I get to see you this weekend, I'm happy. See you later," he said before leaning forward and kissing her lightly on the lips as the first bell rang. This kiss was much improved from their last, and the butterflies returned.

"Good luck at your game tonight," she called over her shoulder. The team was playing an away game that night, over an hour's drive away. Marceline had to work that night; otherwise, she would've gone with her dad.

Upstairs, Marceline walked slowly past the women's restroom. There was a flash of what looked like a blonde ponytail. She blinked, but it was gone. She hoped Kendra stuck to her word.

In the Spanish classroom, she briefly passed the teacher's desk on her way to her seat.

"Marci," she heard. It didn't sound like Profesora Ortiz's voice. Marceline turned.

Profesora giggled in a way Marceline knew Profesora Ortiz did not giggle. It made shivers go up her spine.

Profesora Ortiz cocked her head to the side and smiled darkly. "Don't worry, Marci, I'm keeping my end of the deal. Just make sure you do the same," came Kendra's voice through Profesora Ortiz's lips. If Kendra was willing to possess someone again, making it that much harder for her to find peace, Marceline questioned if peace was even an option for her anymore.

"I will. Just don't hurt anyone." Marceline stared intensely until Profesora Ortiz's eyes closed. She blinked a few times, disoriented. She looked up at Marceline.

"Buenos dias, señorita," Profesora greeted, her voice sounding normal again.

Marceline couldn't force herself to respond before taking her seat.

31

Work was busy, but Marceline kept noticing Joe watching her and darting behind shelves all morning. It was almost like he wasn't used to being more than an observer. She knew he wanted an update on the Kendra situation. When the steady flow of customers died down, Marceline told Sheldon she was taking a bathroom break. Her eyes flashed toward Joe's, trying to subtly beckon him to join her. He floated behind her. She pushed open the door to the women's restroom and waited, but Joe didn't follow. She peeked her head around the door. "Come on, what are you waiting for?"

"I can't, I mean, I've never entered the women's restroom during store hours," Joe said nervously.

Marceline rolled her eyes. "There's no one in here but me. You can come in. Don't you want to hear about Kendra?"

Joe begrudgingly met her inside, his curiosity winning out. He stayed near the door in case another woman entered. "So," he said. "Did Kendra succeed?"

Marceline shook her head, relieved. She told him that aside

from the possession of Profesora Ortiz, Kendra hadn't harmed anyone at school that day.

Joe fist pumped the air triumphantly. "I knew you could stop her, Marci! How did you do it?"

"Well, I just asked her to wait until the next full moon. I promised her I'd figure out a way to help her find peace."

Joe winced. "Be careful of that Kendra. She's a bad seed, and I don't want to see her wrath if you can't keep that promise of yours."

"Why wouldn't I be able to keep the promise? How hard is it to find peace?"

"Marci, I thought your mentor might have told you this by now, but peace doesn't really exist for those of us who got stuck in Catori Springs. Once we hit the lower dimension here, we're here for good."

"I know, I know. Amina told me this place is different. But I'm going to figure out why you all are stuck here and—"

"Well, I can tell you why we're stuck. That's simple. But what no one knows is what to do about it."

Marceline was taken aback, but excited. If she knew the why, that was half the battle. "Tell me, Joe."

"The town's original families, the Webers, the Palmers, and the McCormicks, were all witches themselves, you know."

Marceline shook her head, eyes wide. She had no idea the magical past Catori Springs held.

"The McCormicks were the first of the original covens to reside here. Legend has it, each of the three original Catori Springs covens performed a ritual which created an energy vortex that tied all the spirits who remained in the lower dimension within the boundaries of Catori Springs to be stuck here forever."

"Well, if it was some kind of ritual, can't it be reversed?"

Joe shrugged. "No one's figured out how to break the curse so far, or at least, no one's really tried."

"Why not?"

"Trapping spirits in Catori also traps the energy from all these souls in one place. Catori Springs has become a hot spot for covens for this reason. All types of magic, apart from yours, I'm afraid, can benefit from this amount of energy in one place."

Marceline's head was reeling. She had to put a hand up to pause Joe's rambling. "What do you mean, other types of magic? I didn't know there were other kinds of magic," Marceline said incredulously.

Joe frowned. "Amina didn't tell you? There's celestial, natural, and, of course, sacrificial magic."

Was her magic considered sacrificial? Just that word gave Marceline a creeping sensation under her skin. "Why does this curse benefit the other witches and not Spirit Walkers?"

"Think about it, Marceline. For you, all these souls trapped here do is make you have to constantly produce those shields of yours, or else get some of your energy consumed by spirits. All that takes a toll on you over time. But for the other kinds of magics, who draw energy from either natural sources or from celestial events, having all these extra spirits here packed full of pure energy only makes it easier for them to generate their power to perform magic."

"So, no one will break this curse because they selfishly want more power?" Marceline cried, outraged. "Do none of them have family members trapped here? Do none of them care how awful it is for all of you stuck here?"

Joe offered her a gentle smile. "It's not so awful here, Marceline. Don't you fret over us. I only wish my Gladys could be stuck here with me. It wouldn't be so bad then."

"Gladys isn't stuck with you?"

"She's over the rainbow in the sky, I'd like to believe, thank goodness. After I passed, she moved in with our daughter in Boulder. If she hadn't, she'd be here, stuck just like every other person who dies within the bounds of Catori Springs."

"Everyone who dies in Catori is automatically stuck? Why doesn't anyone warn the people here?"

Joe shrugged. "Same reason no one has broken the curse, I suppose."

Marceline felt sad for Joe. "I'll figure out how to reunite you with Gladys soon," she promised.

"I hope you do, dear, but know the covens won't make it easy for you. They don't want to break the curse and release all this pent-up energy."

Marceline felt herself grow angrier. "How can I speak with these other covens here? Where do I find them?"

"They're everywhere and nowhere at the same time. I'm sure you'll be able to find them with the Coffin Races, full moon, and Halloween coming up."

"What does that have to do with anything?"

Joe winked. "Busy time of year for the covens." Joe suddenly gasped, and Marceline turned around to see the bathroom door opening as a customer entered. When she turned back around, Joe had already disappeared through the wall.

32

After work, Marceline turned Barb2.0 in the opposite direction of her house. Marceline thought she'd check if Amina had finally reappeared. She hoped Amina had a good excuse for not returning earlier, even after Marceline had told her lives were at stake.

At the McCormick Estate, Marceline noticed the shields were back up, and she didn't have to block out any spirits this time. Light was coming from the side windows. Amina was back.

Marceline stomped through the weeds to the side door and threw it open. Six pairs of eyeballs staring back at her greeted her. The group sitting before Amina nearly made her do a double take. Marceline vaguely recognized two of them as store regulars: a bald man with a black mustache, a woman with long blonde hair down to her waist. The other three were the Eyotas, Bijou's parents and Bijou herself. Bijou offered her a small wave and smile. Other than Bijou, none of them looked very friendly or happy about the interruption. The many candles in the room flickered at the shift in energy. All the flames seemed to be pointing Marceline toward the door. Marceline saw Russel floating in the background.

"Out," Amina instructed. "I have a meeting to finish."

Marceline's face was feverish with rage. She didn't know what this meeting was, or why Amina seemed so unbothered, like she hadn't completely bailed on her. Marceline narrowed her eyes, glaring at Amina. Marceline felt a gust of wind propel from her, blowing out a half a dozen candles. Amina raised her eyebrows, and Marceline turned back toward the door, slamming it behind her. Rush floated through the door, joining her on the steps.

"Impressive gust you produced," Rush said.

Marceline rolled her eyes. "It wasn't me. It was the wind from the door." Part of her knew she was wrong. She'd felt the energy pull from inside her, but she didn't want to admit that part of herself was real.

Russel snorted and held his hand out. "Right, because it's so windy out here."

Marceline shrugged. It wasn't breezy in the slightest. "Who are those people in there?" she asked.

Russel hesitated. "Witches, I think."

Marceline was desperate to be back in that room. She moved closer to the door to try to listen, but she heard nothing. What were Bijou and her parents doing in there? "What are they talking about?"

"That, I will leave for Amina to explain."

Marceline shot him an annoyed look. "Why can't you?"

"This is something for you witches to discuss. I'm just a fly on the wall, or a ghost on the wall, rather. Not a messenger."

She wondered if Amina knew what she'd just found out about the town's curse. Maybe she was asking them for help. "Fine, since you won't answer that question, tell me, when did Amina get back?"

"Earlier today. Did anything happen at the school?"

Marceline shook her head. "I took care of it, for now. I'm still going to need Amina's help, unfortunately, or I wouldn't be here at all."

The door burst open, and Bijou emerged. Marceline jogged up the steps, throwing her arms around her.

Bijou giggled with her face pressed against Marceline's chest. "Did you miss me, or what?"

Marceline finally pulled back and smiled. "So much. How's your arm?" she asked, glancing to Bijou's stiff, casted right arm.

"I've missed you too. Arm is healing well. Shouldn't have to have the cast on too much longer, hopefully. How is your head doing?"

Marceline pushed the air between her lips and swiped a hand at the air. "Oh, it's fine. No need to worry about me. I'm glad your arm is getting better," she said, then paused. "So, what are you doing here?"

"Amina requested a meeting with the coven leaders. Anyway, I could ask you the same question." Bijou's eyes flicked accusingly toward the door.

"Your parents are . . . witches?" Marceline asked hesitantly. It still felt weird to say the word out loud, to acknowledge that it was real, not fantasy. Katy would love to hear she was right about the Eyotas after all.

The term didn't faze Bijou. She nodded. "Both my parents are. My mom is one of the heads of the celestial coven, and my dad is one of the heads of the natural coven."

"If your mom is celestial and your dad is natural, what are you?"

Bijou shrugged. "I won't know until I turn seventeen. I've just been trying to learn both my mom's and dad's sides for when I become fully Realized next fall." Bijou took a step closer and took a deep breath. "I know you're a sacrificial witch. I remember what happened that night." Marceline looked down at her feet, preparing to apologize for Bijou's memory of Marceline throwing her down the stairs, but Bijou continued, "You saved me from that bad spirit."

Marceline's head snapped up. "You saw her too?"

Bijou shook her head. "I couldn't see her . . . I could feel her taking over, like I was being frozen from the inside out. Then I lost control." Marceline shivered at the memory of the exact feeling. "The only clear thing I remember after that was waking up in the hospital. But I know you saved me. I keep having a vision, a half-second blip of you surrounded by light, touching me, and pulling me back over the rail. If it weren't for you, Marci, I don't know if I would be here."

Marceline reached for Bijou's hand. "I'm so sorry that happened."

Bijou nodded, her face growing more serious. "I'd been suspecting you were dealing with spirits before, but then it was confirmed." She paused to clench Marceline's hand tighter, as if to pull her gaze down into Bijou's intense brown eyes. "You need to be careful dealing with the spirits, Marci. They're dark. They latch to your soul, feeding on the light."

Marceline shook her head. "They're not all bad, B, some are just lost and feeling desperate."

Bijou tilted her head in the direction of the house. "That's what you've been doing in there, isn't it? Working with Amina?"

Marceline shrugged, not wanting to confirm or deny. "Do you know anything about the town's curse?"

"Curse? In Catori Springs?" Bijou asked, her tone verging on skeptical. "My parents have never mentioned anything about that."

Marceline finally knew something Bijou didn't. "Ask them."

A crease appeared between Bijou's eyebrows. "Amina has been already, but they don't know anything."

"Maybe they'd say more if it's you asking the questions."

Bijou chewed her lip but didn't seem to want to talk more about the curse. "Before I go, I have something for you." She reached into her cross-body purse that hung at her hip, pulling out a tincture. "I've been mixing peppermint oil with other properties that my family and I take every day to protect our energy. It's especially important for a Spirit Walker like you. Come by the store next time you need more."

Marceline hadn't realized how much Bijou had been looking out for her. It almost brought tears to her eyes. "I will. Thanks for this."

Bijou broke her gaze and smiled. "I hope it's been helping." She glanced up at the sunset and let out a breath. "My parents are expecting me. I should probably be going, but it's been great to see you."

"Wait," Marceline called. She didn't want her to go. "Meet Katy and me tomorrow night. We're going to this party; you should join us."

Bijou's face lit up and she laughed into her hand. "A party? I've never been to a real high school party."

"So, you'll come with us?"

Bijou bit her lip, but she couldn't hide her grin. "Oh, what the heck, sure. Where do we meet?"

"Katy and I can pick you up from your place around ten," Marceline said. "I'll text you when we're close."

Bijou let out a squeal and quickly covered her mouth to contain herself. "See you then."

As Bijou made her way back to the house, Marceline could've sworn she heard Bijou still giggling.

33

Russel waited beside Marceline for the coven leaders to make their leave.

"I like Bijou. She seems nice," Russel said to break the silence.

"She's great," Marceline agreed. "I had no idea she was a witch too. I mean, we always suspected, but in a joking way. Makes me wonder how many of them there are here in Catori Springs. I wonder if there's any other Spirit Walkers."

"Lots of witches, not as many who are Spirit Walkers, I'm afraid. From what I've gathered, the energy caused by all us trapped spirits in Catori is great for other magic, but not so good for Spirit Walkers who are fed upon by us nasty spirits. I'd imagine most Spirit Walkers would steer clear of Catori."

Before Marceline could respond, the witches came out. Seeing Marceline standing outside, she made brief but intense eye contact with each of them. None acknowledged her with anything more than a stare, besides Bijou. She knew that Mrs. Eyota knew what she was. She must've known all along. But why didn't that unite them? Why did it seem as though Mrs. Eyota was distrustful of her as a fellow witch?

"Mr. and Mrs. Eyota," Marceline called before she lost her nerve.

All five turned to her, surprised she had spoken.

"Consider breaking this curse. It doesn't need to be like this."

Mrs. Eyota's face colored red. "How dare you—"

Mr. Eyota put an arm onto his wife and stepped forward. "Don't speak on a supposed curse you know nothing about, Ms. Lees."

"Marci," came Amina's stern voice behind her. "Come inside."

The witches made their way through the tall grass. Marceline watched them go, half expecting them to jump on broom sticks. Instead, she heard the click of car keys and saw the flash of headlights. That seemed very un-witch-like. Marceline took a steadying breath before entering the room.

"I see you're getting better at directing your energy," Amina remarked.

Marceline didn't want to waste any time with small talk. "What were you talking with the other witches about?"

Amina shot a glare toward Russel before turning back to Marceline. "For your information, it has to do with dispelling spirits in Catori."

"And did you find out how to reverse the curse?"

Amina's lips flattened into a thin line. "Not yet. Talking to them was like trying to get information out of a stone wall. They tried to act like they didn't know about it. It's like they don't want me to figure it out."

Marceline relayed what Joe had told her about the creation of the Catori Springs curse, and about how the power-hungry witches were likely not going to be willing to help right the wrongs of their ancestors.

"Doesn't surprise me," Amina replied nonchalantly. "If you think normal people are selfish, wait until magic is involved. Once they get a taste, most will do anything to ensure they keep the power to themselves. When they have to do it at the expense of all these other trapped spirits, that's when it becomes a problem."

Marceline was glad Amina seemed as angry about it as she was, but it didn't excuse the fact that Amina hadn't come back when she'd promised.

"What about our other problem? You said you were going to be back before Friday with a solution. If it weren't for me, Kendra would've killed someone today. So, thanks for being entirely unhelpful."

Amina stood up, walking close to Marceline. "What did you do?"

Marceline took a step back, but Amina stepped closer. Though she was significantly shorter than Marceline, Amina's intensity made her feel bigger. When Marceline didn't respond right away, Amina pointed to Russel. "Rush told me you used my spell book to try to dispel him."

"It didn't work," Marceline said quickly. She noticed Russel hadn't spilled her secret about using the spell to drop into the lower dimension. He held her gaze for a moment.

"Obviously, it didn't. But what the hell are you doing trying to cast spells?"

"I had to try something! I couldn't let anyone else get hurt. You were supposed to help me," Marceline roared.

"I told you to wait for me to get back," Amina shot back.

"If I had waited, someone would already be dead. And don't worry, I didn't use any of the useless spells in that stupid book on Kendra. I just told her to wait until the next full moon. I told her I'd be able to help her find peace before then."

Amina slapped a hand to her face. "You really made a promise with a spirit?" Marceline heard Russel sigh in the background. "Great, just great," Amina muttered under her breath, turning her back to Marceline and starting to pace.

"What's the issue?" Marceline asked. "I stopped her from killing anyone."

"Yes, but making a promise with a spirit is dangerous. It ties her to you," Russel explained.

"What does that mean?"

"It means you can't break your promise, or she won't be stuck to the school anymore. She'll be stuck to you," Amina said harshly.

Marceline swallowed. "I didn't know that," she mumbled. Not that it really mattered. If Marceline broke her promise, it was her who would be the sacrifice, anyway. But no one had to know that.

Amina sighed. "I guess I didn't have time to explain much of anything before I left. I'll teach you what I know, I promise, and I will help you dispel your schoolgirl ghost, but I need you to give me my spell book back."

It was in Marceline's bag. She held tighter to the strap. "No," Marceline said firmly. "What if you leave again? I'm going to need something to help me get rid of Kendra."

Amina rolled her eyes. "Aren't you the one who not five seconds ago just called the spell book useless and stupid? Fine, but nothing in there is going to help you, trust me. I've tried it all. I don't need you trying out any more spells and emptying yourself out."

"Emptying myself out?" Marceline asked.

Amina turned her back to Marceline and joined Russel on the couch. She clasped her hands under her chin and leaned forward. "Our magic is sacrificial. Every time you use it, you must either sacrifice something or someone, or a small fraction of your energy is used."

Marceline shivered. That's what was meant by their magic being sacrificial. "Do you . . . sacrifice?"

Amina shook her head. "I don't believe any other creature should have to suffer so I can use my magic."

Marceline's eyes darted down to Amina's gray stripes on her wrists. "Would using a real sacrifice be considered dark magic? Would it darken your stripe?"

"Like I said, it only takes one dark spell to darken a shade," Amina said with narrowed eyes, crossing her arms and tucking her wrists out of sight. "My family practiced dark sacrificial magic. I didn't know different until I was older. Families like mine are why sacrificial magic is often misunderstood by the other witches. They believe our magic to be inherently dark. I suppose it is, but that doesn't mean all of us practice it in that way. Yes, some sacrificial witches do use their powers for bad things, but not all of us participate in dark rituals."

Marceline considered what Joe had told her. "I learned there are other kinds of magic. How are they different from ours?"

"All magic must come from a source. They're pretty self-explanatory. Sacrificial magic comes from sacrifice. Natural magic comes from nature, from the elements like earth, water, wind, and fire. And celestial magic comes from celestial events like full moons and eclipses, things like that. Even the sun coming up and down is enough to give them a little juice."

Marceline shook her head. She couldn't believe there were actual covens who practiced magic right here in her hometown. "Seems like we really got the short end of the stick."

Amina snorted. "You could say that. But, if we practiced our magic to its fullest, darkest extension, we would be far more powerful than the other types of witches. We win some, we lose some."

Marceline thought about what Amina had said about how people are inherently selfish, especially when magic is involved. She shuddered to think of other sacrificial witches taking actual lives.

"I'm leaving again tomorrow for another trip," Amina said. Marceline wanted to be angry, but Amina's face was earnest. "I'll be back Sunday night. Come back, and I'll teach you more. In the meantime, protect your energy. No spell casting."

Marceline nodded. Despite her past absence, Amina had a sort of authenticity to her. Marceline wanted to trust her. She wanted to trust the one person in town who knew what was going on with her, even if that someone was at times unreliable. She hoped Amina was telling the truth this time, that she'd return.

34

"Where did you say you and Bijou met up again?" Katy asked as they walked, arms wrapped around themselves in the breezy Saturday night, toward Moon Opal to meet up with Bijou.

"Oh, you know us witches. We just communicated via cauldron," Marceline teased.

When Katy turned to her, eyes wide, Marceline laughed, and Katy slapped her arm. "Not funny, okay? I'm confused enough already with all your witchy nonsense. How am I supposed to know when you're making shit up or telling the truth?"

"Sorry," Marceline said between laughs. "And besides, Bijou isn't technically a witch yet."

Katy rolled her eyes. "Now that I know you're one, which means that witches are in fact real, there's no doubt Bijou is a witch. I mean, come on, her mom wears those witch hats year-round. I'm sure those magic genes pass down."

"I never said Bijou would never become a witch, just that

she isn't yet. On her birthday next year, she'll become a fully Realized witch."

"Well, her birthday gift is going to be one of those wands from her parent's store."

Marceline laughed along with Katy.

"What's so funny?" came Bijou's voice. She ducked out from the curved ledge outside her parents' shop where she was sitting.

"Marci's being mean to me," Katy explained, then she rushed forward, throwing her arms around Bijou. "I'm so happy you're coming with us."

"Me too," Marceline added, putting her much longer arms around her two friends and squeezing tight.

Bijou giggled in between the double hug. "I'm so excited to come with you both to a real, no-adult party."

"While there may be no adults, there will be adult beverages," Katy said, looping her arms through both Marceline's and Bijou's as she guided them down the street.

"Aren't you driving us?" Bijou asked.

"I may be consuming a few of those adult beverages at this party," Katy explained, "so I will not be driving. And since neither of you can drive, we're walking. Afterwards, we can sleep in the treehouse if we want."

"Sounds like a plan," Bijou said brightly.

"Your parents won't mind if you're gone all night and spend the night at the treehouse?" Katy asked.

"No, they won't mind as long as they don't know . . . never mind," Bijou said, growing quiet.

"As long as they don't know I'm with you?" Marceline guessed.

Bijou shook her head and turned to Marceline with an earnest expression. "I'm sorry, they just don't understand."

"It's okay, really," Marceline comforted her. "I understand why they don't like me."

Bijou nodded, but her face looked like it was clear there was more she wanted to say.

Before Bijou could say anything, Katy interrupted, complaining about how none of it was Marceline's fault, then Marceline's hearing went out.

Her breath became fog in the air, and she felt a creeping cold all over. Sitting at the bench underneath the streetlamp just feet from them was a woman dressed in Victorian attire. Her red eyes made direct eye contact with Marceline. It was just as Nate had described, different from the last time Marceline had thought she'd seen Anna outside of Luigi's. This Anna looked the same as the one she'd seen in the daylight, only more sinister.

Marceline looked to Bijou and Katy to see if they saw what she saw right in front of them. Neither seemed to notice anything, even as the red-eyed woman stood from the bench.

"Anna?" Marceline whispered.

"What'd you say, Marci?" Katy asked.

Marceline kept her eyes locked on Anna. She smiled briefly at Marceline before rising from the bench and taking a slow step forward.

"Anna, I want to break this curse. I want to help you."

Anna stayed silent but continued to move toward her, faster, as her footsteps morphed into a near jog, then a full-on sprint. Anna let out a blood-curdling scream that made Marceline want to cover her ears with her hands, but somehow, the sound was coming from inside Marceline's own ears.

Marceline closed her eyes, envisioning a shield in front of her and her friends. When she opened her eyes, Anna was nowhere to be seen.

"Did you just see the ghost of Anna?" Katy asked. Marceline could see Katy was shaking with fright, but she was trying to have a brave face. "Oh, God, your nose is bleeding again. Let me see if I have a tissue."

Marceline put her sleeve to her nose, then she turned toward her friends. Katy was rifling through her purse, but Bijou was looking intently at Marceline, head cocked to the side. It was a look of knowing.

"I saw her," Marceline said in a low voice. "But she was not interested in talking."

"What was it you said about a curse?" Katy said, handing her a tissue.

Marceline sighed. "For one night, can we please put all this witchy stuff on the back burner? Can I just have a normal night with my friends at a party? I promise I'll tell you about the curse later."

"Okay," Katy said, "but I'm holding you to that. Curse talk tomorrow."

The three girls arrived at Nate's house minutes later. Marceline could hear the music pulsing from down the street.

"Doesn't he have neighbors?" Bijou asked.

"I'm sure all these rich people are away on weekends," Katy said.

Marceline held the door open for her friends. The second she walked in, she felt arms grab her from behind. Turning around, she was immediately pulled into Tag's chest. "Hey—" she barely got out before Tag's mouth was on hers, pressing hard and firm. His lips tasted like beer. As he pulled away, he immediately took another sip from his red Solo cup. Clearly, Tag was already more than halfway to wasted.

Marceline wiped her lips with the back of her hand.

"I'm so glad you're here, Marci," Tag said, slurring slightly. He swayed, and Marceline instinctively placed her arms under Tag's to steady him.

"Do you need to lie down or something?" Marceline asked.

Tag's face cheered. "That's a great idea."

Marceline shot a look to Katy, who nodded, taking Bijou's hand, and headed toward the packed kitchen area. Marceline wrapped her arm around Tag's waist and walked with him toward the stairs. Surprisingly, he climbed the stairs well and pulled her toward one of the many doors upstairs. The first door he tried, when he moved the handle, a voice immediately shouted, "Occupied!"

Tag shuffled to the next door down the hall, finding it empty. There was a made bed, where Tag immediately plopped down on his back. "Join me," he called to Marceline.

She sat at the edge, but Tag put his arms around her waist, tugging her back into his chest. She giggled as he started kissing the back of her neck. "What are you doing, Tag?"

"Kissing my sexy girlfriend. Is that a problem?" he answered, voice muffled against her skin.

Despite everything, she felt goosebumps rising, the good kind, not the scared kind. She closed her eyes for a moment, then opened them as Tag's hands moved down from her waist.

"Hold up," Marceline said quickly, grabbing Tag's hands. She turned to face him on the bed.

"What's the problem?" Tag asked, trying to lean forward to kiss her. She turned her face, and he planted a kiss on her cheek. "Don't you want me?"

Marceline's face immediately grew hot. "I do, Tag, of course I do, but not like this."

Tag sighed and leaned his head onto the bedpost with a thud. "Of course, you don't want to, because we're at Nate's house, and you hate him for some reason," he grumbled.

Marceline sat up straight and frowned, trying to look at his upturned eyes. "That's not true, and that's not the reason.

Didn't you mean what you said before about not wanting to rush things?"

He sat up, coming closer and gently brushing the hair from her face. In a softer voice, he said, "I just like you a lot, Marceline."

"I like you too," Marceline said, unable to say more before Tag's lips were pressed into hers again. She felt her arms do as they naturally wanted to, wrapping around his neck. The sour beer taste was still strong, bringing her back to reality. She pulled away, putting a hand on his chest to stop him. "Tag, I don't want to kiss you when you're drunk."

Tag sat up straight, recoiling as if he'd been slapped. "Just because I've had a few drinks doesn't mean I'm drunk. You just have this weird thing against drinking, against my friends."

"That's not true," Marceline protested. She grabbed his face, getting him to look at her. "Where's all this coming from? Nate?"

"Nate may have brought it up initially," Tag admitted. "But that doesn't mean it's not obvious."

Marceline let her hands fall to her lap, then she stood up. "Well, you can just keep listening to Nate then, since he apparently knows everything, instead of asking your girlfriend what's actually going on in her head."

She stormed out of the room, not caring if Tag followed or not. Downstairs, Marceline scanned the room for her friends. She walked into the kitchen where she saw Bijou sitting on the counter, a red Solo cup in hand. Bijou's cheeks were flushed. Marceline walked up to her.

"Have you ever had this stuff?" Bijou asked her when she got close.

Before Marceline could respond, she felt a hand on her shoulder. "Oh yeah, Marci and whiskey are old friends," Nate replied.

"I like whiskey," Bijou said, giggling. "Nate's been sharing some of his bottle with me."

"Well, it's mostly Coke with a tiny splash of whiskey," Nate said, pulling Marceline and Bijou closer to him.

"Isn't that nice of him?" Marceline said coolly. She didn't like the way Nate had his hand rested on Bijou's lower back. First, he hit on Katy nonstop, now Bijou?

Nate kept his hand on Marceline's shoulder, squeezing it tightly. "Your little witch friend is pretty cool, Marci."

"She is, isn't she?" Marceline replied flatly. She shrugged out from Nate's grasp and took Bijou's hand. "Let's go find Katy."

Nate's hand quickly returned to her shoulder. "Not so fast," he said, spinning her around. "What's your problem with me, Marci? I haven't been anything but nice to you."

Marceline wanted to keep walking and ignore him, but she paused and turned back. "You know, I didn't use to have a problem with you, but I do now. Ever since Tag and I have started going out, you've changed. It's like you think you and Tag are so much better than me. And now you have these thoughts swirling around in Tag's head that I don't fit in with you all," she practically spat, glaring at him harshly before roughly removing her arm from Nate's hold and taking Bijou's hand again. "Stay out of my relationship, Nate."

Marceline dragged Bijou with her away from a stunned Nate. Bijou's eyes were wide. "I didn't know that you and him were—"

"It's fine, B. Do you know where Katy is?"

"I think she went out to the backyard."

Outside, Marceline could hardly hold back tears that were stinging her eyes. Katy immediately made eye contact, then pushed through the crowd to grab Marceline's shoulders. "Hey, you okay?"

Marceline nodded, but her lip quivered. "Tag and I had a fight, and I'm just trying to leave. You and B can stay though if you want, but I'm going to head out."

"No, we'll come with you," Katy said firmly, looking to Bijou for confirmation. Bijou bobbed her head.

"I feel bad. We only just got here," Marceline said.

Katy waved her hand. "Don't worry about it. I stole a bag of wine," she said, patting the inside of her jacket. "We can still have a good night in the treehouse."

Marceline smiled and Bijou grinned, then grabbed at her pockets. "Can we grab my phone first? Left it inside."

The three of them made their way back inside the house. Marceline stopped in her tracks as she spotted Tag, hands on either side of Lacey as she leaned against the counter. Marceline was seeing red as she ignored Katy's words and walked to Tag, crossing her arms in front of him and raising her eyebrows.

"Oh, hey, Marci," Lacey said with a wide grin, peeking around Tag's shoulder.

Tag turned slowly. Seeing her, he dropped an arm and sighed. "Marci."

In her anger, all Marceline could think to ask was, "Why do you keep calling me Marci?"

Tag's brow furrowed. "That's your name, isn't it?"

Lacey laughed and covered her mouth with her hand to muffle it.

Marceline wanted to say, *That's never what you used to call me*, but instead, she just nodded. "Guess so." She turned toward her friends, who each put an arm around her, and they left together.

35

Sunday morning at the Grocery Elf, Marceline's head was aching, but this time, she wasn't sure if it was from the now-usual cause of spirits invading her energy shield, from the overly sweet pink wine she had sparingly drank the night before with Katy and Bijou, or from sleeping on the hard, wooden treehouse floor. Probably a combination of the three, she decided. Thankfully, Marceline wasn't on register this busy Sunday, and she could heal her headache by ignoring people while she cleaned bathrooms and restocked the produce aisles.

Last night, she hadn't gone into too many specifics with her friends about her fight with Tag. For the past year, Tag had always been someone she could count on who would never cause her any pain. He was always kind and lighthearted, but last night, Tag showed a different side to him, one she wasn't sure she wanted in her life.

How could he turn so quickly on her? Just last week he'd been so concerned and sweet about her concussion, and the week before that had been Homecoming, which, before the whole Bijou-and-Kendra incident, was feeling like the best night Marceline had ever had. What had turned everything so sour between them? As much as Marceline wished she could blame all of her and Tag's relationship problems on Nate and Lacey, she knew there was more to it than that.

As soon as the clock struck eleven, Marceline ripped her apron off and headed toward the McCormick Estate, hoping Amina had kept her word. Checking her phone, she saw a missed call from Tag and a text that read, *Call me*. Marceline didn't want to deal with her aching heart, which, as her headache mended, seemed to worsen. She ignored the text, putting her phone in her backpack as she threw a leg over her bike.

Riding up to the estate, Marceline couldn't help but shiver in the cold. Fall weather had been teasing them for a while, but now that it was October, it wasn't being so coy. Marceline could see her breath in her peripheral as she made her way up the hill, her stiff legs protesting the extra effort. She smiled as she saw gray smoke billowing from the chimney of the McCormick Estate. Amina was home.

At the sight of Amina and Rush sitting together in the room, lit by flickering fire and clouded with a slight smoke, Marceline felt the urge to hug them both. She had to remind herself that if she tried, she'd fall right through Russel, and Amina would probably turn her to stone.

Marceline tried not to look too pleased. "Wow, you're actually back," she said to Amina, feigning surprise.

Amina shot her a look but didn't comment, returning her gaze to the altar. Russel smiled and floated over to make room for Marceline at the table.

Amina was mumbling some words under her breath and allowing a small pile of what looked like the dried weeds from outside to burn. There was a strange scent in the air, spicy to the point where it stung her nose.

"What is she up to?" Marceline asked, taking a seat on a floor pillow.

Russel said, "She's trying another way to cleanse this place, hopefully to help her be able to dispel more of us."

"Has she been able to dispel any of you yet?" Marceline asked.

Russel shook his head. "No, and she's never not completed a job."

"So, she is on a job?" Marceline wondered why Amina had lied about that before. Who was she working for?

Russel shook his head. "I should not have said that," he muttered.

Amina let out a deep, frustrated sigh before opening her eyes and tossing the bundle of dried weeds into the fireplace. "I can't get any of these spirits to budge, no matter what I try. This town has a hold on spirits like I've never seen before."

"So, you haven't figured out how to break the Catori curse yet?" Marceline asked.

"Do I even need to answer that question?" Amina said through gritted teeth, rising to her feet and running her fingers through her hair. As she pulled her hand from her head, Marceline noticed a large clump of her hair went with it. Amina's hands shook as she allowed the hair to fall from her fingers. She looked completely spent. Marceline decided not to press the matter of who hired Amina just yet.

"You know, I can come back later if you need to rest," Marceline offered.

Amina's face hardened. "No," she said firmly. "I'm here now. I promised I'd teach you. What questions do you have?"

Marceline smiled at the question that first popped into her head. "I saw the ghost of Anna last night, you know, the Coffin

Race lady? She was trying to scare me, running at me, screaming."

"The notorious Anna," Russel laughed. "She's been here so long she sometimes likes scaring kids."

Marceline continued, "So, my question is, can other non-Sight people see her sometimes, or is this guy I know full of shit?" She wouldn't put it past Nate to have lied about something like this, but his story had been in the exact place she'd seen Anna.

Amina cracked a small smile. "Powerful old spirits like Anna can sometimes make themselves appear to non-Sights. Like during a full moon, or on your Coffin Race day when everyone repeats her name, or Halloween, or on the anniversary of her death. And sometimes spirits can appear to their living loved ones, especially when they're at their strongest around the anniversary of their deaths."

"That's why so many people report sightings of the real Anna at the Coffin Races," Marceline said. She supposed if Nate had seen Anna on a full moon, maybe he was telling the truth after all. "You mentioned Halloween. Someone told me Halloween was the one day a year spirits aren't confined to where they died."

"It's a full-on ghost party," Russel said, grinning.

"Are you serious?" Marceline asked.

"October 31st is the one day every year spirits have freedom. A lot of ghosts will spook the humans just for fun," Russel said, smirking.

"And I'm sure you don't participate, do you, Rush?" Amina teased.

"I would never," Russel said, winking toward Marceline.

"Have you ever met Kendra?" Marceline asked Russel. The mood immediately shifted in the room.

Russel coughed as if to clear his throat, which Marceline

was sure was just an act. Could ghosts cough? Did they even need to if their lungs weren't functioning? "I have. She's quite a . . . bitter girl," Russel said, frowning. "She hates humans. But she doesn't usually hang out with the other spirits very much on Halloween. She always goes to her parents' house."

It made Marceline sad to think of Kendra, still just a teenager, wanting to be home with her family. Even though she wasn't the most moral ghost, Marceline knew Kendra was just desperate. She still wanted Kendra to find peace.

"Kendra possessed someone else at school on Friday. A teacher. It wasn't threatening, exactly, just a warning. Is it still possible to peacefully dispel her?"

Russel shook his head. "It doesn't seem like she wants peace if she keeps possessing others. The more she does, the lower she sinks, and the more difficult it becomes to send her to peace even if we could here in Catori."

"So her only real way out now would be to take someone's life?" Marceline asked nervously.

Russel and Amina exchanged a look, silently deciding who would answer. "I don't know if she has an option for peace at this point," Amina said finally.

"Amina, I know you can't dispel spirits in Catori," Marceline began. Seeing Russel's look, she added, "*Yet.* Could you at least tell me how you would normally dispel a spirit outside of Catori Springs?"

Amina cocked her head thoughtfully for a moment, then she nodded. "Telling you isn't the same as showing you. I have a job on Friday night. It'd be an overnight thing. Meet me here at 3 p.m. Friday if you want to come."

"I'll definitely come," Marceline promised. She knew she had to go. But how would she get away for the weekend?

———

Marceline rode back into town, craving something from the bakery across from the Grocery Elf. As she entered B's Sweet Treats, she paused as she saw a tall figure with his back to her leaning over the front counter. The door had already sounded, alerting everyone in the bakery of her presence, but she still tried to turn back, pushing herself back through the door.

What did a girl have to do to get some muffins without running into her . . . Was Tag her ex? She took the three steps to unlock her bike, her fingers suddenly not functioning. She heard the door to B's Sweet Treats open just as she was able to stuff the lock in her pocket and roll Barb2.0 out. As she lifted her leg, she heard, "Marceline, wait, please."

Marceline wanted to close her eyes, to get on her bike and ride blindly away, anywhere but here. Setting her foot back on the ground, she opened her eyes and looked up into Tag's face. She wished he was harder to look at, but the sun was hitting his hazel eyes just right, and his freckles fanned perfectly across his nose. She sighed and tore her eyes from him to stare at her shoes. "I don't want to talk," she said quietly.

"Then just listen, please," Tag pleaded. When she didn't reply, he offered, "You can have some of these pumpkin spice muffins."

Marceline found herself nodding. He walked toward a bench, and she followed, sitting as far away from Tag as she could. She crossed her arms, but quickly uncrossed them as Tag fulfilled his promise and opened the box of muffins between them.

"What's with the muffins?" she asked.

"Take one. Sister made me get them," he explained. Marceline took a bite and chewed slowly while Tag nervously stared at his hands. He opened his mouth to start speaking again a few times, with no words coming out. He cleared his throat. "I'm so sorry, Marceline. I was an asshole last night. I don't know what got into me. I should never have put you in a position like that, tried to pressure you, or argued with you about the drinking, any of it."

Marceline blinked back her tears, surprised at her sudden emotion. "It's okay, Tag."

Tag sighed. "I know I was throwing my insecurities on you. I love my buddies, but all we ever do is drink and play sports together. I don't have many people in my life who I can talk to like you, Marceline. I've never liked anyone how I like you, and I just want you to like me too. I guess it scares me. The thought of losing you makes me act like a jerk. I know I've been holding onto this anger against you that I wasn't even aware of, and it's so not fair to you. I promise I don't feel that way anymore. I just want us to be happy again so badly."

Tag himself looked on the verge of tears, and it took a lot to keep herself from leaning over the muffin box between them to wrap her arms around him. He took a shuddering breath, and Marceline exhaled deeply. She didn't want him feeling so upset and taking full responsibility when she knew her hiding this new witch-side of her was half the reason for the problems in their relationship.

"I want that too," she said lightly. "And I know I haven't made it easy to be with me. I have a lot going on right now that I haven't been completely honest about."

Marceline allowed Tag to take her free hand. "What's going on?" he asked gently.

She couldn't find the words to tell him. It was too much all at once. At least Katy had been discovering this along with her, and at least both she and Bijou had witnessed proof of Marceline's magic. Tag, on the other hand, was starting from scratch. She sighed again. "Have you heard of that tarot reader who stays in the McCormick Estate?"

"The one you and your friends went to see?"

Marceline nodded. "I've been working with her, and she's been teaching me things."

"Things?" he pressed.

"About myself. About how my life is changing."

"So, she's like a mother-figure to you?" Tag asked.

Marceline snorted at the thought of Amina being remotely maternal. "No, more like she's helping me realize all the things I'm capable of and how to move through life with these new . . . gifts."

"Well, I know you're capable of a lot. I'm glad you have a mentor," Tag said, then paused. "I can tell you don't want to tell me everything right now, and I get it. I hope one day you will be able to share more about what you've been learning."

Marceline let out a sigh of relief and let her head lean into Tag's shoulder. "I promise I'll tell you more about it once I understand it better myself. Thank you for being you, Tag."

Tag leaned over to kiss her on the forehead, then he chuckled. "You know, you don't have to hold on to that if you don't want it," Tag said, looking to the muffin in her hand.

Marceline laughed and took another bite. "I was distracted," she protested mid-chew.

"I want to take you on a date next weekend. You free Saturday night?"

Marceline instantly wanted to say yes, but she remembered her commitment to Amina. She wasn't sure how long she'd be gone. She bit her lip as she considered.

Tag's face fell. "You have plans?"

"I really want to, but I actually have plans with Amina, the tarot reader, this weekend to go out of town. I don't know what time we'll be back."

"Oh, well, just let me know if you want to do something that night."

Marceline felt lighter knowing she had opened up even a little bit to Tag, and he hadn't pressed her to tell him when she wasn't ready. She didn't know when she'd be ready to tell him everything, but she knew she couldn't keep it from him forever if she wanted their relationship to survive.

36

To attend her weekend trip with Amina, Marceline had to lie to get her shifts covered at the Grocery Elf and told her dad she had to spend the weekend away on a school camping trip for her environmental studies class. Katy was the only one who knew the full truth of her trip, but even Katy didn't know about the Catori Springs curse. Marceline really was starting to feel self-conscious about her constant lying or telling half-truths to the people she loved, but it was preferable to them knowing the truth and sending her to the cooky-bin or worse, somehow getting involved in this mess with her.

She'd even lied to Kendra when prompted for an update. Marceline told her that weekend she was finally going to figure out how to break this Catori curse. Kendra had even managed a non-terrifying, genuine smile at this, which somehow made Marceline feel even sicker with guilt. It was like once she'd started, the lies kept flooding from her mouth. She'd had no reason to lie to Kendra and get her hopes up. Well, she supposed that wasn't a lie; she was going to try to figure out how to dispel her, but she definitely shouldn't have made any guarantees. She should've already learned her lesson from her last promise.

Marceline had to skip out of her last class of the day on Friday to meet Amina by three. Leaving early gave her time to race home to grab the bag she'd packed the night before and drop Barb2.0 off before heading to the McCormick Estate. She started the ten-minute walk from her house to the estate, feeling like her heart was beating out of her chest. She was nervous to finally see how this dispelling worked, if it worked at all. If this Sight she possessed was more than the curse it seemed, she was excited to see what could be.

Walking up the hill to the estate, Marceline spotted Amina walking down on the opposite side of the street. She called to her, and Amina responded with her usual scowl. Marceline jogged across the street to meet up with her, but Amina never paused to say hello. For someone whose legs were much shorter than hers, Marceline was out of breath trying to keep up with her.

"You're in a hurry," Marceline panted.

"Yeah, well, you were late," Amina snapped.

Marceline frowned, checking her phone. "No, I wasn't. You said three, it's not even three now." Amina ignored her; her eyes were focused straight ahead. "Can you tell me where we're going?"

"Gunnison," Amina answered shortly.

"How are we getting there?" Marceline asked, though by Amina's walking pace, they might be able to make what was normally a three-hour drive before sundown.

Amina sighed, like Marceline had asked the dumbest question. "The bus," she said.

Marceline wasn't sure why Amina's attitude was so sour

today, but she wasn't about to push anymore of her buttons if she could help it. She'd keep her mouth shut.

They arrived at the bus station, and Marceline reached for her wallet to pay for the ticket, but Amina placed her cold, slender fingers on Marceline's wrist. "Don't worry about it."

As someone who survived on a diet of peanut butter and jelly sandwiches and was pretty much homeless, living in an abandoned estate with no running water or electricity, Marceline thought Amina could use the money more than she could. "No, really, it's fine. I have a job . . . ," Marceline trailed off, realizing with Amina's deepened frown that she'd said the wrong thing.

"Like I don't? And don't think it's me being generous. The client paid for our travel expenses," Amina seethed.

"Thanks," Marceline said awkwardly as Amina paid for the tickets in exact change.

As they settled into their first bus ride of the night headed toward Denver, where they'd have to board a separate bus toward Gunnison, Marceline reminded herself she hadn't completely lied to her dad. She was going to be in Denver that weekend after all, even if it was only passing through for an hour.

Marceline wished she could lean her head against the glass window as they left Catori Springs, but Amina had taken the window seat. The cool pane would feel nice against her constantly hurting skull. Though the pain in her head wasn't always intense anymore like it had been, it was still always there, lingering. Marceline dared a glance in Amina's direction, but promptly turned back toward the window across the aisle at Amina's unwelcoming glare. Here Marceline had been excited to learn more on this long bus ride, but it didn't seem like Amina was willing to offer anything more than grunts.

She had to try. Who knew when she'd get another chance to be alone with Amina for this amount of time again? Marceline took a deep breath. "So, other than dispelling ghosts, what other magic can we do?" she asked.

Amina shushed her immediately. "What the hell are you doing?" she grunted angrily.

"What? There's hardly anyone on the bus, no one can hear us," Marceline said.

"Never discuss these matters in public," Amina scoffed, crossing her arms and leaning her head against the window.

Marceline sighed. At least she'd brought her headphones and the spell book to read through. Glancing over, she saw Amina's eyes were already closed, but she gently nudged her, anyway. "Is this okay?" Marceline asked, gesturing to the book in her lap.

Amina rolled her eyes and put a hand to the book, mumbling under her breath with closed eyes. Opening her eyes again, Amina started coughing, like her throat needed to be emptied. "Now, only those with Sight can read it," she gasped through coughs.

"How'd you do that?" Marceline asked.

"Magic."

"Well, duh, but I meant . . . Wait a minute, everything in this book is different," Marceline said, flipping through the pages. She'd studied this book cover to cover, but now she didn't recognize a single page.

"It only shows what you ask for," Amina explained in a mumbled tone. "I thought these sections may be good for you to know."

Marceline opened to a chapter about mind shields and how they could be projected to also protect those around them. "Is there anything specific I should read before we get there?"

Amina's only response was to clear her throat again and close her eyes, leaning back against the glass. Marceline rolled her eyes. She wouldn't be getting any more questions answered on this bus ride.

The rest of the way, she read about how Spirit Walkers could project a constant shield so that spirits can only appear to those with Sight if they were summoned, either verbally or mentally. Marceline thought back to when Anna had appeared when they were walking to the party last weekend. Had she been thinking of Anna then, or had her shield not been up at that moment? She supposed ever since she'd heard that story from Nate, she thought of it every time she passed a streetlamp with a bench beneath it. Even indirectly, you could call upon spirits. A Spirit Walker could simply say, "All spirits in my vicinity, appear before me." Marceline shuddered at the thought. Why would she want to see a cluster of ghosts in front of her? Even though she knew not all of them were bad, some, like Kendra, were.

Kendra. What was she going to do about Kendra? She really hoped this trip would prove to be enlightening. She'd have to give Kendra an update on the situation as soon as she got back, and right now, she had nothing.

Amina was lightly snoring against the window, suddenly appearing to Marceline as much younger than the wrinkles on her skin and deep under-eye bags revealed her to be. Marceline was so curious about what Amina's story was, how she'd come to realize her Sight, who'd taught her.

Marceline remembered her own mother's words. Was her mother's Sight the reason why she'd left them? In Marceline's mind, it didn't excuse it. Nothing could ever be a good enough reason to leave your kids. Marceline knew it'd be different if in the future she chose to have kids. She'd never leave them.

In Denver, they had a thirty-minute stop before they could get on the next bus. "Want to grab dinner somewhere?" Marceline suggested.

Amina shook her head. "I've got some peanut butter and jelly sandwiches."

Marceline eyed Amina's skinny frame. She knew this woman's grocery order was the same every week. Did this lady survive on a strict PB&J diet?

"No," Marceline said firmly. "Dinner's on me. You need to eat something that doesn't contain grape jelly for once."

To Marceline's surprise, Amina didn't protest. There was a diner across the street from the bus station. They got seated at the only booth in the restaurant with a flickering light bulb above it. The place was nearly empty.

As her eyes briefly scanned the kid's portion of the menu, Marceline started laughing.

"What?" Amina asked, face still down turned.

"You can still order your favorite," Marceline said, pointing to the PB&J on the menu.

Amina cracked a small smile. "It's not my favorite. In fact, I kind of hate peanut butter."

"Why do you eat them all the time, then?" Marceline asked.

Amina shrugged. "Cheap. And doesn't require a fridge to store."

"Don't you get paid decently from these gigs?" Marceline pressed.

"I do. But I have no need to be reckless with money. I'm saving for retirement."

"Retirement?" Marceline quizzed. "You can't be older than what, mid-fifties? What's the normal age to retire from ghost hunting?"

Amina smiled again, this time showing her teeth for a

moment. She didn't look so scary when she smiled. "I look fifty-five, huh? This job really is taking a toll on me."

Marceline's guess at mid-fifties had been to be polite. If Marceline really had to guess, she'd say Amina looked to be early sixties.

"How old are you?" Marceline blurted. Amina raised her eyebrows, and Marceline immediately said, "Sorry, you don't have to answer that."

Amina shook her head. "It's fine, really. What if I told you I was only thirty-eight?"

Marceline's eyes widened and her mouth dropped, but she quickly regained composure so as not to be rude. Amina's skin looked both old and young at the same time. It had the firmness of someone in their mid-to-late thirties, but the deep lines of someone much older. Her hair was already graying, but Marceline reminded herself it wasn't that abnormal for people in their late thirties to start prematurely graying. Mostly, it was the eyes that made Amina seem older. They had dark circles underneath them and looked like they'd lived a full life and seen a lot, in the knowing way a lot of older people seemed to possess. To be fair, Marceline guessed Amina had seen a lot more than the average person ever would. With a stressful job like spirit dispelling, including a nomadic lifestyle without proper nutrition, Marceline could see those factors playing a role in someone's premature aging. "I'd believe it," Marceline replied after consideration.

Amina laughed, and Marceline could actually see her youth shine through.

As Amina lightened up a bit and their meals of tomato soup and grilled cheese sandwiches were delivered to their table, Marceline thought the time was right to ask. "So," she began, setting her spoon down. "Rush mentioned you were on a job in Catori. Could you tell me about it?"

Amina's eyes narrowed, and Marceline saw her immediately withdraw back to her stern exterior. "I was sent to Catori to rid the town of spirits. Obviously, I haven't been successful yet."

"Dispel the entire town's population of spirits?" Marceline asked. That seemed like a massive job for one person.

Amina gave a single nod.

"Why didn't you tell me?" Marceline pressed.

"It's none of your business, that's why," Amina said, glaring at her.

"Who hired you?" Marceline knew practically everyone in town, and she was dying to know which ones cared enough about the spirit population.

"Again, none of your business."

Marceline sighed. "Fine, touchy subject, I see. For this job we're going on tonight, who hired you and why?" Amina let out an exasperated groan, and Marceline reminded her, "You told me you would teach me things. Teaching requires you to answer at least some of my questions."

Amina shook her head but seemed to lighten up a bit at the subject change. "A lot of times the person who hires me likes to remain anonymous. They find me on my website and send me an email, but I usually don't meet them in person. Most of my clients are new homeowners who bought a house for cheap only to realize they weren't alone. I also get a fair number of businesses with lingering spirits. It's rare to get a job to dispel an entire town. Anyway, the woman who hired us today needs help with her house. Apparently, there's an interesting crowd of spirits lingering there."

Marceline nodded. A standard job, it sounded like. Amina didn't seem worried, which made Marceline feel slightly better.

Amina had devoured her entire meal quicker than Marceline had finished half her sandwich. She noticed Amina was eyeing the rest of hers. "We have to get going to the next bus. Could you help me finish this?"

Amina cleaned off the rest of Marceline's plate and bowl in minutes. Marceline had two ravenous, growing brothers, but even she was impressed.

"Time to go," Amina said.

37

Marceline was groggy as Amina shook her awake. "We've made it to Gunnison," she announced.

Marceline stretched her arms overhead and yawned loudly, trying to shake the sleepiness out of her. Now wasn't the time for sleep. Now was the time for ghost hunting, or rather, ghost dispelling.

They walked up the main road from the bus station. The town reminded Marceline of Catori, but somehow, it was even smaller, a quality many might find to be charming, but Marceline found to be confining.

"Do you know what kind of spirits we'll be dealing with?" Marceline asked. She was feeling more uneasy than she'd expected.

Amina, on the other hand, was as calm as ever. "Not sure. I guess the spirits in this house break a lot of things. Dishes, pots, windows. They slam doors, that sort of thing. Could be someone hateful, or could just be someone mischievous."

Marceline sincerely hoped it was the latter.

Sensing her discomfort, Amina added, "Like I said, most spirits I encounter aren't bad, just confused or bored."

"What are we going to do when we get there?"

Amina shrugged. "Just talk to them. There's nothing to be afraid of. You have your shield, and I have mine."

Marceline nodded, and Amina led them down one of the streets off the main road. After walking another block, Amina came to a stop. "This is it," Amina said outside of a tall, three-story house with a steeped, gabled roof and a large round tower.

Marceline projected her energy shield with more intensity as Amina continued toward the house. "Owner said the key would be under the mat," she said, bending down and fishing her hand under the *Welcome* doormat. Coming up with a key, Amina unlocked the front door with a click that was deafening in the silent night.

Amina walked in without hesitation, the floorboards creaking beneath her. She immediately removed her backpack and started rifling through it. "What are you doing standing outside?" Amina snapped.

Marceline came in, closing the door behind her. The moonlight provided only enough light to produce scarily human-like silhouettes of furniture. Marceline took a few deep breaths as Amina lit a sage bundle, handing it to Marceline. "Start smudging, I'll follow," Amina instructed.

Remembering what she'd read about cleansing homes with sage, Marceline walked slowly room to room, making sure to carry the smoke from the smudge stick all the way from the floor to as high up the wall as her arm would reach, hitting each corner of every room. She tried to ignore the sensation of being followed by someone who wasn't Amina.

After Marceline had smudged the entryway, the dining room, and the kitchen, she passed through the butler's pantry to another more formal dining area, where she saw in the mirror the passing figure of a woman in a flowing dress. Marceline stopped in her tracks. "Someone is here with us."

Marceline could hear Amina groan. "Obviously, that's why we're here. Keep going."

Marceline did as she was told, concentrating more on her mental shield than the job at hand. "Can't we turn the lights on in here?" Marceline asked, realizing her voice had grown very high-pitched.

"I usually don't, but sure, if you want," Amina said.

Marceline sighed and shook her head. Of course it was protocol to keep the old Victorian house looking as spooky as possible. "No, it's fine. Keep the lights off."

Amina had Marceline smudge the entire downstairs, which included a living room and an actual ballroom, then the seven upstairs bedrooms, and finally, they made it up to the attic. As they both climbed the stairs, Marceline heard a crash from downstairs. The sound of glass breaking. "Is anyone else in here?" Marceline asked Amina.

"No other living people, if that's what you're asking. Seems like whoever is here with us wants to play. You want to do the honors, Marci?"

Marceline took a deep breath. She was glad she'd just read over the section about how to safely summon spirits. "All spirits in our vicinity, appear before us," Marceline said, then quickly added, "We mean no harm."

Amina clicked on her flashlight, scanning it around the room. "Hello?" she called. "We feel your presence. It's okay, you can show yourself."

As the light moved around the room, it finally settled on the figure of a young woman beside an older woman, both wearing long nightgowns. The younger woman's was stained red with what looked like blood from the waist down. The light from

Amina's flashlight went right through them to the wall behind, casting no shadows.

"Hello," Amina said gently. "I'm Amina. This is Marceline. We're here to help you both move on from this place."

"You can see us?" the younger of the two spirits asked. When both Marceline and Amina turned in her direction, she added, "And you can hear us?"

"Yes to both," Amina replied. "We are here to help you move on from this realm, if that's what you wish."

"God, finally," the younger spirit sighed.

"Don't use His name in vain!" cried the other spirit.

"I wasn't, I was thanking God," said the younger with a smirk.

Marceline shot Amina a look, which she ignored. "Is anyone else living here with you two?" Amina asked.

"It's just us," the younger spoke up. "There was someone else here, Mary, but she left us long ago."

"Where did she go?" Marceline asked.

"I would like to say Heaven, after we've suffered God's wrath being stuck in this place, but we really do not know," the older one said, a somberness streaked throughout her words.

Amina took a few steps closer, shining her flashlight on the ground. "Who are we speaking with?"

The younger spirit floated forward, swaying her hips as she did. She opened her mouth, but the older spirit floated forward assertively. "Go ahead, Gloria," the younger sighed.

Ignoring her, the older spirit said, "I am Sister Gloria. I am a nun at St. Frances Catholic Girls School."

"Was," the younger corrected.

"That is what I said," Sister Gloria snapped.

The tension between the women was palpable. No wonder there were so many broken objects. Marceline guessed it was either the younger doing it to annoy Sister Gloria, or it was the result of their constant bickering. At least neither of these spirits seemed bad, not like Kendra.

Floating in front of Sister Gloria with the same dramatic sway, the younger batted her eyelashes and said, "I'm Lilith. I was working here at the brothel back in my time."

"This place was a brothel and a Catholic all-girls school?" Marceline asked. That was a combination Marceline had never thought possible.

"We cleansed this place with holy water after what dark acts were committed here, but yes, St. Francis moved into this building in 1958," Sister Gloria said with disdain.

Marceline looked to Amina, almost as if to ask permission before speaking. Amina nodded lightly. "How long have you two been here?" Marceline asked.

"I died first," Lilith offered. Sister Gloria flinched at the word. "It happened when I was giving birth to my son in the bedroom below, in the tower. I heard his cry of life. It was my greatest joy, and then I died. I didn't realize it at first. Everyone started rushing over me, panicking, taking my baby away even as I protested. I felt fine, so I sat up, but that was when I realized I was no longer attached to my body. It was surreal as I looked down at what was me, now lifeless and soaked through with blood. I was this transparent specter. From that moment, no one heard me. No one saw me. It was incredibly lonely until Mary joined me. And of course, Sister Gloria joined us as well."

"I'm sorry you went through that," Marceline said. "How about you, Sister?"

Sister Gloria appeared choked up. She took a moment to respond. "My heart stopped beating in 1965, in my sleep."

It was clearly still a sensitive subject for Gloria, so Marceline just said, "I'm sorry that happened."

Gloria shrugged, turning her back.

"There seems to be some tension between you two. Why is that?" Amina asked.

Gloria spun back around. "She is reckless," scolded Sister Gloria. "She strikes fear into the living for fun."

Lilith laughed. "Well, we don't get much other enjoyment in our state. We argue a lot. Sometimes I like to get a rise out of Gloria to the point that she gets so worked up she can make doors slam shut or lamps fly off the table," she admitted, eyes shining.

"Childish behavior," Sister Gloria seethed.

Lilith smiled.

"Can either of you tell me why you stayed here, why you didn't crossover when you died?" Amina pressed.

Lilith answered, "For me, it was my son. I know it was him. I wanted to be with him, to watch him grow up. Of course, he didn't stay in this house long. A family adopted him in town. Every Halloween, when I could leave this awful house, I would go to him. See how much he would grow year to year. What he was up to. It was incredible to see him, but so painful. But none so painful as it has been without him."

"What happened to your son?" Marceline asked gently.

"I do not know," Lilith said, eyes glistening with emotion. "He left before he was eighteen to fight in the Vietnam War. He never came back, and I do not know what ever became of him."

Instinctively, Gloria moved closer to Lilith. "There, there," Gloria muttered lightly under her breath.

Lilith took a shaky breath.

"What about you, Sister Gloria?" Amina asked.

"Teaching, spreading the word of the Lord, was my calling. I suppose I stayed because I was not ready to stop teaching lessons," Gloria answered, then sighed. "Not that I have accomplished much in the years since. All my teachings seem to fall on deaf ears."

"That's not true," Lilith said gently. "You have taught me so much. If it was not for you, I do not know if I would still be here, or if I would have gone down the destructive path to have another take my place. The misery of losing Samuel would have been too much for me. You helped me make peace with the situation. For that, I am so thankful."

At the mention of peace, Marceline glanced at Amina.

"Being candid, I also have learned from you, Lilith. How to enjoy life, how to laugh. You have been a great blessing to me," Sister Gloria said.

"Do you ladies believe in the idea of finding peace after death?" Amina posed.

"I was always so devout, so sure," Gloria said. "And I would still very much like to believe that God would send me to Heaven, but I am ashamed to admit that I am unsure now."

Lilith nodded in agreement. "If there was peace after death for us, somewhere to go besides here, we would have found it by now. Mary did."

"That's not necessarily true," Amina said, stepping forward. "I work with spirits to help them find peace, but I can only help those who want to be helped, who feel at peace with how they are leaving the world. Are you ladies at peace?"

Both ghosts nodded, looking at one another.

"I think we've found inner peace. So why haven't we moved on like Mary did?"

Amina smiled gently. "It sounds to me that what is holding you two here now is one another. Maybe you each stayed for your own reasons, but now, you are both just keeping one another company."

"See, Gloria, I told you it was all your fault," Lilith teased, then she turned serious. "It was your selflessness that got you here, your desire to keep helping people. Now it is time for you to help yourself."

Sister Gloria, if she could produce tears, would have them streaked down her face. "I could not bear to leave you. Only if we could go together." Gloria turned to Amina and Marceline. "What do we do?"

Amina smiled. "Just follow the light," she whispered. "Release any energy that is no longer serving this space."

Marceline felt tears on her cheeks as a cloud appeared with yellow rays shining through it. It was warm, like a summer day. Their backs were turned, and Sister Gloria and Lilith floated hand in hand until they got far enough away that their legs touched a distant ground, and they walked their separate ways. Distantly, Marceline could hear voices calling each of them as they walked, welcoming them.

As the portal closed, Marceline felt like whatever was holding her upright instantly let her go, and she stumbled, catching herself against the wall. Amina also fell back, as if her knees couldn't support her. Marceline felt dizzy, and she held a hand to her head as she rose from the wall.

"Wow. That was amazing," Marceline said. When Amina remained motionless, Marceline rushed toward her, kneeling beside her. "Are you okay?" Amina's eyes stayed closed, and her nose was bleeding profusely. "Amina," Marceline said, shaking her lightly.

She touched Amina's face and suddenly felt a cold sensation creep across her body. The pitch-black room suddenly felt darker. "Amina," Marceline said again, her voice faltering as she grew dizzier. Marceline felt herself swaying, her hand still on Amina's face, until Amina's eyes snapped open. Amina slapped Marceline's hand from her face, and Marceline almost immediately felt better.

"I'm fine, don't touch me," Amina growled, quickly pulling herself to her feet.

"You passed out," Marceline countered.

Amina ignored her and started down the stairs. Marceline followed slowly behind her. Did Amina really have to be this aggressive toward her all the time, especially after they accomplished such a beautiful thing?

At the bottom of the stairs, Marceline stopped as her boots crunched on a broken glass vase shattered on the ground—Lilith's last trick. The floor was wet with the water that had once been contained, and Marceline crouched to pick up the bundle of fresh flowers now splayed on the floor. Marceline held them thoughtfully as Amina opened the front door, and, on the porch, she turned around. "What are you waiting for?" she snapped.

Marceline hung back. "What the hell is your problem with me?"

"I don't have a problem with you," Amina said between clenched teeth.

"You've been short with me and treating me like I'm stupid this whole night. And anytime I show any sort of concern for you, you instantly lash out at me. Did you not want me to come with you?"

Amina sighed and leaned her weight onto her right leg. "Do we have to do this here? Right now?"

"Yes, we do." Marceline stood firm, crossing her arms with the bundle of flowers pressed against her chest.

Amina gritted her teeth against the pain Marceline knew she was feeling in her head. Marceline was feeling it, too. "Honestly," Amina finally spoke, "no, I didn't want you to come with me on this trip."

"You invited me," Marceline shot back.

"It's not you, Marci. You're not the problem."

"What is the problem, then?"

"I don't want to teach you these things," Amina said quietly.

Marceline felt like she'd been slapped in the face. She hurried out the door, shoving past Amina, and walked down the path in front of the house. Why had Amina told her to come if she didn't want her to come? Why had she bothered to teach her anything at all?

"Marci, wait," Amina said. Marceline didn't turn around. "I don't want you to become like me, to embrace your Sight, to help spirits, because I want to keep you safe."

Marceline rolled her eyes. "You said it yourself. As long as we have our energy shields up, we're totally safe. Why wouldn't I want to use my Sight to help people find peace, to make a difference in the world?"

Amina sighed and struggled to produce words for a while. In a quiet voice, she said, "Because every time you use your power to dispel a spirit, part of your life goes with them."

38

The silence was heavy for a moment. Marceline dropped the flowers she had been holding, hardly noticing as they floated gracefully to the sidewalk. "What does that mean? Part of your life goes with them?" Marceline finally asked.

Amina sighed. "It's the reason why I look much older than I should. Why my hair is falling out and soon my teeth will too. My body is aging at more than double the speed because of how I do magic. It's why others like us, who possess this sacrificial magic, often will use other innocents as their sacrifices. I draw power from myself only. But it has its price."

Marceline felt like her stomach was in her throat. "Why do you do it if it's literally killing you?"

"For that same feeling you had back when we allowed Lilith and Sister Gloria to finally find peace. Helping others has an almost addictive quality. I started this when I was your age, when I didn't care about myself, when I felt it would be selfish not to use this power for good." Amina paused and walked close to Marceline, clutching her arm. "Marci, I want you to know it's not selfish to choose yourself, to choose your health over this life. I wanted to show you all the sides of it, the good and the bad, so you can make an informed decision, but you don't have to choose the life I chose. I wish someone had told me that when I was your age."

Amina released Marceline's arm and turned away, but not before Marceline saw the glint of tears in Amina's eyes. The air outside the now empty house was so still, so at ease. The silence of this town at a moment like this when her life was being changed made Marceline want to scream, just to disrupt the peace. She should have known possessing magic was too good to be true. Nothing was ever easy for her.

"Do you regret choosing this life?" Marceline asked quietly.

Amina immediately shook her head. "I don't regret it. But I wished I'd known to use my power more sparingly. You see, I grew up with a family who believed in real sacrifice. I didn't know this until I was older, the blood they had on their hands," Amina growled, scowling in disgust. "Because those monsters took the lives of others, their lives were protected. Their bodies didn't take the damage mine has taken."

Marceline didn't know what to say. She had never known this vulnerable side of Amina. She only knew her hot-headedness, her stubbornness. It reminded Marceline that you can never judge a book by its cover. You could never know what made a person the way they were. "I'm sorry," Marceline said after a long pause.

Amina nodded. "I wish I hadn't already taught you so much. I should have just taught you enough to protect yourself and left you with that."

"I don't regret knowing all this. I'm glad I do," Marceline said fiercely.

Amina looked her up and down, looking sad. "We should get going."

Marceline followed slowly behind Amina, unsure of where

they were going, but not having the energy to ask. She couldn't imagine what time it was. It had to be early morning. Amina took a right on the main road, headed toward one of the few buildings with lights on in the windows, the Pine Grove Motel.

Marceline noticed once they were in the light of the motel lobby just how disheveled they looked. Amina's nose had bled again, red drips dried to her face, and her eyes looked blood-shot. Marceline was sure she didn't look much better. The man at the front desk looked hardly phased by their appearances, but he did pointedly direct them toward the motel's no drugs policy.

In their motel room, Amina took off her shoes and lied on the bed, closing her eyes.

Marceline hesitated beside her bed. "Amina?"

"Hm?" Amina mumbled.

"How did you send them to peace? How did you open that portal?"

Amina kept her eyes closed. "Once I get to know them, understand why they're still here, and they're actually ready to leave the earth, I project the portal. Like how you would project your energy shield, but it's a stronger force."

"I get you need to know those things, but how did you *do* it?" Marceline pressed.

Amina yawned and rolled to her side. "It's just something we can do."

Marceline rolled her eyes. "But where do they go?"

"Don't know," Amina said, yawning again.

"How do you create a portal to somewhere you don't know?" Marceline asked, growing more frustrated.

"You just do."

"You're not a good teacher, you know that?" Marceline snapped, storming into the bathroom. Clearly, Amina didn't want to help her anymore. She was going to have to figure it out herself, as she always seemed to have to do.

Marceline decided to take a quick shower before bed. With the hot water raining on her, she had the idea. She was going to dispel a spirit all on her own. There were bound to be some spirits floating around this old motel, right? She needed to prove to herself that she could and prove to Amina that she didn't need her help.

She quickly toweled off before throwing on sweatpants and a hoodie. She peeked out the bathroom door and heard soft snores coming from Amina. Taking a deep, steadying breath, Marceline whispered, "All spirits in my vicinity, appear before me." Glancing into the steamy bathroom mirror, the fog instantly cleared as the temperature in the bathroom dropped. In her reflection, she saw multiple figures floating beside her, calling to her.

Marceline felt the icy presence as the hands of several spirits clawed out to her, fingers reaching through her. Marceline shuddered. Then she remembered reading in the spell book what she could add. She closed her eyes and said, "I ask the universe to please remove all negative entities from this room. You are not welcome here, so please go back to where you came from."

Marceline felt relief as the icy hands vanished from her skin. Opening her eyes, she saw behind her one man. He looked to be in his mid-to-late twenties. The shirt he wore had a bloody hole through it. As she made eye contact with him, he frowned.

"Hello," she said nervously. "I'm Marceline. I'm here to help you."

The man narrowed his eyes and crossed his arms over his chest. "How can you see me?"

"I'm what's called a Spirit Walker. I can see and hear spirits."

"Then how come you're only talking to me?" the man asked.

"Because I sent away the negative spirits," Marceline explained.

The man cracked a smile. "Glad I made the cut. It's nice to talk to someone other than the other morons here with me."

Marceline smiled back. "What's your name?"

"Brian Allen," he said, offering his hand and looking hopeful she would take it.

"The only thing I can't do is make physical contact with spirits," Marceline said. She thought of the spell she'd done with Russel to make physical contact, but now wasn't the time to waste her finite power.

Brian nodded, looking embarrassed. "Right, just a habit I still have from, you know . . . before."

"If you don't mind me asking, how long have you been stuck here?"

"Long time," Brian said, pressing his lips together in a thin line and nodding. "Too long. I took this bullet here in 1989." Brian gestured to the hole in his chest.

"I'm sorry that happened to you," Marceline said.

Brian blinked at her. "You know what? Thank you. No one has ever said that to me. Not that I've been able to have many conversations with people who are alive since then, but thank you for acknowledging that. It sucks being dead."

Marceline nodded. "I'm sure it does."

"The worst part is that it was the guy I considered to be my best friend who did this to me, shot me right through the heart. I was the night manager here, filling in at the front desk when he came in. He pointed that thing at me and said, 'Sorry it came to this.' Then he fired it. Just like that. No hesitation."

"That's awful. Why would he have done that?"

"All these years later, and I still couldn't tell you. Maybe it was jealousy. I was the one who got the best-looking girl, who had the nicer truck, the better house. Maybe he was just psychotic. I'll never know. He wasn't a suspect for a while. The cameras were mysteriously off that night, and they had no evidence. He even came here with the cops and my girl. That prick really had the nerve to flirt with her. Right after I died."

"Did he get arrested?" Marceline asked.

"That's the craziest part of this whole story. My girl, Lisa, man I love her, she worked here too. I don't think she was like you, a Spirit what-cha-ma-call-it, but she had some sort of sixth sense. She kept working here after, and I could have sworn sometimes she saw me, but only for a moment. And she never could hear me, no matter how much I yelled. And I couldn't touch her, obviously, couldn't touch anything. My hands float right through everything. But I was so pissed, I needed someone to know it was him who killed me. Maybe it was the anger coursing through me, but one day, when Lisa was here, I got the urge to give her a message. I focused all my energy on the computer keyboard at the front desk. I couldn't last long, but I managed to type, 'L, it was D.' You should've seen her face when the keyboard typed that in front of her. She put it all together. She's the one who got him convicted. It took a long time, but she got him. I don't know if that sack of shit is still alive, but I hope when he dies, he stays in jail as a ghost, rotting forever."

"That's an amazing story," Marceline said. "Not the you dying part, but the fact you were able to convey your message." She thought back to how Amina had controlled the conversation with Sister Gloria and Lilith, how she'd brought it back to the why. Marceline needed to know why he was still there, and if he was ready to go, to open the portal. "So, your best friend murdered you back in 1989, and you stayed in order to make sure he was convicted, and he was, so why are you still here?"

"Isn't that the golden question?" Brian laughed.

"No, really, Brian. Think about it. There's got to be a reason you're still here," Marceline pressed.

Brian shook his head. "Just bad luck, I guess. Not everyone goes to Heaven. I'm not saying I was a saint when I was alive, but I wasn't some terrible guy either. But the way I see it, if I was going to go to Heaven or wherever, I probably would have already by now."

"Is it Lisa?" Marceline asked.

"Lisa?" Brian asked.

"Is Lisa the reason you're still here? Do you still see her sometimes?"

"Sometimes," Brian said. "She owns this place now. She's married with kids. Of course, she's still absolutely gorgeous." Brian could not keep the smile off his face when he spoke about her.

Marceline nodded and smiled. "Is she happy now?"

"Seems to be," Brian replied, voice turning somber. "It's bittersweet. I wish it was me who could be the one making her happy, who was her husband, the father of her children. But her husband is a good man. He takes care of her, and that's all I could have wanted."

Marceline understood. Brian was ready. His mission had been accomplished. It was just a matter of letting go now. "She's taken care of," Marceline said gently. "You don't have to worry about her anymore or stick around for her. I think Lisa would want you to find peace."

Brian's eyes glimmered with non-existent tears. "I don't know if I can leave her. Even if I could, I don't know how to."

"I could help you," Marceline said. "But you have to want to go."

Brian's body shook with emotion.

"You shouldn't feel guilty for choosing yourself," Marceline added, repeating the advice Amina had given her.

Brian nodded. "I love her, but she'll be okay without me. I think I'm ready to leave this place."

"You are." Now was the part Marceline wasn't so sure how to do. She closed her eyes, envisioning a golden ball, like her shield, but bigger, deeper, full of joy and peace.

When she opened her eyes, she was surprised to see the portal in front of her, Brian having already floated through. He turned back for a moment. "Thank you for listening to me, Marceline," Brian said before continuing through the warm tunnel. He floated until his feet touched a distant, solid ground and started walking.

There were voices calling to him, and suddenly the portal closed. It was as if Marceline had been standing in front of a heater that was abruptly shut off in a freezing cold room. Her head pounded, and she lost her sight and hearing for a moment as she stumbled back against the sink and slowly lowered herself to the ground. She took a few breaths with her head tucked between her knees, watching as blood from her nose dripped onto the tile floor.

"You did it," came Amina's voice.

Marceline looked up to see Amina leaned against the bathroom door frame. Somehow, she looked equally proud and disappointed.

"You were right," Marceline said.

"About?"

"The portal. You were right, it was just something I could do. It didn't take much thought."

"Well, I'm usually right about most things," Amina said with a smirk.

Marceline smiled, then her face fell. It had been a

marvelous feeling, helping Brian. So good, that it scared her. "You were also right that it's addicting. The feeling of helping someone find peace is indescribable. It's like I found my purpose, and that's to help people."

Amina's smile fell like it was suddenly too heavy for her mouth to handle. "I know the feeling."

39

In the morning, Marceline and Amina took the bus to Denver before going their separate ways. Amina had a few jobs in the city to take care of, but she promised she'd be back by Wednesday. Part of Marceline wished she could join her, but part of her was relieved to be going home, to try to recoup the energy she knew she'd lost in dispelling Brian. She wasn't sure if it was in her head, but she felt weaker all the way to her bones. She felt almost frail, like her body had experienced something incredibly traumatic, but her brain felt the opposite, like she had accomplished something amazing, which, of course, was also true.

Still exhausted, she fell asleep on the bus back to Catori.

She woke up to the sound of the bus doors opening, and when she opened her eyes, the sun greeted her with a massive headache. Rubbing her eyes, she looked outside the window. Her stomach did a flip-flop. She didn't recognize this stop. She stood, grabbing her bag as she asked the bus driver, "Excuse me, sir, what stop are we at?"

"Last stop, Havtree Park," the bus driver, Craig, according to the nameplate, told her.

"So, we passed Catori Springs?" Marceline asked. She knew the answer, of course, but she hoped feigning stupidity would help her in this situation.

"Yes, ma'am," he said.

"Oops, that's where I was supposed to stop. My dad's there to pick me up," Marceline explained, smiling innocently.

Sensing what her motive was, the bus driver, with a flat face, said, "Well, ma'am, either your dad can pick you up here, or you can purchase another bus ticket back down to Catori Springs."

"It's only a twenty-minute drive," Marceline protested.

The bus driver raised his eyebrows. "That's the tone you should be taking with your daddy, not me."

Marceline sighed. The bus driver stared her down until she took the steep steps off the bus, pulling her phone out of her pocket. As she got to the bottom and took a step off, she realized her phone was dead. She turned around as Craig closed the bus doors. She knocked on the door with her knuckle, but Craig put the bus in drive and pulled away from the curb.

So she was stuck in the town past Catori, her phone was dead, and the only phone number she had memorized besides her own was her father's. Even if she could convince some stranger to let her borrow their phone to call her dad, she had no good reason to tell him why she'd been stranded in Havtree Park and not with the rest of her school trip.

Buying another bus ticket it was. Walking to the outdoor bus station counter, Marceline told the attendee what she needed.

"Seven dollars," the cashier said, smacking a bubble with her gum.

Marceline nodded, fishing in her bag for her wallet but

finding nothing. "One second," Marceline said, kneeling on the ground as she removed everything from the bag. "I have money." A line was starting to form behind her. She told the woman behind her to go ahead. She scooted her belongings to the side. "Come on," she mumbled.

After shaking the entire bag upside down, it was determined there was, in fact, no wallet in her backpack. She sighed as she packed up her bag again, cheeks burning with embarrassment. "I'll come back," she told the cashier.

Marceline walked back down to where the bus had dropped her off and sat on the bench. Should she try to walk along the dangerous, curving mountain pass with cars flying around the sharp edges to get back to Catori? No, that wasn't really an option. She dropped her head in her hands and looked to her right. To her surprise, she saw Lacey, holding an ice cream cone, walking with what looked to be her mom.

Marceline bit her lip and thought. This might be her best chance to reach someone from home. *But did it have to be Lacey?*

Marceline sighed and stood. She and Lacey made brief eye contact, but Lacey looked down quickly, suddenly fixated on her ice cream cone.

Marceline cleared her throat. "Lacey, hi," she called.

Lacey glanced up. "Oh, Marci, funny seeing you here," she said, as if she hadn't just tried to pretend Marceline didn't exist.

"Friend from school?" Lacey's mom asked with a surprisingly charming smile that did not match her daughter's.

"This is Tag's girlfriend," Lacey said pointedly.

Lacey's mom's smile faded, and she and Lacey both cocked their heads to the side with narrowed eyes and pursed lips. Marceline could definitely see the resemblance now.

"Yes, that's me." Marceline laughed nervously. "I was actually wondering, could I use your phone to call him really quickly? My phone is dead."

Lacey's eyes narrowed. "How did you get here?"

"The bus," Marceline said. "I was supposed to meet someone here, but they had to cancel. Now I'm stranded." She wasn't sure why she said that. It was like her brain was now programed to lie about every detail.

"How unfortunate," Lacey's mom said in an unsympathetic tone.

Marceline glanced at the phone in Lacey's hand. "So, can I, please?"

Lacey and her mom exchanged a look, but Lacey rolled her eyes and started dialing, making a point to put it on speakerphone. Tag answered on the third ring. "Hey, Lace, what's up?" came Tag's voice.

"Hey, Tag," Lacey responded, twirling her hair around her finger. "Thanks for answering so quickly, you always do. I have someone who needs to talk to you." She held the phone out to Marceline but wouldn't allow Marceline to hold it herself.

"Tag, hey, it's me," Marceline said into the phone. She wished she could take the phone and walk far away from Lacey's and her mom's judgmental stares, but she couldn't. "I'm kind of stuck in Havtree. Do you think you could come pick me up?"

"Havtree? I thought you were with Amina?" Tag said. The volume of the speakerphone was all the way up, and Marceline couldn't bear to look up to see Lacey's and her mom's reactions.

"I was, but she stayed back. I took the bus, and I fell asleep on the way back and missed the stop. And my phone died," Marceline said.

"I thought you said you were going to meet someone here in Havtree," Lacey said loudly.

Marceline let out a nervous chuckle, feeling her cheeks

continue to burn. "No, I wasn't meeting anyone. I don't know why I said that."

There was an awkward silence, then Tag said, "I'll leave now. Where are you?"

"Outside the ice cream shop on Main," Marceline answered. Her throat felt like it was closing in on itself.

"I'll be there soon," he promised.

"Bye, Tag," Lacey said quickly, hitting the end button.

Lacey's mom and her both shot her the same, biting look, then Lacey's mom said, "It was a pleasure, Marci. We should be going."

Marceline was thankful to see them turn away, but Lacey turned back. "You know, Tag doesn't like liars."

"I'm not a liar," Marceline protested. "I just didn't want to say I fell asleep on the bus, I don't know why." But even that was a half-truth.

Lacey turned on her heel and continued up the sidewalk with her mom. Marceline sat at the tables outside the ice cream shop, waiting in shame.

When Tag pulled up twenty minutes later, she was both relieved and nervous. She climbed into the passenger seat of his truck, avoiding making eye contact. "Thanks so much for picking me up."

"Of course," he responded, putting a hand on her thigh. "How was your excursion with the tarot reader?"

Marceline hesitated. She wanted to share what an amazing trip she'd had in terms of dispelling and the unfortunate truth she'd learned about herself, but she couldn't tell the whole truth, could she? She glanced at Tag and wished she could share everything. Only she knew the complete story, about how important it was to break the curse in order to dispel Kendra, and it was weighing on her. She was used to sharing everything with Katy, but even Katy didn't know it all. Marceline felt tears form in her eyes.

Tag gave her a concerned look. "Did the trip go badly? Is that why you came back alone without Amina?"

Marceline shook her head and wiped a stray tear. "No, it's not that. I learned a lot from Amina, but I also got some not-so-good news, and I still don't know how to fix some things, that's all." Even as she said it, she knew how vague and confusing those details were to someone who had no context.

"You can tell me anything," Tag said, trying to momentarily catch her gaze before turning his eyes back to the road.

Marceline nodded, but she knew she couldn't. "Tell me about your game last night," she said instead.

Tag launched into the story of the game, which won the Catori Springs Cougars a spot in the state finals. Marceline congratulated him and asked if he'd thought more about which school he wanted to go to for football. Tag's entire demeanor darkened, and he was quiet for a long moment.

"I don't even know if I want to play in college," he said. Marceline's brow furrowed. This was the first she'd heard of this. "It's not fun like it used to be, but I know my grades aren't good enough to get me into a decent school without football, let alone get me a scholarship."

"You don't like football anymore?" Marceline asked.

"It's just been my identity for so long. I've always been the football guy; I've always been good at it. I don't know who I am without it. Recently, I've had this thought, like, what if I didn't play in college? What if I just took that time to see what else I like, what else I'm good at? But then I think it'd be dumb to pass up on a football scholarship to a good school. I've already gotten some great offers, full rides too. I've got to make a decision soon."

Marceline reached over and took his hand. "That's a hard

decision. But you know, to me, football isn't what defines you. You're not just Tag the football guy. You're also Tag the thoughtful, funny guy. The guy who likes peanut M&Ms and hates mushrooms on his pizza, and who will do anything for his friends. You're so much more than football, Tag. So, whether you choose to play in college or not, just know that. And either way, I'm sure you'll learn a lot about yourself once you're away at school."

Tag smiled and pulled her hand up to his mouth, pressing her palm against his lips. "I like you a lot, Marceline."

40

The roar of Tag's truck when they turned onto her street made Marceline cringe. Dad had a sixth sense for detecting that sound. He could be sound asleep and wake up to the sound a block away. If he wasn't at the store, she knew he'd be waiting for her.

"Are you going to tell him where you were?" Tag asked.

Marceline chewed her lip. She wanted to be more truthful with the people in her life, sure, but it wouldn't really hurt her dad if she just let him think she went camping for school, would it?

"I think you should," Tag added.

Marceline smiled and gave him a quick peck. "Thanks for being my moral compass. And for picking me up. I really, really appreciate you."

"Anytime," he said, giving her another kiss. "Good luck."

Marceline grabbed her bag and walked up to her house, entering through the garage as she always did. Everything in her house seemed at once unfamiliar and familiar. Even though she had been gone only twenty-four hours, it had felt much longer. She breathed in the scent of her home. Funny how she couldn't smell it on a day-to-day basis, but being away for a short time could make the scent so much sharper. She could see her brothers playing soccer in the backyard through the kitchen window.

"With Tag?" came Dad's voice from the living room, startling her.

"Oh, he just picked me up from the bus," Marceline replied.

"How was your camping trip?"

"Good," she called, setting her bag on the counter.

"You look surprisingly clean for sleeping outdoors," Dad remarked.

"It was pretty much glamping," Marceline said weakly. She could tell something was up. He sounded suspicious.

"You know what's funny?" Dad asked, rising from the recliner.

His tone didn't suggest anything was funny or would ever be funny again. It was confirmed; the jig was up. She braced for the impact. "You?" she replied, trying to crack a smile.

Dad's expression didn't budge. "Well, yes, of course, but that wasn't what I was referring to. It's funny that you seem to be the only one in your entire school invited on this environmental studies class camping trip." Dad held up her sleeping bag. "You didn't even bring your sleeping bag, bean. You could've made this more convincing."

"How did you—"

"Well, I saw your environmental studies teacher at the store this morning, and when I asked why she wasn't on the camping trip, I realized there were some discrepancies in your whereabouts this weekend."

Marceline clenched her fists. Why, of all people, had her dad run into her teacher this weekend? Any other weekend, and it would have been fine. Marceline supposed lying to her father about being with someone, when her dad was the owner of the town's main grocery store and knew the entire town, had been her first mistake.

Dad continued, "You couldn't have been with Tag because he had a game last night, great game, by the way. You couldn't have been with Katy since I called her mom and Katy wasn't with you. You certainly weren't on a school camping trip. All of this begs the question," Dad took a dramatic pause and removed his glasses. "Where the hell were you last night?"

"Do I have to tell you everywhere I go?" Marceline countered. Seeing Dad's expression, she quickly realized her error.

"Yes, Marci, you do. You're not even a legal adult yet. You wanted to learn how to drive? Forget it. As long as you continue to lie to me and go on your little solo adventures, you're not going anywhere. As a matter of fact, you're fired."

"I'm fired?" Marceline cried incredulously.

"You're no longer an employee at the Grocery Elf," Dad said, crossing his arms. "That way, you go straight to school and straight home. You're on lockdown."

The thought of spending all her time stuck in her room made her want to scream. "What about paying you back for Barb2.0?"

"You're not fired forever. You'll be able to pay me back eventually," Dad said firmly.

———

At school, Marceline's locker got slammed the moment she got it opened. On the other side of the locker door was Katy, eyebrows raised expectantly.

"So, how was your ghost adventure?"

"I dispelled one all by myself," Marceline reported, smiling.

"Aw, baby's first dispelling!" Katy squealed. "I should make you a t-shirt. I'm so proud of you."

Marceline's smile fell. "There's something else I learned, though."

Katy, matching Marceline's tone, frowned. "What is it?"

"The type of magic," Marceline whispered, the m-word hardly perceptible as she didn't even want any lip-readers to pick up on it, "I possess is sort of dark. It's called sacrificial magic."

Katy shushed her, looking around for a moment, then pulled her into an empty classroom. "Go on. What is this sacrificial magic?"

"It means that I can only use magic if I sacrifice."

"Like, sacrifice people?" Katy said, eyes wide. Marceline could tell she was trying to keep a brave face.

Marceline shrugged. "Any form of life, I guess."

"Is that what you've been doing this whole time?" Katy asked in a high-pitched voice, taking a slow step away.

"God, Kat, no. Do you really think I would do something like that?" Marceline said. Katy cracked a small smile of relief. "But, since I don't actually sacrifice any life to use magic, whenever I use magic, I sacrifice a part of my life."

Katy's face fell again. "You mean, you're, like, killing yourself every time you do one of your witchy spells?"

Marceline nodded. "Magic takes energy. In my case, the energy comes directly from me. I have this spell book, and there's so much I want to practice and try, but I can't be wasteful with my life or energy. I've been reading the spell book cover to cover, but I can't practice. Maybe one day this knowledge will come in handy."

Katy's furrowed brow grew concerned. "It seems like maybe it would be better for you to separate yourself completely from this magic stuff. If you can't even practice it anyway, what's the point of learning all this stuff?"

"It's interesting to me. But it's hard. I can kind of understand the temptation to do what it takes to have unlimited magic, but I would never stoop to sacrificing others." Marceline shuddered at the thought.

"What does all this have to do with Ken—" Katy started to say.

Marceline covered her friend's mouth with her hand. "Don't say her name." The first class bell rang, signaling they had five minutes until class started. Marceline knew Katy hated being late, but she didn't budge from the room, staying focused on her. Marceline went on to explain how she'd been working with Amina to learn about her magic, how the spirits in Catori were stuck, how she had, all by herself, helped Brian find peace.

Marceline hardly looked up as she spoke, the words coming up like vomit. It was a relief to spill all these secrets she'd been harboring, to release some of this stress and pressure. Once she started talking, she couldn't stop. When she glanced up, Katy was looking at her thoughtfully, but with a sadness in her eyes. "So?" Marceline said nervously. "What are your thoughts?"

"That's amazing you can help spirits," Katy said slowly. "I know you're a selfless, giving person, and you want to help people, but I don't want you to do it at the expense of yourself. You matter too."

Marceline nodded. "I know, and I'm going to be safe about it. But if I have this gift to help people, I feel like I have to use it. I'm just one person, and I can use these powers to help so many others find peace. Now that I know I can do this, I don't know how I can stop."

"But if you can't even dispel any spirits in Catori, then

maybe you can just stay here and not have to feel the pressure to dispel anyone," Katy said.

Marceline shook her head. "The energy is building up here to too high of a level. The spirits can't be stuck here forever, they'll be desperate, they'll start taking other's lives to leave this place."

"Is that what K," Katy started, looking up and back at her, "tried to do with Bijou? Take her life to free herself?"

Marceline nodded. "That's the other thing. I made a promise to K. If I can't figure out how to dispel spirits in Catori and help K find peace by the next full moon, then she's going to sacrifice someone." She didn't want to tell Katy the part about her promising herself to Kendra to save Katy. She'd never want Katy to feel any sort of guilt.

"By the next full moon? That's in, like, a week. Do you have any idea how to break whatever it is that's holding everyone here?"

"I have no idea. Amina is helping me, though," Marceline said.

Katy wrapped her arms around her. "I'm sorry you've been dealing with all this on your own."

Marceline felt a lump in her throat as she hugged her tight, resting her chin on Katy's head. "I'm sorry I didn't tell you sooner."

Katy pulled away and held Marceline's hands firmly. "I'm going to help you figure this out, what might be causing this energy magnet that's holding all these spirits here. I'll start researching."

"Well, I know how the spirits are stuck, partially, I guess. There's a curse in Catori Springs that was created by the town's founders centuries ago."

Katy shook her head. "Great," she muttered flatly. "A curse too. This is very tricky. Have you asked Bijou about this?"

"She didn't know anything last time I asked. I told her to ask her parents, but I don't know if they'll tell her anything if they know I'm the one asking about it."

"Well, I'm no expert on magic, but I am pretty solid on Catori Springs history. I've never read any lore about a town curse, but then again, I've never looked. I'll do what I can, but in the meantime, maybe you could try talking to Anna?"

Marceline was confused. "Anna?"

"I figured you've been seeing her a lot, and she's been here for over a century. Maybe she knows something and would be willing to help."

Anna's red eyes and menacing laughter reminded her of Kendra, only worse. Marceline sighed. Maybe Katy was right. "I can try to talk to her."

The bell rang, signaling the end of first period.

"Thank you for your support. I'll let you go to second period," Marceline said. "Oh, and you can call me after school if you want. I'm unemployed now. My dad fired me."

Katy held a hand over her mouth as she covered her grin. "Fired by your own dad from the Grocery Elf? That's going to look great on your future job applications."

Marceline rolled her eyes, but she couldn't help but smile.

41

Marceline was starting to feel like a bad person skipping class and being chronically late. Then, she remembered, there was a worse person in the world, and she was in the third-floor bathroom.

With her deadline three weeks away and falling on Halloween, the day that would strengthen Kendra and let her loose from the school, Marceline knew she had to give Kendra some hope that she had kept up with her end of the bargain. In reality, Marceline knew she hadn't made much progress at all in figuring out how to dispel spirits in Catori, but Kendra certainly didn't have to know that.

Wanting to hurry to not be *that* late to second period, Marceline ran up the stairs. On the third floor, slightly out of breath, Marceline burst into the women's restroom. "Kendra," she called.

"You rang," Kendra said from behind her. Marceline turned around and had to move out of the way to avoid Kendra's icy form floating right through her.

"I wanted to give you an update on what I've been working on."

"And? Spit it out, Marci."

Marceline took a deep breath, trying to put on a happy face. "I was able to help a spirit find peace, to move on, to leave the realm you're in."

"Really?" Kendra said, her voice sounding hopeful as she moved closer. "Here, in Catori?"

Marceline hesitated. In an effort to be more honest, she said, "Well, no. But I'm learning."

Kendra's eyes darkened. Marceline realized now might have been a good time to actually continue to improve her lying skills. "So, you haven't made any progress at all."

"Well—"

Kendra spoke over her. "That wasn't a question, that was a fact."

"I'm working on it," Marceline said firmly. "I'm working with a very skilled Spirit Walker. She's going to help me help you."

Kendra pursed her lips. "Is she *pure* like you?"

Marceline didn't know the word "pure" could sound so awful until it came out of Kendra's mouth. "What does that even mean?" Marceline asked.

Kendra shot her a look like Marceline was an idiot. "Does she self-sacrifice like you, or does she actually use the true extent of her power?"

Marceline hadn't known Kendra knew anything about Spirit Walkers or about how sacrificial magic worked. Sensing it was time to use her half-truth-telling skills again, Marceline said, "She's teaching me both."

"Well, well, that is interesting information," Kendra said, floating in a circle around Marceline. She stopped right in front of Marceline. "But remember, your deadline is only a few days away. Since you've been putting in some genuine effort, I'd agree to amend my offer now, if you'd like. Instead of sacrificing you, I could sacrifice that Lacey girl you seem to despise. Or how about Nate? He's rather annoying."

Marceline didn't like hearing others' names from Kendra's mouth, even if they were names Marceline wasn't a big fan of. "No, if anyone is going to be sacrificed, it'll be me."

"Quite the martyr, aren't you?" Kendra said flatly. She crossed her arms. "Maybe your life at stake isn't enough to motivate you. Maybe it has to be one of your friends. Katy, is it? Or what about the handsome boyfriend, Tag?"

Marceline's heart dropped in fear, then rage filled her. Hearing her loved ones' names in Kendra's voice made the risk of something happening to them seem that much higher. "That wasn't our deal. I'm the sacrifice. And, you know, if you stopped possessing people for like two seconds, maybe that would motivate me. You stooping lower and lower is only going to make it harder for me to peacefully dispel you."

Kendra's eyes lit up at Marceline's change in energy. "In that case, I've changed my mind."

"What do you mean?"

"Now that I know you're not as pure as I thought you were, and that my *missteps* in possessing the idiots in this school has decreased my chances of this supposed peace, I want you to do something else for me. I don't want to be stuck here anymore, but I don't want to die either. I don't want to find peace, or whatever you call it, I want to be brought back to life," Kendra declared.

"That's not possible," Marceline countered.

"I've heard it is," Kendra shot back. "And if you're learning how to use your powers the right way, not the pure way, you'll be able to do it for me."

"I don't think—"

Kendra interrupted her again. "Ask your teacher. She'll know," she said before floating back through the door. "Don't forget, October 31st I'm leaving this place one way or another, and either you, or one of your friends, will be my sacrifice," came Kendra's voice, echoing in Marceline's ears.

42

"You can never bring a spirit back," Amina said sternly.

Marceline sat on a pillow opposite Amina and Russel. The candles, a new lavender scent as opposed to the usual unscented candles, stung Marceline's nose. She'd snuck out after midnight on Wednesday, or rather, very early Thursday morning.

"Like, it isn't possible or . . . ," Marceline trailed off, ending her words with a metaphorical question mark.

"Something like that would disrupt the balance of the world," Amina said.

With Amina's back turned, Marceline looked at Russel. "How does it work? From what I've been taught, I thought there were only two ways for a stuck spirit to be freed. One, they find peace. Or two, they find darkness by killing someone to replace their energy in the place where they died."

Sparing a quick glance at Amina, then looking back to Marceline, Russel said quietly, "There is a third way."

"Don't, Rush," Amina warned.

Marceline glared at Amina. Russel argued, "Marceline

ought to learn it from us rather than from the wrong people."

Amina crossed her arms and gave a single grunt, which Marceline took to mean she woefully gave her consent.

Russel continued, "Rumor has it, when you don't die instantaneously, your energy gets split, neither here nor there, which is why we get stuck in this lower dimension. That means those who are dead but stuck still have a hold, a tiny hold, on the dimension of the living. With enough power, a Spirit Walker could grasp that last remaining thread of life and bring someone back to life."

Marceline's eyes widened. "How is that possible? To reverse death?"

"It's not always possible. It has to be a death that was somehow preventable. You can't just put a spirit back in a dead body. You have to completely reverse time and stop whatever killed them from killing them," Russel said.

Amina sighed and all the candles around her shot higher. "All that occurred since the death would be altered. History itself, people, events, some of it will cease to exist or be forever changed," Amina said forcefully.

"So, it is possible," Marceline mumbled. "Kendra was right. She said she didn't want to die, she wanted to live."

"Well, that's not her choice to make. She's already dead, there's no turning back, there's only completing the course of nature," Amina snapped. Since she had returned from her long weekend of dispelling, her eyes were more bloodshot, and Marceline noticed she was significantly more irritable, if that was even possible.

"So, it's not exactly bringing them back to life, it just brings them back in time to the point they died? How much power would need to be generated to do that?" Marceline asked, incredulous.

"A lot," Amina said darkly. "It comes at a cost, as I

mentioned. Another life must be taken to produce enough of a sacrifice to make the transition possible."

"A life for a life," Rush confirmed sadly.

"How is that fair?" Marceline asked. "Why would anyone do that?"

"Three reasons: love, money, and power," Amina replied. "Some may pay a Spirit Walker to save the one they love. It also gives the Spirit Walker greater power, but it's dark power, fueled from the underground."

"What kind of power?" Marceline asked.

"The power you and I already possess, but without the physical toll. It allows those who sacrifice to perform all kinds of spells," Amina explained.

"Like?" Marceline pressed.

Amina's eyes narrowed. "It doesn't matter, because without a sacrifice, you won't have the power to be able to do them, anyway."

"I just want to know what's possible," Marceline said quietly.

"Unless you turn to darkness, nothing is possible." Amina crossed her arms. "Are you willing to turn to darkness?"

Amina's and Russel's stares burned into Marceline's face. She thought of what Kendra had said about being pure versus using dark magic. "Of course not," Marceline replied quickly, feeling her cheeks flush.

"I sense her honesty," Rush vouched.

Amina kept her arms crossed and her head tilted. Marceline sensed that Amina didn't trust her.

"Believe me, I would never," Marceline said. "I'm pure."

Amina's eyebrows raised at the term, but she kept silent. After another prolonged stare, Amina finally nodded. "I know," she said softly.

"So, if we're not going to bring her back to life, what are we going to do about Kendra? She threatened my friends. Her deadline is in two weeks," Marceline said. She felt tears sting her eyes, a mix of her anger and fear. Amina stayed silent, staring down and avoiding Marceline's gaze. "Earth to Amina," Marceline snapped.

Amina wouldn't look up.

"Amina?" Russel asked in a gentle voice.

Amina's lips trembled, then she finally looked up. "I don't know yet, alright?"

"We don't have time. We need a plan, now."

Amina's head fell back down, and Marceline stood. There was no use waiting around if Amina couldn't help her. Russel watched her go.

———

"Anna?" Marceline called on the street she'd seen Anna. She'd hoped saying her name would be enough, but no one in Victorian attire appeared. In a more demanding tone, Marceline said, "Anna, I summon you."

"What do you want, Spirit Walker?" came Anna's voice from behind her.

Anna no longer had her red, glowing eyes. Instead, she had haunted, sad eyes. Everything about her had a grayish-blue tint, and she was slightly see-through. Her feet hovered off the ground.

With Anna's sad, blue eyes glaring at her, Marceline suddenly felt at a loss for words. "I'm sorry about this whole Coffin Race," Marceline stuttered. "It must suck to have a whole town remember your unfortunate fall."

Anna narrowed her eyes. "Every year, everyone in this town gathers, calling my name, dressing like me. Every year, on this day, I am reminded over and over that I am not forgotten, when being forgotten is all I really want." Her voice sounded so desperate it hurt Marceline to listen to it. She wanted to help her.

"I'm working on reversing the curse that holds you here."

"Is that why you seek me, Spirit Walker?"

"Yes," Marceline said, hoping her voice sounded even. She took a step toward Anna, even as she felt herself shake with the coolness radiating from the icy figure. "Is there anything you can tell me about the curse?"

"I'm afraid not," Anna said. She spun to drift away, but Marceline couldn't let her get away without offering any answers.

"Anna, wait. You must know something."

"Nothing worth telling."

Marceline found it odd she didn't elaborate. "So, you do know something, but you just won't tell me?"

Anna's eyes were slowly turning from a blue to a purplish, nearly red hue. She kept her lips pursed.

The desperation made Marceline's voice crack. "I need to break this curse before Halloween's full moon. To save my friends . . . To save myself. I'll do whatever it takes."

"You aren't the first to make such a claim, and I can assure you, you aren't the last to tell me this. I do not need any more false hope from you Spirit Walkers. Stay away from me," Anna said sharply, continuing to drift down the side-street.

Marceline followed her. "Anna, wait. I can do this."

Anna spun faster than Marceline could take another step. Her eyes were fiery red, and she screamed directly into Marceline's eardrums, "Do not follow me."

Marceline held her hands over her ears, closing her eyes. When she looked up, Anna was gone. She sighed, the overwhelming feeling of dread melting over her. What was she going to do?

43

It was a lot more difficult to solve a curse when you were grounded.

The next two weeks, Marceline's dad watched her like a a hawk the moment she got home from school to the moment she retired to bed. Marceline never thought she'd see the day she actually missed working at the Grocery Elf. Although, practically anywhere would be better than the confines of her house, where she was constantly taunted by her kid brothers, forced to make shallow small-talk with her step-mom, and dodging glares from her perpetually angry father.

With no way to leave the house other than to go to school, Marceline had to put all her faith in Amina to break the curse. The upcoming Coffin Races, the day before Halloween, was the only day she'd be allowed outside of the house. The only reason was so she could play the "Anna" in the Coffin Races. She didn't think her dad had the heart to tell the boys they couldn't participate again this year.

Thankfully, the Coffin Races was exactly the place she needed to be. That was going to be the day she'd have to make everything happen. If only she could communicate with Amina before then. But alas, Amina didn't have a phone.

The Friday night before the Coffin Races, Marceline was a bundle of nerves. With the lights off in her room, she tried to sleep, but it wouldn't come with the impending doom of the weekend. What if she couldn't keep her promise to Kendra? What if this weekend was her last in this dimension? Then she'd really have to have faith that Amina could break this curse. If Marceline couldn't handle being locked in her house for two weeks, there was no way she could handle being a ghost stuck in the high school for eternity.

Her exhausted brain was beginning to shut off when the buzzing of her phone startled her wide awake. The vibrating continued, and she frowned. She hardly ever got phone calls. Grabbing her phone, she almost didn't answer. She was tired and feeling dejected, but it was Katy.

"Hey, Kat. I was almost asleep."

"Well, you can sleep later. You're going to want to hear this. I was reading one of those Coffin Race informational flyers, and they tell you the history of Anna."

Marceline sat up. "Anna?"

"Yeah, you know, ghost Anna? Coffin Races Anna?"

"What about her?"

"Well, we've always known her as Anna Thompson, but did you know she was married into that name? Her maiden name was McCormick."

Marceline's eyes widened. "So Anna was a part of one of the founding families of Catori Springs? But I thought she'd only come here to cure her tuberculosis?"

"That's the story we've been told, but I found this thread online. Apparently, there is no record of an Anna Thompson or an Anna McCormick ever checking into any of the tuberculosis treatment centers here in town. We know she died in 1891, and her cause of death was supposedly tuberculosis, but who knows for sure?"

Marceline was silent as she pondered. Joe had told her the town's original families were witches. If Anna had been one of the town's original founding families, that meant there was a high chance she had either been a witch herself or at least some members of her family had been. Perhaps Anna knew more about the town's original curse than she let on. Even still, Anna had refused to talk.

"So, what do you think, Marci? Are you going to try to find Anna?"

"I already did a couple weeks ago," Marceline admitted. "But she wouldn't tell me anything."

Katy clicked her tongue. "That makes me think she's got something to hide. You're going to have to get her to talk. Maybe Anna is the first string we need to pull to solve this whole mystery."

———

Saturday morning, the Lees household was active much earlier than usual. When the sun had barely started to shine through her curtains, Marceline heard her dad hammering away in the driveway, making last-minute repairs to the coffin. Marceline wanted to go back to sleep, but she heard her brothers' footsteps stomping through the hallway and groaned. She wondered how two small boys could sound like a herd of baby elephants walking through the house.

Marceline sleepily came downstairs. Delilah, who looked like she had been awake for some time, was in a sewing frenzy, having been given the task of making Marceline's Anna costume. The costume consisted of a flowing white skirt and a vintage-looking, corset-like red velvet jacket with intricate button embroidery, as was tradition. The boys were eating cereal at the kitchen counter.

"Nice hair," Peter scoffed at the sight of her.

Marceline reached up to touch the curlers she had forgotten Delilah had made her put in the night before. She stuck her tongue out in response.

"We were about to wake you up," Theo said.

"Well, Dad beat you to it. Probably woke the entire neighborhood up too," Marceline muttered on her way to the coffeepot.

Delilah's hand snatched her wrist on the way by. "Marci, can you try this on, please?" Delilah's tone was a mixture of defeat and pleading. Marceline had never seen her so frazzled.

Marceline nodded.

Delilah said, "There's a pair of stockings for you on the counter as well."

Marceline held back her sigh as she gathered the clothes in her arms and clambered back upstairs to change. She ripped the stockings as she pulled them up her legs. Luckily it was the upper thigh, so no one would see. She pulled the skirt up, which would have to be laced in the back, and put the jacket on, which surprisingly fit like a glove.

Back downstairs, Delilah quickly got to work lacing up the back of the skirt. "Everything fits," she cried appreciatively. She started removing Marceline's curlers, spritzing them with hairspray. Normally Marceline would have hated Delilah doing her hair like this, but she was still too half-asleep to protest. "Boys, go put your costumes on. They're in your rooms. Your hats are all down here." The boys did as they were told, scrambling as they tried to race one another up. Delilah put her finger on a paper she had on the table, tracing the words on the page. "We just have to give you the traditional rosy cheeks and red lips, put your hat on, and you're good to go."

Somehow, the five of them managed to get out of the house in their costumes; Marceline as Anna, and the boys, Dad, and Delilah dressed in the classic tuxedo with matching top hats. It was drizzling and foggy that morning, which of course was not ideal on a day when half the town was going to be outside. All the main roads were blocked off on Race Day, so they walked into town, carrying their decorated coffin, despite the fact it had wheels on the bottom. Dad didn't want the wheels getting "worn out" before race time.

Marceline saw several more Annas on the way, who shot her icy glares. Normally a friendly place, the Catori towns-people became competitive beasts on Coffin Race Day.

"Alright, Lees," Dad said, out of breath from taking on the brunt of the coffin-carrying. "Remember, place in all categories. Marci is a shoo-in for best Anna. Our coffin is one of the best, if not the best, coffin out here. The race itself, just focus and run. We're going to have Delilah and me in the back. Boys, you're pushing the front. Marci, try to be as light as possible inside the coffin."

Marceline rolled her eyes while the boys laughed. "Yeah, Marci, you might make us lose if you don't lighten up," Peter taunted.

Up ahead, Marceline saw Katy waving at her. Katy put her camera to her eye and snapped a picture of them walking down the street. She jogged to meet them. "Beautiful costumes, Lees family," Katy chimed. "Mind if I use your picture in the school newspaper?"

"How about you use the pictures of us winning first place in all categories as your newspaper picture?" Dad asked.

Katy laughed. "I'll be posed by the winner's podium." Leaning into Marceline, she whispered, "Bijou's here with her family. She's also an Anna."

Marceline's eyes widened, and she nearly dropped her

grasp on the coffin. "We have to talk to her."

"I already did, a bit. She wants to see you," Katy breathed.

As they got to the main street, Marceline took her hands off the coffin to grab her pulsing head. "Marci!" Theo complained. She projected her light shield in front of her, taking a deep breath. She had to be careful with her mind shields. Marceline wasn't to the point of being a seasoned Spirit Walker who could keep up a shield without intense concentration. She still had to focus on the projection part of it.

"You okay?" Katy asked.

Marceline nodded, putting her hands back on the coffin to lift it up. Finally, they were close enough to the start line to set the coffin down. "Let's go find Bijou," she said to Katy, then to her family, she called, "I'll be right back!"

Dad raised his eyebrows.

"It's for the newspaper," Katy assured him.

He didn't look convinced, but he waved a hand. "Hurry back!" Dad shouted after them. Marceline could hear him begin to lead the rest of them through a pre-race warmup, which she was glad she wasn't a part of.

Katy took her hand and led her down the street. "I figured you needed an excuse to get away and find Anna."

Marceline nodded appreciatively. "After we talk to Bijou."

Outside of Moon Opal stood Bijou in a nearly identical attire to Marceline's.

"Hey, Anna, I like your outfit," Marceline called.

Bijou turned, then broke into a wide grin. "Thanks, Anna. I like yours too." She ran to Marceline and threw an arm around her.

Marceline suddenly felt eyes burning into her. She turned to see Bijou's parents shooting daggers at her. "Speaking of Anna. Bijou, do you know anything about her? You know, the real Anna?"

Bijou turned nervously toward her parents, then back to them. "I know the same story as you both do."

Marceline narrowed her eyes. "I think you know more."

Bijou bit her lip, ducking her head and turning slightly. *They're listening*, she mouthed. Marceline crinkled her brow, seeing Katy do the same. *Magic*, Bijou mouthed as an explanation.

Marceline nodded.

Straightening, Bijou continued in a strained voice, "All I know is that shortly after Anna was married, she died of *tuberculosis*, and she was buried the near the top of that peak until, well, you know the story of the coffin sliding down. If I were curious to know more, I might make my way toward the hills."

Marceline caught the rise in Bijou's tone at the mention of tuberculosis. "Right. Well, thanks for the history, B." Marceline turned to look the Eyotas in the eye. In the past, she would've never been so bold, but her anger was raging. "I wonder if Anna has anything to do with that curse I told you about." Mrs. Eyota looked as though she could strangle her. Marceline smiled and turned back to Bijou. "Anyway, good luck in the races."

Katy leaned closer to Marceline as they headed back. "What was all that about?"

"Bijou's parents must have been doing some sort of enhanced hearing spell to pick up our conversation. It sounded like there was more to it than what she could say with them listening."

"At least Bijou kind of confirmed what we suspected. There's definitely something fishy going on with Anna."

"I guess I'll look for the ghost," Marceline said, sighing.

Katy shook her head. "I don't envy you. Meet up after you talk to her? I'll be by the finish line."

"I'll find you later," Marceline promised.

"Don't forget, your race starts in about fifteen minutes."

44

Marceline walked quickly toward the base of the mountain where Anna's coffin had once fallen. She passed the bench where she'd seen Anna before and noticed it start to get colder. By the time she was beside the bench, she could see her breath.

Looking up, she saw a blurry figure walking toward her, wearing the same hat, red jacket, and white skirt combo. Another Anna. Blinking, Marceline held her breath as she realized this wasn't just any Anna.

"Anna?" she asked.

The real Anna looked right past her, floating by her.

Marceline wondered if she had heard her. "Anna," she called again.

This time, Anna let out a long sigh. "What do you want?" her voice echoed around Marceline, filling her ears with that terrifying whispering sound.

"Why didn't you tell me you were a McCormick?"

Anna stiffened, turning her neck to the side while her body remained opposite from Marceline.

"Because I'm a Thompson."

"But you were a McCormick. And you came from a family of witches. Maybe you were even a witch yourself."

"So what if I was?"

"You have to know how to break this curse, or at least about its origin."

"Its origin." Anna let out a screech that Marceline wasn't sure if it was intended to be a laugh. Anna's eyes focused on her. "I was the sacrifice who made it possible."

Marceline's blood ran cold. "The sacrifice?"

"Death by tuberculosis is the lie that has been passed down for over a century. The truth would be far too tragic. It's true, I did return to Catori Springs in 1889 with my husband, James, but it wasn't to cure my tuberculosis. It was at my family's request."

"What happened?" Marceline asked gently.

Anna's lips quivered. "I was only nineteen, you know? I had just gotten married. Mere days following the ceremony, I woke with a gag around my mouth and my arms being bound. They carried me up the mountain, and I knew I wouldn't make it down, not alive, at least," Anna said bitterly.

Anna had only been two years older than Marceline was now. It made her shiver to think of her own life ending so young. She stayed quiet, seeing Anna ready herself to continue.

"They took me to a stream up in the trees. Each of the covens were there, apart from my own. The only person of my blood who was there was my uncle. The other covens needed two Spirit Walkers to complete their plan. Myself, as the sacrifice, and my uncle, as the spell caster. Together, the leader of each coven, sacrificial, celestial, and natural, created the curse which you speak of that traps us all here."

So the McCormicks were Spirit Walkers. "But why would they do that?" Marceline asked.

"My uncle did what he did because he thought it would help unite the covens. Little did he know, he and the rest of my family would soon be forced out of our home. As for the other covens, once they realized the trapped, dead souls enhanced their powers, they wanted everyone to be stuck here, to make this place a magical vortex. Over the years, the energy has only continued to build as more souls have continued to be trapped here, with no chance of peace."

"Why did they need you as a sacrifice? A Spirit Walker?"

"A sacrifice of someone magical was the only way to produce enough energy needed for the spell. For those of us with sacrificial magic, even after we pass, our bodies take in the energy of our sacrifice. My uncle was able to absorb the energy from the sacrifice and from my body and merge his power with two others from the other covens."

Marceline suddenly felt as though there were cotton balls lining her throat, filling her ears. She could hardly breathe or hear. A magical sacrifice was needed? The chills on Marceline's arms weren't just from Anna's presence anymore.

Anna turned away. "All I know is I woke up as my body was being buried in a coffin they'd already brought up there for me. Maybe I was unconscious, or maybe the memory of my death has been erased from my mind, but either way, I am glad. That is not a moment I want to relive."

"The rest of your family, your husband . . . did they know what was going to happen?"

"No. At least, based on their reactions, I don't believe they did. The only perk of dying as a sacrifice or as a Spirit Walker, I'm not sure, is that I was never confined to the place I died. At least I have an entire town to roam."

"I'm so sorry that happened to you. And about your coffin falling . . ."

Anna smiled bitterly. "It was my doing, I suppose. My

husband knew my horror of cemeteries, formalities, and anything low or gloomy, even death. He knew if I died, I'd want to be carried high to sunshine and pure air. Of course, Mother Nature had other plans for my body. My coffin was washed down only thirty years later. And now, as a painful reminder, I am forced to watch the townspeople mock me year after year." Anna took a sharp inhale. "I just want to be gone from this place for good. Forgotten, as I should be."

Although part of Marceline didn't want to know this answer, fearing it might be in the creation, she had to ask. "How can I send you and everyone else trapped here to peace? How do I break this curse?"

Anna spun her back to Marceline. "It won't happen, I can assure you."

"Surely it can be broken," Marceline prodded.

The surrounding air grew even cooler as a gust of wind blew from Anna's blue form. "It can," she admitted quietly. "But it would require something I know to be impossible in this town."

"What is that?"

"Cooperation," Anna replied with a dark grin. "All three magics worked together to establish this curse, now all three magics need to work together to end this curse."

"It's time to break this curse," Marceline said fiercely. "I can convince the other covens."

Anna turned her head. "Even if breaking the curse comes at the cost of another life of a Spirit Walker?"

45

Marceline tried to swallow the lump in her throat as she made her way back to the races. Her heart felt heavy. She still wasn't sure how she was going to deal with Kendra. One of the main reasons she needed to break this curse and dispel Kendra was to prevent more deaths. Now, no matter what, a life must be lost.

Seeing her family waiting for her near the starting line, she took a deep breath, trying to remind herself to be present, to enjoy this tradition with her family, even when her mind was racing in a whole other dimension, quite literally.

Dad scolded her for being late, and she mumbled an apology. He pulled back the lid of the coffin, holding a hand out to help her in. Marceline hesitated. Getting into this coffin dressed like Anna, after speaking to the real Anna, felt strange and sickening. The side of the coffin said *RIP Anna Thompson* in red letters.

"Marci, hurry up, we need to get on the starting line!" Peter snapped.

Marceline clambered in, situating her legs straight in front of her and trying not to panic.

Her family wheeled her to the starting line.

"Those first place medals have got our names on them," Dad said. The rest of the family let out cheers. Marceline tried to smile.

The gunshot signaling the start of the race nearly made Marceline faint. The coffin started rolling, though only a few steps in, she heard a grunt and a smack against the pavement. She turned. Theo was down, holding his skinned knee. His shoelace was untied.

"Come on, Theo," Dad shouted.

Theo thrust his chin forward, blinking back tears, and returned to his spot at the coffin, continuing to push.

They were the last coffin over the finish line, but Dad assured them all there were other categories they could potentially win, like best Anna costume and best coffin decoration.

As soon as Marceline heaved herself out of the coffin, Bijou raced up to her, holding her skirt as she ran. Bijou's hat rammed into Marceline's chest and flipping off the back of her head. Bending down to pick it up, Bijou said, "I've got to talk to you."

Marceline could sense the urgency. Dad and Delilah were busy attending to Theo's injury, so she took Bijou's arm and led her through the crowd.

Once they had separated themselves as much as they could in a crowd, Bijou asked, "Did you hear what happened at the school last night?"

Marceline felt the blood drain from her face. "What?"

"A janitor fell down the stairs last night."

The possibilities danced in Marceline's head. "Is he . . . Did he . . ."

"He's alive, thank goodness. He got hurt pretty bad though, broke a few bones and smashed his head," Bijou said.

Marceline could hardly hear anything through the ringing in her ears. Kendra had broken her promise. She must have tried to kill someone else. The full moon wasn't until tonight. Kendra hadn't even given her the opportunity to turn herself in like they'd agreed. Marceline wanted to go right now, but the curse had yet to be broken. She was powerless.

Marceline gripped Bijou's arms tightly. "Bijou, we need to break this curse. Today."

Bijou shook her head. "As far as I know, no one knows how."

"I know how," Marceline said strongly. "And I'm pretty sure the coven leaders know too, but they don't want to do anything about it. They don't want to lose the power here in Catori caused by the abundance of trapped souls."

Bijou shook her head firmly. "My parents wouldn't intentionally keep spirits trapped here."

Marceline squeezed her shoulders. "Ask them about it. We need someone from each magical coven to perform a ritual to break the curse. Maybe you can get them on our side." She left out the part about the sacrifice as her mind filled in the details. She couldn't allow any other soul to be lost due to this curse. If it was her seeking to end this curse, it was her blood on the line, and no one else's.

"Marci, when I asked my parents about the curse, all they told me it was that it was Anna who was the sacrifice. Does that mean someone else will have to die to break this?"

Marceline looked down. "I think so."

Bijou's mouth opened and closed several times as she processed. "A magical sacrifice?" she asked in a small voice.

"Yes," Marceline replied meekly, still unable to look up.

Bijou sighed. "The covens won't help you. Especially if they know a sacrifice is involved."

"Maybe if we can get enough witches to band together, and

with the full moon tonight, enough power can be generated to avoid that." Marceline didn't know if Bijou believed her or not. Marceline certainly didn't believe herself, but Bijou held her stare.

"I'll try to convince them to help."

Marceline left Bijou in the crowd, feeling herself reeling, falling down a mind spiral. She chewed her lip as she walked, not paying attention to her surroundings. *Get it together.* There were tears in her eyes. She was on the verge of panicking.

Her blurry vision came into focus for only half a second before she connected with a solid torso. Looking up, she saw Tag's familiar sideways grin. His arms instinctively supported her. "Excuse me, Anna, I'm looking for my girlfriend. Have you seen her?"

"Not since your girlfriend was laced up in this costume this morning." Marceline hoped Tag wouldn't pick up on the shakiness of her breath.

Tag frowned at the sound of her voice and her watery eyes. "Hey, you okay?"

Marceline couldn't help but crumple when someone asked her that question when she most definitely wasn't feeling okay. Tag pulled her into his chest, and she felt her knees buckle, but his arms supported her. As much as she wanted to be strong, to pull away and try to be the brave hero of this story, storming in, guns blazing, and take care of Kendra herself, she was scared. She melted into the comforting arms of Tag. "I'm okay," she said unconvincingly. She couldn't fall apart, not now. Marceline stood, straightening herself and pulling her velvet jacket more firmly around her.

"What is it?" Tag asked gently.

"It's nothing," she said, trying to look anywhere but his face.

Tag frowned. "Marceline, you can tell me." When she said nothing, he sighed with frustration. "I've given you space, but at a certain point, you can't keep leaving me in the dark. I'm your boyfriend. I'm here to support you. Why do you always push me away when you're struggling?"

He was right. But now wasn't the time to tell him everything. She blinked back tears. "I'm sorry, Tag."

Tag took a step away, annoyance replacing his concern. "Don't do that. Don't make me have to comfort you when you're the one who won't tell me the problem."

"I'm not making you do anything," Marceline said. It hurt her to think of him comforting her out of obligation rather than want.

Tag almost took a step forward at her pained expression, but Marceline could see him pull himself back. "I can't help you if you don't let me in."

"I know," she whispered.

"How can I be in a relationship with someone who doesn't trust me with their problems?" Tag asked in a choked voice.

The hurt in Tag's voice was like a punch to her gut. She was hurting him when she only wanted to protect him. Marceline tried to swallow, but her throat felt like a fist was lodged in it. "I do trust you, Tag."

Tag put his hands in his pockets and let out a breath that appeared in a cloud around his mouth. "It doesn't seem like it."

She flinched at the sound of the commentator roaring over the intercom that the winners were about to be announced.

"You should probably find your family," Tag said. "Good luck, Marceline."

Marceline turned away. He didn't know how much she'd need that luck. She took a step, but she hesitated. This couldn't be how they ended their last conversation, and there was a very real chance it could be her final words to him.

Spinning back around, Marceline said, "I don't deserve you. Thank you. For everything, Tag."

46

Marceline didn't know what she'd find at the school, and that frightened her more than she wanted to admit. *Be brave*, Marceline reminded herself. *Be the hero.*

Even though she was grounded and technically not allowed to leave the races, and even though she had no idea what she was walking into, this was more important. She had to convince Kendra not to take another life. With the full moon and Halloween tomorrow, which would release Kendra along with all the other spirits to leave the locations they were bound to, Marceline knew they would have to break this curse tonight. Of course, that only worked if Kendra didn't kill someone before then.

She walked as quickly as she could in the high-heeled boots Delilah had lent her that pinched her toes. The pain almost made her mind sharper, more focused on the task at hand rather than her own fear. The more she walked, her boots tapping rhythmically on the sidewalk, the more her confidence grew. Her confidence, she realized, was fueled by an anger she hadn't allowed herself to feel until now.

Marceline burst through the front doors of the school, surprised to find them unlocked. Maybe no one had remembered to lock them after the janitor had been evacuated.

She called Kendra's name in the front hallway. She knew Kendra could easily float through the floors to meet her, but she was nowhere to be seen. In her ears, Marceline could hear Kendra's laughter, like she was wearing headphones on full volume. "Kendra!" Marceline shouted again.

She ran up the stairs two at a time to the third floor. The windows that normally streamed in light over the staircase were darkened by the clouds outside. Marceline wasn't out of breath at the top of the stairs like she normally would be. Her energy tank was being fueled by a static rage.

Kendra was waiting for her at the top of the stairs, arms crossed.

"How could you?" Marceline spat.

Kendra's eyes narrowed. "Well, it's nice to see you too, Marci."

"Cut the crap, Kendra. Why did you try to take the janitor's life? I told you I was going to help you find peace, and maybe even help bring you back to life. Why would you do this?"

"Believe it or not," Kendra said, floating in a small circle around Marceline, "I didn't try to kill him. It really was an accident."

"Please," Marceline scoffed. "You expect me to believe that?"

Kendra paused her circles to put her hands on her hips in front of Marceline. "I don't appreciate your accusation. Why would I lie about this? If I had managed to successfully possess and nearly kill someone not on a full moon, when I'm not at my strongest, I would be *bragging*, not trying to act all innocent. I didn't do anything; it really was an accident."

Marceline crossed her arms. "I don't believe you."

Kendra laughed, the sound piercing Marceline's ear drums. "Fine, don't believe me. He didn't even die here, so it doesn't matter. I'm still going to be stuck here. Not for long, though." Kendra's eyes flashed as lightning struck outside. Marceline could hear the raindrops starting to drum against the window-panes. "I'll be alive again soon, right?"

"If you think I'm sacrificing another to bring you back to life, you're crazier than I thought you were."

Kendra's entire body quivered as her tint grew red. "We had a deal."

"We had a deal that I would send you to peace. I never agreed to bring you back to life."

"Well, have you broken the curse yet?" When Marceline didn't respond, Kendra continued, "In case you forgot, your deadline is quickly approaching, and something about your nervous, twitchy movements is telling me you still have no idea how to break it or how to satisfy your promise to me."

"I have a plan."

"Really? A plan? What a vague answer."

"No, really, Kendra. I'm gathering witches as we speak to perform a ritual that will break it."

Kendra laughed again in her high pitch that made Marceline wish she could stick duct tape over her mouth. "I never really had faith in you, Marci. I knew you would never be able to break the curse. But since you made that promise, well, at least I'll have you to sacrifice."

Marceline kept her mouth stuck in a firm line, even as Kendra floated closer, sending chills up her arms.

"Did you know I don't even need to fully possess someone to kill them? All I have to do is enter someone's brain, fry their blood vessels, and zap, just like that. I thought it would be poetic to have my victim die in the same way I did, but I'll give you the choice, Marci. Which would you rather do?"

Marceline clenched her fists. "I—"

"Marci?" came a voice from down the stairs. Marceline and Kendra made quick eye contact. It was Katy's voice. Marceline felt the blood drain from her face.

"We've got a friend," Kendra chimed.

"No," Marceline said. Without thinking, she reached out to grab Kendra's arm to stop her. To her surprise, Marceline made contact with Kendra's cold wrist.

Kendra's eyes widened at the touch. "You are learning your powers," Kendra said, smiling appreciatively.

Marceline didn't know how it was possible for her to be holding onto Kendra without verbalizing the spell, but she held firm.

"Marci?" Katy called again from down the stairs.

"Go, Kat, I'm fine. Leave!" she shouted, unsure if Katy could hear her or if her voice was also in the lower dimension. Marceline felt blood start to fall from her nose again, dripping onto the tile floor. She couldn't hold on for much longer.

"You know," Kendra said with a smirk, "now that I mention it, Halloween is only a day away. Maybe I'm feeling stronger than I thought." Marceline's hand fell through Kendra's once-solid wrist, connecting with air.

"Katy!" Marceline screamed as Kendra slowly began to drop herself through the floor. Marceline rushed down the stairs, sprinting as fast as she could.

As Marceline jumped down the last steps, she turned to see Kendra, head tilted and a thin smile on her face, floating behind Katy. Katy couldn't see the ghost in her shadow, and she smiled with an unknowing ignorance and sighed with relief.

"Marci," Katy said as she started to jog to her.

Kendra and Marceline made tense eye contact.

"Maybe I don't have to wait for you to fail. Maybe my next

victim is right in front of me," Kendra said, the words only audible to Marceline.

"No!" Marceline shouted.

Marceline and Kendra took off toward Katy, who looked confused by Marceline's reaction. Moments before Kendra's outstretched hand reached Katy, Marceline grabbed Katy and projected a glowing, white energy shield around them. It was the strongest Marceline had felt. The energy radiating from her made her skin tingle. Katy's wide eyes made her think even Katy felt it. The force of the shield shot Kendra down the hallway until not even Marceline could see her. Marceline knew Kendra was still there, watching, even if her shield made the ghost invisible.

Marceline's nose instantly gushed, and her vision went blurry. Katy grabbed her arms to steady her. "Was that Kendra?"

Marceline nodded, wiping her nose. "We need to get out of here."

They reached the doors of the school, but before they left, Marceline called back into the hallway, "I'm going to dispel you, Kendra, if it's the last thing I do."

"Tick-tock," was Kendra's response, echoing down the hall.

47

O utside, the heavy, cold raindrops thudded against Marceline's skin, soaking through her Anna costume in moments.

"What were you doing going in there alone? Are you crazy?" Katy scolded loudly over the storm.

Rather than respond, Marceline threw her arms around her friend. She'd been so close to losing her. Katy's head fit perfectly under Marceline's chin, and Marceline leaned down, pressing her cheek against her hair. After a moment, she pulled back and turned quickly to not let Katy see it was hard for her to swallow the unexpected lump in her throat.

"Hey," Katy said, her voice softening. "Are you okay? What happened in there?"

"Nothing," Marceline said, fixing the hairs on Katy's head she'd knocked out of place. "I just told her I have a plan to break the curse. But we're going to have to hurry. Kendra's not going to give me another extension. How did you know where to find me, anyway?"

"Well, I was looking for you to take a picture of you for Best

Anna Costume, which you won, by the way, and I found Bijou instead. She told me what she'd told you about the janitor, and I knew where you'd gone."

"Speaking of, have you heard anything about that janitor?"

"I looked into it. As far as I know, he's still recovering in the hospital. There haven't been any news updates since this morning."

Marceline bit her lip and ran her hand up and down her velvet jacket. "Kendra says it was an accident."

"Do you believe that?"

"I'm not sure. But either way, she's not happy, and I need to figure this out tonight. I need to find Amina."

"We," Katy said firmly. Marceline shot her a questioning look, and Katy took her hand. "*We* will figure this out. *We* will find Amina. You're not doing anything alone anymore."

Marceline smiled, squeezing Katy's hand. "I love you, you know?"

Katy winked. "You'd better."

———

Marceline could immediately sense Amina was not home, as the shield around the property wasn't up.

Katy hesitated as they took the dirt path past their usual cut off for the treehouse. Marceline realized Katy hadn't returned to the McCormick Estate, apart from the treehouse on the lot, since the tarot readings.

As they neared the stone building, which looked more ominous surrounded by gray storm clouds, Katy hooked her arm through Marceline's. "This place still gives me the creeps."

Marceline thought it best not to tell her about the large spirit population on the lot. "Amina's not here. How about you wait in the treehouse so you're not out in the rain while I go inside?"

Katy glared at her. "I just made that entire speech about you not being alone, Marci."

"I won't be alone."

It took a moment for Katy to register what this meant, then she winced.

"It would probably be weird for you to watch me have a conversation with someone you can't see or hear," Marceline said.

Katy tried to manage her horrified expression. "Who exactly will you be speaking with?"

"His name's Russel. He's a friend." As she said his name, Marceline saw Russel appear on the porch, smiling even as raindrops hammered through him. "I'll come find you after."

Katy climbed the ladder to the treehouse, probably faster than she normally would, as Marceline crossed the weeds to reach Russel.

"Why, hello, Marceline. Or shall I say, Anna?" Russel said, gesturing at her costume.

Marceline smiled back weakly, but couldn't hold her cheeks up for long. Russel's smile instantly faded. They continued in silence the rest of the way into the house.

Inside, Russel sat on the couch while she stood by the door.

"Would you happen to know where Amina is?" she asked.

"She's out on a trip. Said it was an emergency."

Marceline swore loudly and began to pace. Of course Amina wasn't here. Why would she be here when Marceline needed her most?

"What's going on?" Russel asked.

Marceline explained how they needed to break the curse today. Then she paused, looking up and feeling Russel's calming presence. She knew she could trust him.

"And there's something else. I wasn't completely honest when I told you about my promise to Kendra." Marceline took another deep breath. Without concentrating on her inhales and exhales, Marceline wasn't sure she could trust her chest to keep filling her lungs. "I didn't just promise Kendra that I would help her find peace. I promised that if I didn't, she could use me as a sacrifice instead." Saying the words for the first time made it feel real. Marceline felt light-headed, like her breath had been stolen.

Russel rose from sitting and floated around the room. "Marceline," he muttered under his breath. "This is not good."

Marceline had tears in her eyes. "I couldn't let Kendra take the life of my friend, or anyone else, for that matter. And yet here we are again, needing to lose another life just to break this stupid curse."

Russel nodded solemnly. "It's a vicious cycle, isn't it?"

"That's why I need to find Amina to serve as the sacrificial witch in the ritual, to end this once and for all. Do you have any idea where I can look for her or how I can reach her?"

Russel narrowed his eyes at her. "Wait a moment. In theory, you don't need Amina for this at all. You could be the sacrificial witch that is needed."

Marceline couldn't look him in the eye. She stared at her feet. Somehow, he knew what she was planning.

"Marceline," he drawled. "You aren't thinking of volunteering yourself as the sacrifice in this ritual, are you?"

She felt the tears in her eyes again as she avoided his gaze. If there needed to be a sacrifice, Marceline wouldn't allow anyone else to lose a life besides herself.

"That's . . . what I thought," Russel said in a small voice.

She hoped he wouldn't try to talk her out of it. "It has to be a sacrificial witch who is the sacrifice. It's not that I have a death wish," Marceline choked. "I don't. But it's only fair. I promised myself to Kendra in the first place. At least my sacrifice in this ritual would serve a far greater purpose. It would be the means to send so many others to peace."

"That doesn't make it fair. You don't have to do this, Marci."

"I'm hoping the full moon tonight will generate some extra power for us tonight. But I will if it comes to it."

Russel's hue had turned an even darker shade of blue, almost black. He looked sad.

Marceline couldn't stand to look at him anymore. It would only bring her to tears. She wiped her nose. "So, how do I find Amina?"

"I suppose a locator spell could work. It's not in your wheelhouse by yourself, because it requires multiple sources of magic, so you'll need another witch to perform the spell with you." Russel's voice sounded hollow.

"So, I need another witch."

"Yes, but the covens won't exactly welcome you with open arms. In their eyes, you use dark magic, even if you don't sacrifice life forms other than yourself. Be careful when you approach them."

"I will," she said.

"Marci, wait," Russel said. She turned to face him. "If it comes to that, it'll be quick. Dying, I mean. The final action of your soul leaving your body is not painful."

Her throat was suddenly burning at his words intended to be comforting.

"You're a very good person, Marceline. I do hope that you can find another way."

She turned her back, so he wouldn't see her quivering mouth. "Thank you, Russel."

"Be well," he said.

48

The rain had stopped by the time Marceline made her way to meet Katy in the treehouse, but she was shivering in the cool, post-rain chill.

Marceline could have cried with relief as she remembered she and Katy had stored extra clothes in the treehouse. She was ready to be out of this dripping wet Victorian costume.

Up the ladder, she could see Katy had had the same idea, having changed into dry clothes. She had Marceline's pile ready for her.

"As great as you look in that sopping wet velvet jacket, I thought you might like some dry, modern-day clothes."

"Thanks," Marceline said. "You read my mind."

Marceline took her phone out of her pocket, seeing a long scroll of texts and calls from her dad and a few from Tag. She sighed but decided to at least send a quick text letting her dad know she was safe, but that she was doing something important. Dad responded immediately, confirming she was going to be in big trouble when she got home. But, in fact, Marceline wasn't sure she'd return home to receive her punishment at all. Holding back tears, she responded, *I'm sorry. I love you, Dad.*

Her thumbs hesitated over the texts from Tag. What would she say to him? What could she?

She didn't have time to think about her potential demise. As Marceline changed into a different jacket and some jeans, she explained to Katy about the locator spell.

"Can't you just have Bijou help you do the spell?" Katy asked.

"I don't think so. She's not a fully Realized witch yet. I'm guessing I'll need someone with more power."

"Maybe her mom . . ." Katy didn't finish her sentence as Marceline shot her a look that said, *In your dreams.*

Katy crossed her arms over her chest. "You never know. Bijou could have convinced her to help."

"No way. That woman despises me."

"You know, Marci, you once said there was no way magic and the supernatural existed. Never say never."

———

Marceline took a deep breath before pushing open the door to Moon Opal. The familiar, vague scent of grass, dirt, and flowers floated through the air. Once again, no one was at the counter to greet them.

"What's that smell?" Katy asked with a crinkled nose.

Distantly, Marceline heard voices coming from the back of the store. She held a finger to her lips to signal Katy's silence as she tip-toed toward the beaded curtain.

"Why didn't you tell me?" came Bijou's voice. It was the loudest Marceline had ever heard Bijou speak. She sounded upset. Marceline and Katy exchanged concerned looks.

"Because it didn't concern you. It still doesn't. You're not even a witch yet!" Mrs. Eyota shouted.

"How does it not concern me? It concerns everyone in Catori! What about Nana and Papa? Are their souls trapped here too?"

"No, they passed over. We don't allow our own to die within the Catori Springs border, if we can help it," Mr. Eyota replied in a deep voice. "But if they do, their spirit only serves to strengthen their descendants in Catori for years to come."

"At the cost of them never finding peace," Bijou cried. "I can't believe you're all okay with this. We need to break this curse."

"The curse has only been strengthened by time, Bijou. Even if we tried to break it now, it would require an unimaginable amount of power."

"We have a lot of witches, and it's the full moon tonight. Is that not enough?"

"A sacrifice is required, my dear."

Katy's eyes immediately shot to Marceline questioningly. Marceline couldn't return her gaze.

The beaded curtain swished and clacked as Bijou came barreling through it, wiping tears from her cheeks. She didn't see Marceline and Katy until she nearly ran into them.

Bijou quickly took each of their hands and guided them outside.

"Are you okay, B?" Katy asked gently.

Bijou shook her head. "I'm sorry, Marci. I tried. They won't help. I had no idea they were keeping this from me."

"It's okay," Marceline said, trying to keep the panic from her voice. "We'll just need to find others who can help us break the curse. We can't be the only ones in town who think it's wrong, right?"

Bijou nodded. "I think I know someone from the natural

292

coven who will help us. You guys know Brennan from school? He was homeschooled like me, and this was his first year too."

Marceline vaguely remembered a guy named Brennan who sat in the back of her biology class, and she nodded. "Are you saying this Brennan guy is a natural witch?"

"That's exactly what I'm saying," Bijou said. "He's in your grade, and he became fully Realized only a couple months before you, Marci, but he's been studying magic for many years."

"Sorry to get off topic here, but Bijou," Katy said, lowering her chin, fluttering her eyelashes, and smiling. "Why do your cheeks get so pink whenever you say Brennan's name?"

Marceline hadn't realized until then, but now Bijou's cheeks were noticeably flushed.

"No reason," Bijou said quickly, putting her hands to her cheeks.

Katy giggled, then put her serious face back on. "Is Brennan going to be powerful enough to help break this curse if he's so new?"

"New witches actually have a lot of power, sometimes more than older witches. It's only a matter of directing that energy. Young witches usually don't have the skill or focus to cast as powerful spells as more experienced witches," Bijou explained to Katy then turned to Marceline. "If Brennan knows the spell, he'll be able to concentrate enough to do it, I know he can. He's more disciplined and stronger than other young witches."

"Brennan it is then," Marceline said. Not like they had any other options. "But what are we going to do about the celestial witch?"

Bijou's eyebrows knit together thoughtfully, then she said, "Tonight, for the full moon, the celestial coven will gather in the town center to perform their monthly power-generating ritual. I usually attend to watch my mom. We can try to find someone there."

"We *will* find someone there. We have to," Marceline said.

"The only problem is, even if we do find a celestial witch willing to help us, we still don't know the counter-curse spell," Bijou said.

"I think I know someone who does," Marceline said. When her friends looked up, Marceline quickly explained, "Amina. She's been trying to solve this case for weeks. I'm sure she's at least found something out. I need your help, though, B. I need to do a locator spell to get to her."

Anna had agreed to provide the counter-curse spell if Marceline provided the witches, but Marceline didn't want to explain the true reason why she needed Amina, a sacrificial witch, there. Amina would be the one doing the spell, and Marceline would be the sacrifice, if need be.

Bijou chewed her lip. "So you need a witch like right now."

"I guess that means we're going to have to call *Brennan*," Katy said brightly. "Bijou, I'm sure you have his number?"

Bijou blushed again. "Yeah, I guess we should call him." She pulled out her phone, and Katy snatched her wrist.

"Is that a picture of him saved with his contact? How adorable!" Katy squealed.

"He set that, not me," Bijou muttered.

"Oh, he did? How is this the first we're hearing of this? Bijou has a boyfriend," Katy sang.

Bijou was the color of beet juice. "No, I don't," she insisted.

Marceline put an arm around Bijou. "You should've seen Kat when I first told her I was partnered to do a class project with Tag." Marceline's stomach flipped, thinking of all the people she'd never see again if the sacrifice were to happen. Tag. Her family. She shook her head. She couldn't allow herself to think of this now.

Bijou cracked a smile before dialing Brennan's number. Katy reached over and pressed the speaker phone button. Before Bijou could protest, a voice said, "Hey, Bijou."

"Brennan," Bijou replied in a shaky voice, unable to make eye contact with either of them. "I'm here with Marci. We need your help."

"Spirit Walker Marci?" Brennan asked.

"Come on, Brennan, how many other Marcis are there in Catori Springs?" Katy blurted as if she couldn't help herself, then she said, "And hi, by the way, this is Katy."

Brennan laughed. "I guess you're right, Katy. What do you girls need?"

"A locator spell," Marceline answered. "And more, but we'll explain later."

"Can you meet us at the McCormick Estate?" Bijou asked.

Brennan didn't miss a beat. "Sure. I'll be there in ten."

49

Moments after Marceline, Katy, and Bijou had crossed over the front gates of the McCormick Estate, the sound of footsteps made each girl turn around.

"Bijou Eyota, I didn't class you as a trespasser," Brennan teased. He came toward them with his hands in his pockets and long, dark, nearly black hair in his eyes. His tall, lanky form towered over Bijou's as he stopped before them. "I mean, I can expect this sort of thing from feisty Katy and her best friend, Marci, but Bijou?"

"Don't let her cute, rosy-cheeked, button nose appearance deceive you. Bijou's a real badass," Katy said, winking.

Bijou looked as though she wanted to crawl into a hole.

Brennan laughed and looked toward Bijou warmly. "I would never underestimate her."

Bijou and Brennan locked eyes for a prolonged moment.

"Before you make me vomit with all this cuteness, I think you have a spell you need to help Marci with," Katy said.

"Right," Brennan said, pulling his gaze away from Bijou. "Who do we need to find?"

Out of the corner of her eye, Marceline saw Russel watching them from just outside the stone mansion. "Her name's Amina," Marceline answered. "She's another Spirit Walker, like me."

"Can I get any other details?" Brennan pressed. "I've never met or seen her, so it's difficult for me to channel her without knowing anything about her."

Marceline struggled to think of other details she knew about Amina. She realized she didn't even know her last name.

"She's about my height," Bijou said. "She's Japanese, with short, black hair peppered with silver."

"Maybe late-fifties," Katy offered.

"She's actually only thirty-eight," Marceline said quietly. "And she eats peanut butter and jelly sandwiches almost exclusively. She's kind of rough around the edges, but she's a deeply caring person once you get to know her."

Brennan nodded and rubbed his hands together. "Okay, an old-looking, middle-aged Japanese woman who eats a lot of PB&Js." He turned to Marceline. "I think we can find her if we work together."

"I don't know the spell," Marceline said, feeling embarrassed.

"It's okay," Brennan said gently. "You can repeat after me."

Marceline didn't even want to bother asking how this was going to work. She just nodded. "I'm ready."

Brennan clasped Marceline's hands and closed his eyes; Marceline followed suit. Together, they spoke in a language Marceline was slowly starting to pick up from her spell book and from hearing Amina speak it.

In the middle of Marceline's vision, the blackness of her eyelids became like a movie screen as a scene started to appear. Shots of minor details. A tree, a road, a bus stop. *But where is Amina? There.* On the bench beside the bus stop was Amina, balled up with a jacket thrown over her. Her body was shaking with the cold. Beside her was what looked to be a liquor store with posters for beer and a blinking *open* sign. Marceline looked left, reading the street sign. Nevada Ave. *Where was that?*

Before Marceline could investigate further, Brennan released her hands, and the back of Marceline's eyelids returned to black. She opened her eyes.

"You saw Amina; you saw the street. You can find her from there." Brennan turned away and held his temple.

Marceline rubbed her eyes, feeling strangely fine for the first time after using magic. "We could've kept looking."

Brennan shook his head. "You were siphoning magic from me. It's hard enough to support a difficult spell like that, let alone just with my magic. Normally, it takes at least two witches."

Marceline reached under her nose, feeling no blood. "Oh, I'm sorry. I didn't know I was using your magic. We could've used my own."

"No, you didn't have to sacrifice yourself," Brennan said with a sad smile. "I know how your magic works."

Marceline couldn't help but wish it was as easy for her to use magic as it was for Brennan. "Thanks," she mumbled.

"So, what did you two see? Where is Amina?" Katy asked.

Marceline answered, "I don't know exactly. I just saw her asleep on a bench by a bus stop. On a street called Nevada Ave."

"Is she alright?" Bijou asked.

A crash of thunder struck the sky, signaling another rainstorm was likely on its way. Marceline bit her lip. "I honestly don't know. She looked cold, and she was passed out."

Marceline described as many details as she could, but before she'd finished, Katy held her phone up, showing a

Nevada Avenue in Redwood, a town no more than a forty-minute drive away. Katy had also pulled up a map of the bus stops along Nevada Avenue.

"There are twenty-one bus stops," Katy reported. "So, we should probably narrow this down if we can. Did either of you catch the name of the liquor store?"

Marceline and Brennan looked at one another and shrugged.

After a quick search, Katy found eight liquor stores on Nevada Avenue, three of them were close to bus stops.

"Great, I'm glad that worked. But what was this other spell you needed help with?" Brennan asked.

Marceline exchanged glances with Bijou and Katy as if to ask one another, *Who's going to tell him?*

"It's a long story," Marceline finally said.

"If you join us on our road trip to Redwood, I'm sure we'll be able to explain everything," Katy suggested. "It's a thrilling story, with curses, ghosts, betrayal, and witches, of course."

50

The girls and Brennan piled into Katy's Subaru hatchback. Marceline took the passenger's seat to allow Brennan and Bijou to awkwardly sit beside one another.

They'd explained the curse and how to break it to Brennan, and he'd nodded determinedly. He was going to help them. At least they'd checked off one piece of the puzzle on Marceline's list.

"Can you stop shaking your leg?" Katy said to her, putting a comforting hand on Marceline's knee. "We're going to get Amina and be back before midnight. It will all work out."

Marceline tried to offer a smile, but the corners of her mouth wouldn't lift. Bijou shot her a sad, knowing look. Marceline looked at her fingernails, picking at the skin.

Katy sensed her mood and turned up the music blaring from the AUX. It was one of their favorites. Katy sung along loudly as she drove, letting her shoulders sway up and down and her head bob to the rhythm. As the chorus got close, her eyes flicked to Marceline.

"Come on, Marci, you know the words!"

Marceline couldn't help a genuine laugh from coming out. She shouted the familiar words along with Katy, and in the rearview mirror, she even spotted Brennan and Bijou mouthing along, loosening up.

As the song concluded, Marceline blinked back tears. If this was the last car sing-along with her friends, she was grateful she'd gotten to experience it one last time. Marceline had to put her impending death out of her mind. She had to concentrate on the now, on the task at hand. Right now, it was finding Amina.

Brennan's hand reached through the middle console to lower the volume. Katy complained, but Brennan said, "I'm sorry to spoil the fun, but I've got to ask. A curse-breaking spell like this must require a massive power-generating ritual. A sacrifice, I'm guessing. Have we considered that?"

Marceline briefly met Brennan's eyes in the rearview mirror. Her throat was dry. The first time she tried to speak, only a croak came out.

Bijou responded for her. "Perhaps the full moon and the spirits out and around from it being Halloween will be enough."

"Maybe," Brennan said, unconvinced. "But what if a sacrifice is required? What will we do then?"

"Then the curse won't be broken," Bijou answered firmly. "Right, Marci?"

Marceline swallowed the lump in her throat. "But what if Kendra kills someone, anyway?" *Or kills me, anyway?*

The silence hung heavy in the car.

"Hopefully it won't come to that," Brennan said quietly.

The stares of her friends were going to burn holes in her. "Amina will know what to do," Marceline said in a hopefully reassuring voice.

They'd been driving for a while. They passed a sign that announced they had entered the city of Redwood. Nevada Avenue was two miles away.

"Take the Nevada exit," Marceline instructed.

Katy grabbed her phone from the middle console and tossed it to Marceline. "Find the list of liquor stores on Nevada Avenue I made."

Instead of choosing the first on the list, Marceline closed her eyes, trying to force whatever magic she had in her to help her make the right choice the first time. She opened her eyes. "Let's try Lots a Liquor first. It'll be on the left in three miles."

The thought of Amina, cold, motionless on that bench in the pouring rain, terrified Marceline. She'd tried not to picture it, but she couldn't help but wonder, what if they were too late? What if Amina was . . .

"There, on the left."

A figure was lying on the bench as Marceline had seen in the vision. Katy parked, and Marceline quickly jumped out, jogging to the bench. It was so cold Marceline could see her breath puffing in little clouds. As she got closer, she recognized the slight form who was drowning in an oversized black hoodie, the hood pulled over her head, and her hands clenched inside the sleeves. Her jean jacket was draped over her legs. The laces on her black boots were untied.

Amina was lying so still, the exposed skin on her face so pale and drained, Marceline was scared she'd frozen to death.

"Amina," Marceline called. She placed a hand on Amina's bony shoulder. Amina didn't stir, but Marceline saw her release a shaky, shallow breath.

"I can warm her," Brennan suggested.

Marceline jumped; she'd almost forgotten he was there. "Are you sure? Do you have enough power?"

"We had a long rainstorm today. I'm feeling strong," he replied.

Brennan closed his eyes and laid a hand on Amina's arm, brow furrowed in concentration.

More footsteps approached behind them. "Is she . . . ," Katy trailed off.

"No," Marceline snapped, practically growling. Amina couldn't be . . . Marceline lightly shook Amina's body. "Come on," she muttered. Marceline let out a sigh of relief as Amina started to shiver, which Marceline took as a sign her body was working to continue to produce more heat.

Brennan was now shaking in the cold after transferring some of his body heat.

Marceline pulled Amina up from the bench, leaning her limp form against her shoulder and cradling Amina against her.

Brennan removed his coat and wrapped it around Amina's tiny shoulders. "Let's get her in the car," he suggested. He leaned over to lift Amina into his arms and as he did, Amina's hood slipped off, revealing her short hair. Marceline gasped.

Amina's hair had completely grayed over. What had been a black head of hair with streaks of gray the last time she'd seen her was now a gray head of hair with silvery streaks.

"She's sacrificed too much of herself," Bijou said sadly.

Amina's eyelids fluttered as Brennan slid her into the back seat.

"Amina," Marceline said gently, hopefully.

Amina's eyes turned toward her, widening, then narrowing. Her face seemed to have aged as rapidly as her hair had, with thick lines sagging under her eyes and cheeks. "What are you doing?" Amina hissed.

"Saving you," Marceline said. She never thought she'd be so happy to hear Amina sass her.

"Who's this?" Amina said to Brennan, eyeing him defensively.

"Brennan," he said, offering a hand. Amina just stared at it until Brennan awkwardly retracted his outstretched hand. Bijou patted him before climbing into the back seat beside Amina. Marceline slid in on the other side of Amina.

"Do I need to go to a hospital?" Katy called back from the driver's seat. She cranked the heat dial as far as it would go.

"No," Amina croaked, pulling Brennan's jacket tighter around her shoulders.

"Back to Catori," Marceline instructed Katy. Marceline turned toward Amina, gravely serious again. "I need your help."

Amina cleared her throat. "Is that why you did a locator spell to find me?"

"Well, you're welcome for saving your ass from freezing to death," Marceline snapped. "What were you even doing there, anyway?"

"I had my client drop me there after my last . . ." Amina's eyes flashed toward Brennan and Katy. "After my last job. I guess I must've passed out and missed the bus."

"You're lucky we came to get you."

Amina raised her tired-looking brows. "It seems to me it's luckier for you that I wasn't frozen solid by the time you came to get me."

"We need you to help us break the curse. All it takes is someone from each coven to work together to perform the counter spell. We have us, Brennan as the natural witch, and we're working on getting a celestial witch. Then we're ready."

"You conveniently left out the sacrifice that's needed to break the curse," Amina said coolly.

All eyes in the car found Amina, then Marceline.

Marceline once again offered the same full-moon-plus-Halloween energy as a plausible alternative to the sacrifice.

Marceline hoped her eyes conveyed her desperation for Amina not to confirm what they both knew, not out loud to her friends. Someone was going to have to die, and it had to be a Spirit Walker. Amina was quiet, then she took a deep inhale, looked to a confused- and concerned-looking Katy, and said, "Driver, I need a drive-through."

Katy nodded obediently and took a right.

"There's no time for fast food," Marceline said through clenched teeth.

"Maybe it's not such a bad thing to build up our strength before the spell," Brennan said.

Marceline crossed her arms and slumped in her seat. "Says the always-hungry teenage boy." Even though she was pouting, her stomach grumbled as the smell of french fries entered the vehicle. She realized she hadn't eaten since her rushed breakfast that morning before the races.

Katy ordered Marceline her usual without asking. Marceline devoured her meal quicker than she ever had, and she was ready to talk. Amina, however, was slowly savoring every bite.

"So, are you going to help break the curse?" Marceline pressed. "You promised."

Amina didn't react immediately, as if no one had spoken. Amina tossed a french fry into her mouth and chewed thoughtfully. After a minute, Amina slowly turned to Marceline and said, "I said I'd help, so I will."

"Are you strong enough to help?" Brennan asked. "No offense, you just seem a little . . . spent."

Amina cracked a smile. "What do you mean? I just took a long power nap on a bus stop bench, I feel fantastic."

Marceline locked eyes with Amina. Amina wasn't blinking. "Seriously. Can you?" Marceline whispered.

The smirk faded from Amina's lips. Their stare lasted until Marceline finally looked away first. "You know I don't break promises."

51

Midnight was approaching. As the sky got darker, it only seemed to taunt Marceline, reminding her of her deadline. Time moved quicker when you were in a hurry.

"So, what's the plan to obtain a celestial witch for the spell?" Amina asked.

Bijou started, "Well, the witches gather around eleven in the town center for the full moon and—"

Amina snorted. "That's your grand plan? You think these witches, who are incredibly loyal to your mother, the leader of the coven, who very strongly opposes breaking this curse, are just going to come running to help you?"

"Someone will help," Bijou said, unfazed even as Amina's gaze challenged her.

"If you say so," Amina relented.

Katy parked her car across the street from the park that made up the town center.

"The coven should be here by now," Bijou said.

The group got out of the car and started crossing the street.

Marceline noticed Amina hanging back, and she lingered by the car door.

Amina looked up. "Performing a spell like this and taking another life would scar you forever as a dark witch. But you're not planning on sacrificing another, are you? You're planning on being the sacrifice."

Marceline hesitated then slowly nodded her head.

"Is it worth your life?"

"It's worth it to save another's life," Marceline said firmly.

Amina took Marceline's hand in an uncharacteristically gentle and comforting hold that made tears form in Marceline's eyes.

"Promise you'll get rid of Kendra for me," Marceline said.

"You do it yourself," Amina said, using Marceline's hand to pry herself out of the backseat with a grunt. Marceline shot her a confused look, then Amina rolled her eyes. "You're not dying tonight, Marci."

"You have to let me do this," Marceline said in a loud whisper, trying to keep her voice from carrying.

"I don't have to let you do anything."

Marceline eyed Amina up and down, noticing her obvious deterioration. When it came down to it, Amina couldn't beat Marceline. Marceline would get her way.

Their stare-down was broken by Katy calling to them, telling them to hurry up.

From across the street, there didn't appear to be any sign of activity in the park, which seemed odd, but Marceline supposed the witches probably wouldn't want to be easily visible from the street.

The group made their way across the grass. As they walked for a minute, past the playground and the creaking swing set, Marceline spotted flickering candles in the distance. She could see cloaked individuals moving about in the darkness. They were skipping in a circle, chanting words she couldn't comprehend.

"This is insane," Katy breathed. "What language are they speaking?"

"It's an ancient witch language. But you wouldn't be able to understand it even if it was plain English. They put a spell on their words to make them gibberish to anyone outside their circle," Bijou explained.

Katy went to take another step forward, but Bijou took her hand to stop her. "The coven has likely set up a protective border around themselves. If we move closer, they'll know we're here. Just let me go. I'll talk to them."

Though invisible, Marceline could sense the energy forming the protective barrier around the witches.

"I'm coming with you," Marceline said.

"The coven won't help you," Bijou countered. "It has to be me."

Before someone could stop her, Marceline stepped into the celestial coven's protective bubble. The vibrational hum of the witches' incantations made Marceline's insides feel like every cell was moving. Marceline took a deep breath. At once, every hooded head looked up at her, stopping their chanting. The abrupt silence was jarring. The wind picked up as if it was complaining.

"Get your dark magic away from us, Spirit Walker," a woman's voice seethed. Marceline recognized her as the librarian at the local library. Other men and women in the circle were also familiar, even if she couldn't place their names.

Marceline held her hands up in an attempt to appear non-threatening, her sleeves falling down and revealing her white stripes, but the group all geared up defensively. "No, please. I don't practice dark magic. I'm here because I need your help."

Bijou came forward, joining her in the bubble.

"Bijou?" Mrs. Eyota called, stepping forward and allowing her hood to fall. "What are you doing? I told you to stay away from the Lees girl."

"She needs our help, Mama. We need celestial witches to help break the curse that holds all spirits here. It's time to allow our town's dead to find peace after we've denied them for so long."

"It's not worth the sacrifice," the librarian shouted.

"But what if I told you that there was going to be a death tonight, regardless?" Marceline said. Her words seemed to at least garner the attention of the coven. Marceline took another small step forward. "A ghost in the school has threatened to take another's life to replace her own. She's not the first desperate enough to do that, and I can promise you she's not the last. One sacrifice tonight, and there will never be another innocent death at the hands of a spirit here in Catori."

Mrs. Eyota and the outspoken librarian held their unwavering glares, but the other witches seemed to consider this for a beat.

"I'm trying to use my supposed dark magic for good," Marceline continued. "If you all stand by, continuing to benefit from the energy from dead souls you intentionally keep trapped here, then who are really the ones using dark magic here? Who are the ones benefiting from the sacrifice of others?"

One powerful voice sounded above the others. "We will not help you, Ms. Lees," Mrs. Eyota boomed. "We do not associate with dark magic."

"Please," Marceline said again. She would beg if she had to. She'd do anything.

Before she could say anything else, in unison, the witches said, "*Shun.*"

Marceline felt herself thrown back by a strong force, tossing her several feet away to land on her back. She could still see the witches, picking up their chanting and dancing where they'd left off, as Bijou spoke passionately, waving her hands. Marceline rose and made her way back to the circle, yelling and pleading, but this time the barrier was solid, and she couldn't enter. How could they not give her a chance?

She fell to her knees, out of breath from shouting and the force of her fall. How could they be so heartless? How could they ignore her pleas?

"Marci, are you okay?" Katy cried, bending over her.

"They won't help," Marceline said, shaking her head. "We can't break it."

"Bijou's still in there," Brennan said. "She could convince them."

Amina slowly walked to where Marceline was crouched, not saying a word.

They waited for a few minutes on the grass. When Bijou finally emerged from the circle, her face was somber. She shook her head.

Marceline felt her heart drop, and she buried her head in her hands. She was going to die tonight after all, but it wasn't even going to be for a good purpose. It was going to be at the hands of a vengeful spirit.

"We still have three witches. Maybe that will work?" Katy said weakly.

"There has to be one from each form of magic, or it doesn't work," Amina said.

Marceline whispered, "It's over."

"Don't say that," Katy said gently.

"There's nothing else to say," Marceline said, angry now. She stood with her back to the witches. "Let's go."

"Not so fast," a voice called.

Marceline turned around. A wrinkled, white-haired

woman had just appeared from the witches' circle, her hood pulled back.

"Hazel?" Bijou asked incredulously. "But Mama said . . ."

"I'm banished from the coven," Hazel replied matter-of-factly, then she smiled gruffly. "I've had my fun with the coven these last fifty-some-odd years, but enough is enough. It's about time this damn curse gets broken."

"Thank you," Marceline breathed.

"I have a condition, though," Hazel said.

Marceline nodded. "Anything."

"Once this curse is broken, promise you will peacefully dispel my husband."

Marceline offered a smile and looked pointedly to Amina, who would have to be the one to do this if Marceline didn't come out of this alive. "I promise."

52

On the way out of the park, Hazel returned to her car to grab a bag of candles they'd need for the spell. Marceline hadn't thought that far ahead, but it was all happening now.

Now with six passengers, Katy's Subaru was nearly dragging as they piled in. Still, Marceline urged her to go faster as she guided Katy to the hill Anna had been sacrificed on. She knew that was where the curse began and where it must be broken. Time was ticking. Midnight was only slightly over half an hour away.

"Stop here," Marceline instructed.

"The Aspen Leaf Cemetery?" Katy asked. She sighed. "Why does it have to be a graveyard?"

"We're dealing with ghosts and witches, that's why," Amina snapped.

The hike began in the graveyard where, only a month ago, Tag had asked her to Homecoming. Marceline had only turned seventeen a month ago, and yet it felt like her entire life had changed, like she was so much older. Back then, the leaves had been glowing gold, orange, and red. Now, the leaves had fallen, brown and crunchy beneath their feet. Marceline always thought the cycle of life was best visualized by looking at the patterns of leaves. The transformation, the fall, the regrowth, and repeat. No more repeating of the seasons for Marceline. There was only the fall to go.

She looked again at her friends. She was glad not to be alone, but she knew she couldn't allow them to watch. Forcing herself to inhale and exhale, controlling the tears from forming, Marceline turned to Katy and Bijou.

"You two should probably wait here."

"No way," Katy said. "I told you, you're not doing anything alone anymore. I'm coming with you, and so is Bijou."

Bijou nodded, but there were tears streaming down her cheeks. She threw her arms around Marceline, and Marceline willed herself to stay strong, even as Katy's eyes widened in realization.

"No. Absolutely not," Katy yelled in more of a high-pitched squeal.

"Katy—"

"No," Katy shouted again, face twisted in a panicked rage. "You are *not* sacrificing yourself. You can't."

"It has to be a Spirit Walker sacrifice to generate enough power, doesn't it?" Bijou asked quietly.

Marceline bobbed her head slowly.

Katy shook her head. "There has to be another way." The desperation in Katy's voice was enough to make Marceline break. She blinked rapidly to hold in her tears.

"There is," Amina spoke up.

"No, there's not," Marceline countered angrily.

Amina narrowed her eyes and set her jaw. "I'm not going to allow you to die."

The pre-emptive grief visibly hit Katy as she started trembling. "Marci, I—"

Marceline took Katy in a hug. "I know," she whispered, then she pulled away. "I love you both," she told Katy and Bijou. "I'm so sorry. Tell my family, tell Tag, I . . ."

Marceline couldn't finish, but Bijou was nodding. Katy couldn't stand. She crumpled as sobs wracked her body.

Turning to Amina, Brennan, and Hazel, Marceline cleared her throat. "It's this way."

Marceline held a flashlight from Katy's emergency kit in her car as she led the trek up the stone steps in the graveyard. She took a deep breath at the bottom; it was going to be a rather steep hike. Turning back, Marceline saw Amina bent over Katy and Bijou, whispering softly. Almost as if she could sense Marceline's gaze, Amina turned and followed.

Though she wasn't entirely sure how she knew, Marceline was certain of the way to go. There was a slightly overgrown trail on the right that Marceline took.

No one spoke for the first few minutes, until Brennan said, "Marci." She looked back. "I'm so sorry."

"Thanks, Brennan." Marceline couldn't think about it, or her legs would stop working. All she could focus on was the next step. One at a time.

They climbed the hill quickly until it leveled out slightly. The soft lights of Catori Springs could be seen from this vantage point.

"You found me," came Anna's ethereal voice, traveling only to Marceline's and Amina's ears. "I didn't think you had it in you."

"I'm willing to do whatever it takes," Marceline said.

"Who are you talking to?" Brennan asked, looking around. "A ghost?"

"Anna," Amina answered.

As if given permission, Hazel busied herself setting the tall candles she'd brought in a circle around them.

"So, you've got your witches. Which is the sacrifice?" Anna asked.

"Me," Marceline and Amina said in unison as they both stepped forward.

Amina grunted in frustration. "How many times do I have to tell you, Marci? You're not dying today."

Marceline shook her head. "There's something I never told you about the promise I made to Kendra. I didn't just promise I'd help her find peace. I promised if I didn't by the full moon, she could take me as her sacrifice."

Amina looked up at the sky and clasped her hands beneath her chin. Without looking at her, she said, "Why would you do that? How stupid—"

"It wasn't stupid. It was to save my friends or any other innocent life. And I'd do it again, which is why you have to let me do this. I made the promise. My life is already as good as gone. I'd rather die to break this curse that will benefit everyone in Catori than just to send an evil spirit to Hell or wherever they go."

"I don't care about whatever promises you made. You're not keeping them," Amina said, drawing a knife from a sheath strapped to her waist. "Before I made any promises to you, Marci, I made a promise to someone else. To protect you."

Marceline's eyes widened. "Amina, don't."

Amina smiled sadly. "I'm so weak, I wouldn't be strong enough to do the spell anyway, even with your sacrifice. It has to be me, Marci."

"I can't kill you," Marceline cried. As she spoke, the surrounding candles lit simultaneously.

"Marci," Brennan said gently, stepping forward. "It's almost midnight. If we're going to do this, we need to do it now."

Marceline could hardly breathe. "I can't, I . . ." Her sentence ended with a gasp as she watched Amina plunge the knife into her stomach.

"No!" she screeched, running forward and catching Amina before she fell. Marceline gently lowered Amina down, holding her breath. Marceline's shocked brain couldn't comprehend the blood on her fingers, the blood pouring from Amina.

Amina's breaths were ragged. "Don't let my sacrifice be for nothing," she breathed.

Marceline jumped as she felt hands on her shoulders.

"We must get started, dear," Hazel said, firmly using both her hands to pull Marceline to her feet. "Can your ghost tell us the spell?"

Marceline looked around at the scene as if she were watching from above. She made eye contact with Anna, who nodded before floating toward her slowly, then quicker. Marceline could hardly recognize what had happened as her insides seemed to freeze from within. Anna was inside her.

"Repeat after me," Anna's voice, spoken through Marceline's lips, said.

The words poured out of Marceline's mouth, and Brennan and Hazel followed along while Amina lied still in the middle of their circle. The flames around them shot higher the louder their voices chanted.

The wind blew around them, but not at them, swirling around the circle like the start of a tornado. Marceline wasn't Marceline. She was a passenger in her own body, but even she felt the physical effects of the spell draining her.

They were full-on shouting the spell by the end, until Marceline's vision went black.

<h1 style="text-align:center">53</h1>

From the ground, Marceline opened her eyes and saw Brennan and Hazel also collapsed. The candles had extinguished, and the wind gusted through the circle once more.

She sat up quickly, feeling fresh blood from her nose trickle down her chin and neck. "Brennan? Hazel?"

As soon as she said his name, Brennan gasped, putting a hand to his chest and coughing.

Marceline couldn't find the strength to stand, so she crawled over to Hazel, fearing the worst. What if the spell had taken too much out of the sweet old woman? Brennan followed her lead and met her at Hazel's unmoving body.

"Hazel," Brennan said, gripping her shoulders. He closed his eyes, and Marceline could tell by his concentrated look he was doing magic.

"What are you doing?"

Brennan released Hazel as she took in a deep inhale. His eyelids drooped with exhaustion. "I just projected some of my life onto Hazel. She's okay."

Marceline's eyes shot to Amina lying in the middle of the circle. She made a move toward the body.

"Marci," Brennan called weakly. "She's gone. Amina's gone."

Even though the rational side of Marceline's brain recognized what he said as true, she had to at least try. She owed it to Amina, her mentor, the one who'd taught her everything she knew about who she was now. Reaching Amina, Marceline took Amina's cold, lifeless hand and visualized sending some of her life to Amina.

She couldn't tell if it was working, but Marceline could feel the drain on herself. Her nose started bleeding again, but she kept her eyes pressed tightly shut.

"Marci," Brennan said again. "It's no use, she's . . ."

Another soft breath sounded in the quiet air, this time from Amina's lips.

"That can't be possible," Brennan muttered incredulously.

Marceline reached for Amina's wrist, feeling a faint pulse. "She's alive," Marceline confirmed breathlessly.

"I don't understand. I've never heard of a sacrifice not actually dying," Brennan said.

"Sometimes," a voice said from behind Marceline, causing her to jump, "someone who whole-heartedly, willingly sacrifices themself can be spared, but at a cost."

"Did it work? The curse is lifted?" she asked Anna.

Anna smiled. "It worked. After all these years, spirits in Catori Springs are free to find peace. Thank you, Marci."

Marceline couldn't believe it. Somehow, they'd managed to break the curse without a single life lost. Then Marceline remembered there was still someone at risk; whoever Kendra's next victim would be if she couldn't find Marceline.

She stood, dizzy as the blood rushed to her head. "We need to get these two to a hospital," Marceline said to Brennan.

Brennan looked at her helplessly. "I'm not strong enough right now to carry them down the hill."

Marceline swallowed nervously. "Stay with them. My phone is in the car. I'll go down to call for help."

She turned toward the trail, but Brennan called her name, and she looked back. "What about the ghost in the school who wants to kill you?"

"I'll get to her before she gets to anyone else."

"But that spell just took a lot out of you," he argued.

"I still have some power from the sacrifice," she lied.

Brennan seemed to believe her, or he didn't have it in him to continue arguing. "Be careful."

She just nodded, as words seemed too much effort.

Marceline climbed down the steep path as quickly as she could manage in the dark, having left the flashlight with Brennan.

Katy and Bijou were waiting in the graveyard.

"Marci?" Bijou asked, squinting in the dark.

Katy, who'd had her head in her hands, snapped up. Seeing Marceline, Katy ran to her.

Marceline's legs collapsed under her, but Katy's arms supported her. "What happened? Where are the others?"

Marceline could hardly speak. "They need an ambulance," she gasped feebly.

Bijou pulled her phone out, immediately dialing 911.

Marceline was still unstable on her feet. Katy tried to get her to sit, but Marceline shook her head, trying to straighten herself. "I have to find Kendra. Can you take me to the school?"

"Marci, you're hardly functioning. You're not in any state to take on a spirit who's at full-strength."

"I don't have a choice, Kat," Marceline said, closing her eyes. "I promised her, and you can't break a promise to a spirit."

Bijou walked toward them, holding her phone. "The ambulance is on its way. What did I miss? Did you break the curse?"

"We broke it," Marceline confirmed weakly. "Bijou, stay here for when the ambulance arrives. If you follow that path up, it's the first flat section on the right. Katy, take me to the school. It's time to dispel Kendra once and for all."

She didn't wait for confirmation from either of her friends, and instead made her way to the car. Katy begrudgingly followed.

The cool passenger's seat window was a welcome relief for the pain in Marceline's skull. She rested her cheek against it on the drive, suddenly unable to keep her eyes open.

"Marci?" Katy called, the sound breaking through Marceline's mental haze.

"I'm just building my strength to fight Kendra," Marceline replied, with her eyes still closed.

"No, Marci, it's midnight. It's officially Halloween."

Marceline's eyes shot open, and she sat up straight. Sure enough, the time on the dashboard clock read 12:00 a.m.

Katy shot her a concerned look, her hands white-knuckled on the steering wheel.

"I'll be okay," Marceline said. "Just hurry."

Without warning, the pain in Marceline's head transformed into a searing, stabbing sensation. She cried out, gripping her head and closing her eyes. Distantly, she could hear Katy's voice, but the words were muffled and incomprehensible. Marceline forced herself to open her eyes, realizing they were passing the McCormick Estate. The dozens of spirits once trapped in the estate were streaming out at once, taking their leave on the one day a year it was possible.

"Drive," Marceline forced her mouth to say. "I can't . . ." She couldn't finish her sentence as her brain seemed to get unplugged, and all her senses turned off.

54

Marceline woke in Katy's car and rubbed her eyes, trying to get them to adjust to the darkness. It took her a moment to remember what had happened, but as she grew more alert, she turned to find Katy wasn't in the car anymore. The car was parked in front of Marceline's house, and Katy was knocking rapidly at the front door.

Taking a deep breath, Marceline pushed the door open and stood, gritting her teeth against the dizziness.

"Marci, sit back down," Katy said, turning around and jogging down to meet her. She took Marceline's hand. "You passed out. Don't move so quickly."

"It was just all the spirits from the McCormick Estate. They overwhelmed me, but I'm okay. What are we doing here? We need to be at the school," Marceline protested.

"We were right by your house, so I came to find your dad to get you to the hospital, but I don't think anyone's home."

Marceline frowned. "What do you mean, no one is home? At this time of night?"

The girls' heads turned simultaneously toward the familiar

roar of Tag's truck coming from up the street. Marceline's heart raced. What was he doing here?

Tag parked and ran out of his truck, leaving the lights on and the door open in his haste.

"You're back," Tag said, reaching Marceline and embracing her tightly. The hug nearly crushed her, but it made her feel safe in the way Tag always made her feel. "We've been looking for you for hours."

Marceline pulled away from the hug. "Looking? I told Dad I was doing something important."

"That was hours ago. He got worried when you never came home. Especially since both you and Katy were missing. They brought your brothers to the neighbor's house, and your dad, Delilah, and I have been out looking."

Even after the way they'd left things, Tag had still gone out to look for her. "We're okay," Marceline said, trying to shoot Tag a reassuring smile. "But we have something else important we need to do." Marceline reached to take Katy's hand to pull her toward the car, but Katy wouldn't budge.

Katy turned toward her. "Go get your spell book. You may need it."

"Spell book?" Tag asked. "And what is so important you have to go at midnight?"

The girls ignored him, and Marceline sighed impatiently at Katy. "I don't need the book. I know how to dispel, and now that the curse is lifted, I can do it."

"But what if Kendra doesn't deserve peace?" Katy said. "Before she went up for the ritual, Amina told me there was a way to banish a spirit rather than send them to peace. She said something about how your book will tell you what to do."

Marceline remembered Amina and Russel talk about banishing spells.

Tag was watching them like they were speaking another

language. Marceline turned to go inside, but Tag grabbed her arm. "What the hell is going on, Marceline?"

For the sake of time, Marceline blurted, "I'm a witch, Tag."

Tag released her a took a step back, dumbfounded.

"I don't have time to explain everything right now, but I promise I will." If he still wanted anything to do with her after tonight. Based on his stunned face, Marceline wasn't so sure if he'd want to speak to her ever again. She jogged to the garage to enter the code to open it.

"It's a long story," she heard Katy say to Tag.

Marceline moved as quickly as she could upstairs, grabbed the heavy book from beneath her bed, and met them back in the driveway. She was out of breath, but she marched to the passenger door of Katy's Subaru.

Katy hesitated. "Are you sure you have to do this right now, Marci? You're not at your strongest. What if what happened to Amina starts to happen to you for sacrificing too much of yourself?"

"It won't," Marceline said quickly. "And I'm strong enough for this. Katy, come on."

"Where are you going?" Tag asked, grabbing Marceline's wrist again. His face desperately pleaded for answers.

"Just stay here," Marceline told him. "I'll be back soon to tell you everything."

"I'm coming with you," Tag said firmly.

"No, Tag, the fewer people there, the better."

"Marci," Katy called. Her voice shook with fear. "She's here."

Marceline turned to where a horrified Katy was pointing and saw Kendra floating at the edge of the driveway. Since it was Halloween, Kendra must have had the energy to make herself visible to humans.

Tag followed their gaze and jumped at the sight of the

transparent, glowing-red ghost of an unhappy-looking teenage girl with her arms crossed over her chest.

"Who is that? Why is she floating?" Tag stammered. "Marceline?"

Kendra shot Marceline a sinister smile. Before she could utter a word, Kendra floated forward, cutting through Marceline's weak shield like a knife, bee-lining for Tag.

Though she tried, no light shield sprung. Marceline could only watch in dread as Tag's body shuddered. He tried to resist the internal attack, face straining until it relaxed into a smirk.

"I thought I might find you here, Marci," Kendra's voice said through Tag's lips. "Didn't realize you'd have guests, though. What a treat!"

"Get out of his head, Kendra!" Marceline shouted, trying again to blast a shield over Tag. Kendra was too powerful.

"Happily," Kendra said. "But only if you come to the school so you can give me what was promised."

"Why the school?" Katy asked.

Tag turned to Katy and smiled sweetly, in a way entirely unlike his usual smile. "So I can kill your best friend, of course," Kendra replied.

At Katy's shock, Kendra-as-Tag turned toward Marceline. "You didn't tell her about the promise you made me, did you, Marci? I thought best friends were supposed to share everything. I'll tell you what Marci wouldn't, Katy. She promised me her life if she couldn't bring me to peace by tonight's full moon. But since the curse is still up, Marci owes me. She's going to take my spot in the school."

Marceline and Katy made quick eye contact. Kendra didn't know the curse was broken.

"You know, just for fun, I could kill your boyfriend here at your house, Marci. Or how about your bestie, Katy? Ghosty slumber parties every night!"

Marceline watched as Kendra exited Tag's body. He collapsed, and Marceline ducked to break his fall. Bracing his head was all she could do to keep him from crashing onto the pavement.

Kendra shifted into Katy's body, sending Katy shivering as if blasted with an intense cold. Kendra spoke through Katy. "Who would you rather die, Marci? The doting boyfriend or the loyal bestie?"

"Stop, please," Marceline begged, crouched over Tag. "Leave them alone. I'll come with you to the school."

"Then come now. I'm done playing around."

Tag's body was motionless in Marceline's arms. "Why isn't he waking up?" She squeezed his hand. He didn't squeeze back. She looked up accusingly.

Kendra, as Katy, huffed. "He's fine. Just going to have a killer headache tomorrow is all. Likely a concussion."

Marceline ran her hand over Tag's cheek. She gently laid his head on the driveway. At least he was breathing. "Leave Katy's body unharmed, then I'll come."

Katy tilted her head and narrowed her eyes in the familiar way Kendra always did. "I'm not leaving this body until we get to the school."

Marceline tried to control her breathing as her heart hammered in her chest. Even as she rose to her feet, she felt lightheaded. She needed more strength if she wanted any chance of winning this fight for life against Kendra.

55

Kendra, using Katy's body, walked toward the Subaru, jingling the keys in her hand.

"I haven't driven in almost twenty years. This should be interesting."

Marceline silently chewed her lip, considering her options. Even if she used all the power in her body, she didn't think it would be enough to take Kendra down. She needed an energy source. For the thousandth time since she'd found out about the other sources of magic, Marceline wished she had something she could draw power from that wasn't *alive*.

Katy hopped in the driver's seat, eyes on Marceline.

She couldn't get into that car without knowing if she could produce a portal to dispel Kendra, peacefully or not.

Out of the corner of her eye, through the darkness, a figure was emerging. As the silhouette of a woman in a long gown and hat got closer to the porch light outside Marceline's house, Marceline could make out who she was. Anna.

Kendra didn't seem to notice the extra ghost as she struggled to get the key in the ignition.

Anna drifted directly toward Marceline. "You can send her away now."

Marceline let out a shaky breath. "I'm not strong enough. I don't have enough in me to sacrifice."

Anna smiled. "All you need is something alive."

Marceline frowned, not understanding. Then she contemplated, what exactly was considered alive? Did that only apply to humans and animals, or did it also apply to other forms of life? She glanced down at her dad's well-manicured flower beds beside the driveway. Would that count as a sacrifice? Anna nodded, almost as if she'd read her mind.

Analyzing the situation, Marceline realized she'd dropped the spell book in the commotion. It was flipped open but blank, since she hadn't thought of a spell for it to open to yet.

She crouched to grab it.

"Marci, we go now, or the deal is off," Kendra called from inside the car.

"You know what to do, Marceline," Anna whispered.

Marceline closed her eyes and focused on a spell to banish spirits. When she looked again, the words appeared across the page.

She heard footsteps nearing and saw Katy's boots standing beside her. "You. You have no business here, Anna." Katy's face was twisted in an unrecognizable rage.

Anna scoffed. "I've been around here far longer than you, girl."

Marceline needed to act quickly. First things first, she needed Kendra separated from any human body. Marceline crushed one of her dad's marigolds in her palm and projected the strongest shield she could muster at Katy. As the white shone over Katy's body, it was as if Kendra's spirit was being ripped out by invisible arms, and Katy stumbled, crashing to her knees with a yelp.

Kendra was the deepest shade of red Marceline had ever seen. "How dare you?"

Looking down, Marceline realized the flower she'd held had crumpled, as if she'd been holding a long-dead, dried flower. It had worked.

Katy held her head, looking disoriented as she glanced at the scene in front of her. She made eye contact with Marceline, nodding to indicate she was okay.

Kendra shot for Tag's limp body next, but Marceline increased her shield, blocking Kendra from reaching either of them.

"We had a deal!" Kendra cried, floating higher than the usual inch off the ground, trying to appear taller.

"I broke the curse, Kendra," Marceline said. "I can fulfill my end of the deal, and no one has to die."

Kendra slowly floated down, glowering. "That's not possible."

Katy spoke up. "Actually, it is."

Kendra glared at her.

"I reversed the curse that didn't allow us to dispel trapped spirits in Catori, which means I can send you to peace, or wherever else is more fitting for the likes of you," Marceline said.

"Banishing spells are dark. You don't do dark magic," Kendra seethed.

Marceline pushed her jacket sleeve jacket up and revealed her stripe. Only now, Marceline realized, the stripe was no longer bright white. It was gray, the same color as Amina's. Breaking the curse, using a sacrifice, had darkened her forever.

Kendra's eyes widened, but Marceline could see her attempt to regain composure. "Breaking a century-old curse must have weakened you," came Kendra's voice. She laughed. "Go on, try to banish me. I doubt you have enough power."

Marceline's nose was bleeding. Even with the sacrifice of

the plants, she honestly didn't doubt Kendra's statement. Marceline looked to Anna. Was she strong enough?

Katy shot her a questioning look.

As she hesitated, Kendra made another move, this time breaking past Marceline's shield, aiming for Katy again. This time, Katy cried out in pain.

With a yell, Marceline projected her shield again, taking Katy in her arms before her body collapsed beside Tag's. She laid them side by side. Katy's chest rose and fell, but she too was unconscious. The sight of two of the people she loved lying so still nearly stole her breath. She felt like her entire body had frozen over.

"I told you to leave my friends alone," Marceline growled. When she saw Kendra's face again, it brought back her fiery anger, thawing out the chill of seeing her loved ones harmed. Even as Kendra pushed against the shield with all her strength, Marceline held firm. "I'm stronger than you."

Marceline walked to the edge of her shield, taking Kendra's wrists. This time, Kendra wasn't slipping away. Kendra's face held an emotion Marceline hadn't seen her show before. Fear.

Another hand gripped Marceline's wrist. Anna. She nodded confidently. Marceline could feel Anna's energy strengthening her.

With the spell book open, Marceline chanted. Anna joined her. Together, their words built on one another to create more than just sound. The air formed a thick barrier around the three of them. Marceline wasn't breathing, but it was like she didn't need to. The power of their chants grew, and Kendra was shrinking. Marceline bled from her nose, her eyes, and her ears.

Kendra was only growing smaller, narrower, thinner, until Marceline wasn't grasping anything at all. Kendra had literally faded to nothing. Though she didn't know exactly how she knew, Marceline knew Kendra was gone forever.

As Kendra vanished, the air was at once forced back into their circle. Only now, it was suffocating to Marceline's lungs. She fell to the ground, writhing, as her brain screamed for oxygen, but her lungs refused it. After a few panicked breaths, she allowed the air to settle into her body. When she opened her eyes, color in the surrounding world flickered in and out. It was as if seeing color required too much energy for her brain to process. "We did it," she wheezed.

Anna floated beside her. Marceline couldn't lift her head to look past the bottom of Anna's dress. Behind the ghost, Marceline noticed all the flowers and grass in the yard were crumpled and dead.

"Thank you, Marceline. For freeing me. For freeing this town. My debt to you can never be paid, though I hope my contribution helped in some way."

Marceline couldn't form words. She had tunnel vision. Darkness was closing in on her, but the last thing she saw was a glowing passageway, the silhouette of a woman in a long gown with a red jacket floating deep into the light, walking until she faded out completely, and the portal closed. Marceline felt the last remaining energy in her body drift away. Her eyes closed, and the world fell into nothing but gray clouds.

56

For the second time in a month, Marceline woke up to the sounds of subtle beeping and a sterile, chemical smell. Before her eyes opened, she knew. She was in the hospital again. As she slowly started to put her memories back together, her eyes snapped open, blinking a few times in the bright fluorescent light before settling on a startled-looking Katy.

"You're awake," Katy said. She beamed at Marceline and took her hand.

Marceline instantly wanted to throw her arms around Katy, but the IVs hooked into her arm prevented her from reaching even an arm's length away.

"Easy, Marci," Katy cautioned with a gentle laugh. "I'm happy to see you awake."

Her brain still couldn't make words come out, so Katy continued, "Your dad just slipped away for a few minutes to take a shower and change his clothes. He's been here nonstop." Katy paused and gave her a grave look. "Marci, your dad is super freaked out. We're going to have to come up with an explanation for what happened. Your dad found us all passed out in front of the house. By the time he got there, Tag and I were awake, but you . . . you weren't."

Marceline's chest tightened at the thought of disclosing any of this to her father. What had he thought when he'd discovered his daughter, passed out, bleeding from multiple places?

"I'll figure something out to tell him. What about Amina? Hazel? Are they alright?" Her voice was croaked and broken. She cleared her throat, and Katy handed her a cup of water.

"They're both fine. They're here resting too. Amina seemed to have been in worse shape than you, somehow." Katy shifted in her chair and leaned closer. "Listen, Marci, I don't know what happened with you and Kendra. When you came in here, you were completely depleted. Dehydrated, low on iron, low white blood cell count, low on electrolytes, everything. Was it Kendra?"

Marceline's eyes closed as she recalled Kendra shrinking and shrinking until she disappeared completely. "Kendra's gone forever."

Katy smiled until her lip quivered. "That's good news. But I didn't know it would come at such a physical cost to you. Marci, I don't want to see you like this ever again." Katy's eyes filled with tears. "When I woke up, and I saw you just lying there, barely breathing . . . it was the absolute worst."

Marceline squeezed her hand. She remembered how she'd felt seeing Katy and Tag lying so still. Katy must be feeling how she'd felt. When Katy turned back up to look at her, she started crying. "Do I really still look that bad?" Marceline said.

Katy laughed and laid her head on Marceline's shoulder. "I love you, you know?"

"I love you, you know."

———

Marceline felt herself regaining strength over the next days in the hospital. She'd managed to keep her protection shield up the whole time she'd been at the hospital, but she knew that having to keep it up all the time wasn't helping her heal any faster. Dad, understandably, was worried about her. Tag was too. It made her weary to think of Tag and all she'd have to explain to him. He knew she was a witch and could speak to ghosts, but that was about it. He was being patient, as he always was, and not pressuring her to speak about it while she was in the hospital.

Once she was cleared to move around, Marceline went straight to Amina's room. Whereas stuffed animals and flowers from her friends and family surrounded Marceline's hospital bed, Amina's room was bare. Marceline wondered if Amina had any friends or family she remained in contact with. Of course, if Marceline's family had been full of dark, sacrificial monsters, she wasn't sure she'd keep in contact with them either, but still, it made her feel sad to see small, prematurely-aged Amina lying alone in her bed.

At the sight of her, Amina's face brightened slightly, but she didn't smile. Marceline still offered a small smile and pulled a chair that hadn't been used beside Amina's bed. "How are you?" Marceline asked.

Amina looked tired, but she always did. Perhaps the wrinkles in her skin were less pronounced. "Good. The doctors had me pegged as a Jane Doe for a while. When I finally woke up and told them my birthday, they thought I had brain damage," Amina snorted. "I ended up having to tell them a year far later than my actual birth year just to shut them up. Told them I was joking. Now they think I'm just some middle-aged lady trying to act like I've turned thirty-eight for the twelfth time."

"Now that you mention it, I'm going to need some proof you're actually thirty-eight."

"If I could punch you right now, I would," Amina said, lifting her arm into a boxing position. As she did, both of their eyes fell to where Amina's stripes should have been.

Marceline's eyes widened in shock at Amina's glaringly bare wrists. Amina's stripes were gone. There was no sign of the once glittering gray stripe. Amina's pale skin was suddenly so dull.

Marceline's own stripes were a shade of gray, slightly darker than what Amina's had been. She didn't really know what it meant for her as a Spirit Walker other than it being a major hit to her reputation as a witch.

She thought of what Anna had said. Sometimes, a willing sacrifice could be spared, but at a cost. "Amina, what happened out there? To your stripes?"

Amina looked up at Marceline and shrugged. "Just what you're thinking happened, but you're too afraid to say it out loud. I've lost my magic, maybe forever. I'm no longer a Spirit Walker. The sacrifice killed that part of me."

Marceline's eyes widened, and her mouth fell open.

"Hey, don't look at me like that, okay? I've found peace with it. It's better than dying, really dying. And besides, all this time, I've been helping the dead. Pouring so much of me into my work. Since my eighteenth birthday, I have never slowed down. I honestly didn't think I'd reach my fortieth birthday, and I'd accepted that. I'd thought I'd die a Spirit Walker. And then I went and poured into helping the living for once," Amina said, looking intensely at Marceline and offering a small smile. "I'd never done that before."

"And look where it got you."

"Yeah, thanks a lot," Amina laughed, then she grew serious again. "But really, thank you, Marci."

"For what? You almost died because of me."

Amina shrugged. "Yeah, but I didn't. And now I get to live a real life. One without the obligation to help the dead. I'll probably start helping the living now, knowing who I am, but it's freeing. I've never had options before. It was always dispelling after dispelling. Now I get to choose what I do."

Marceline nodded and smiled. "Well, when you put it like that, I'm happy for you. Glad I could help you by almost killing you." Marceline paused and looked down at her hands. "I banished Kendra."

"All by yourself?"

"Anna helped me. I don't know how. I know she was a Spirit Walker before she died, but I didn't think she could still do magic."

"She can't," Amina said gently. "Dead people can't do magic."

Marceline shook her head. "No, she said the spell with me. We did it together."

"Maybe Anna chanted along with you, but it must have been all you, Marci."

Marceline couldn't accept that. "No. I was so weak. There's no way I could've done it on my own. I could feel a power outside of me helping."

"Don't be so hard on yourself. Maybe it was all you. You're one strong Spirit Walker, you know."

Marceline swallowed. She couldn't believe she'd done that all on her own. "I think I used the plants, the grass, the flowers. I didn't know we could use other forms of life to generate magic."

Amina's brow furrowed. "That's not possible. Sacrificial magic doesn't work like that. It has to be a living, breathing sacrifice. Or at least, mine did. I've never heard of another Spirit Walker being able to use anything but sentient life as a power source."

How could Marceline have taken the energy from other, non-sentient forms of life? The thought of yet another part of her that couldn't be explained was verging on overwhelming for her. She distracted herself as another question came to mind. "What exactly did I do to Kendra? Where did I send her?"

"You didn't send her anywhere. That's the point of a banishing spell," Amina scoffed, rolling her eyes like Marceline was an imbecile.

"What do you mean?"

"With your spell, you banished Kendra from existing at all. Right now, she's not in the lower, lower dimension, Hell, or whatever you want to call it. She's definitely not up in Heaven. She's just gone for good."

"Oh," Marceline said quietly. She supposed that was what Kendra deserved. After trying to murder her friends, Kendra didn't deserve peace, but Marceline also didn't think Kendra deserved to suffer eternally. Kendra's spirit ceasing to exist altogether was the best possible outcome. Kendra had been removed from all dimensions, permanently. "I think I've got a lot of dispelling to do in Catori now that I've reversed the curse."

"I wish I could help you with that. That's the one job I wasn't able to finish . . . ," Amina trailed off and shook her head. "Speaking of the Catori Springs job. Marci, I should probably tell you now who sent me here in the first place."

Marceline felt her heart skip a beat. "Who?"

Amina didn't hesitate, looking straight into Marceline's eye. "It was your mom, Apolline."

Note to Reader

Dear reader,

Thank you so much for taking the time to read the first part of Marceline's story. She has had a special place in my heart for a long time, and I am happy to share her with you. I hope you enjoyed reading as much as I enjoyed writing.

If you didn't know, I am an independent author, published through my own small publishing company, WIP Publications. As an indie author, there are a few easy things you can do to support me and your other favorite authors.

1. Leave a review

If you have a few minutes to spare, please consider making your way over to the online retailer you purchased the book from to leave your honest review. This is one of the best ways to show support to your favorite books!

2. Sign up for my newsletter (and get free stuff!)

Keep up to date with new releases and hear more from me by signing up for my newsletter at KaileyUrbaniakAuthor.com. From there, you can sign up to receive a free copy of *Apolline*, the prequel novella in the Spirit Walker universe you don't want to miss!

3. Follow me on social media

I love to hear from my readers, so if you'd like to catch up with me (or tell me your ghost stories), please follow me on Instagram, TikTok, and/or Facebook. You can find me if you type in @KaileyUrbaniakAuthor.

4. Buy Direct

Be sure to purchase book two of the Spirit Walker series at KaileyUrbaniakAuthor.com, as it really supports me as an author.

Thank you again for reading. I look forward to hearing from you. In the meantime, keep reading, and keep shining your light.

With love,
Kailey

Acknowledgments

It's difficult to put into words what publishing my first book means to me. I've wanted to be a writer all my life. Since I was a young girl, while other kids wanted to grow up to be astronauts, princesses, or professional athletes, I always said I wanted to write books. And here I am. Though I wouldn't be here without my support system.

To Jared, my number one fan. Thank you for allowing me to spit ideas at you nonstop. I'm so thankful for your critical eye, for your ability to provide feedback in a kind but helpful way, for your reminders when I'm overwhelmed that it's okay to step away and breathe fresh air once in a while. I couldn't have finished this without you.

To my mom, an author herself, L. K. Urban. Thank you for paving the way and being a huge inspiration for me, not only as an author, but in everything you do. You've been my biggest cheerleader. Your encouragement throughout this process has meant the world to me.

To Jenn, the other half of my twin heart. In all of life's inevitable peaks and valleys, you are always and have always been the voice of advice and reason. If I ever feel stressed or down, you manage to find a way to make me see through the smog. You are the shining light that guides me out of any darkness.

To my Western master's cohort, past and present. When I joined the program, a shy and unsure twenty-one-year-old, I knew zilch about the publishing industry. Kevin J. Anderson, your program gave me the base knowledge and connections I needed to not only grow in my career, but to make my dreams of publishing a novel come true. There was a time when I thought this career wasn't possible for me, that I wasn't cut out for it. But this program showed me the way.

And a huge, huge thank you to all my other friends and family members for your unwavering support. You know who you are, and I hope you know how valued you are.

About the Author

A self-identified logophile—someone who is obsessed with words—Kailey Urbaniak works as a writer and editor. She was born and has lived most of her life surrounded by mountains and beneath sunny skies in Colorado Springs, Colorado. For as long as she can remember, she has always wanted to be a writer and professional reader; hence, she became an editor. After graduating with her bachelor's in English Literature, she went on to study the industry and earned her master's degree in Publishing from Western Colorado University. For the past five years, she has worked closely with best-selling authors and first-time authors to edit, write, and publish a diverse range of projects including novels of all genres, short stories, blogs, and social media content. *The Sight* is her debut novel. When she is not writing, reading, watching ghost-hunting videos, or working with clients, she finds peace being outdoors and appreciating nature with her labradoodle, Charlie.

If so inclined, please feel free to reach out to Kailey on social media and sign up for her newsletter for updates on all things writing (and more) at KaileyUrbaniakAuthor.com.

facebook.com/kaileyurbaniakauthor

instagram.com/kaileyurbaniakauthor

tiktok.com/kaileyurbaniakauthor